Wakefield Press

# Sincerely, Ethel Malley

Stephen Orr was born in Adelaide in 1967, studied science and education and taught in a range of country and metropolitan schools. One of his early plays, *Attempts to Draw Jesus*, became his first novel, shortlisted for the Australian/Vogel's Literary Award. Since then he has published eight novels (most recently, *This Excellent Machine*) and a volume of short stories (*Datsunland*). He has been nominated for awards such as the Commonwealth Writers' Prize, the Miles Franklin Award and the International Dublin Literary Award.

Stephen Orr is married and lives in Adelaide.

# Sincerely, Ethel Malley

# Stephen ORR

Wakefield Press

Wakefield Press
16 Rose Street
Mile End
South Australia 5031
www.wakefieldpress.com.au

First published 2021

Excerpts from *The Darkening Ecliptic* by Ern Malley used with permission from
the Estate of Max Harris.
*Exiles* by James Joyce, first published 25 May 1918, first performed 14 February
1926, Regent Theatre, London.

Edited by Jo Case, Wakefield Press
Designed by Liz Nicholson, Wakefield Press
Typeset by Jesse Pollard, Wakefield Press

ISBN 978 1 74305 808 4

A catalogue record for this
book is available from the
National Library of Australia

Hear the sum of the whole matter in the compass of one brief word – every art possessed by man comes from Prometheus.

Aeschylus (disputed), *Prometheus Bound*


The whole problem stemmed from a misunderstanding as to where the truth left off and imagination began.

Frederick R. Ewing


For it is not good to be a god on earth
Not knowing the language, nor the dinginess of men,
Unable to petal the paper flowers of flesh,
To call a prayer and hear return 'Amen'.

Max Harris, (from) *At the Circus*


It is finished
It is finished
IT IS THE MERCY.

Donald Crowhurst

# 1981

Ben McDonald walked his dog toward the hockey oval. It was a cold morning, with a blue sky and frosty camellias, but he didn't care about that. He just wanted to get home, see how George Frazier was holding up, eat a decent breakfast, make his way to the bus stop on Parramatta Road, deal with another day of Pythagoras and advanced calculus at The King's School, come home and do it all again. That's all he wanted.

But it wasn't what he got.

The story he'd tell Max Harris (a few hours later) was light on details. There were reasons for this. Mainly, that he was in a rush and, despite finding a body, still had to get to work. But mostly, this is how it happened. He saw the body of a woman (mid-sixties) dressed in a frock and cardigan, and muttered to himself, 'Isn't that Ethel?' His first thought was, I could turn, walk home, pretend I didn't see her. Otherwise, there'd be the drama of applying first aid, or dealing with a body (he'd found his uncle dead on the toilet), calling the authorities, answering questions for the police. He didn't like the idea of this. Being a teacher, he knew that life was all about paperwork.

So he stood beside the body, looking around, realising there was no one else he could share the drama with, wondering if he'd later feel guilty if he chose to do nothing. All of these thoughts passed in the minute he stood watching Ethel Malley, hoping her chest would rise and fall, or she'd stand, brush herself off, and it would all be over. But she stayed as stiff as a statue. And he mumbled, 'Jesus, not now.'

He knelt, placed his hand in front of her open mouth and felt for breath. Nothing. His dog strained to get away, continue her walk, despite the body. He said, 'Ethel, you okay?' But there was no reply. Shook her. Nothing. He felt for a pulse, but couldn't find one. Wondered if he should massage her heart, breathe into her mouth, like he'd seen at first-aid training (not that he'd really been paying attention). But then he thought, What's the point of that if she's already dead? She must have been, because she was as cold as the pavement she'd probably slid or fallen onto from the bench behind her, although it was hard to say.

Ben McDonald waited on the bench and said, 'Bad luck, old girl.' Like that, like he'd already dealt with it, moved on, found something else to worry about. The dog sat on the grass beside him, still surveying the selection of trees. That was life. The living and the dead, and the way dogs dry-pissed on long walks.

Eventually someone came along and Ben explained that he'd found her dead, and could he (the other bloke) wait while he went and called someone. The other bloke said he'd go call while Ben waited, but Ben had had enough of the body, with its laddered stockings and implications for his own existence, so he said he'd go, and that was that.

So he went home, called an ambulance, returned and, as he and this other man waited, went through Ethel's handbag, found a copy of a magazine called *Angry Penguins* and leafed through it. Autumn 1944. Featuring a poet called Ern Malley. Inside the front cover he found a handwritten name (Max Harris) and an address and phone number in Adelaide. He said, 'Ethel was sort of like the local . . .' The other man didn't seem to care. He, too, had to get to work. He (Ben) found Ethel's purse and said to the other man, '. . . apparently she was, you know, nutty.'

And this other man said, 'Maybe she was related to the fella on the cover?'

Ern Malley. They agreed this was likely. Ben thought he remembered something about a brother, long since dead. As the sound of the ambulance grew louder, Ben McDonald found one of Ern Malley's poems in the magazine (its yellow pages and cracking spine) and read: '*It was a night when the planets were wreathed in dying garlands* . . .' He said to the other man, 'Never much fancied poetry.'

This man agreed. If someone wanted to say something, they should just say it. None of this fucking around with dying garlands and (later) the autumn of my Valhalla. What did it mean? Who knew? Who cared? This was a great country, with yachts and plenty of jobs and skilful sports people, and engineers good enough to build an opera house when the architect spat the dummy. So why poetry? Why make life difficult?

At which point Ben McDonald placed the magazine in his back pocket and, as the ambulance men arrived, said, 'I suppose I better tell Dad . . . and this Harris fella.'

# 1943

# 1

'Got yer card, Ethel?'

Mr Moore was my butcher, and had been for years. Pot belly, drainpipe legs (you'd see them in summer, under his apron) and half a little finger (I was there when he did it).

'Yes, Mr Moore.' Sometimes, cheekily, I wouldn't offer it, and he wouldn't ask for it. But with things going so bad in New Guinea you had to make an effort. So I gave him my ration card, and he snipped off the coupon with his bloody fingers.

'Everything sorted?' he asked, smiling, returning it.

I wasn't sure what he meant. My order? The bindii his brother-in-law had sprayed for me? Ern? Yes, probably Ern. So I said, 'I think so, Mr Moore.'

He just looked at me, like he wanted to keep going, but didn't. Cared, but had to tread carefully. 'I always thought he was a gentleman.'

'One of the last.'

'I even told him, anytime . . . there was work on offer.'

He had. Mr Moore's son had started at fifteen, never smiled, always listened to the wireless. He was hopeless: fatty cuts, too much or not enough, and the sausages he made were like old men's . . . can I say it?

I'm new to this writing business. I've been told how it's done. Learnt a thing or two from my brother's poems. But I'm still feeling my way. Like finishing sentences with prepositions. I remember the nuns telling me off for that. But Max would say, Na, don't worry about rules, Eth. Just write it like you feel it. Be honest.

So that's what I've decided to do: be honest. About the whole dirty affair. About Ern, and his scribblings, and me discovering them and sending them to Max and him being so kind and seeing, *realising* Ern's talent. And his belief in him, and me, during all the time those bastards said dirty things about us. The sleepless nights and endless worry. Until, in a way, we were . . . no. Max said never give anything away. Maintain the suspense. So I will.

Back to Mr Moore's son – Justin, I think his name was. You'd see him scratch himself, then handle the meat. I wanted to say something, but dared not. In the end, it didn't matter. He joined up, shipped out and was sent home, dishonourably. What that meant, I never found out. But sometimes you'd see him out the back of the shop, smoking, listening to the races, and once he said (something like), Hey, Dad, where the f . . . did you put those keys? Mr Moore turned to me, embarrassed, and said, I dunno, Ethel. We've tried. What do you do?

And now, he said, 'Nice send off, was it?'

'Yes.'

'I was wondering if I shoulda come, but I wasn't sure.'

'No need for that . . . (half pounda mince, if you could).'

'Just gotta get it over and done with, I suppose. What I mean's . . .'

'I know.'

'My sister, Janice, you know what happened to her?' He wrapped my mince, clipped the book, smiled.

'Bali, wasn't it?'

'Yes. No giving way to pedestrians over there.'

'Mother shouldn't have to bury her child.'

He placed the meat on the counter, and I slipped it into my bag. As we both waited, thinking of the boy, and the bemo, or scooter, or whatever it was.

'Long as you keep smiling,' I said, and he agreed, wiping the blood from his hands, gathering the coins in his long, bony fingers and dropping them into the till without counting.

Back down Byron Street. I'd often walk this way with Ern. My Ern. My only brother. A loving, giving, and reflective man. The baby I nursed, the boy I cared for. Although, if you listen to some, he never existed. Never. What a *strange* thing to say. How could you claim someone who'd lived, hadn't? You can play with words, reference the Greeks and Romans, ghosts and spectres, but what's real's real. One man said he was a figment of my imagination. I replied, This scar here, see, where he conked me with a cricket bat. That's my imagination, is it?

Ern, in uniform, so handsome, as we turned from Byron into Dalmar Street, saying, The critics never liked Byron either, Ethel. *Tis pleasant, sure, to see one's name in print. A book's a book, although there's nothing in't.*

In what? I asked.

A book. Seeing yer name in print. All overrated. He had a bit to do with his half-sister, and that caused a stir, too.

That's filthy.

What it was like back then.

I never understood why they'd named a street in Croydon

after him. I preferred wood: pine, oak, mahogany. Or flowers (a suburb needed a Rose Street). But Ern had always liked his stuff. Keats, too. Who, like Ern, never lived to see the success he deserved. Twenty-five – that seemed to be the age. Only a bit of a life.

There's nothing in it, he said, smiling, walking with his hands behind his back, as he always did when he got pensive.

Of course, back then, I had no inkling about his poems. He'd never mentioned them. I didn't think he was that sort of person. You know, off with the fairies, like Byron and his sister and half the Greek navy.

In what? I kept asking (I remember, I kept asking).

Fame, he replied.

Well, we needn't worry.

He just smiled at me, knowingly.

What are *you* gonna be famous for? I asked.

Having a sister like you, he replied, trying to kiss me, although I always pulled away, and he chased me a few steps, laughed. That's how it had always been with us. No complications.

You were famous once, I said to my brother.

When?

At school . . . you got the certificate for poetry, remember?

But he just walked, smiling at the bolt-upright sun above our house.

Dad reckoned you were onto something. What was it about? A horse?

A dromedary. A drowning dromedary.

But it got ashore, didn't it?

It did, Ethel.

That conversation seems ironic now, although Max said a

good writer never points out things like that – he or she hides his or her technique, but what the hell, I'm just an amateur.

Graves' Disease. If he'd never lived, how could he have died? And he died, angrily, I can tell you. But maybe that's not for now.

I mustn't dwell on the past. That's not what you want to hear about. That's for me. Pissy-pants Ern, sitting under the jacaranda at lunch, until I came along and said, What, you done it again? Him nodding. Me going to fetch one of the many pairs of pants Dad had left at the office. Changing him, under the tree, the purple fluff settling on our shoulders. Like grace. As the Lord said, *Give unto he who needs you the most* . . . Or something like that. Acts, was it? Either way, Ern'd piss his pants all the time. I'd change him, otherwise he'd just sit in wet undies.

Onwards and upwards. Dalmar Street. Every house the same, pretty much. Claret-coloured castles with neat yards. A rose, an aggie, a sundial, just in case. There was something about that in one of his poems. A Greek afternoon. Too much of the Byron, leading you up to Parramatta Road. Nice neighbours. We always had nice neighbours. Few fruit trees. Blocks were never wide, but deep, so the kids had somewhere to play.

'Hello, Mrs Kynoch.'

'Hi, Ethel.' Though she remained bent over, pruning, refusing to succumb to conversation. She, too, had failed to appear at the funeral. Bit of a shame, really, because Ern would often pop over (she being a war widow) and help her change a globe or knock a hen on the head. That warranted one afternoon, surely. It wasn't like she had much else to do. Except fertilise, and feed her hens. Though, I promised myself, I won't get nasty.

'Still warm,' I said. She just smiled. It wasn't even warm, but you had to make an effort. She'd had a rough trot, too. Not her, but her family. Story was her sister went missing when she was three. Mrs Kynoch was four or five. Anyway, no trace, and everyone assumed the worst, until Kerry (Mrs Kynoch) was finishing her Intermediate. There was a new girl starting school. Kerry looked at her, and knew right away. Mentioned it to her mother, who came to school to check, called the police and next thing, it was all over the news. But the sister refused to believe, or return to her family. Ern mentioned it once, over a cuppa, but she didn't say much – just, You don't always get to choose how things work out.

I left Mrs Kynoch with her mock orange, her little mock life. Walked home, along the road that sloped, gradually, towards Croydon. Ern, in his cart, racing down with no brakes. I knew it wouldn't end well. Called out, Ern! Stop yerself.

I can't!

Number forty. A little gate that creaked. I always knew when he was home from town, taking care of 'business' (although he never explained), from the Three Bells, although he was never a heavy drinker. A beer on a warm night; a sherry with his sister. Some poets, as it turns out, drown in the stuff. Apparently they need it to write, although that was never the case with Ern. Just a smoke on the back porch, late at night, studying the bright stars, mumbling (I can hear him, from the lounge room), If that's the case . . . it's so fuckin' futile. Yes, he used those sorts of words, but never in mixed company. Just when he was talking about the price of things, and how a war couldn't explain how a piece of rib eye cost a day's wage.

In we go. New carpet, because the old stuff wore to a thread. To your left, the sunroom. A little table where I'd sew. Would. Sometimes I'd find Ern in there, scribbling, and when I'd ask, he'd say, Letter to a fella I used to know.

Who's that?

No one you'd know.

That was Ern, always secretive. See, some thought him the soldier. And he did his bit. Never shirked. Some the insurance salesman, but he never liked that. He told me it was just for money. National Mutual treated him poorly, held back his retainer, never trained him properly. Then, when he left, lost all his records, payslips, the lot. So when people went looking for proof that he was real, they couldn't find anything. Weren't interested in what I had to say.

Little hallway. Leading into a lounge, with a wireless, where we'd sit charting the progress of the war. Ern'd say something like, Hitler's had it now.

Why?

You can't fight a war on two fronts. Look at him, England, America, Russia – it's just a matter of time, Eth.

Yes.

In the interim, a lotta mums are gonna lose their boys.

More's the pity.

Us two, sitting in our recliners with our Penfolds. If only I could get those days back.

Further along the hall: the kitchen on the right, the diner on the left; and further, my bedroom, and Ern's sleep-out, left like it was.

Pop your head in, you can smell it. And him. The Capstan and poppy oil, the old papers he'd pile in the corner, his never-quite-washed clothes. That'd be up to me. Waiting until he went out, gathering his jocks and shirts and putting them in the wash. Couldn't smell himself, I suppose. But men can't. Unless it's piss, and then they know, and sit waiting to be helped.

# 2

Ern got sick. Quick, too. He'd only just moved home when the worst of it started. Sleepless nights (I'd hear him switch on his wireless in the early hours, searching the static for a song, or voice; I'd think of going in, but had to sleep, because they were long days, caring for him), diarrhoea (back where we'd started, all those years ago, me washing his underpants), hot flushes (sweating, his sheets wet in the morning, and I'd have to wash those too). His heart would race. The doctors said that was part of it. Sometimes, sitting on the lounge at night, he'd turn to me and say, Jesus, Eth, I think I'm gonna explode.

And irritable. God! He'd call me into the sleep-out, ask me to get his food, and I'd take a few minutes too long, and there'd be a voice down the hall: Come on, Eth, what are you doing?

Me appearing: I'm goin' as quick as I can.

Who was that on the phone?

None of your business who it was, Ern.

I can't be gettin' up all the time.

I'd just look at him, and he'd realise, but never apologise. Just say something like, It's pretty crook, havin' to sit here all day.

Still, that was unlike Ern. The *real* Ern. The gentleman

Ernest Malley. That's what I had to remember, every time he raised his voice or thumped the wall or played the races up loud (no doubt to annoy me). I'd say, That's not my brother. I'd remember the boy, as he was. Climbing Dad's ladder, launching himself into space, expecting me to catch him. Up and down. Carn, Eth, one more time.

You're too heavy.

He'd stand in front of the mirror (I'd see him, through the crack in the door), all rib and bone, flat chest, sunken belly, razorback cheeks, eyes empty, dark.

You alright in there?

Got any powder?

I'd see him, feeling his ribs, and the bits where he used to have tits.

Cruel, what a disease can do to someone. But a sick body's nowhere near as bad as a sick mind. At least you can still see, understand, feel bad, or hopeful. The other happens without you realising. Like those people (I read about one woman) who think they're someone else. Invent a whole new person in their head, play out the scenarios, even talk and walk and behave in such and such a manner. See, that'd be worse.

He'd lie there, most of the day, morose. I'd try and cheer him up. Take in the *Weekly* and read to him. Katharine Hepburn. Judy Garland. But I guess he didn't care about all that. Had other literary interests, as it turned out.

He liked Keats. All that business about an interstellar zodiac. I have no idea what that was about. But he was probably sitting there thinking, Judy Garland – *please!* As I babbled. Not knowing. He could've told me. I would've been interested, or at least pretended. He could've explained the flowers on the goat's horn (was that something Greek? Max once explained, but I can't remember). Instead, he chose to keep it from me. Perhaps he thought I wouldn't get it, or maybe, maybe it was something so personal he couldn't bring himself to . . . confess. That's probably it: what he wrote in his poems.

It affected his thyroid. Which grew and grew, until it was a goitre, which was a bit distressing to look at, if you went to the shops, or down the street. But it wasn't his fault. Eyes popping out all over the place. That could unsettle people. Funny at first, like he was putting it on. But then people realised.

Poor old Ern. Seeing the end, I guess. Like a hallway that goes on and on, getting darker and darker. He must've sensed something. Max said it was there, in his poetry, his colloquy. *I have lain with the Lion, not with the Virgin, and become He that discovers meanings*. See, meanings. That's what he was working out, at three in the morning, searching the white noise. Although I don't know if he ever found anything. Probably just the next day's scratchings.

Ern was a sensitive man, but brave. A few days before he died, I got up to find him dressed in his uniform, tie done up, shaved (although he'd cut himself pretty badly). He said, Can't stand another day sitting in there, Ethel. How's about we go for a walk?

So off we went. The whole morning. Along Dalmar Street, Lang Street, through Centenary Park (I can still remember them pruning the trees) and down Queen Street towards Central Home Science School. He'd hobble, I'd help him, he'd sit at a bus stop, get his breath, and we'd be off again. At one point he said, Funny, isn't it, Eth, when you think of the thousands that've walked along here.

18

I wasn't happy when he got bogged down in dark thoughts. But I humoured him. What do you mean, Ern?

What I mean's – how the present's only interested in itself. Now. Maybe in the future, a bit, but hardly ever the past.

He explained, all the mums and dads and kids and everyone who'd walked along Queen Street, but now were pushing up daisies. That's the funny thing, he said. How quickly we forget.

You won't forget me, Ern? I asked.

Then he went all serious. You won't forget me?

I refused to answer.

Past the school. The kids were all out on the oval, eating lunch, practising hockey. A group of three or four girls sat close to the fence and watched us pass. They giggled, spoke, tried to look away. I knew what it was. Ern's eyes. Like he was the opening act at the Tivoli. Ern didn't seem to notice, but I did. I've always been aware of that sort of thing. The way people can study you, make notes, form theories, discuss them: all minus any respect for the truth of the matter.

Ern was too tired to walk home. Out of breath, sweating. I said, We shouldn'ta come. He said, What's the alternative?

That was it. I'd had enough. Self-pity; that's what he'd learnt from all those poets. *My name is writ in water*. Bullshit. No Malley's ever succumbed to a shitty liver. Especially Ern. In 1933 he left school to become a mechanic. We needed money, so off he went. I guess he had regrets (up to the end) about not being able to go to university, where he would've studied the greats, become great himself, perhaps. But that was Ern. Family first. Not long after, he got an offer to sell insurance. Did that for a while, lost interest, taught himself how to repair watches. Then came the war, and me and him standing outside Victoria

Barracks. In, and he had to strip off, and they thought him suitable, gave him a uniform, a gun, sent him to learn how to fight the Japs.

I noticed a man in his garden, approached him and said, My brother, Ern, seems to have had a turn.

Should I call an ambulance? He looked for Ern.

No, but you wouldn't have five minutes to drive us home?

Is my story dragging? Thing is, I need you to know about Ern. Exactly the sort of man he was. Once you know, the rest of the story will make sense. But if you come to see him as some sort of ghost, it'll be too confusing. You won't recognise him. The smell, the way he combed his hair, kept his sideburns just so. I need you to know he was a man of strengths and weaknesses. Complex. Sometimes confusing (proud one minute, whimpering like a puppy the next).

These were difficult days. One night, as I sat in the front room, I saw him, in his pyjamas, fertilising the roses (along the fence with number forty-two). I opened the window and said, What you doing?

They smell better at night.

Come on, Ern. Come in.

But he just sprinkled his granules, mumbling, maybe a poem, to each rose.

Ern.

I could see it running down his legs, the finely digested steak, egg and chips. Sliding, caught in the hair, dribbling down to the sock line, into his sandals. I ran out, grabbed him, whooshed the fertiliser from his hands and said, Come on. As he yielded. As he always had. Into the shower. The jamas into the copper, again.

Then, later, when he was clean, and felt better, I put him to bed. What would Dad say?

He didn't have this bloody . . . sickness. Mum didn't.

Doesn't matter. Dad's mum might've . . . or it coulda just happened. Doesn't need a reason.

Everything needs a reason.

No, Mr Moore's son didn't turn out like Mr Moore.

That seemed to get him. Life just drifted, like the tide, bringing debris.

This all started when we were four and seven. Dad'd take us to Dee Why and North Curl Curl, sometimes as far as Narrabeen. We'd walk along the beach for hours, gathering bits of wood, a shoe, or a chunk of someone's surfboard. Then we'd load it all in the car and head home and Dad would take it into the shed and throw it onto his pile of shitty things. He'd glue and wire them together, make sculptures, call them things like *Epiphany 1923* or *The Sunken Brow*. Me and Ern'd go out and look at them and I'd say, What's that about? But Ern wouldn't say a thing. He'd just study the rubbish, stuck together, like he understood what Dad meant.

Dad and Ern continued collecting. Mona Vale, Avalon Beach. I stopped going. After a couple of years the shed was full of stuff they'd made. One day, Ern came home from the beach, excited, throwing his arms about, and said, Look, Chile!

A soccer ball, with a single word written on the Side. *Farsa*. He said, What do you reckon it means?

No idea. Why Chile?

Where else?

Newcastle . . . New Zealand, perhaps?

No, Chile. *Farsa*. I wonder what it means?

Although I don't remember him checking. The ball was enough, still pumped up, ready for a game. He placed it in his room and it stayed there, beside his bed. *Farsa*. As I tucked him in that night, he asked, Who do you think owned it?

Some kid.

Chile, eh?

Yeah, I reckon, Ern.

I've been thinking. We should make some effort to find him.

How?

He had to think. Not sure. But it'd be nice, wouldn't it, returning it. Maybe it was a tsunami. They suck things out to sea. Maybe it got him, too, Ethel?

Maybe, Ern.

# 3

A blustery morning. I walked west along Parramatta Road, hair in my face, grit in my mouth, carrying a box of Ern's old things. Traffic everywhere, tooting and weaving, like they had to be there yesterday. I turned into the shop. The bell rang and I said, 'The devil's making that blow.'

'I don't know what it is,' Peggy Wright said. 'A cyclone, perhaps?'

'Wouldn't that be funny? You and me, trapped in here, the roof blowing away?'

She giggled. We both giggled, like we always did, most of the morning, when it was our day at the Legacy shop. Every second Tuesday: me and Peggy (she'd lost a husband on the Somme), staunch supporters of the recycled (like us, she said: bits of leftover lives no one wanted to pay full price for). Drinking our bullocky tea, with caster sugar; eating rock buns (that could break a horse's teeth), remembering husbands, brothers, neighbours and friends. From ten till four, supporting Legacy, like it supported us. Peggy was old enough to be my mother, but when I was with her, she felt more like a sister (the one I'd always longed for, perhaps).

I noticed a pile of shoes moving and, from behind them, a pair of eyes.

'Don't mind him,' Peggy said. 'Shelley asked me to have him again. I told her it was my Legacy day, but she was desperate.' She shook a finger at him. 'As long as you stay out of the way, right?'

But the small boy didn't reply. Just piled the shoes higher, to make a castle.

'How are you, David?' I asked.

'Good.'

'*Thank you*,' Peggy said.

'Thank you.'

He never said much. This I thought strange, although I'd never say anything like that to Peggy. I wanted to ask if he was okay: hard of hearing, perhaps, or dumb? I placed the box on the table and started unpacking. Shoes, pants, a couple of shirts and a pair of old reading glasses he'd needed towards the end.

'His?' Peggy asked.

'I was gonna pop them in the incinerator.'

'Someone'll buy them.' She picked up the first shirt and slipped it onto a coat hanger. 'How much do you reckon?'

'Two and six.'

Wrote the tag and attached it.

'How's Michael?' I asked.

Her ex-teacher son, who'd recently decided he didn't like children, or teaching, or anything, really, and had taken to the lounge.

'What can you do?' she said. 'Shelley's on at him but . . .' She stopped, noticing David. 'You don't need to listen.'

David stood, walked over to the bookshelf and started browsing. Took down a *Boys' Own*, sat, and opened it in the little valley of his legs. Peggy whispered, 'I said to him, How you

24

gonna pay the bills? But he didn't care. Just lay there, looking at the ceiling.'

'Is he ill?'

'No. Well, not that I know of.'

That's what Ern could be like, some days, I told her. Like he'd fall into a puddle of his own gloom, then thought about it, and climbed out. Like he was getting free from some Johnny Weissmuller quicksand that was setting around him. But he'd always manage to get out. Always.

The boy studied the pictures. Page after page. Checking we were still there, continuing.

'It's like he's given up on caring,' Peggy said.

'Why?'

'I don't know. Nothing's changed. Same people, same job, same everything.' She seemed perplexed, determined to work it out, here and now, perhaps with my aid.

'Sounds like a bita . . . depression.'

'*No*. We've never had none of that.'

'Just creeps up on people.' I thought of referencing Mongolism, or Graves' Disease, but guessed they weren't relevant. 'Men, especially. How old is he?'

'Thirty-five.'

'Well, that's the age. One day they see sunshine, the next, storm clouds.'

She thought about this. Maybe it had to be accepted: her son was depressed.

'And what if . . .?' she said. 'What do you do about it?'

'They give them an electric shock.'

She looked horrified. 'You don't reckon it's that bad?'

'From what you're saying.'

'No, if it was depression he'd just need to . . . I mean, we'd need to get him out a bit.'

'That's it.' I took over pricing Ern's things, as she'd lost interest. 'Take him out. Manly, for the day. And a hobby. Has he got a hobby?'

'No.'

'Fishing, crystal sets . . .' Come to think of it, Ern was the same. He never really had a hobby. I suggested darts (the Butcher's Arms have a competition on Wednesday nights), cycling, but he never . . . I descended, again, but pulled myself from the sticky mess. 'No, that's what he needs, Peggy. A distraction.'

She seemed convinced. Threaded Ern's dacks onto a hanger and said, 'Maybe we'll take him somewhere on the weekend. It's a shame to see him sitting there.'

Then she remembered David, still on the floor, but not turning pages anymore. 'You haven't heard any of this, have you, boy?'

He just stared at her – then the book.

Peggy whispered (although still loud enough for the boy to hear), 'I hope this doesn't mean *he's* gonna end up the same way.'

'Don't be ridiculous. He's just quiet – aren't you, David? Quiet?'

I put on the kettle and we sat at a table in the back room and talked until the first customer came. Some old girl after a coat.

'We're all out of coats,' I said. 'With all this cold weather, people haven't been donating them.'

She left, shitty, but I wanted to explain that we were just volunteers and had no control over what was brought in, or wasn't.

We straightened racks, moved shirts, trinkets, frocks. That's what most of our job was: straightening things, keeping order in the jungle. Back to the counter: more tags, more sorting, and

Peggy (who'd been preoccupied this whole time) said, 'The shame was, they'd just made him head of English. He was going to conferences, talking at meetings, even wrote a paper for some teachers' association. Then one day he came home and told Shelley, I quit.'

'That musta come as a shock.'

'Yes – they still owe a fortune on that house.'

David had had enough of literature. He stood, replaced the book, and looked around.

'What you after?' Peggy asked.

'Can I go outside?'

'No, you can't. Someone'd steal you, and I'd have to explain to your mother.'

He didn't seem put off. Approached the men's jackets, took one from the rack and tried it on.

'Careful with that,' Peggy said. 'We gotta sell it.'

The last of his shirts. As I examined it, I noticed a spot of blood below the collar. Peggy saw, but didn't say anything. 'We can't sell that one,' I said.

David was parading around the shop, stopping, saluting.

'It'll do for rags,' Peggy suggested.

A spot of blood, that wouldn't do. It had come at the end: Ern trying to sit up, coughing, most of the blood going into his handkerchief. But he was so hot, and sweaty, and the blood around his mouth and nose mixed with the perspiration and rolled down his face, his neck, onto his shirt. Just coughed, for two hours straight. One hanky after another, then, when they ran out, a bedsheet I'd ripped into pieces. As he stared at me, terrified, his eyes all aglow (even more than usual).

Peggy told her grandson to stop acting like an idiot. He sat on the floor and said he was bored and this got her angry, so she led him out to the storeroom and told him to stack the boxes of new donations.

Eventually Ern would get to sleep, but towards morning, that last morning, I heard a sort of gurgling. I wondered if I should go in, but left it. Left him, alone. Until the noise subsided, and there was silence (apart from a few birds starting up), and I knew. Knew I wouldn't have to look into those same eyes, hear that same voice, pleading for help. No time for maudlin behaviour. There'd already been enough of that. So I said, 'I've been meaning to set those books right.'

Problem being, people would come in, take a Nevil Shute, put it back under A; take a Joyce Cary, put it under T. Why? I can't say. You'd think a person'd think, Well, the next fella won't be able to find that. But people are lazy; getting lazier. With an endless capacity for self-deception. Happy to drop a piece of rubbish on George Street, but if someone did the same in their front yard ... So I began. Removing; replacing. But then the inevitable happened. 'A lovely book,' I said to Peggy, who was busy counting the pieces of a jigsaw someone had left at the door. I showed her. *Tortilla Flat.*

'Oh, I love Spencer Tracy,' she said, coming over. 'It was a lovely film.'

Lovely? She'd been? Without me?

'And a nice story.' She saw it in my eyes, stopped short. 'My sister-in-law asked.'

I just smiled. Returned to the books. A few Old Testaments, and Homer.

Peggy. If I thought about it, my only friend, Peggy. That's what happens. You lose touch with people, your circle diminishes, and you rely all the more on the few. To invite you to the movies every so often. Like I'd invited her: the Legacy dance (we two, waltzing in a hall full of war widows), a trip to the Botanic Gardens, Mrs McArthur's seat. But no, stop, I said to myself. That sort of thinking gets you nowhere. Sunny skies or stormy skies. We choose, every day. She was the only one who'd stood by me.

When Ern got sick – there every day when I couldn't go out, bringing meat from around the corner, eggs, and the sago pudding she made. She was the only one. None of Ern's old mates (what had happened to all of them?). And after he died, she was the only one who came to the cemetery. A light rain, makeup running, and Ern waiting to descend, again. A priest the bookmakers had paid for (fitting, considering what they'd taken from him).

Me and Peggy. *The Lord walked across the green, green grass . . .* She didn't say much, but she was there. Back into the chapel, and a room set out with a tea urn and cups and biscuits, although we didn't eat many.

'Me and you should go see something,' I said.

She lit up. 'We should.'

'Lena Horne, *Stormy Weather*, just opened at the Tivoli.'

'*Life is bare, gloom and misery everywhere,*' she sang, and smiled, just like the small service, *abide with me* and dimly remembered Keats. '*Stormy weather, just can't get my poor self together . . .*'

Though we never did get to see it.

Events overtook me.

# 4

The 297 to Burwood. Some sort of frump beside me with her head in a magazine. Would it have hurt to talk? She wasn't even reading, just drooling over photos of slow-cooked lamb shanks. Go, stop, go, but I had my window open, so I could descend into the city. Outside, spreading, settling across footpaths and lawns. And the smell (my eyes closed, the bus revving), taking you back to . . . me and Ern. My brother pushing me over, covering me with Dad's wheelbarrow, sitting on it, waiting. Me kicking, him laughing; slow-cooking with the sweating grass, dandelions, dogshit. Yes, Ern could be like that. A little terror. Couldn't see the harm he was doing. But then me, with my powerful legs, kicking him off, giving him a mouthful, and him saying, It was just a joke, Eth. And you couldn't stay angry at Ern for long.

Breathing in, as the old girl turned the page, and I smelt the front yard of forty Dalmar Street. Me, in bed on a spring morning, the sheets tossed off, the low sun on my face and legs. And him, moving closer, kissing my neck, and further down. The rustling of leaves from the path, the cockatoos in the jaca, and the thought of . . . (goodness, should I write it? Max said everything!). And soon, sleep turning to other things. A hand on my left breast, as I felt the desire, but sensed the limitations.

Still, once begun. Him against me, making his intentions known (and still the smell of lawn, the dark heaven of the barrow). Me, turning, accepting him. Until there were two bodies, busy, like a pair of fighting cobras.

'Would you like this?' the woman said, offering her magazine.

I attempted to recover. The smells, all of them, gone. 'Ta.' Pretended to look through (there was nothing that satisfying), as she stood, got out on Parramatta Road. Although the bus was full, no one else sat next to me. I wondered why. Did I smell? Were people worried about conversations they didn't want? Or maybe it was me. Maybe I'm an *unpleasant* person.

There was a soldier on the bus. Older than Ern would've been. He just sat, with his leg stump bandaged, like he wanted us to see. I wondered how it might've happened. Something heroic: trumpets, newsreels, Jap machine guns and men splayed dead across cycads. I could've got up, asked him, but you don't, do you? There were a lot of limbless men around back then. I just noticed the dried blood on the bandage. I wondered if it hurt, or whether they'd given him something. If he was holding in the screams (Ern did at first, too, but you can't for long). Had someone hacked off the offending limb one afternoon on the Kokoda? Had he wondered if he'd survive, or end up on the 297 to Burwood?

I noticed fresh blood. I couldn't look, or look away. It was repulsive.

Another stop, and plenty of people got on, but again, none of them sat next to me.

My stop! I got up, fought the crowd, alighted and hurried home. Past Mr Moore, busy setting out his window (managing a wave, at least); Mrs Kynoch on her porch smoking a cigarette.

31

Up the drive, fumbling for my key, in the door, a string bag full of things on the bench (they could wait) and I lay down on the bed. The stump still in my head. And Ern calling: Eth, I'm feelin' pretty crook.

Coming.

Reckon we should call someone?

I'm coming!

Well, perhaps we could've called someone, but would it have made any difference? More pain relief? And if he'd been admitted to hospital, what then? There was nothing they could've done. Although it would've allowed me to get some sleep.

I stormed down the hallway into Ern's room. The made bed (clean sheets), the mopped floor, but he was still there, lingering, calling, making demands. I grabbed his case from beneath the bed (the day he arrived at the front door – Just a couple of weeks, Eth – although there he was months, a year, later, expiring), placed it on the duvet and flung it open.

Right! What's left? The idea being, I could clean it all out – every trace. Turn the room into a hobby nook, another sewing room, or maybe even take in a boarder. Bita company. Although, what were the chances I'd find someone suitable?

The damn postcard! On the wall behind his bed, since he'd arrived. Innsbruck. When did he go to Innsbruck? He'd never mentioned Innsbruck, Austria, Germany. I took it down and noticed writing on the back: *Ern – The plot is sprung the Queen is took, One night enjoyed the next forsook. Remember? Lois.*

*Lois?* Ern and Lois in Innsbruck? *Lois?* Unless she was the girl he'd had in Melbourne. He'd mentioned her a few times. Oh, just someone I met. Used to go to the pictures. Nothing came of it, Eth.

That's a pity.

You work out, quick smart, if you're suited to someone. Too sanctimonious for me, Eth. Loved the sound of her own voice . . .

But what was Lois doing in Innsbruck? What plot? Sprung? Which queen? Was this some sort of break-up postcard? *Lois*. You never really knew with Ern. He only told you what he thought you needed to know, or wanted to hear. Maybe there was no Lois. Maybe he'd written the postcard as some sort of joke. On whom? Me? But I'd only ever been a decent sister.

I found a bottle of iodine in one of his drawers. Half full; it might've done him some good. Not now. A book I'd missed: Thorstein Veblen's *The Theory of the Leisure Class*. I flicked through, searching for more clues about Lois, Ern, the life that might've happened, or been made up. The book outlined contemporary practices of barbarian-tribe consumerism: the subjugation of women, the popularity of sport (and a lot of other dribble), but no more clues. Nothing handwritten, underlined. Maybe it had been Lois's book – maybe she'd read it to him, at night, beside the wireless?

I sat down on the bed and cursed my brother. There was no trace of him left in the front room. He'd censored himself, fed me clues, lies, left a few pieces of driftwood, the Chilean soccer ball. I put it in the case, but then stopped, removed it. I'd need something to remind me. He was still sitting on the barrow, keeping the world from me. Cruel Ern! Didn't I love you enough, Ern? Should I have been there, at the end, when you needed me most?

The case looked funny. The bottom was flat, the sides pushed out, splitting, but the top was bulging, heavy, full of something.

I lifted it, examined, smelt it, felt it. Newspapers, perhaps? The interior was protected by a piece of masonite. I fiddled with it, and it popped out. Revealing a collection of handwritten pages. I read the first one. 'Dürer: Innsbruck, 1495'.

*I had often, cowled in the slumberous heavy air,*
*Closed my inanimate lids to find it real,*
*As I knew it would be, the colourful spires,*
*And painted roofs, the high snows glimpsed at the back . . .*

I read it through. Not so much a diary, a travelogue, a description, as a poem. Finishing with, *I am still the black swan of trespass on alien waters.*

*Alien waters?* What did that mean? I looked through the pile and there were more. 'Night Piece'. 'Petit Testament'. Each with its stanzas and rhyme, rhythm, assonance and alliteration. All of the gear I remembered from Mr Wallace's Intermediate Poetry. *The swung torch scatters seed, iron birds and intuitive arms.* Poetry. Things that might've been, but weren't. Were, but couldn't have been. *Poetry?* For God's sake. Ern? I'd never noticed, seen, heard, read, discovered. But maybe there was more, not less, to this stumpy man.

I kept searching the collection, each poem named, printed neatly as if a third or fourth draft, like he'd taken the time, made a real effort to write words that expressed something . . . Well, I couldn't tell. I was no judge. Although some of the lines were pleasing: *Reserving to myself a man's inalienable right to be sad.* That sounded true enough. Like something Ern might've said, on a bad day. *Scrubbing my few dingy words to brightness.* Come to think of it, it was a nice bit of writing. Pleasant enough, as it

34

sat on the tongue and ear, as the smell of mown lawn sits in the nose, and memories in the head. *There is a moment when the pelvis explodes like a grenade.* Well, that was something that'd happened in the war. Something painful.

These poems seemed to be the real Ern. *Spain weeps in the gutters of Fitzroy.* Maybe he'd meant we had our Franco? Who knows, when you travel so deeply into a man's mind? That is all rhyme and riddle, and doesn't, and shouldn't, make sense. Nonetheless, it flowed, it enchanted, and it was written by my brother.

I assumed.

# 5

I found Roy McDonald at the Canterbury Library. Hidden between the encyclopaedias and periodicals, in the musty, never-much-accessed small bowel of rare books, acid-free, lignin fibres with their million meanings. Explanations, and rhymes, mostly forgotten (although Ern'd survive the ages). I noticed this man, playing with his beard, approached him and said, 'You're Karl's brother?'

He just waited.

'He said I might find you here.'

He didn't look happy. 'He did, did he?'

'Didn't think you'd mind.'

I had once given Karl McDonald (whose Queen Street house backed onto mine) eggs, but hadn't received a thanks; seen him sunbathing naked; heard him singing to himself as he pruned. Of a night, his wireless too loud, Count Basie coming into my bedroom as I tried to get to sleep. I'd remembered him saying something about a brother who'd taught English, who'd been head of department at King's, who knew every poet from Cicero to cummings. He'd said, Oh, yes, what he doesn't know about English . . .

So, poems in hand, I'd walked around to Queen Street. Knocked. Waited for the answer. Karl?

Yes?

Ethel, from Dalmar Street.

He'd lit up, sort of, but mainly confused as to what I was doing on his porch. I mentioned Ern, how he'd recently passed, and Karl seemed sympathetic (as much as a near-stranger need be). I said, I've just made this discovery. You wouldn't read about it . . . Showed him the poems, and he said, Now Roy's retired he spends most of his day at the library, writing.

Writing?

This novel. He's been talking about it for thirty years.

So I caught the bus again, found him, and explained how Ern and I used to have plenty of decent Rhode Island Reds, but how we'd lost interest. As he sat, clutching his pen, thinking (probably), What the hell do you want from me? I told him about Ern. About leaving home early, working as a mechanic, fixing watches, and the poems. I said, 'You never really know a person, do you?'

'How's that, Ethel?'

'To look at him, Ern seemed the least poetic person you could think of. He was practical, always working with his hands.' I noticed the blank page in front of him. 'You're working on something?'

'Trying.' He covered it, like I might notice the lack of words.

'When I think back,' I said, 'I realise there were signs.'

He didn't encourage me. Just sat waiting. Maybe he was between ideas, words, sentences, books?

'He *did* read – nothing highbrow – but I do remember him sitting on the back lawn. Maybe it was *Ivanhoe*. I remember Dad had that in the house, not that he ever read it. Dad was also practical. He could fix anything, although he did have a creative bent, too. Made sculptures out of . . .' I stopped, wondering. 'You probably don't want to hear about this.'

'You came all this way for . . .?'

'I'm probably disturbing you.'

There was a pile of pages, but I couldn't see anything on them.

'I'm still at the planning stage,' he said.

'Karl mentioned.'

'When I've got it all worked out, I'll start.'

'What's it gonna be about?'

'Not sure. I've got a few ideas. Daisy Bates, she's an interesting woman. I'd like to write about her.'

'That's the one lives with the blackies?'

'Yes. Years she's been out there, helping them, hundred-degree heat. You wonder what's going on in her head.'

'Well,' I said, happy for a way in, 'that's the same with most people, isn't it?'

'How's that?'

'I had no idea my brother was a poet. Never said a word, but when I found the poems . . .' At which point I took the sheath from my handbag, laid the sheets on the desk and said, 'There you go. And I never knew.'

He took his time, read through them, one by one. Started whispering, reciting: '*the careful spider spins his aphorisms in the corner* . . .'

I couldn't tell what he was thinking. He worked through the pile, then said to me, 'Your brother was a modernist?'

'Was he?'

'Was he?'

'I'm not sure. What's a modernist?'

'Someone's who's thrown off the past. Who wants to start again.'

'Perhaps he was.' Although I'd never thought Ern particularly modern at anything: the way he dressed, what he talked about, the films he saw or the music he listened to. 'Where would he have got all that from?'

'He would've had to read widely, I suspect. A lotta influences in here.'

'He never read much at all. Well, what I saw, anyway.'

'Of course, bits are . . . derivative.'

That didn't sound good at all.

'*One oasis and the next mirage* . . . and other bits are just strange, like here, *In the twenty-fifth year of my age, I found myself to be a dromedary.*' He looked up. 'I'm not sure what that could mean. Did he have an interest in camels?'

'Not that I know of. I'm unsure whether he made it as far as Africa during the war.' I wondered, where did he fight? Innsbruck? Kokoda? Martin Place? 'In what way would he be a dromedary?'

The poet, or novelist, with the whole world still in his head, said, 'You tell me, Ethel.'

'I'm no poetry expert. That's why I asked Karl. I thought it might be shorthand for something. You know, like a lark, or a nightingale?'

'No, I don't reckon. A camel's a camel.'

'Right.'

He kept reading.

'But do you think it's any good?' I asked.

'Bits, I guess. And you reckon this is ridgy-didge?'

'How do you mean?'

'He wasn't taking the piss, or having a bit of a laugh?'

'Why?'

'You tell me. Playing a trick on someone. Someone who liked modern poetry?'

No, a poem was a poem, surely. You wrote it to be a poem. You didn't compose a symphony to make fun of other people who composed symphonies, did you? 'I couldn't tell you, Roy. All I know is that when Ern set out to do something, he did it well.'

'Well, just a thought. Nice poems, some of them. Bits of them.'

I felt a little angry with him. Who was *he* to tell me Ern was derivative? What had *he* done? Why did he come to the library every day to write if he didn't write anything? That was just putting off writing. Maybe that's why he'd taught for thirty years – because he knew he wasn't really up to it. Still, who else did I have to ask? Croydon was no Montparnasse, Parramatta Road no 13th arrondissement. 'They obviously *meant* something to him.'

'I think so. Where did you find them?'

'Hidden in his suitcase. Like he didn't want anyone to see.'

'Why would that be?'

'He was a modest man. Maybe he was scared of people finding out. Maybe he thought I'd laugh at him. Maybe that's why people hide away.' What I meant was because they're scared of failing. You couldn't fail if you hadn't tried. Like me, never getting around to entering my marmalade in the Easter Show.

'I could just keep it,' I said. 'No one much I could show it to. Our parents are long dead. Quite frankly, I'm not sure what Ern got up to.'

'Kept a low profile?'

'I think there was a woman in Melbourne. Lois. Ever heard of a poet down there? Lois something?'

'No.'

'Right.' I tapped my nails on the table, thought of thanking him, and leaving. It'd been a long shot, but I'd tried. I'd owed it to Ern, and I'd tried. 'I better let you get back to work.'

He thought, wiggled his head a bit then said, 'It doesn't matter. I've finished for today. He sounds like an interesting fella, your brother, Ethel.'

'I reckon. Bit of a mystery man, but now he's gone, I'd like to know more.'

'Of course.' He checked the poems again, like he was deciding, then ripped a corner off his blank page, scribbled the words: MAX HARRIS, ANGRY PENGUINS JOURNAL, ADELAIDE, and passed it to me. 'This is the latest and greatest. Send it to him, maybe he'll publish it.'

'*Angry Penguins?*'

'A literary journal. Specialises in everything modern: poems, stories, art, philosophy. I have a feeling it might fit in.'

'You mean they might publish one?'

'You can only try.'

I thought about this. What a way to honour my brother. Put him in print. Tell him (wherever he was in the aether) that he was a bloody good poet, after all, and he shouldn't have been ashamed, shouldn't have hidden his gift. Yes, it seemed like just the thing to do: tell the world about Ern Malley. Shout his name from the rooftops. *The Darkening Ecliptic* (or so he'd called his collection). Brightening. Filling the world with whatever it was that made a man modern.

# 6

I never understood Ron Dalrymple. He was a strange man, always staring at you like he wanted something, or wanted to do something to you. Tall, with a too-thin moustache, and the nose of some pantomime witch. He sat opposite our cake stall, watching me and Peggy, or me, I guess. I called, 'How you going, Ron?' He just smiled, like he was thinking, You'll soon see how I'm going . . . *Ethel*.

Legacy had been running the stall for years, once a month, and me and Peggy took our turn each October, before it got too hot, after it'd been too cold. Peggy didn't see the point: twenty-five women having to bake a cake or two, the men setting up the table (outside Coleman's shop on Parramatta Road), then us sitting in the sun all day, packing up, ten quid in the till, and what were you going to do with that? She'd explained, in cost-benefit terms, it just wasn't worth it. Surely I had to agree? But I didn't. After all, you had to do your bit, make an effort. What was the alternative? Not having a cake stall? Not raising money?

So we sat on our wicker chairs, waiting, as old men and homemakers, with their little tribes of jam-smeared kids, walked past, stopped, felt the cakes, asked if they were fresh (*of course, yesterday afternoon!*), passed on (leaving indentations). As the sun warmed and the cakes sweated and I called to Ron, 'Can we organise some shade?' And he just shrugged and said, 'Not a lot we can do.'

Some people would stop and admire a sultana bar or tea cake and say, I can give you so much, and I'd say, but that's the price, as marked, and they'd say, I haven't got that much, but I can give you x amount, and I'd say (getting the shits on), As marked, thank you, taking it back before they squeezed it to death. Once, a woman slipped a rainbow cake into her handbag and I saw her go and called to Ron, and he walked after her and confronted her but she wouldn't give it back. I guess that's what Peg meant. Cost-benefit. And where *were* all the widows? Wouldn't have hurt them to pop by, offer a word of encouragement.

Still, you could only try. Even when it got boring, sitting, watching the cars drive by. So I opened my purse and got out the paper I'd brought. And a pen. Cleared a spot on the table and started writing: *Dear Sir, When I was going through my brother's things after his death, I found some poetry he had written . . .*

The librarian had given me the address. He'd had a copy of *Angry Penguins* under the desk (this was never explained) and showed it to me. I had a quick look. Nothing much: a few poems, a bit of tattle about Mallarmé and Rimbaud, whoever they were, a story, some strange artistic pieces. But this is what Mr McDonald reckoned was modern. So I copied the name and address, and said to the man, 'You reckon they take poetry submissions?'

'Oh, yes,' he said, smiling strangely, like he was undressing me there at the counter. 'Write a few poems, do you?'

'My brother did. I thought this Max Harris might like to see them.'

'Righto. It's very modern, cutting-edge stuff. No Henry Lawson or Banjo Paterson.'

'Ern was no Banjo Paterson, from what I've seen. But I suspect it's worth submitting his stuff. I think he'd want me to.'

Although I wasn't sure if this was true. Why'd he gone to so much trouble to hide the poems, avoid telling me? Not a word. Not a hint. But he was dead, and the living carry the dead, don't they?

*I am no judge of it myself, but a friend who I showed it to thinks it is very good and told me it should be published . . .*

'What do you think your chances are?' Peggy asked, leafing through the poems I'd brought along to show her.

'Well, I don't know how good they are, really.'

'You shoulda shown Michael.'

'He's too busy.'

'He would've had some idea. He's not too busy . . . sleeping.' As she went from one to the other, unsure, mumbling, 'Can't see it myself.'

'What's that?'

'*I snap off your wrist, Like a stalk that entangles.*'

'Well, it's *modern.*'

'How's that?'

'I dunno. We can't be expected to . . . it's just modern. Some people get it, some don't. Maybe if you've spent a lotta time reading poetry.'

'*I was a haphazard amorist, Caught on the unlikely angles . . .*'

I was getting shitty with her. She could make you feel that way sometimes. 'Listen, Peg, either you get it or you don't. I don't. You don't.'

'Either it *means* something or it doesn't.'

'Not necessarily. What about Picasso? Who knows what that's about?'

'You can still tell it's a woman, or a bull, or whatever, but *transmuted to a troll?*'

Peggy was nice enough. But a person needs some degree of subtlety. It's no fun if what you see is exactly what you get. A person has to be a bit of a mystery (like Ern, as it turns out). Otherwise they, you, life itself, becomes dull and predictable, like the recipe for a banana cake (sweating in the sun). Like Ron, still watching us (I'd called out, 'Ron, you can go home and come back later', but he hadn't even replied, just sat there, grinning).

*On his advice I am sending you some of the poems for an opinion . . .*

A nice woman bought a beef pie (although I'd warned, cakes only, *meat will turn*). I served. Peg was busy with the poems, her face twisted, tortured. 'It's nice if you can *enjoy* a poem.'

'You don't think there's anything pleasurable about them?'

She checked, to make sure, then said, 'Not really.'

'I don't know. Here, in this "Sweet William" one: *My blood becomes a Damaged Man, Most like your Albion . . .*'

'What's an Albion?'

'It doesn't matter.'

'Then you can't understand it.'

'You don't need to. You don't understand everything Shakespeare says.'

'Most of it.'

Although I doubted she'd ever read any.

*It would be a kindness if you could let me know whether you think there is anything in them. I am not a literary person myself and I do not feel I understand what he wrote, but I feel that I ought to do something about them . . .*

I stopped, surveyed the cakes. There were still a lot left, and the afternoon was dragging – as was my mood, patience, tolerance.

'A secret poet?' Peggy said, smiling at me. 'Though, it was, is, nothing to be ashamed of, I suppose. A hobby. An amusement. Like a person plays the piano, or makes sculptures.'

I saw Ern and Dad busy in the shed, cobbling a load of old shit together, the wireless blaring, the laughter – more than anything, the laughter they shared as they worked.

'You don't write poems for your own amusement,' I said.

'Yes, you do.'

She was right; you do. The hammering and nailing, the sawing, the welding of metal bits together, *Samson that great city, his anatomy on fire*, until Ern'd come in and get me, and they'd reveal what they'd done, and I'd think, What the hell is that? Both of them grinning, then laughing, like they were taking the piss out of me, and wanted to take it out of the world.

*Ern kept himself very much to himself and lived on his own in late years and he never said anything about writing poetry . . .*

'Still, it's a funny thing to do,' Peggy said, poking a friendship fruit cake.

'What's that?'

'Writing poetry. A bit . . . inward looking.'

*He was very ill in the months before his death and it may have affected his outlook . . .*

Mr Dalrymple approached, picked up a slab and said, 'Seems fair we take a few home, for the effort, if no one's gonna buy them.'

So we decided. Packed the butter half cakes and orange dream cakes into the boxes they'd come in, wiped down the

46

table, folded it, carried it to the boot of Ron's car. As we went he said, 'I've been waiting for a moment all day, Ethel.'

'How's that, Ron?'

'This might seem out of the blue, but me being a widower, and you . . .'

He couldn't say it; avoided eye contact, packed the table away, closed the boot and then had nowhere else to look. 'I find myself going to the movies.'

'You do?'

'I like war movies, and spy thrillers, like Alfred Hitchcock. But I'm happy seeing almost any type of film, Ethel.'

I processed this information. The way he could meet my eyes from so far away; the way he just sat in the sun, sweating, when there was shade a few yards away; the way he didn't mix, make conversation with me and Peggy, perhaps because he didn't want Legacy knowing his business, or perhaps because he didn't want to sound stupid in mixed company.

'I was just thinking,' he said. 'No point a person going alone. By the time you get cleaned up, shaved, get on a bus.'

'No, going anywhere by yourself's a bit . . . I mean, I've been doing that for years.'

'So, if I was going to a film, at the Five Ways say, it'd make sense to stop by your place and see if you were interested.'

'I'm like you, Ron. Not fussy.'

'Good.' He smiled; almost rubbed his hands. 'So, say, next Saturday night?'

God! A dog after a bone. But what could you do? 'If it's just about a movie, Ron.'

'That's it, just a movie.'

We stood, wordless. The cakes in their boxes, still sweating.

The till, almost empty. Peggy, waiting, watching. When I got back to her, she said, 'What was all that about?'

'Some people just take a bit of understanding,' I said.

# 7

It took me three buses, but I was determined. Point being, can you really know someone? Or just the bits they choose to show? For instance, if I studied myself in the mirror, what would I see? A not-so-young woman, stocky, flat-faced, with a Roman nose with a hint of upturned tip. Straight hair, not bad-looking, or good-looking. Plain, perhaps, but with a touch of the Nordic, or maybe Norman? A positive, almost cheerful outlook on life, although not blind to the dark side (the side, I think, Ern was exploring). A rational woman, but with a Catholic bent, although I rarely go to church anymore. Not an atheist, but agnostic. A doubter, some nights when I lay in bed, but then morning, sunlight, and the voice of God in the almond tree.

That's what you'd see. Someone very average. Unlike Ern, with his bent. I had no such urging. I'd tried several hobbies: ballroom dancing, crochet, knitting, even a course of leather-work at the Croydon Institute. But nothing had stuck. Except Legacy, but that was more a duty.

Three buses, through a warm morning, a boiling afternoon, until I arrived at Victoria Barracks. I had to walk half a mile to the gate, and when I got there I said to the guard, 'I rang earlier, about my brother.' I clutched my string bag full of spring onions. 'He was in the Second Third Battalion. I spoke to . . .' I put down my bag, found the envelope in my pocket and said, 'Warrant Officer Jim Tabor.'

'I got you, missus.' And he called. 'Bert.'

A soldier appeared, and the sergeant said, 'Take this lady to Records and Pay, will you?'

So there we were, the corporal and me, walking across the asphalt. I studied the parade ground, the living quarters, administration buildings, flags and old cannons and jacaranda trees. 'It's a big place, isn't it?'

'There's a war on.'

I wasn't sure what he meant. 'Terrible thing, conflict.'

'They start 'em, we finish 'em.'

That seemed reasonable. 'Lotta mothers won't see their sons again.'

This time he didn't reply. Maybe I was becoming too emotional, or political. Maybe he thought I was some sort of journalist, or German spy, fishing for information.

'That Hitler,' I said. 'If it wasn't for him . . .'

He turned to me. 'If it wasn't him it woulda been someone else. It's just the way it works.'

'What's that?'

'People. There's always a scrap.'

'I guess that's true.' As we plumbed life, with all its awkward angles and uncomfortable bits.

The corporal delivered me to a white building with white walls and a white door. There was a counter and a bell, but no sign of anyone in the office. He rang, waited and said, 'Maybe they've gone to lunch.'

'You wouldn't think so. Not with a war on.'

But he just glared at me strangely, like he couldn't fathom what I meant. Eventually the warrant officer appeared and the corporal left me, without so much as a goodbye. Like I'd been some unpleasant task.

Warrant Officer Jim Tabor had a badge confirming who he was. A walrus moustache, oiled hair and a freckle trembling in the corner of his regulation face. He kept licking his lips, but I wasn't sure if he was nervous or thirsty. Drill-sergeant eyes that measured the world in twelve-inch paces, and double time.

'I rang earlier,' I said.

'Ethel Malley?'

'You said you might know something about my brother?'

'Right.' He approached a desk, searched a pile of folders and returned with Ma-Mo (1941 Enlistments). He looked me over (like my buttons weren't polished) and said, 'What did you say his name was?'

'Ernest . . . Ernest Malley. Of Croydon.'

He opened the folder, ran a finger down a list of names and said, 'Ernest?'

'Yes.'

Repeating. Mumbling: '*Ernest Malley?*'

'Ernest *Lalor* Malley. Though everyone called him Ern, obviously, except me, when I was angry with him, then it was . . .'

Well, to cut it short, there was a lot of mucking around like this, a lot of chatting, but in the end the nice warrant officer found Ern's file (ENLISTED 20 JANUARY 1941), but really, considering the war, couldn't tell me any details. Just a basic record. He was there. He'd served. Don't you worry about that, missus. But . . . you could be anyone, he said, and I told him I was Ethel, Ern's sister, but he said you can't just say that, you've gotta prove it, and I said what about my ration card, but he said anyone could've written Ethel on that. I asked if Ern had been overseas but he just laughed and said he could be shot for telling me. I said Ern kept his military service to himself, but he said, That's common, for Returned men. I even told him about the poems, but he didn't see the relevance.

So I thought, Bugger you, mister. I placed my string bag on the desk, searched through, said, 'I just have to find my tablets.'

'You okay?'

'You haven't got a glass of water?'

And when he turned, and when he walked back to get me water, I checked the file, I saw a name: *Lois* . . .

'I can feel my breakfast coming up,' I said, gagging. 'But I have antacid here somewhere.'

*Lois Fauske, Kew.* I repeated the name a few times to make sure. Then closed my purse, took my bag and said, 'I must've forgotten them. Not to worry. Thanks for your help, Mr Tabor.'

I left him at the counter, with the water, and the file. Walked back to the front gate, said good afternoon to the guards, and almost ran back to the bus stop. *Lois Fauske, Kew* . . . At last, a name; someone who might know more about my brother than me. Surely he hadn't hidden himself from someone he *loved*.

I stopped at the GPO and asked a lady and she checked and said she could put me through. I was directed to a booth, where I sat waiting for the call. The smell of leather and varnished wood; the bakelite phone; a fly, managing circuits of decreasing circumference until he or she gave up and sat beside me, waiting. I thought about all the things I wanted to ask her: Did he tell you about his poems? Did he talk about the war, where he'd been? Did he talk about me, Ms Fauske? Was that you, in his

'Perspective Lovesong'? *I have remembered the chiaroscuro of your naked breasts and loins* ... Oh, what a thought. I hadn't realised Ern had it in him.

The bell tinkled and I picked up the phone and waited. 'Hello, is that you Ms Fauske?'

Then a sleepy voice. 'Is that you, Mary?'

'No, this is Ethel Malley, Ern's sister.' I waited. Did she even know he was dead? Surely they'd stayed in contact.

'Mary?'

'Ethel ... Ethel Malley.'

'Ethel ... can I help you with something?'

'I was Ern's sister.'

'Who?'

'Ern, my brother, your friend.'

'Ern?'

'Yes. I'm calling from Sydney. I found your name in his file at Victoria Barracks, and was wondering if we could have a chat.'

'Why?'

'To talk about Ern.'

She sounded like she was still asleep, or drunk, or on some sort of medicine. Maybe she was just simple. I imagined her, lying in bed, clutching the phone, some new fella (perhaps) clawing at her chiaroscuro breasts. 'I found a postcard you wrote to Ern.'

'A postcard?'

'From Innsbruck. I thought, perhaps, you'd travelled together.'

'With Ern?'

'Yes.' Recognition. She'd used his name, she was remembering him, although it all seemed a bit dim and distant.

'I've never been to Innsbruck.'

'But you . . . you must have.'

Silence.

And then I recited: '*The plot is sprung the Queen is took, One night enjoyed the next forsook.*'

'Is this some sort of joke?'

'Ethel. Ethel Malley. Sister of Ern, who you went out with, didn't you?'

'Never heard of any Ern. Sure you're not getting me mixed up with another Lois?'

'Lois Fauske, Kew?'

'Yes, but maybe it's a different Lois Fauske? Sorry, I can't help you.' And without so much as a goodbye, she hung up.

I was left holding the phone to my ear, then the fly managed a second wind and landed on the receiver. Either Ern was lying, or she was. I wondered whether I should call her back, demand an explanation. But what if she was right? What if there'd been no Ern and Lois?

I caught the bus home. All the way imagining Lois and Innsbruck and Warrant Officer Tabor's baby-bum skin and hearing their various voices, none of them reliable, it seemed. I smelt freshly cut lawn, but it didn't register. Viburnum and pittosporum, both of which gave off the smell of childhood (one outside Ern's room, one outside mine). I walked up Byron Street without thinking of Byron, although I could hear poetry, and not just in the branches of Mrs Kynoch's golden elm. I heard the love song, thought of the Princess of Princess Street. Finally, as I approached number forty, I thought, Damn it, what's it matter? If the past doesn't want to be known, I don't want to know it. You, Ern. Your girlfriend (if ever she was). You want secrets, you keep them. I just don't care.

I searched the letterbox, and there, a postmark from the Adelaide GPO. I opened the letter, hoping Mr Harris would agree: Ern Malley was no poet. But that's not what happened.

*Dear Ethel,*

*Thank you for sending me the MSS of your late brother. I read it through carefully and I was very much impressed with it. I should have no hesitation in publishing the poems you sent me in the January issue of* Angry Penguins *. . .*

I didn't know what to think. Pleased, shocked, and disappointed that maybe he was the great poet I, and others, had suspected. Either way, confused. My brother was still taunting me, still sitting on the wheelbarrow. Mr Harris went on to explain how he and his committee might want to publish Ern's work in a book, and send it to America, to England. He asked for more of his poetry (was there any, hidden somewhere else?) and 'details of his life, his work, the nature of his illness, his interests in architecture and art, and so forth'.

Right, I thought, standing at my gate, my hand shaking with excitement, the roses (suddenly) smelling, the children (all at once) shouting down the street. Ern Malley, genius. Bugger me bloody well dead.

# 8

I worked out there was a fuse in the box, and fixed it. Went into the shed, fighting my way through the piles of junk me and Ern had deposited over the years. Hot, too, so you could imagine yourself descending, abandon all hope, as Ern might say (not to me, it seems). Old paint tins that had fallen over, so I stacked them in a corner. A tea chest of tools that had come apart, so I gathered them in a pile. Three boxes full of someone's toys, children's books, party decorations. I wondered, Whose children? Someone must have left them with us, and forgotten to reclaim them. But that would've been decades ago.

Hell. That's what it was. Somewhere no one wanted to go, but where we had to, eventually. As kids, me and Ern were given hell banknotes by the Chinese woman around the corner. Cheap, nasty-looking things, printed on tissue paper: flat-headed emperors and dragons, denominations of death in fifty million slashes of a sharpened razor. She said, 'Burn them for good luck.' So we went home, told Dad, dragged him outside and lit them (Ern managing to scorch his blazer). We stood watching, the smoke taking war, cancer, whatever it was that had killed Mum, the perve at the athletics club, long division, fruit and everything else evil out of our lives, up, up, into the Croydonside layer, dissipating in the smoke from the glass factory. We watched, deciding all our misfortunes were gone, and only luck and love lay ahead.

There were some smaller boxes, and I checked inside. If Mr Harris wanted more, I'd find more. If Ern had hidden poems in his case, chances were there were others. He couldn't have just started with 'Dürer: Innsbruck, 1495'. There must have been earlier yearnings, hidden from me and Dad. Maybe that's what he was doing, sitting on the shed roof? Or in the toilet?

The first box contained primers, grammar books, Greek and Latin. I stopped to admire the Malley copperplate, the neat lines and precise columns of debt and credit, like a ledger we were still using. BREAD 5d MILK 7d BUTTER 2d – and the red numbers in smudged ink. A little doodle of a bird, or was it . . .? No, the dirty bastard had written, *a vaginer*. And its owner, with her slit eyes: Mrs Wu (Ern singing, *Wu, Wu, how do you do? Nail and hammer and reversible screw*). But that was Ern, puerile, none of the modernist poet back then (or was it?).

I kept searching. Another box. A few old atlases, dictionaries, *Gulliver's Travels* and . . . hold on, what was that? No. Manuals. Mower. Our old Austin. I stood, surveyed the shed and realised how big a job this might be (and me in my good dress, ready for *Tarzan*) and wondered if it was worth it.

Another box, and another, more magazines, knitting patterns, and the knitting itself: moth-eaten jumpers and cardigans. I shook the box and it fell apart. Wondered what Mum would say. But she was long gone. Unless there were ghosts, it didn't matter. The old dining-room chairs, the table with the broken leg. And there we were, the family Malley, all of us, so I couldn't have been more than seven. Dad reading the paper, Mum telling him not to, me playing with my peas, Ern hiding his boiled carrots under his mashed potato. Mum saying, I can see what you're doing.

They're disgusting.

Turning to Dad for support, who only said, Eat yer carrots!

The surly eyes, the screwed-up nose, the carrot on the four prongs – sniffing it, tasting it, Mum repeating, Eat the damn thing!

He tried. Then coughed, gagged, spat it out in his hand, and Mum said, Don't be so dramatic. Looking to Dad for support, who only said, No one's ever died from lack of carrot.

Mum standing, taking Ern's plate, saying, If you couldn't be bothered eating the damn things. Storming out to the kitchen, as Dad watched us, eyes saying everything: Careful, kids, don't say a word – she's about to explode.

I think, in a way, my mother did explode. Or implode. Through disappointment. A husband who didn't seem to care about anything; a son who showed no respect; a daughter, me, plain, slightly unappealing, perhaps. That was her life: we three moons circling in an orbit of crocheted cardigans and tea cosies. None of us ever as thankful as she wanted, expected, and finally, demanded. Enough to kill anyone, perhaps.

There were more poems, I knew there were. Maybe he'd scribbled a novel, something autobiographical. I realised you weren't born good at writing; it took practice. So there must've been apprentice pieces. Or had he burned them, like Mrs Wu's hell notes? Maybe I was in one? Disguised as an old maid. *The widow Eth blew her bottle top in an explosion of Bren guns in the Portarlington dew?* Well, it wasn't *so* hard . . .

58

*Dear Mr Harris,*

*Thank you for your letter of reply and your kindness in giving your opinion of Ern's poems. I am very glad to know that you think they are so good . . .*

The wheelbarrow, with its rust holes for air. Thankfully. I was still under it, kicking, shouting for him to let me out, and he was still laughing.

There was an old pedal car. I used to drive it from the top of Dalmar Road, and Ern'd be in the back. Although it wasn't much of a hill, it was enough for us to get a good head of steam. Flying down the street, Dad calling, Put on the brake, Ern! Although we were going so fast it didn't matter. Ern calling something like, What d'yer reckon, Eth? Me saying, Stop the bloody thing. While I could see the possible outcome, it didn't occur to him. Nothing much did, really. Until we hit the gutter, tumbled a few times, rolled on the grass, grazed a few shins, got more dog shit on our clothes.

I gave up. I was getting too dirty. Didn't want to ruin the evening. Just shouted into the rafters, 'Thanks a bloody lot, Ern!'

No reply. Bastard.

'Who was she, eh? Yer bloody girlfriend?'

Living in a conspiracy of silence, with her Mallarmé and vaginer, a transfigured parrot he could spend his evenings fingering. I saw him, down the back shed, busy with his quill, invisible to the world.

'There was no one, was there? Lois, my arse. You made her up. Like you made it all up.'

Silence. Although the shed was still full of ghosts. Dad, with his pipe, a business shirt, vest and suspenders; me; Ern, sitting cross-legged on the ground. Yes, it was a different shed back then. Neat, little stacks of things around the walls, all the pipes and timbers suspended in the trusses, a shadow board for the still-living tools. The Aztec ceremony: a couple of oars we'd found on the beach, crossed, lashed together (Ern and his fisherman's friend); a couple of old buoys; wire and timber, twisted into tree shapes, and bits of old rubbish hung like fruit. Then Mum coming in. What, you doin' another one of those?

Dad only smiling.

Ern saying, Tell her what it's called, Dad.

*Baroque Exterior.*

Righto. Arms crossed. You two kids need to come in for a bath.

That was it. There was no chance she'd say it was any good. She had no idea what it was, what you could do with it, what it was worth. It was just one in a long line of pieces of shit that Dad had wasted his evenings making. She must have been so disappointed in him, me, Ern – all of us, hanging off every word our idiot father said.

'Ethel?'

Christ, I'd forgotten. 'Back here, Ron.' I went outside, brushed off, and met him in the drive.

He was wearing an old suit. 'I heard you talking to someone.'

'Me? No, just looking for something in the shed. Come in a minute while I clean up.'

He was hiding something behind his back. Produced a bunch of red roses and said, 'Something for the kitchen.'

I wasn't sure what to think. We'd only agreed on a movie. Roses, weren't they romantic? I just wanted Johnny Weissmuller. But I took them and said, 'They should cheer the place up.'

I went to the bathroom and wet a flannel, wiped my face and arms, cursed Ern for almost ruining a nice evening. 'Get yerself a drink,' I called. 'There's a beer in the fridge. We're not running late, are we?'

'No, plenty of time. Just show newsreels, and you know what they're like. I mean, not saying I'm not *patriotic*, but you go to the movies to get away from it, don't you?'

I emerged, and we sat across from each other at the breakfast table. Like me and Ern, on an autumn evening. He said, 'Live alone, do you?'

'Well, now. I used to live with my husband, Evan, then later, Ern. I told you about Ern?'

'Yes.'

Descended. But managed. 'Maureen O'Hara, isn't it?'

'No, Frances Gifford this time.'

Silence. As the sun set, Dad worked in the shed, and Ern snored from the front room.

'Quiet, I bet,' Ron said. 'Alone, I mean.'

'Yes, Ern was company.'

Ethel, he was calling, Bring us some water, will yer?

I examined the roses, sitting in the vase I always kept handy, just in case. 'You shouldn't have, Ron.'

'Well . . . not much to spend me money on anymore.'

'No?'

Eth?

Shut up!

The letter to Mr Harris lay on the table. Unfinished. I'd meant to include some more poems, if I found them in the shed, but I hadn't.

'Your brother served?' Ron asked.

'Yes, but he was also a poet.'

'Don't say?'

*I never knew that Ern wrote poetry. He was a great reader and told me he did a lot of study in Melbourne. He said he often used to go to the public library at night . . .*

'He said he often used to go to the public library at night.'

'Right. Why was that?'

*I wouldn't have thought Ern was interested in art and architecture as you say . . . He did have a coloured postcard pinned up in his room which I haven't included because the writing on the back seems to be personal . . .*

'Well, Ron, you think you know someone.'

'How's that?'

'As kids, we were close. He told me everything.'

*I am sorry I can't tell you much more about Ern, but as I said before he kept very much to himself. He was always a little strange and moody and I don't think he had a very happy life, though he didn't show it . . .*

'You're right, Ron, it's quiet without him, but it's always quiet when people go. You take them for granted. Sometimes there's a reminder (like when people are sick, and you think they might die), but soon enough you're walking past them, not noticing . . .'

He waited a moment, then said, 'It's a seven-fifteen bus.'

'Right. Enough time for a bit of lippy?'

'I reckon.'

I realised I'd become bad company, so I made a decision to blow off the dust. I slipped on my best shoes and a cardigan and locked the front door. As we walked, I sang: *'Thou hidden love of God, whose height, whose depth unfathomed no one knows . . .'* And he joined in: '*I see from far thy beauteous light* ...' A couple of old Methos, we, as we walked, the full moon strained like curd through muslin, smoke from a fire somewhere, and the smell of frangipani. 'So much nicer than *those* poems,' I said, dreamily.

'Which?'

'Ern's. Modern, I guess, but not something you can sing along to ... *my heart is pained, nor can it be at rest, till it finds rest in thee* ...'

A twenty-minute trip to town in a crowded bus. A couple of boys hogged a seat, and Ron cleared his throat, but they didn't care. Maybe we weren't old enough. Crippled enough. Like Ern, with the walking stick he used in the last few weeks. Demanding I take him to Repin's Quality Inn for a Vienna coffee (his favourite). Full uniform, people assuming (I suppose) he'd just got off the boat from Normandy. But it didn't matter – he wasn't doing anything wrong, as such. He had one little decoration, and I asked him what it was for. He examined it, read the inscription and said, Everyone gets one.

What for?

Turning up.

Ron sat squeezed in the same spot, gazing out, wondering. 'What battalion did you say your brother was in?'

'Second Third.'

'You musta misheard.'

'How's that?'

'They were on the Malayan Peninsula. Still up there somewhere.'

I waited, surprised. He looked at me, maybe to gauge my reaction.

'He was medically discharged.'

'That explains it.' Although his expression suggested it didn't, really. 'Bit of a mystery man, your Ern?'

'Could say that. Mr Harris reckons those poems of his might make him famous.'

'Bit late now, eh?' Trying to smile.

Down George Street, into the cinema, and he bought me ice cream. The newsreel, Rabaul, poor old Darwin bombed again. Women and children sheltering in holes as soldiers ran for their lives, manned anti-aircraft guns, and one of them (Look, I wanted to say to Ron), one of them resembled Ern. 'How long ago was this?' I whispered.

'Few weeks.'

'Right.' And again, the spitting image of my brother. 'That one looks like Ern.'

'Isn't he dead?'

I didn't reply. Then the man talked about Tojo, and Himmler, and it was too late to tell.

The movie started. Johnny Weissmuller wasn't so fit anymore. Maybe it was the war. He had little paunchy tits, like Ern, and a gut he seemed to be sucking in. I whispered to Ron, 'He's seen better days,' but he ignored me, lost in the film, following the progress of the German paratroopers who, for some reason, had seen fit to land in the jungle, kidnap Boy, and slap a lot of people around. Tarzan wasn't about to take it. He was shot at, tied to a tree, but none of it mattered. None of it. I just saw Ern, with his shirt off, swinging from the vines, muttering to the monkey.

All at once, I felt out place. In this cinema, with this man I didn't know. I wanted to stand, go home, sit on my brother's bed and smell him, talk to him. I remembered. Opened my purse and took out one of Ern's poems. *The evening settles down like a brooding bird* ... The words seemed more real than anything. Than Tarzan (and the Nazis with their uniforms that didn't look right); Ron; the fake jungle that we'd played in as kids. I just wanted to pull Ern from his foxhole.

And when it was all over, I did. Sat at the table at one o'clock and wrote:

> *I've got so much to tell you about Ern. A marvellous man. And as you say, a genius, perhaps. I've checked the timetable and there's a train gets in next Wednesday, three-fifteen, if you'd have the time to meet me, share a cup of tea and discuss my brother?*

I walked to Queen Street in my dressing gown. No one around, of course, though I thought I saw Mrs K looking from her window. I was happy, beaming, full-mooned and Methodist, singing lusty lines to my God, and Ern's. And home again, to bed (never mind Ron). And lay there, reciting the lines that'd stuck in my head: *If this be the norm of our serious frolic there's no remorse.*

# 1944

# 9

It wasn't the most promising start. Hardly a city: a few small towers sitting in the sun, a river that was really a creek, overgrown with reeds, full of brackish water. There were several camps of men, washing hung out, little fires on the banks of despair they'd colonised. I said to the man next to me, 'I've never been to Adelaide before.' He just grinned.

It'd been a long trip. Across some nice country, with fruit trees and mountains, then paddocks, plenty of sheep, before it dried out. Broken Hill, but I didn't bother getting off. Bleached desert; as we rheumatically clanged past. Not much to look at, really, and I wondered why I'd come. Did I need to? Still, I'd be able to explain it all: Ern, the private man, the larrikin, the trickster, the thinker, the poet. More wheat country, towns with proud little ovals, tractor dealers, a few cars, dogs, pubs. Before slowing into Adelaide Railway Station: a paling roof, each of the timbers rotten, cracked, giving way. Wide platforms with baggage trolleys and a few porters, although most of them stood talking, smoking, their shirts undone to their nipples, pants down around their hips. I gathered my few things and got off. The crowd, as it was, dispersed, and I was left alone with my case (Ern's), my umbrella and a blend of body odour, smoke and beer.

I sat on a bench that didn't want to take my weight, picked up an old newspaper ('*Janus* sunk off Anzio') and wondered what to do. He'd said he'd meet me. What did he look like? I'd seen a picture. Had I? Had I seen a picture? Either way, I was the only one on the platform. Eventually I gave up, wandered down to the concourse and looked around. Turned a circle, and said, 'Where are you, Max?'

'Ethel?'

There he was, smiling, a sort of younger Claude Rains.

'Mr Harris?'

'Max, please.'

We shook hands. He took my case and said, 'Sorry I'm late, but I couldn't get a park.'

'That's alright.' Too nice, as usual. I should've given him a mouthful then and there, set the tone, but I didn't.

He walked and I followed. 'That's one of the few advantages of living in Adelaide, Ethel. You can always get a park, but today . . .'

'I was only waiting a few minutes.'

'Good trip?' He stopped and bought cigarettes, offered me one, lit up. 'D'yer mind?'

'No, go ahead. Ern smoked, but when he moved back in I told him, not in my house, and he said, Well, it's not just your house, is it, Ethel?'

He seemed happy to listen. Led me up a ramp that disgorged into the guts of the city. More little towers and pubs, a few cars on the wide street, a bus blowing smoke.

'That's where we grew up. Croydon.'

'Funny, isn't it,' he said, 'a man who wrote poetry like that, growing up in Croydon. He never travelled much?'

'No, not that I know of. Lived for a time in Melbourne, but I mentioned that.'

'With this . . . *Lois*?'

'I believe. He was in the army, but he never said much about that. I think he might've served up North. Darwin, perhaps. I think I saw him in a newsreel.'

'Don't say?'

Not a dismissive *don't say*; but a sort of, *I might be interested, but you'll never know.*

We walked past Parliament House. Big, ambitious columns; like someone had wanted the place to amount to something. The crowd thickened, but they all smelt of talcum powder, poppy oil, sweat.

'I was drafted,' Max said, as we waited at the lights. And waited. Always green the wrong way. 'I told them I wasn't good for much but they signed me up anyway, sent me off for Basic, and I ended up at some godforsaken camp digging latrines.'

'They didn't think you could fight?'

'I told them. I didn't want to get killed, Ethel.' He managed a grin I'd get to know; the do-you-believe-me-yet grin, the raised eyebrow (one side), the tilted head. Maybe he was a smart-arse. That'd make it a long stay.

'Eventually they got sick of me and sent me back to town, and I was put in charge of a spotlight.'

I waited. Was he for real? A spotlight? Was that code?

'See, there.' He pointed to a department store. 'I was on the roof, every night between one and seven, but Göring hasn't sent anyone our way yet. Which is surprising,' he grinned again, 'cos you'd think Hitler'd be interested in Adelaide.' But then he stopped, and seemed to be having proper thoughts. 'Do you reckon Hitler would even know about Adelaide, Ethel?'

'He might.'

'Anyway, I still go up there when they're desperate for someone.'

We crossed the road and headed along North Terrace, beside a high wall surrounding an old mansion. Max said, 'That's the governor's place.'

'Very posh.' As I tried to see over the wall.

'You a monarchist, Ethel?'

'Well, you gotta be, don't yer, with a war on.'

'Perhaps. Politically, I'm undecided. I like the idea of communism, but they shoot poets, generally.'

I tried to laugh, but it was too hot.

'At least Ern did his bit,' he said. 'Which is ... well, Ethel, it's all a bit strange.'

Now we were waiting at another set of lights.

'How's that, Max?'

'The way you described him, Ern seems, seemed, like such an *ordinary* man.'

'He was. Simple. Very few complications. Sometimes he was moody.' We crossed.

'So where do you think he got the inspiration?'

'I couldn't tell you.'

'Maybe he was just born with it?'

'Like Mozart?'

He didn't seem sure about this. 'Perhaps. I suspect there was someone influential. Someone he mightn't have told you about?'

'This Lois? You heard of anyone with a name like that, in Melbourne – a poet, writer?'

'Na, although ... I reckon he wrote about their relationship.'

He sat on a bench beneath a plane tree. Told me he just wanted to get his breath. The street was lined with proud little sandstone buildings with wide porches, shutters, lights that burned in the day. One, taller than the rest, had a SHELL sign, with the S faded beyond what you could see. Max said, 'When you mentioned Lois, I re-read the sixteenth poem.'

I waited. No, he seemed alright. Not a smart-arse, just a clever sort of chap. He took out a sheet of paper, and I recognised one of the copies I'd sent him. He read: '*In the same year I said to my love (who is living), Dear, we shall never be that verb perched on the sole Arabian tree . . .*'

'Makes sense,' I said.

'*. . . so I forced a parting, Scrubbing my few dingy words to brightness.*'

'Goodness, I'd never thought about it that way. You reckon he broke up with her?'

'I reckon. Thing is, Ethel, you study these poems, they reveal a lot. The Arabian tree is his poetic . . . sense, his essence, as a man and poet. Maybe she was the problem, not the solution. Maybe coming home to live with his sister was the solution.'

'No?'

'It's just an interpretation. You can agree or disagree. But it seems clear to me. Here was a man – a genius, I reckon – who knew his creative powers, but also knew he had no chance of expressing them. So when he got sick . . .'

'He saw it . . . clearly?'

'Perhaps.'

And I did. Clearly. It was like Ern had written in some foreign language, and Max was the only man in the world who knew it. 'I just thought he was a scribbler, Max.'

'No, a scribbler couldn't write this.' He shook the paper (finished his smoke and stepped on it). 'Look at these words here,' and he searched another page. 'Bourdon, enteric, crenelated, valency . . . they're not words you find in the average car mechanic's vocabulary, Ethel. It's like he's sat for years, reading a dictionary.'

'He often talked about Keats and Byron.'

I sat back, took in the warm, afternoon air, smelt the chlorinated fountain spray. Maybe the place wasn't so bad. More than a whiff of civilisation, along with the body odour. 'So you reckon you'd like to publish him, Max?'

'Of course.'

He reached into his jacket and produced a copy of *Angry Penguins*. He seemed to have everything in his jacket. This was something I'd discover, given time. Max was a Renaissance man. He had his finger on (and in) everything. You never knew what he was thinking, what he'd planned, what surprises he had in store. An old head on young shoulders (although it was a young-*looking* head). Like his brain was a giant butterfly net, catching everything, classifying it, describing it in his little journal. Which I studied. Him, the editor (along with Mr Reed, who I'll tell you about later); Sid Nolan, the decorator.

'I want to publish all sixteen poems in the one edition.'

It didn't seem a longish magazine. 'That'd just about fill it.'

'So?' His quizzical but defiant look (more about that later). 'If I print one I gotta print them all. They go together, Ethel.'

'You'd do that? For Ern?'

'For *art*, Ethel.'

There were some strange paintings: someone called Tucker, and one called Perceval. Birds, perhaps, but their bodies were as big as houses. Still, these weren't the local watercolourists.

'I wouldn't want any payment,' I said.

'You wouldn't get it, either. It's not exactly *The Robe.*'

There were a few other poems. More modern ones, by the look of it. *The lash of eyebrows on my melted moments, and you, smelling the cordite of our misfortune* . . .

Max said, 'Not as good as Ern's.'

'You reckon?'

'I tell you what, Ethel,' and he lit another cigarette. 'I was sitting there at eleven at night and I opened this letter from some woman in Sydney called Ethel Malley, and she says, *Dear Mr Harris*, and I'm thinking, Here goes, if the brother writes like her, god help us. I read them all in twenty minutes, and I knew. I wrote to John straight away. Then I went to bed, but I couldn't sleep, so I got up and read them all again.'

'*No?*'

'I did. I wouldn't joke with you, Ethel. I say it like I see it, which is why I've got my enemies.'

'Really?'

'You don't have to look far. Small town, big fish with a modernist brush. Still, I don't care. If it's good . . .'

It seemed too good to be true. All of my life, I'd never known anyone as clever as Max Harris. The doctor, perhaps, but he treated me like I was simple. 'Thanks, Max.'

'Haven't done anything yet. But when people read these poems . . .' He patted his pocket. The rest of them must have been in there. 'I want to get them read overseas – London, New York – these are as good as anything anyone's writing over there. Better. Fresher. With a real Australian voice.'

Of course, he might've been joking. An elaborate, staged event for his amusement, and my destruction.

Then he turned to me with an old-fashioned, no-nonsense smile and said, 'You must be tired from that trip?'

'Come to think of it . . .' I felt my head rolling on my shoulders, my eyes refusing to focus; the excitement, the newness of it all, fading. 'Sleep for a week.'

We made it to his car – an old Austin with windows that wouldn't wind down, and a steering wheel you could remove while driving. He didn't stop for lights, unless there was something coming towards us. Unnerving at first, but I got used to it. Rules, he explained, were for those stupid enough to follow them. Man, he said, had the power of free will, logic, even (as Ern had proved) abstraction. So why would you wait at a light if nothing was coming?

He sped past a tram depot, the sorry-looking red and gold boxes sitting sweating, like everyone, in the sun. Turned down a side street and pulled up in front of a small flat with an over-grown garden. We went in through a camellia and pepper tree jungle, me tripping on a path of broken concrete; a cat at the door, licking a dry saucer. It followed us in. To a lounge room (of sorts) with a couch buried under books, papers, clothes and wine bottles, which spilled onto the ground, and a rug (I could just see) drowned by a life (bohemian, I guessed, different to how Ern had lived) of free-living and sloth, plates of food scattered like unexpected dog turds.

'Have a seat.'

I couldn't see where, so I moved some books and cushions and sat, crammed in my own excavated hole. 'Nice place you got.'

'Hold on.' He went back out, returned with my case and said, 'I've put you in my room. I'll take the couch.'

'No.'

'That's okay, I can sleep anywhere. Had Sid over a few weeks ago and . . . oh, did I tell you? He's agreed to do the cover for the Ern Malley edition.'

'Sid?'

'Yeah, it's gonna be great: Ern, a few paintings, my introduction. Oh, that's right, I's thinking, we need a photo of Ern.'

I reached into my top pocket, flattened the snap and presented it to him. He studied it, but didn't seem sure. 'He's quite young here.'

'Yes. Four, five, perhaps. I like that shot. Not long after Mum passed. You can tell – he's dressed in rags, his face is filthy. I mean, Dad tried his best, but it was a lot: two kids to school, work, mortgage. Mostly, I ended up caring for Ern.'

'That must've been tough?'

'You do what you have to. I remember standing on the piano stool, stirring the stew (I'd made) because Dad didn't get home till late. And Ern, god bless him, always asking for something.'

'You were close?'

'I guess so. And stayed that way, till he went away. Then, like you said, he became a bit of a mystery man. But we were always close, and he knew, when he was sick at the end, his sister would look after him. That's why it's sort of strange . . . why he didn't choose to share more with me.' I waited for some understanding, but Max seemed confused. 'Can you see what I mean, Max?'

'Yes.'

'It wouldn't have hurt him to say, Hey, Eth, listen to this thing I wrote.'

'Right. Although, it'd be good to get something a bit more recent. So people'd know what he looked like.'

'I did try to find one, but couldn't.'

Max went into the kitchen and fiddled about, filled the kettle, lit the stove and put it on. 'That's strange,' he called. 'Everyone's got a few lying about.' He returned, found a spot on a piano stool (not that I could see the piano) and said, 'Like a ghost, our Ern. Doesn't even photograph. Like he didn't want anyone knowing about him. But the poems, the way they were prepared, suggested he knew they'd be published.'

'How's that?'

'Margins, titles – why wouldn't he have just scribbled them?'

'Maybe you're right.'

'A man of contradictions. And you reckon he fought up North?'

'I don't know. Towards the end, I sat with him and asked, but he didn't want to talk. Then,' I joked, smiling, 'one day he says to me, Alright, Eth, you got me. I was working with Special Ops. (I knew when he was jesting, Max.) I said, How's that, Ern? He says, We were dropped into Norway at night and had to hike seventy-three miles. Deep snow. German patrols. Eventually we sighted the heavy water factory, prepared our explosives, hiked down the hill, knocked off a few sentries, got in and . . . well, that was Ern, always the entertainer. Like when we were kids – he memorised that speech from *Hamlet* and presented it on the front porch one night. Dad was watering, talking to some neighbour, and out he comes: *To be or not to be . . .*'

Max was intrigued. 'Watch repairer, motor mechanic, actor, spy?'

'He was no spy. Although . . .' I returned to my pocket, found the scrap of paper I'd recovered from under his bed, and handed it over. 'I was meaning to tell you, I found this between his mattress and the bed slats.'

Max read: *The wind masters the waves, As the waves the sea, And all of it entire, And none of it to me – I had thought it was finished, And now it is useless, Like the writing on graves, Empty of future, Renew . . . the sign . . . At the moment of . . .* He looked up. 'The moment of what?'

'Death?' I said.

He re-read it. 'I reckon you're right, Ethel.'

'He was writing it at the end, see? A spot of blood on the corner. I reckon he wanted to say his last hurrah, but then . . . I can hear him, calling me, Max. See him, slipping that beneath the bed, with his last ounce of energy. That's what I reckon.'

'*All of it entire . . . none of it for me.* You might be right. It's more personal than the poems. Not as good, but personal. *Writing on graves* . . . That's a beautiful sentiment.'

I waited as he re-read. 'Of course he wasn't a spy, but in a way, a story's more interesting, isn't it, if you gotta fill in the blanks.'

'Yes,' he said, intrigued.

'And even more interesting when you don't know how it ends. And none us do, do we, Max?'

'No.'

The kettle boiled. I'd had enough of sitting in the crevice. I jumped up, went out and turned it off. 'Where do you keep the cups?'

He appeared behind me, brushed past, close, and I could feel his heat. He opened a cupboard, found two cups, blew out the dust and placed them on the counter. Beside more grey and green, bubbly, black and blue food. Another saucer full of butts, smoked down to various stages. Then he moved closer, and I felt his leg, and arm; strong, unwilling to compromise with my soft, flabby body. We jostled, as he made the tea. As I peered out of the kitchen window at the backyard that was more jungle, a fence, and behind this, some sort of factory. 'Got this place to yourself?'

'Mum helps with the rent.'

'That's nice.' I could smell his breath, smoky but minty, although I hadn't seen him eating mints. Then he turned, leaned to get something, and brushed my chest. I just waited for the chaos to pass; for the heat from the kettle and cups to dissipate. All the time, forgetting poetry.

'Me,' he said, taking milk from the fridge and filling the cups, 'I'm a bad egg.'

'How's that?'

'A very minor poet, although I have ambitions.'

'I'm sure your stuff's very good.'

'Sugar?'

Soon we were sitting in the backyard. There was a half-dug air-raid shelter, a few sheets of iron nailed to wood, and Max explained how he'd tried, but given up, unable to see how it would protect him from any bomb. He lit another cigarette, offered me one, and I thought, Why not? No more Dalmar Street. Mrs Kynoch's remarkable roses, Mr Moore's economical cuts. So I took one, and he lit it (softly, graciously), and I inhaled, coughed, but continued.

'You're still young,' I said to him. 'A few more years, you'll be writing poetry just as good as Ern's, if not better.'

'Na, I don't reckon, Ethel. I look at what I've done and I think, So what?'

'Like Ern.'

'*He* was different. Although my mother had great expectations. *She* was the original Miss Havisham.'

I wasn't sure; I waited. No point appearing too stupid.

'Clarris Harris.' Grinning, again.

'Clarris?'

'Yes. *Clarris Harris*. Although she was always the first to laugh. She said she was going to do the same to me, but there were no boys' names that rhymed. She was a big reader. Everything from the local rag to Dostoyevsky. She encouraged me.'

I tried the tea. The milk was beyond drinking, so I replaced the cup and waited, hoping the cat might drink it. Still, the cigarette was working. It seemed to slow the heart, the senses.

'She was determined to make something of me, so she took me to the Mount Gambier library every Saturday and left me there while she went shopping. And (this is without a lie, Ethel) by the time I was fourteen I'd read every book they had.'

'*No?*'

'I promise. I was a voracious little bastard. Which, of course, got me beaten up at school, until I discovered . . .'

He was quite the storyteller. There was no way you couldn't listen, or believe him.

'. . . if I played footy, they'd leave me alone.'

'You, football?'

He looked around. 'I didn't like it, but, you know, boys being boys, they assumed I was okay, despite spending my weekends reading *books*. Cos, you know, books, that was a sure sign that . . .'

I didn't know. A bit pink, perhaps?

'I was a top goal scorer.'

'In Mount Gambier?'

'Down south. Big lake. You heard of it?'

He never seemed happier than when he was remembering. He told me how he'd attended St Peter's College on a scholarship, become school captain, topped Leaving Honours and ended up reading his way through the university library. Like life was just a cycle of ever-bigger libraries.

'But what about your interest in poetry?' I asked.

'Ah.' He stood, went in, upturned piles of papers and returned with a newspaper clipping. 'Listen, the *Possum Pages* from the *Sunday Mail*, March 1924: *The Masefield Affair. Once, in the doldrums of the offing, offering grief and joy in equal measure, Herr Masefield set off with rod and reel in search of carp and carping . . .*'

He read, I listened. Blew smoke into the twelve feet of sky the backyard afforded. I felt happy; like I'd arrived somewhere I belonged, met someone I'd always known. The ground was covered in cat shit in various states of decay, but like Max might've said, why clean it up if it's not doing any harm?

He finished and I realised I hadn't heard it. But said, 'That flows nicely, Max.'

A grin, again, as if he knew something I didn't, although the opposite was probably true.

# 10

Max slept in this room, apparently. The walls peeling, mould on the ceiling, and cobwebs full of bits and pieces I couldn't make out in the half-light (from the bulb that flickered). Piles of musty clothes, a collection of Buddhist statues and more books, papers. He'd told me this is where he did most of his editing, propped up in bed with a gin, a typewriter in his lap. I wasn't sure he'd changed the sheets, but I was so tired I could've slept anywhere. Despite the myna bird (it didn't stop for breath) in the hibiscus outside my window, I fell into dreams of wide roads, sparking trams and old men in bow ties (was the whole city like this?).

Max woke me at four-thirty. I could hear him from the living room, droning: *Om mani padme hum*. Over and over, as incense drifted into my room, the smell of burnt fruit, the bird, still. 'Is that you, Max?'

*Om mani padme hum.*

Eventually he came in with a cup of tea and a bowl of cooked peaches. I sat up, tried the tea (the same milk) and attempted the peaches, but they tasted like the bottom of an ashtray. I doubted (even then) that Max had any culinary skills. Wondered how he stayed alive. Cans of Campbell's, perhaps? He sat on the end of my bed, looked me over, and I covered myself.

'Sleep well?'

'Yes. And you?'

But he wasn't interested in sleep. 'Do you meditate?'

'No.'

'I can teach you.'

'Well . . . if you think?'

Ten minutes later, the both of us sitting on an old mattress in the living room, legs crossed, repeating the chant, focusing on a big red ball that was (but wasn't) moving across the kitchen wall.

I showered, got dressed, and we set off for the university. Max had a lecture, although he wasn't sure if he'd attend. He explained it wasn't necessary; you could buy the notes, memorise them, slap a few words down for the exam. As long as you passed. Distinctions were a waste of time; everyone got a degree in the end. In the meantime, you could've been writing poems, essays, stories. He (he explained) was the only student with his own journal. Most of his friends lived in a sort of extended childhood. But that wasn't the Harris approach: you had to make your own way in the world (even though he'd told me his mother was paying his rent). As we drove towards the city, he said, 'My father doesn't see the point of books.'

He was weaving through traffic, ignoring red lights, nearly knocking over pedestrians crossing on green. 'He's always on at Mum – *stop mollycoddling that boy.*'

A long stretch, as I sunk into the seat, but then sat bolt upright as a mum and kids tried to cross, and instead of slowing, he went around, pressing his horn (that didn't work).

'When it comes to parents,' he said, 'we prosper despite, more than because. Especially creative types. They live on short rations, Ethel.'

'How's that?'

'A kind word can keep a poet writing for years. Which is why you've got to be nice to kids.'

Ern. Nailing an inner tube to *Psychosis III*, as Dad smiled and said, That's just what it wanted.

Brakes. He avoided the bumper bar in front of us by inches. I tried to smile, and he said, 'Don't worry about that. Never so much as a dent.' Setting off, he said, 'You musta lost the photos of Ern?'

I took a moment. 'I must have.'

'Pity.' He glanced at me again.

'Like I said, Max, he was morose at the end. I suspect he found them, disposed of them without me knowing. Maybe that's something troubled people do?'

'Maybe.'

'He had a hard time of it.'

'I'm sure he did ... whatever happened. Up North, I mean.'

'Someone so shook up, self-loathing, that they'd destroy their own photos. Like they didn't want the world to know they existed. That's sad, isn't it?'

He gave me that strange look again, and said, 'Dad's a commercial traveller. When he was away I used to sit in my room and read and draw and write stories about cowboys. That's when you're most happy, Ethel. When you're left alone.'

'My mother had the same streak ... although Dad had her under control.'

'When I was seventeen I wrote my first story. It was called *The Syphilis Museum*. About this dad that wants to scare his son, so he takes him to a museum of ... *syphilis*.'

Was he making this up? Did, could, such a place exist?

'Old dongers, pictures of people with sores, that sort of thing. I must let you read it some time. Anyway, I showed Dad, and his jaw dropped.'

He was enjoying it. I'd already learnt, this was his thing – his *thing*.

'He said, What the bloody hell's all this . . . *filth*?'

Max laughed, turned into what I assumed was the university, and found a car park. 'Museums for *sy-phi-lis*? Is there something wrong with you, boy? He threw the story in the bin, then said, If you ever do anything like this again.'

I wasn't sure. It did seem a strange thing for a child to write. But it was modern; he was modern; the world was modern – so who was I to judge?

'But I didn't give up. I got it out the bin, stuck it back together, and kept it, to remind me.'

'Of what?'

'That you have to pay a price.'

'For what?'

'Originality. If your writing's worthwhile, most people will hate it.'

We walked through a sea of young bodies, all smelling minty, nice, edible. Max took me through the back door into a theatre. Again, lots of young people standing around smoking, someone asking Max who his new girlfriend was. Him explaining Ern, the poems, and me, the sister from Sydney. We climbed a set of stairs, navigated a passageway crammed with scenery, and emerged onto a stage. Empty, except for three people sitting with scripts in hand. Max said, 'Sorry I'm late.' He introduced me, we sat in the circle and he said, 'What's the consensus?'

The consensus was that none of them liked Cocteau. They'd

read the play, as promised, made an attempt to understand it, flesh out the characters – but, in the end, they explained, there *were* no characters, no plot, no setting, no sense. The world of talking mirrors and eight-armed butlers just didn't interest them.

'What do you want to do?' he asked a young woman who seemed to be the most opposed to the choice of play.

'We talked about *Arms and the Man.*'

Max glared at her. 'But we'd be the first in Australia to do the Cocteau.'

'But no one would come,' a young man said.

'*Everyone* would come. Interstate, overseas. Everyone.'

The young woman said, 'Even if you could follow the storyline . . .'

'What's that matter?'

'Are you joking? People pay money, come out for the night, they want a story.'

'Bad luck. They'll have to deal with it.'

And the young man. 'They won't have to. They just won't come.'

'That's their problem.'

And the third person, an older girl, said, 'It'll be our problem. We'll still have to pay for the theatre.'

Max just studied them, shook his head. 'Ethel's brother, Ern, wrote *modern* poetry. *Modern.* Before he died – see, he died trying. And you want Shaw?'

'Yes,' the first girl said.

'Go on, tell them, Ethel, about *The Darkening Ecliptic.*'

'Well,' I sat, uncomfortable, with my handbag in my lap. 'I think he was trying to do something new, with language.'

'See?' Max said. 'He didn't redo Keats. Something *new*. If we don't, what's the point? A thousand people will put on Shaw this year. You want to be like everyone else?' They sat, waiting. 'Why don't we just do *Macbeth*?'

The older girl lit up. 'You reckon we could?'

'But this, this,' and he indicated the script, '*this* is worth our time.'

Nothing. Just the sound of hammers on scenery, someone reciting lines, loading drinks into the fridge.

'Fine.' He stood. 'You decide. Let me know. But I'm not doing Shaw.'

He turned, stormed from the stage, and I said, 'He does have a point.' But no one acknowledged me. I almost ran after him, along the passage, down the stairs and out the stage door. 'Max, wait.'

He turned, waited. 'Sorry, Ethel. I've had enough of that lot.'

We walked across a sort of park, littered with dozing bodies, books, rugs.

'You've got quite a task there,' I said.

'I put out an ad for a modern theatre group. They applied. But, apparently, modern stops around 1910.'

We entered a grimy-looking building, waited for a lift and made our way to the Union bar. There were already a dozen people sitting around, drinking (before it was allowed), slouched over tables, most of the chairs still up, the cleaners busy with vacuums. Max said, 'I know it's a bit early but ...' What he meant was, who cares? Who made the rule that you could only drink after six? The liver worked anytime.

He bought me a shandy and we sat at a table overlooking the Union lawns. I told him I preferred full strength and he made some sort of joke about Greeks and ouzo. He topped up his beer with something from a hip flask, skolled, shook his head and said, 'Now I'm ready for another day.'

A tallish man entered and approached the bar. Stood, waiting, waved to Max and smiled. Max said, 'He's a rotten bastard.'

'Why's that?'

'I'll tell you *why's that*, Ethel. He's a professor of *Australian* literature. But, *but*, he's a Pom. Came here for a contract, hated the place, hated Australian literature, said – get this – said there is really no such thing as Australian literature.'

'*No?*'

'He refused to teach Australian authors (except *Kangaroo*, that was *sort of* Australian, by a proper, English writer).'

'But how can he be teaching—'

'There you go.' He leaned forward, sipping his drink, topping it up from his flask, all the time watching the professor.

'Philip Dunk, but he calls himself PIM Dunk.'

I wouldn't say I saw jealousy in Max's eyes, more a contempt for everything ordinary.

'He tells his class, he says, Oh, you know, I'd like to return to England, but with the war on it's safer here, for now.'

'He can just bugger off,' I said.

'I wish he would. Anyway, when your brother's poems first arrived, I thought, Okay, I'll show him.'

'*Him?*'

'I thought he might like them. I mean, Ern writing in a modern European idiom.' He smiled at the man at the bar again. 'But you know what, Ethel?'

'What?'

'He sent them back with a note.'

'Go on.'

'Saying, *This sort of thing is highly derivative, I'm afraid.*'

'Derivative?'

'*Rather incomprehensible verse that young men and women are writing in Europe. You know, Maxie, it's rather unfortunate that it's catching on here too.*'

'Rotten bastard.'

'See, that's what I'm up against, Ethel: PIM. Although, I shouldn't have shown him, only I thought he could be convinced.'

I watched as Dunk took his drink, paid, laughed with the girl, passed time until he could escape the world of koalas and fake modernists like *Ern Malley*.

'All the more reason to do what we do,' Max said. 'He said, *You Australians should stick to sunburnt countries and rolling plains.*'

'Drongo,' I said (and I think Max might've smiled).

This man, this PIM, took his drink and approached us. And in some sort of posh accent, said, 'Starting early today, Mr Harris?'

'Late,' he replied. 'I missed a lecture, so I thought, Why not?'

'Why not indeed?'

*Indeed.* As I sat glaring at this man, my inner Vesuvius bubbling.

Max said, 'This is Ethel Malley.'

He extended his hand, but I didn't offer mine.

'Ern Malley's sister.'

His face lit up. 'Ern, the poet?'

'The derivative one,' I said.

He looked at Max. 'I didn't say that, did I, Max?'

'I think you might've.'

'I just meant, you have to be careful with this new sort

90

of versifying. If things don't make sense, then they don't make sense.'

'Maybe,' I said, 'if you don't understand them, you should keep your opinions to yourself.'

He didn't seem in the least bit shocked. 'But Mrs Malley, I was asked.'

'Sounds to me like you might've already made up your mind.'

He just grinned. But not a Max grin, which was okay. More, a clever dick grin, which wasn't. I said, 'I think time will tell, Mr Dunk.'

'I think so too.'

'And when all of Australia and England knows who Ern Malley is, you might regret your words.'

'Quite possibly, Mrs Malley.'

'And in the meantime, maybe you should keep your trap shut.'

# 11

That night, it continued. Max had promised me some culture, Adelaide style. *Culture*, like he was clearing his throat. Back in the Austin, along North Terrace, down King William Street – Miss Tonkin's Toilet Salon and a few frock shops. Lights, every hundred yards, red, waiting, Max saying, 'Oh, bugger this.' Taking off, and then, at last, lights and a siren.

We pulled over and Max got out, walked back and talked to an officer in an old Buick. I watched in the rear-view mirror as they laughed, shared a few words, and Max returned, got in and said, 'All taken care of.'

'No problems?'

'No.' He pulled into the traffic without indicating.

'He let you off?'

'Don't worry about all that, Ethel. I knew him when I did the police rounds, when I started at the *News*.' He indicated a tall building to his right, a honeycomb of shuttered offices and smog-blackened sandstone. 'That was my job. Me and this fella called Rattle. We'd get a call, and they'd be pulling someone out of the Torrens, and we'd ask the coppers, you know, for the *real* information.'

'I didn't know you were a journalist.'

'I wouldn't call it that. A gatherer of tidbits and gossip, a photographer of bodies and debutantes – that's another thing they're big on here. They like to see their kids in nice frocks. Anyway, I did it for twelve months, and got to know most of the coppers, as you can see.' He turned left, found a park, and pulled in.

'But you didn't become a journalist?'

'No, God help me. Could you imagine that? *World's biggest pumpkin, grown by Norm Smith of Fullarton.* I decided, if that's the best I could do . . . So I applied for university.'

The Establishment were gathering in the Town Hall foyer. Men in old suits, stiff ties and polished shoes. Women in dresses down to the marbled floors, diamante clavicles and heads bee-hived in the nastiest sort of way. A few men wore navy and air force dress uniforms, medals clunking beside glasses of spumante. A sort of marked-down respectability, smelling of mothballs and dry-cleaning fluid. Max said, 'I've started writing a bit of an introduction to Ern. I got so far, but was wondering what I could say about him. You know, something only his sister might know.' He sat, lit a smoke, and waited for me.

I'd already found his introduction. I'd got bored (he'd gone out to buy smokes, milk and bread). I'd sat at the table, picked the first sheet off the pile: *Ern Malley prepared for his death quietly confident that he was a great poet, and that he would be known as such.*

I sat beside him, lit my own cigarette. 'I think I've told you most things.'

'Right. Although it's hard to get a sense of the man. He's quite a mystery.'

'Not so much. He was no big deal at school. Never got into trouble or anything but, no big deal. Used to piss his pants.'

'*Ern?*'

'He had a nervous disposition, or a weak bladder. But he grew out of it. He was happiest around Dad, and he was his favourite. You know how it is, as a kid; your dad talks, but he's looking at your brother.'

Max pointed out a young officer with badges and bars and a pencil moustache, and said, 'They're always the easiest to understand.'

'Who?'

'That type – what you see's what you get. But the interesting people, you have to pull back the layers.'

'When you reported?'

'I was never interested in the obvious, which is why I spent my days at the races, my nights with Cavafy. That's what . . .' He turned to me. 'It's almost like, Ern mightn'ta written a word of those poems.'

'No?'

'Like there was another Ern, and you and me don't know him.'

I had no idea what he meant. 'Then who wrote them?'

'Ern, of course. But the inner Ern.'

The introduction continuing: *He prepared his manuscript to that end – there was no ostentation . . .*

'He might've been a spy,' I said.

'No. Less obvious.'

'He could fix watches. He fixed mine; he was very good. He could get a car started, change its bits. He was a good tinker; him and Dad, in the shed for hours. And at the end of the day, his poems are . . . collections of words.'

*It was an act of calm, controlled confidence.*

'Yes, I see your point, Ethel. Was he a particularly . . . *sexual* person?'

Max; shocking, as he tended to be.

'Not so he told me. Although, afterwards, I discovered a few postcards in the shed. Nothing special. Just women with, you know . . . down below.'

'Vaginas?'

'But tell me about a man who doesn't . . .'

He winked. Did he mean Evan? Is that what he meant? And what did he want to know about Ern? If I'd seen anything? Because, as a matter of fact, I had. Poor Ern saying, Just looking for a globe in the shed. And the way the light was cast, the shadows thrown from the door, you could tell.

'If you mean him and this Lois,' I said. 'I wouldn't know. They had a secret life.'

'That's funny, isn't it? You'd think he'd want to tell you. What was it about this woman?'

The bell rang and we went in, sat towards the front, and waited as the crowd settled.

'Sex,' Max said, loud enough to be heard for a row or two, 'drives nearly every human behaviour. I was telling you about the syphilis museum.'

'Yes.' Whispering.

'There was an actual syphilis museum, near Naracoorte. This old fella, he'd made papier-mâché dicks and covered them with Vaseline to make it look like . . . you know. And sores, pus, the lot. A friend of mine, his father took him, three, four times, because the old man'd had the clap, but it'd miraculously disappeared. And this friend . . .' He looked around. 'Anyway, point is sex isn't a choice, is it, Ethel?'

'No.'

'You give in, regardless. Ern, he was a man of spirit, but also of body, you can tell. But if he felt the need to hide that then . . .'

The string quartet came out, started tuning up. I didn't like the topic much, but that was Max, always after the subtext, the hidden story.

'Masturbation,' he said. 'It's still the one thing we're not meant to talk about. But I read some research saying ninety-seven per cent of people do it. Ninety-seven. And we all go around pretending we're one of the three. Unlikely, eh, Ethel?'

As the warming notes tumbled, tuned, and faces turned away from us.

'Either way, I'll just have to find something to say,' he said. 'Shakespeare, look at him. Some people can't believe a country bumpkin wrote what he did, but that only made it the more remarkable.'

As the strings found concert A.

'But even he had a wank, I guess.'

The lights dimmed, the musicians waited, the last of the crowd settled. I reached into my pocket and retrieved the letter I'd found in the bedside drawer (not that I'd been looking). To John Reed, his co-editor (more about him later), asking if he'd set the letter to type, and if he could see the proofs. Then: *He's a marvel, this Malley, but I think we should check, don't you? Someone in Melbourne must have a connection to National Mutual. If he worked there for so long, they'd know. Apart from anything else, might be able to tell us something personal . . .*

And folded in with this, the reply. *I guess you're referring to the Randal situation in the UK. Those two poets were ratbags, and the stuff they wrote was ordinary. Nothing like Ern's. I shouldn't worry, Max. I don't think it worth chasing up, and shan't, unless you insist.*

*This stuff is good, genuine. Why would you try it on, if you could write that well anyway?*

I handed the letters to Max, and he flattened them on his knee as the Ravel began. Then he turned to me with a sort of silent horror. Folded them, put them in his pocket, and listened to the music. We sat like this for nearly an hour. No looks, no whispered words.

This Randal business. Trying to make editors look stupid. Surely he had more faith? There'd been an instance like this. I remembered. A fellow writing a novel, pretending he was an Armenian, and he'd been in the Turkish massacre, but survived, crawled out of a pit, onto a boat, to Australia. He'd sold thousands of copies, the press had interviewed him; on the radio, the *Weekly* even. But someone had got suspicious. He didn't look particularly Armenian, or Turkish. Some of the facts in the novel (he'd said he was five, standing with his mother, and a machine gun had opened up, but it had missed him; he'd fallen under his mother's body, and they'd shot the few survivors, but hadn't seen him; he'd got out, found a friendly family, been hidden for years, went to school, before being smuggled out of the country on a freighter) were Hollywood. The author had been asked some difficult questions, and supplied inadequate answers. One reporter had asked him to speak Armenian, but he only knew a few words. And on and on until, eventually, this man had admitted he'd never been out of Footscray. And the book was pulped. Money (some of it) returned, a mea culpa and he was never heard of again. Forgery at its best and worst, which is the same thing. One man saying to another (many millions), *Really, this is a funny sort of game, and I'm better at it than you. And here's proof.* The thing being, I guess, there must have been a thousand forgeries and fakes every day of the year: paintings and poems and songs, and the Kaiser's monocle. Most of them acceptable, because they're never uncovered. Secret. Intellectual masturbation, carried on by ninety-seven per cent of us, apparently.

Back to the foyer, in silence. Max turned to me and said, 'I didn't mean . . .' He sat, and said, 'That night, when I opened your letter, that was a whole new world, Ethel. I read "Dürer" and thought, This is the real thing.'

'But you had doubts?'

'Never. You believe me, don't you?'

As the furs were paraded in front of us; dead foxes smelling of naphthalene and cheap perfume. All so fake, although no one thought to question this.

'I was reading about Randal,' he said, 'and I wrote that in a moment of confusion.'

I didn't know what to believe. But I wanted, needed, to know that Max was with me.

'He didn't check,' he said. 'He was right. I was wrong.'

And then I added, 'Even if you had've checked, they would've said he hadn't worked there.'

'Why?'

'I checked. They said they had no record, but probably wouldn't anyway, as he worked casual, and they only had records of permanent people.'

'But someone might've known him?'

'Might've . . . I didn't ask.' I sat beside him. 'Because by that point I didn't care. Who was I to doubt my brother?'

We both watched the parade of people and powder, bubbly and bangles.

'He was the only person I had, Max.'

This time he seemed real, genuine, like this was the authentic Max.

'Me and him, listening to the wireless, in Croydon. Hardly anyone visited us. Just like it had been when we grew up. Dad out in his shed, and me and him playing checkers.'

And that, I guess, is how Max and I began. Having to accept the little frauds in each other's lives. Him, roaming his museum of ecstatic pox. Me, lying in bed listening as my brother called. Both of us peas in a pod, and yet, in no pod, because Max was just as much a missing person as me.

# 12

I eventually attended a lecture with Max. Ethics and aesthetics. In which poets and painters were named, explained, illustrated with slides. We sat at the back and he provided a running commentary. Homer was on mescaline, apparently, busy with boys, their poetic limbs shimmering in the Mediterranean light. Kant was an alcoholic, Hegel a narcissist who only wrote to spite his mother. From there to the bar, again, which seemed to be his favourite place. An early gin and tonic, then over to Miller Anderson & Co., where he bought a scarf on credit. Up to the roof, the woman in the lift laughing with him. He seemed to know everyone, and everyone seemed to like him. She said, 'You coming back any time soon?'

'When I run out of money.'

'It's not the same without you.' She explained how Max had been their best storeman, spending his days in a broom closet where he held court over the world's longest poker game.

'All that lifting wasn't good for my back,' he told her, and she smiled, like they shared some dirty secret.

Up to the roof, and the spotlight, sandbagged into position. A few seats waiting for the spotters, a rangefinder, a radio – all covered with canvas.

'This is it,' he explained, walking towards the edge, peering down at the city streets, the ant people, five stories below.

'Exciting work?'

'If the light worked.' He showed me where the diesel would go, if there was any. 'So we'd just sit here, waiting. Not that there was any point. I mean, the Stukas are out of range, aren't they?'

'What about the Japs?'

'Adelaide?' He stood on the edge, balancing.

'Careful, Max. It's a long way down.'

'It'd make a mess, wouldn't it?'

Me wondering what he was capable of. Did he have some maudlin streak, like Ern (some nights, when the memories returned)? 'A breath of wind, you'll be over.'

'No great loss to the world of poetry.' He pretended to jump, smiled at me, laughed. 'What d'yer reckon, Ethel? My brains'd end up all over someone's suit.' Indicating below.

'*Max.*'

'It's tragic, isn't it? So angry he jumped from the roof of Miller Anderson's department store. Come to think of it' – and he stepped back – 'that doesn't have much of a ring. Could you see it, in the history books: Max Harris, minor poet, dead on the pavement?'

Then to the cafeteria, where we met Mary Martin. I must say, I didn't like her from the beginning. Mean eyes and mouth, and a mousy voice that only ever hinted at things, never said the thing itself. Not my type. But Max was taken by her. They discussed everything: lectures, politics, Göring, Sid and Albert and the rest of the crew in Melbourne. She, in a sort of Indian shawl thingy, always throwing it about.

We sat with tea, and she showed us the final proofs. Starting with Nolan's painting, reproduced on the cover in full colour. A green sky and a sort of rainbow-coloured tree, with rocks and desert and other bits and pieces. I didn't get it. I thought we could've done better, but this Sid Nolan, they loved him. I suggested something more evocative, but they wouldn't hear of it. A nice Heysen, perhaps, with a stream and hills and a cow or two. This thing, this lollipop tree, would put people off, I explained.

But Mary just admired it. 'Put *what* sort of people off?'

'*People* people.'

'It'll put the dullards off, Ethel. But the people *we* want, it'll be right up their alley.'

'Who are these people?'

'People who realise we're living in the twentieth century. That things are going on – a war, perhaps. That art needs to respond.'

'Ern responded.'

'He did.'

'And we want people to read him.'

'But not with a Heysen on the cover.'

Max supported her. 'It's a new way of seeing the world. Just like Ern. That's what we're about, eh, Mary?'

'Or else I'd get a job with the *Weekly*.'

What's wrong with the *Weekly*? I wouldn't have minded if they'd published Ern. Then everyone would have known about his gifts: Mr Moore, Mrs Kynoch, the prime minister. But I doubted the prime minister read *Angry Penguins* (more's the pity). 'I'm quite happy with Mr Nolan's painting, if you think it suits.'

'Happy?' Mary asked. 'Do you know how lucky we are to have him?'

'I've never heard of him.'

'And without a fee. Do you know how many people are working to make sure that Ern Malley—'

'As we should,' Max said, moving a hand, an arm between us.

But Mary just glared at me. 'Anyway, it's in the poems, isn't it?' She turned to the page proof of 'Petit Testament' and read: '*Dear we shall never be that verb, Perched on the sole Arabian tree . . .*' And looked at me. 'That's all Sid had to work with: a sole Arabian tree. I quite like the line myself' (as she conceded the smallest nugget) 'but as to what it means?'

'It needn't mean anything,' Max said. 'If the line works. Don't you agree, Ethel?'

And this woman's face said, *Malley is no Mozart, or Byron, or Keats, or anyone, much*. But I wasn't going to be drawn. 'Yes, I think that'll do nicely for the cover. You're right, we're after a certain type, aren't we?'

'Yes,' Max said.

'Thinkers, intellectuals . . . although it'd be nice if Ern connected to the common man.'

'Given time,' Max said. 'Few poets register in their own age. Decent ones, that is.'

Mary agreed, as she searched the text (not only Ern, but the other contributors, and Max's introduction). Then she arrived at the photo of the boy Ern, in a park. 'This is the most recent?'

'Well, obviously not the most recent,' I said. 'But as I told Max, he must've done something with the rest.'

'He destroyed them all,' Max said to his offsider, secretary, whatever she was.

'He was very thorough,' Mary said. 'You'd think he would've missed one . . . or the army would have a record. Didn't you say you checked with them, Ethel?'

'Too late,' Max said. 'It's going to the printer today. Anyway, I like the idea – the man of mystery. We should cultivate that. Don't you think, Ethel?'

'Yes. People can imagine. I've had to. Never had any idea my brother was a poet. He never let on, you see, Miss Martin.'

'Mary. Still, it'd be good – if people could get some idea.'

'He was in a very dark place,' I said. 'I would've liked to help him, but he was all alone.' I waited. Admittedly, for effect, but if she could play some silly game so could I. 'And to think, one day, when I was at the shop, he got out of bed, found these photos, put them in a pile in the yard (perhaps) and set a match to them, almost like he wanted to destroy *himself*.'

'The will to negation?' Max said, because that had got a mention in the lecture.

'Yes. We all feel that way at times, don't we, Miss Martin? That we're no good, and the world would be better off without us. That we could step over the edge. He was suicidal, I'm sure. He only wanted one bit of Ern Malley left in the world.' I indicated the proofs. 'And now that's all there is. So, in a way, he'd be happy to be dead.'

Mary said, 'I'm not sure if anyone's happy to be dead, Ethel. Your range of emotions is limited once they bury you.'

Little bitch! That's the sort of sarcasm I had to deal with.

Then she said, 'This is a funny-looking photo.'

'Why?' I asked.

She indicated a dome in the background: Ern, lawn, a few old buildings. 'It looks like the Berliner Dom,' she said, showing Max.

He checked. 'A cathedral of some sort?'

'The Berliner Dom. I've been there, climbed to the top with my parents. I tell you, it's nearly exactly the same.'

'No, that was Brisbane,' I said.

'*Brisbane?*' she asked.

'A family holiday, early on.'

'Doesn't much look like Brisbane,' Max said, examining it more closely.

'Or maybe Melbourne, we went there too.'

'Where in Melbourne?'

'I can't be sure. Somewhere out of the city . . . Geelong.'

Mary almost laughed. 'Geelong, some sort of medieval city?'

'That's not medieval. It's somewhere we went, I can't remember.'

Then I had two faces staring at me: Max checking the photo, me, trying to work it out. Mary said, 'It's funny, too, how it's not really picture quality.'

They examined it more closely.

'See, Max . . . like newsprint?'

'Dad took that with his Brownie,' I said. 'A family holiday. We were so young, I can't remember. Well, you can't at that age, can you?'

Max said, 'All part of the mystery, eh, Ethel?'

'Not so much a mystery. He was a bit of a porker at that age, you can tell – see, the big, fat legs? But he stretched out when he was a teenager.'

There were a few typos, and Mary said she'd correct them before returning the pages to the printer. Then, in a moment of grace she said, 'I'm sure Ern will have a big impact on *his* readers.'

Civility, at last.

That night there was a poetry recital. Not as modern as I thought. A few university students with flannel jackets and ties (askew, admittedly), and their girlfriends, like the little ballerinas people made to cover their toilet rolls. Some sort of society dame who, Max explained, bankrolled the event.

Max was up first. Welcomed everyone, said he might as well get the party started. Read one of his own, the pelvic rose *'unfolding in the flesh, gropes its roots into the germs of life, esoteric beings around the root hairs of cells.'* On and on, although nowhere as good as Ern. Then his girlfriend, Von, sat next to me and said, 'This is his best one. He's learnt it by heart. I told him to pop it in *Penguins*, but he won't.'

'Why not?'

'Says it's not good enough. Says he wants to keep room for the *real* discoveries, like your brother.'

'This is every bit as good as Ern,' I said, although it did go on a bit, and at least Ern made a *bit* of sense.

'Max has taken to you,' she said. 'Talks about you all the time. Ethel said this, Ethel said that.' She smiled at me strangely. 'You enjoying his bed?'

'Sorry?'

'Comfortable, is it?'

'Yes.'

'See, that's Max. Do anything for anyone. You keep him in line. Make sure he eats his meals.'

'I will.'

'I've tried. There's no point. He doesn't listen to me. Clean up, I say. But he won't.'

Where was this going? Was I some sort of threat? I hadn't meant to be, didn't want to be.

'And be warned, he gets up to some strange things.'

'He does?'

But Max had finished, and the small crowd was applauding. He said, 'I've written a new one, on the theme of nipples.' And he produced a scrap of paper from his jacket pocket. '*The geography of nipples is uncertain. Explorer Mawson found three types in his travels: the residual nipple, so small and faint it can hardly be seen . . .*'

'He likes to shock,' Von explained.

'I've noticed.'

'I think that has to do with his father. He was ignored mostly; he's still trying to get his attention. Although you can't, can you?'

'What?'

'Be noticed, by your parents. They ignore you for a reason.'

I wasn't sure what she meant.

'*. . . secondly, the volcano nipple, reaching into the sky, erupting like hot marmalade . . .*'

'What reason?'

'I think he likes you, Ethel. And not just because of your brother. He sees you as a sort of, country girl. Although – you're from Sydney?'

'*. . . thirdly, the spreading nipple, its areola so vast that Mawson, short on food, was worried he'd never find his way out . . .*'

'Me,' Von said, 'I'd rather be dancing. Mary's more his literary muse. Although they're not close, in a physical sense. She wouldn't have any of that. I think she's asexual.'

More applause. I thought they'd be laughing, but they took him seriously. How could you write a poem about a nipple?

'Keep him in line,' Von said, looking at me sideways.

'I'll try.'

Max said, 'Edition four is nearly out. I'm not giving much

away, but *this* is the big one. I'll give you a hint: Ern Malley.'

Silence, as everyone hung off his every word.

'Ern is *the* great discovery. If anyone's been reading Eliot, this is better. So we're going to give you a taste. But not me.' He motioned for me to come up. 'Come on, Ethel. Ethel Malley, the late poet's sister, here tonight from Sydney.'

Light applause, and I tried to tell him I didn't want to get up, but by then I had no choice. Von encouraged me. 'Go on, this lot'll love you.'

I squeezed onto the stage, and Max explained how I'd sent Ern's poems to him, and how he hadn't slept for days, overcome by the joys of Ern's 'Palinode'. Which he placed in my hand, and invited me to read. '*Now we find, too late, That these distractions were clues, To a transposed version of our too rigid state.*'

Von was sitting with her arms crossed, grinning; and Max was smiling, ecstatic, and the folk were listening, intrigued. At the end I said, 'He'd be very glad if you could buy a copy.'

Max proposed a toast to the late Ern Malley, and it was like everything I'd ever wanted had come true.

# 13

A few days later, Max woke me from a deep sleep. 'They've arrived!' He fetched my dress from the back of a chair, stockings, shoes, pulled back the sheets to reveal my nightie. I barely blushed (but wondered what Von would make of it). There hadn't been any sign of her since the poetry reading. Maybe they were having difficulties? It wasn't my place to ask, but as we drove through another pine-scented morning, I said, 'It was nice to talk to Von the other day.'

Along a road lined with plane trees, a storm of rusted leaves, picture-postcard Innsbruck, a mile of flat-mown couch with a chorus of sprinklers going round and round.

'Von's mother can't see why she would be attracted to a *poet*,' Max replied. 'The other day she said, And what *do* you think you'll be able to stick at, Max?'

'Rotten old . . .'

'I never knew you had to decide.'

'Of course not. Look at Ern and all his jobs. Men need to make their own mistakes, their own discoveries. Like you, with your *Penguins*.'

'That's not a mistake.'

A tyre blew and Max wrestled the car between lanes, up a

median, back across the road, up a footpath, coming to rest on top of a shrub. 'Shit!' He thumped the dashboard, then said to me, 'What do you mean, *their own discoveries*?' But got out before I could answer. I wasn't far behind, standing back, as he searched the boot for a jack.

'I just meant . . .'

'You should be grateful.'

'I am.'

'Who else would've published your brother's poems?' He had the jack, and the spare tyre. Lay on the ground beside the car, connected the tab and started turning the crank. 'Christ, Ethel, sometimes . . .' His hand slipped, grazed the gravel, and he sucked the blood and skin. 'Jesus!'

'Can I help?'

'No, you cannot! You've already . . .'

He glared at me and I wondered what he was going to say. You've already wasted enough of my time? Made me look stupid? He had the car up, searched for the spanner, and started removing nuts. 'Sometimes, Ethel, your arguments are arcane.'

I waited for him to calm.

'Strange, nutty.' Removing each of the nuts, as I stepped back, refusing to provide more evidence. I'd thought he was insightful, but he seemed like every other man: angry, searching for someone to blame. He slipped the old tyre off, the new one on. Didn't say a word.

'I can rattle on a bit,' I said.

No reply.

'Peggy, at Legacy, is always telling me to shut up. But we're stuck in there all day and you gotta make conversation, otherwise it's uncomfortable. Anyway, people were designed to talk.'

He seemed to have no idea what I was going on about. Tightened the screws.

'I'm not the world's most intelligent person, but I mean well, Max. And what I do, I do for my brother.'

Tighter, tighter.

'We were close, and ever since he died, it hasn't been the same. Perhaps I'm trying too hard.'

'Perhaps you are.' Throwing the old tyre in the boot, the jack, spanner. Most of his anger. Before wiping his hands on his pants and looking at me. 'Arcane, like someone's writing your lines for you.'

'Well, maybe they are. God, perhaps?'

'Don't start on that, Ethel.'

'Ern, then?'

'He's dead.'

'Not really. And anyway, my dad used to say, Ethel, you're an old soul. I guess that's it.'

'It is,' he said. 'And life's a book of proverbs.'

He studied me, but I didn't care. Saw my weaknesses, but I wasn't hiding them. That I was proud, defiant, and set my mind on a thing and did it; that I was old-fashioned, because I was a child of the pre-wireless era, when the world was smaller, friendlier; stubborn, like braised steak too long in the oven; arcane. 'You can never really know a person, Max.'

'No.'

'You can make up your mind, but unless you've eaten, slept, argued . . . look at us, arguing now. Perhaps we'll be good friends?'

'Perhaps.'

'I thought I knew Ern, but I had no idea what he was up to.'

Half an hour later we arrived at a small warehouse, cinder blocks, skylights and high ceilings. Maybe it was a garage, because there was a covered pit, high fans clunking under an acre of asbestos sheeting. 'Mary's father owns it,' Max said, walking in, looking around.

There were two old cars in the corner, doors and boots removed, wheels stacked high, bits of engine on a rug. I saw Dad and Ern pulling the Indian apart, cleaning the ... carburettor? I don't know what the bits were called. I could go look it up, find one of Dad's old manuals, incorporate the names into my story, like I really knew. But I'd be pretending, wouldn't I? Trying to convince you of an untruth, and (as Max has said) the most important thing is the truth. So believe me, there were two old cars, taken apart.

'Here!' Max said.

There was a staff room and, inside, the boxes from the printers. We brought them out into the garage and placed them on a trestle table set up for the task. Then Max opened the first, held a copy up to the light and said, 'Do you think Ern'd be proud?'

I took it from him, examined Mr Nolan's tree, flicked through the pages, smelt the ink, the paper; admired how the type was set out, the pictures placed on full and half pages. I closed it, and read the cover: *1944 Autumn Number to Commemorate the Australian Poet Ern Malley*. 'I don't know how to thank you, Max.'

'Nothing to say.' He took another copy from the box, examined it, smelt it himself. 'This is the beginning, Ethel.'

'You reckon?'

'When people read this they'll want to know more about Ern. He'll be famous.'

Rightly so, I thought. Ern was the most deserving man of all. I could see him, knobbly-kneed up the viburnum tree, reaching for the power line that ran through the foliage. Me saying, Ern, don't touch it ... But he had. And stood in a fork, smiling. It can't kill you, Eth – not unless you're touching the ground. Or the both of us, breaking into the Jesus house. The porch, the furnished reception, a library full of hundreds of books about Jesus. And a seat for the great man, when He returned. Ern saying, They can'ta been that stupid. Me: That's what Mr Kynoch reckons. It's all ready for Him, when He comes back. They're weak in the head. Upstairs, the bed made, the toilet and bathroom cleaned. For when Jesus returned, had a chat with the Alexanders, and Mister said, I suspected you'd be along, so we built a house, got it ready.

I examined the contents. I hadn't been interested up to now. Only Ern, whose *Ecliptic* took up 35 of the 108 pages. But there were book reviews, art, a story by a man named Cowan, some Smith putting in his two cents about an exhibition, and this Geoffrey Dutton fellow, whom I'd met. Who were they? Unfortunates, to have to share the issue with Ern. Like Max said, *he* was the star.

I felt so proud of him. He was swinging from the skylight, Dad yelling at him to get down. Farting into a bottle, holding it under my nose. A boy. That's how I'll remember him: a boy. In my mind Ern will always be six: a cut on his knee, Peter Pan with Vegemite around his mouth. With Dad, and the Indian, asking, What's this bit for? Dad telling him to put it in the kero, scrub it with the toothbrush, until the grease came off. All of it. I could see them, sitting in the corner, working without words.

Mary arrived. Unfortunately. It would've been nicer without

her, but she seemed attached to Max at the hip. She was efficient, no-nonsense, a modernist warrior in search of . . . what, I couldn't say. Max? Did she want to conquer him? She skimmed through the magazine, gave me a sort of hug (as best she could) and said, 'I bet you're feeling proud.'

'For Ern,' I said.

Descending. Me in bed, the rattle of lungs, my brother calling, Ethel? Me thinking, What do I do? Call an ambulance? Draw out the suffering? Although maybe I could've kept him alive long enough to see his poems in print.

My job was to address the envelopes. One for Faber in London, for Herbert Read and Stephen Spender, who had some clout, apparently. The Gotham Book Mart in New York and the Grolier Book Shop in Cambridge, Massachusetts. Four boxes to Mullen's in Melbourne, and stores in Sydney, Brisbane, Perth. Someone in Launceston had even ordered a copy.

That was my morning. With a black pencil, as Mary inserted copies, Max sealed them, added the postage, packed them in a tray.

And still, in the corner, Ern and Dad, putting the Indian back together. Dad holding it up while Ern screwed something on. Me watching and smiling, I guess, because Mary said, 'What are you thinking about, Ethel?'

'Dad'd be proud. Ern was his favourite. They were always in the shed.'

'He was a mechanic, wasn't he?'

'Yes, like *his* dad.'

They were attaching a petrol tank. A bigger one, because the Indian would have to go a lot further.

'Did he work for him?' Max asked.

'He might've,' I replied. 'But it never came to that.'

'Why?'

'Cosa what happened to Dad.'

Now they were tightening the tank, and the Indian looked ready for the race.

'What was that?' Max asked.

I wasn't sure if I should say. Was it anyone's business? It was the worst sort of tragedy, one a family never recovers from. 'Dad had his own machine shop, but he got into debt.'

They just waited. Packing, sealing, sorting. I felt like I should keep going. It was a grimy, honest sort of place, some-where that made you want to speak the truth. 'He had a patent on this new fuel pump, and spent hundreds – more, we'll never know – developing it. In the meantime, the work stopped. Then Dad's in debt and the bill collectors are at the door.' I could see Dad working. I wanted to ask him if it was okay to tell them, but he was just a ghost: in overalls, busy with a spanner. 'He sees this ad for the Esso Reliability Trial. Port Augusta to Ayers Rock, and back. No support (there were fuel stops). First prize a thousand pounds. So, he says, That's it. That's our way out, kids.'

They'd stopped working. Perhaps I'd said too much.

'Anyway, he entered. Bought this Indian, and him and Ern spent weeks in the shed doing it up.' I wasn't sure I wanted to say any more. 'It didn't end well.'

Well, that was that. My family, my life. There was no one in the corner. When a person's dead, they're dead. There are no ghosts. Whatever happens, you get used to it and move on.

Mary had stopped work, and started reading the poems again. '*It was a night when the planets were wreathed in dying garlands . . .*' She looked up. 'It really is quite beautiful, Ethel.'

'My word.'

'The more you read it. And since we're being honest ...' She checked with Max. 'The first time I saw them, I wasn't sure.'

'No?'

'Dromedary camels ... I thought your brother was playing some sort of joke.'

'On whom?'

'Max.'

'Why would he do that?'

'You know the types ... bleached bones and swaggies humpin' their ... whatever they hump. Some still haven't come around.'

'To?'

'Ern. They think it's nonsense.'

'And you thought Ern was one of *them*?'

'It crossed my mind. Like you said, Ern sitting up in bed, bits of this and that, thrown together.' She read: '*Princess, you lived in Princess Street, Where the urchins pick their nose in the sun ...* It's a nice bit of imagery, isn't it, Ethel?'

'I reckon so.'

'Because the thing is, your brother wouldn't use his own sister to make a point. That'd be the cruellest thing, someone to do your dirty work.'

Now, I wasn't so sure. Max, too. But there was a table of books, and the envelopes, and boxes. Mary said, 'I can see it, Ethel. *You thought that paying the price would give you admission to Valhalla. But I, too, invented faithfulness.*'

# 14

Handbills (Max said) were crucial. Three hundred, printed on the Arts faculty letterpress, an explanation of *Angry Penguins* issue four, excerpts, the photo of Ern beside a sample of his poetry, six by four inches on lemon-coloured paper, hand-torn. One day, Max said, each will be worth a fortune.

As we walked around the campus, Von followed with her arms crossed. 'People will either read it or they won't.'

'You've gotta give them a taste,' Max said.

He took a handful from the box I was carrying and stormed the conservatorium – pigeonholes, the office, rehearsal rooms, and into a studio where a dozen girls were singing. 'Issue four!' he called, but they just stared, and one said, 'Can we help you?'

'*Angry Penguins* – a journal of modern thought and poetry, featuring this woman's brother, Ern Malley. Have you heard of him?'

'We're trying to practise.'

'Monteverdi, I know. But it's the twentieth century, isn't it? And some composers are writing *new* music.'

Next, Arts. More pigeonholes, offices, common rooms, noticeboards. Max said, 'Not much use here. They haven't got past Shakespeare. And the lecturers are all failed writers, so you can't expect much from them. Failed, but trying to teach the next generation how to write.'

Science. A lecture theatre with a hundred undergraduates waiting to learn about Ohm and Tesla. Max climbed the platform, stood behind the podium and said, 'My name's Max Harris, and I'm the co-editor of *Angry Penguins*.' Silence, except for a few pencils being sharpened, fountain pens unscrewed. 'A small magazine devoted to modern thought. If you need something for the spirit.' He almost laughed. 'I understand the brain needs a bit of exercise, but if I could just read you a few lines from our latest issue? This is a poem by a fabulous new poet . . .'

'Don't bother,' someone called.

'It's no bother. You'll appreciate this one. "Palinode". Does anyone know what a palinode is?' Checking. 'Well, if you listen . . .'

'No one's interested.'

Followed by a growing chorus of complaints.

'Come on, gentlemen, ladies – are there any ladies?' Looking out again. 'Well, it doesn't matter. Here goes. *There are ribald interventions like spurious seals upon a Chinese landscape . . .*'

One young man came forward and tried to remove the microphone. Max resisted, wrestled it back, and they started pushing, harder and harder, while Max kept reading. '*We have known these declensions . . . have winked when Hyperion was transmuted to a troll.*'

The young man pushed him over. Max stood, returned and threw a fist at his face, but missed. Then they were both at it, and the lecture theatre was animated: cheers, most people on their feet. I looked at Von, saw no need to intervene. Max returned to the microphone and said, 'You can buy your copy at the Union office,' before backing away and leaving the theatre.

As we walked, Von said, 'You could've been hurt, Max.'

'You either believe in something, or you don't, Von.'

'I believe, but not to the point of violence.'

'Look what happened to Stravinsky and Diaghilev.'

I noticed blood on his lip, pointed it out, and he started blotting it with a handkerchief.

'Stravinsky was a radical,' she said.

'So's Ern.'

'Ern's Ern . . . no offence, Ethel.'

We tried a few more departments, distributed more flyers, then went up to the top balcony of Union House and scattered the rest to the wind. Watched as they floated, settled; people looked up like it was snowing. Night pieces and love songs.

Then we returned to the Barr Smith lawns and sat in the sun as Max studied the latest copy of the university magazine, *On Dit*. He'd paid for a full-page ad, but they hadn't put it in. Cursed the editor, who (he explained) was an idiot, a mummy's boy with a taste for Adam Lindsay Gordon. I told him he should ask for his money back, but he just stood and stormed across the lawns.

'Where's he going?' I said to a reclining Von.

'He'll be back, when he's had another grizzle.'

I watched him go. 'He is amazing, isn't he?'

'Yes . . . amazing.'

'I've never seen anyone so determined.' But I wasn't sure what Von was thinking. 'You don't seem interested.'

She was lying flat, her eyes closed, her hat partly over her face. 'In what? Ern?'

'Max's work.'

'He doesn't need anyone's encouragement.'

'If you don't mind me saying, you two don't seem very . . . compatible.'

She sat up. 'You've got a nerve. How long have you been here?'

'A week.'

'And you reckon you know Max? Me? Us?'

'I was just saying—'

'*Old* Eth, from Sydney. And Ern, and his girded loins.' She lay down, and covered her face again.

'I know it's none of my business—'

'It's not.' She moved her hat, glared at me, closed her eyes. 'Now it's published, you'd be headed back to Sydney?'

'Soon.'

'Tomorrow?'

'I haven't decided. I thought I'd stay long enough to help Max promote the issue.'

'Long enough?'

'A few days . . . a week.'

'I wouldn't bother. As you can see, he's perfectly capable. I'd guess you've got things to get back to.'

'Not a lot . . . the shop, perhaps, but Peggy's alright with that.'

You're not going to get rid of me that easily, I thought. So you can stick your claws in, get him in a suit and tie, cut his hair, a job with the government. No, that's not Max. You and him have nothing in common. 'You two . . . and your words.'

She sat up again. 'Our words?'

'It seems obvious.'

'Perhaps this afternoon, Ethel. I can help you pack, drive you to the train.'

'I'll be staying as long as Max's happy to have me.'

Max returned, grabbed my arm, pulled me up and said, 'Quick.' Dragged me towards a small office block, into a foyer, and pressed the lift button. 'You can tell this bastard,' he said.

Von followed, amused; as confused as me, I guessed, but knowing a fight when she saw it. We travelled to the third floor, down a passageway, and into an office of some sort of tweedy academic. He had a woollen vest and tie, a beard, and glasses too big for his face. Max threw his *On Dit* onto the man's desk and said, 'You want proof, here it is. Ethel Malley, Ern's sister.'

The man just shrugged; he didn't care about me. Smug. And this seemed to piss Max off no end.

'Well, ask her,' he said to Brian Elliott (according to a little tablet on his desk).

Elliott said, 'Always the dramatist, Max.'

'What, you think she's putting it on? Tell him who you are, Ethel.'

'My name is Ethel Malley, from Croydon, Sydney. I've come to Adelaide because my brother left a pile of poems—'

'I don't know what this proves,' Elliott said. 'So, if you don't mind, I'm busy.'

Max picked up the newspaper, turned a few pages and read: *'It's nice of Mr Harris to attempt such a hoax. In my honour, no doubt. But if he thinks I can be swayed . . .'* He leaned on the desk and said, 'You flatter yourself.'

'That's yet to be seen.'

Max turned to me again. 'Tell him about the poems, Ethel.'

'I didn't know he'd written them,' I said. 'I found them hidden in his case.'

Elliott was getting shittier, but he stuck to the facts. 'Listen,

Max, I appreciate that you've gone to so much trouble, but as I explained in the article, it's patronising, offensive, and juvenile. You can make all the private jokes you want, but to go to the trouble of writing these poems, publishing them, calling yourself *Ern Malley*.'

'He was my brother!' I said.

He just surveyed me; dismissed me.

Max said to me, 'This man, Ethel, writes modern poetry. He thinks I hate his work. He thinks I wanted to make a point about it . . . and that I went to the trouble of writing the poems, calling myself Ern Malley.'

'I beg your pardon,' I said to Elliott. 'Ern only recently died of Graves' Disease. I wasn't aware he wrote, and when I made this discovery and sent the poems to Mr Harris, and he was generous enough to publish them . . .'

Max read from *On Dit*. '*This sort of behaviour can't be excused. Just because Mr Harris resents my work, can't see the context, doesn't understand trends in modern poetry* . . .' And shouted at him. 'That's just the thing. I do! Don't I, Ethel?'

'My word, Max.'

'*If Mr Harris is unwilling to supply a public apology, I'll have no choice but to seek legal amends.*' Max slammed his fist on the desk. 'You think I'd waste months of my time on you?'

But Elliott just sat there.

'Ern was a soldier,' I said. 'He had no time to sit about writing poetry. So, I guess, what he did, he did secretly. I guess he thought it was something a working man doesn't do.'

Still nothing.

'But when I found the poems, I thought, Ern's entitled to have them seen. Maybe they're no good? But Ern was as real as you and me, Mr Elliott. He fought in the war. He killed Japs (I reckon). So you can sit there, teaching people about poetry, but to say he wasn't real . . . shame on you, sir.'

Max stood with his arms crossed; even Von seemed impressed. But I wasn't finished.

'You could've asked Mr Harris first, before assuming he'd done something so nasty. And now *you've* published this accusation. *You* should be the one publishing an apology, to Max.'

But he just said, 'Ern, eh?'

'This is no joke, Mr Elliott.'

I knew he was crumbling. Behind those crossed arms, there were doubts. Not that he'd admit it; he didn't seem the type. At least Max was always truthful.

'Well?' Max said to him.

'Only one person could've written those poems, Max. And published them. Only one person had a reason to.'

So we left the office, the building, and followed Max home across Botanic Park. Me, and Von, almost laughing. And I called, 'Max, why are we walking? Didn't you drive?'

# 15

So the play was eventually decided. *Exiles*, by James Joyce. I told Max I'd heard of him. Some book (*Ulysses*, as it turned out) that had been banned all around the world. Pornographic, apparently. This, of course, appealed to Max no end. A bit of smut's never hurt no one, he told me. Problem being, it left the cardigan set squirming in their seats, with little model erections and the sweats, prized thoughts avoided (not something for the public sphere).

So there we were in the 'Hut', me and Max, and the actors: Ted, playing the lead (the writer Richard Rowan). This, I thought, was Max's attempt at autobiography. The free-thinker, intellectual, tired with the world, the sleepy, round-vowel cast of his own life. Although Ted was taller than Max, better-looking, funnier. Still, we all trade up to our dreams, and nightmares. A young girl called Trudy played an old servant, Brigid, and an older woman called Georgina played the younger Bertha.

The actors stood on stage waiting for the director. He'd already given them the talk about Joyce, the characters, their motivations, and now stood, script in hand, surveying the empty space. Explaining Richard Rowan's drawing room at Merrion. Trudy and Georgina already seemed bored. Like drama was just a matter of remembering a few lines, stepping on stage, repeating them, getting to the end and going to the bar for a tipple.

Max told Brigid and Beatrice where to come in, and they moved like a pair of old sows. Then Brigid said, '*The mistress and Master Archie is at the bath ...*' But before she could finish the line Max was into her. 'I don't think that's how she'd speak. An old servant ... slower, frumpier.'

Trudy, who couldn't have been more than twenty-two or -three, just looked at him like, *I have acted before, you know.* 'She's just stating a fact. She'd be ... plain, without any drama?'

'Admittedly,' Max said, 'but there'd be *something* in her voice, surely?'

'Something?'

'Some warmth.'

'Telling her the kid's in the bath?'

'No, yes, listen, just try again.'

And she did, exactly the same way.

I sat towards the back, by myself, listening and watching. What else could I do? There was still more Ern to promote, and I couldn't imagine going home yet. And yet, the deed was done (or so Von kept telling me).

Brigid welcomed Beatrice, who was a very weathered-looking twenty-seven-year-old. '*Sit down and I'll tell the master you are here. Were you long in the train?*'

I wasn't sure about cutting edge, or the slightest bit radical. A couple of women standing on a stage making small talk. And pretty ordinary small talk at that. Even Max thought so. This time he said to Beatrice, 'Make sure the audience knows the difference in social status. Maybe with your chest out, head up a bit ... superior?'

The way it had been in our own theatre: the Jesus house. Most of the time it was empty (except for the cleaner that came every Thursday). So me and Ern would go in a basement window, sit in the drawing room and pretend we were Lord and Lady Muck. We'd make tea (the fridge was always on, the milk always stocked), sit in the two big armchairs He'd sit in (with Mary, who'd come too), and say things like, Listen, Ernest, this womanising can't go on, you're bringing shame to the family. And Jesus/Ern would reply, It's my life, to be lived as I please. No fake accents or stagey walks. It could go on like this for hours. Me chasing Ern upstairs, across beds, in cupboards, a bath, even (and yes, they'd left soap and shampoo, like, when He arrived, he'd need a good scrub before meeting the masses).

Back on stage, things were progressing slowly. Beatrice asking about eight-year-old Master Archie (not yet cast). '*Did he practise the piano while I was away?*'

Brigid explaining, '*Practise, how are you! Is it Master Archie? He is mad after the milkman's horse now.*'

Max explained how this line would need to be delivered with more emotion, like these two women had a secret war going on; like they really hated each other. He demonstrated: '*He is mad after the milkman's horse ...*' But Brigid didn't seem impressed. She just said, 'Max, I thought we were working on the blocking?'

'But since we're here.'

'It'll take days if you keep this up. It can come later, can't it?'

Max didn't say a word. This was the worst thing; it meant he'd been offended, and was sulking, retreating to the corner of a lounge room in protest; his boyish eyes, face pouting with uncried tears. Ern was a sook, too. Under the jacaranda tree, changing his dacks, turning away so I couldn't see anything. Me saying, You shouldn't get so worked up over things.

Him saying: I told Mr Sasse but he didn't do anything about it. They keep on at me, but he just says, Stand up to them. But there's Tristan and all his mates and only one of me. How am I meant to?

Perhaps not so much a sook. He had cause to be upset. But, one day, I confronted Tristan, asked him what he'd been up to, and he said nothing, so I smacked his face and his lip bled and there was a red mark in the shape of my hand. Ern said he backed off after that, and all was good, but I wasn't sure. Sitting in the Jesus house, in His bed, a few days later, Ern said, We could live here.

How?

You and me, in this place. We could go out when they come to clean. They'll see the food and drink's gone and think it was Jesus.

Don't be ridiculous. They'd know it wasn't him.

We could buy our own food, live here, never go to school (as he thought, I guessed, he'd never have to see Tristan again), read books, make a fire at night . . . what do you reckon, Eth?

What would Dad think, if we never came home?

We could go see him sometimes.

He'd be lonely.

I guess you're right . . . that wouldn't be any good, eh? Although he could come here.

But it's all ready for Jesus.

There's no Jesus.

Might be.

Then Mum'd be alive.

Richard Rowan entered. After a few formalities, he said to Beatrice, '*I had begun to think you would never come back. It is twelve days since you were here.*'

Woody, woody, woody. I couldn't stand it. A perfectly good stage, and script, and they were squandering it. I stood, walked up the aisle, the steps to the stage and said, '*I had begun to think you would never come back. It is twelve days since you were here.*'

They all seemed shocked. I made it clear. '*It is twelve days since you were here.* See, too long. You're upset. Make it known.'

Max stood, arms crossed, realising, at last, the actors would get what they deserved.

'And Beatrice,' I said, 'on that line, *I thought of that too. But I have come.* I sense a real frustration, but not so much in your voice.'

'As we said,' she explained. 'We need to block the play first.'

'Nonsense. We need to learn how to *act*.'

Max went down the stairs, walked towards the back and sat and watched. 'Just checking projection.'

I took this to mean I could continue. I'd read the play three times; most recently, the previous evening. I thought I understood Richard, especially. In terms of Ern. A man who gave little away, but was a deep river, gushing through the bowels of the earth (calling, Ethel!). So I said to him, 'This line, *Have you thought over what I told you when you were here last?* This suggests a secret. You know what I mean?'

His face suggested he didn't.

'Have you read the play?'

'Not all of it.'

'First rehearsal and you haven't read it?' I turned to Max, who said, 'Just keep going.'

I said to Richard, 'You at least know what's happening?'

'Of course.'

Although he had the script in his hand, ready. I guessed he was some sort of lecturer or tutor, a semi-intellectual with a bent for the European, like Elliott, or Dunk, a couple of second-raters sitting out their personal wars with Australia, and its (lack of) culture. 'Well, you'll have to learn it quick smart,' I said to Ted/Richard. 'We can't stage a play with you holding the script.'

'We?' Beatrice asked.

'Just a hand,' Max called, from the back.

'We only need *one* director,' Brigid added, raising an eyebrow, and this, of course, was like a red rag. So I said, 'Mr Harris didn't ask ... but I thought, since I *know* the play.' I looked at Ted/Richard.

'I agree,' he said. 'One director.'

And Beatrice.

'I have a few ideas,' I explained. 'Like later, when Archie—'

'Max!' Ted/Richard called.

'She does know the script.'

And the three witches backed off, for now. The old/young maid said, 'Right then, shall we continue?'

I set them, and moved them, and said, 'Walk it through.'

As they did, I saw Mary enter through the back of the theatre in a rush. Approach Max, sit next to him and whisper something, excitedly. I wondered what. Something nasty, no doubt.

Richard said to Beatrice, '*I told you also that I would not show you what I had written unless you asked to see it. Well?*'

'Angrier,' I said.

'*Well?*'

'You're not going to tolerate this woman much longer, Richard. No emotion. Like you'd like to slap her.'

I could see Tristan holding his face, the welt rising. Tears pooling, as he broke down, cried, but I pushed him against the wall, watched him slide to the ground, placed my foot on his cock and said, If you touch Ern again, I'll kill you. I'll break into your bedroom, and slice your throat open with my mum's bread knife. Got it?

Although I could hardly expect this much from Richard. But I said, 'You can overact for now . . . we can pull it back later.'

But you had to act before you could overact. I felt like I had this man on the ground, and my foot was on his cock, and it felt good. Not the cock, because that just felt like a pound of mince, but that I had control. That fear worked.

Mary was still talking to Max. Talking, then looking at me.

'Ten-minute break.' I walked from the stage, back to Max and Mary, and said, 'They'll need a bit of work, Max.'

'I'm not expecting much.'

'Hello, Mary.'

'Hello, Ethel.'

And we sat and stood, waiting.

'The poems are already getting interest,' this *woman* said.

I didn't know how she meant it. 'From whom?'

'Sid Carpenter, at the *News*. He was intrigued.'

'How's that?'

'You know, Ern Malley, coming out of the blue. He was surprised he hadn't heard of someone so talented before.'

'I explained.' I waited for Max to speak up, but nothing. I hated this about him. How he could step back, study you forensically, and you could hear the cogs in his head turning, grinding. I said to her, 'That's why Ern is unique. Because he just appeared.'

'Poets, artists, composers, take years to develop a voice. It's a lot of hard work. A lot of study, reading.'

'Oh, he read alright. We'd go into the Jesus house, and it had thousands of books: poetry, novels, scientific books about the body, filled with pictures of livers and kidneys, *A Thousand and One Nights* – everything.'

Not true; just Jesus books, but I guessed you could become a decent poet from reading them too.

'I could tell Sid that,' she said. 'That he read books in the, what was it, Jesus house?'

'We couldn't afford books. Our money went on food (just that, after Mum died). So books, forget it. We weren't lucky, like *some*.'

'My dad was a boilermaker,' she said.

'But you got a nice school, I bet . . . so's you could come to university?'

She conceded; for a moment.

'You got to read, Mary, and spend years studying (whereas Ern, he had to go out, work). Anyway, perhaps it's born into a person.'

Max faced Mary accusingly, like I had a point.

She wasn't finished. She was the real Beatrice, convincing without trying. 'Sid spoke to someone in Sydney. Said you'd had a rough trot, Ethel. Spent time in prison.'

The minx! Prison? 'I most certainly was not . . . where did you get that from?'

Max was shocked. 'Mary . . .?'

'It's just what he said.'

131

'Well, he's wrong. I've never broken a law . . . never so much as dropped a piece of paper. How dare you! Going behind my back. Why?' I guess I was loud. The actors were listening.

'It must have been someone else.'

'But to say it . . . to check? *Why?* You think I'm some sort of crook?'

I could've slapped her, pushed her over, stood on her privates. Ern was urging me, too. Ern, with his Jesus books, cross-legged in front of the floor-to-wall bookcase.

'I shouldn't even expect an apology,' I said.

'I'm sorry, Ethel.'

Max was still listening, deciding.

'You've found someone, talked to them, they've checked (making the most horrific of mistakes and accusations), you've rushed here, told Max, tried to make me look . . . What sort of person are you, Mary Martin?' I'd had enough. I turned and stormed out of the theatre, Max following.

As we walked, he said, 'Ethel, ignore her, she has this nasty streak. We've all had to put up with it.'

I turned on him. 'Well, why would you?'

'She's useful.'

'*Useful?*'

'Her heart's in the right place.'

I waited, studied him this time. 'Her heart . . . really? You can't think that, Max. She's a horror.'

'She can be.'

I continued. Across the Barr Smith lawns, unsure, myself, where I was going.

# 16

Max was summoned back to the roof of Miller Anderson's. We drove to town, parked and climbed the fire escape. After four floors I'd had it. Stopped and asked if we could use the lift, but the place was locked up. Eventually we arrived on the roof, greeted by an old lady with bad teeth. 'You don't mind helping?' she said.

How could you mind? The spotlight sat waiting. I asked if it was working and the woman said, 'It might.' She didn't seem to care, either way. Just returned to a canvas chair, her knitting, a thermos she offered around. 'I know you're busy, Max, but if the worst happened . . .'

I wanted to know what the worst was. The Japanese had barely dented Darwin. And there seemed to be a lot of desert between us and them. I said, 'What sort of range do those planes have?'

The woman, whose name I never discovered, but let's just call her Merl, said, 'If they can bomb London from Berlin . . .'

'But that's not very far.'

'Same principle.'

As she continued knitting someone's jumper, sipped tea, sang to herself: *'Take me back to where the River Shannon flows.'*

Max slipped on a coat and helmet and stood surveying his city. One, I guess, he hated and loved in equal measure. Aimed to improve, perhaps, with a dose of culture, although I couldn't see it happening, Ern or no Ern. It seemed to be small in the way it thought. The way it drove, parked, shopped, made conversation, sought useful education – talcum-scented people drifting towards the Gardens, or Myer. Like some sort of perfection had been achieved, and now had to be preserved. Formaldehyde people, charting the war on pin-up boards in their lounge rooms, worried about (but proud of) the sons they'd provided to defeat Hitler and Tojo. It was a perfection I could see now, looking out. Not too many lights along the roads, lined with cat-pissy hedges and lawns edged at thirty degrees to the horizontal.

'Does the spotlight have a globe?' Max said, examining it.

She checked. 'Maybe they bring it up when needed.'

'This is ridiculous,' I said to Max, but he replied, 'It was either this or New Guinea.'

This seemed strange. There was a war on. There were stories of what the Japs did to people, their kids. 'You don't *want* to?' I asked him.

'Not a case of want . . . I wasn't fit.'

Merl said, 'They gotta leave a few men behind, I guess.'

'Ern wasn't fit either,' I said.

Max returned from the edge. 'What did they have him doing?'

'Rabaul.' Trying to remember what I'd already said. Rabaul, that was as good, or likely, as anything.

'Thought you said you didn't know?' As he sat beside Merl, poured himself a cup of tea.

'Or something secret. Which is why he couldn't tell me.'

'You would've thought they'd have him fixing trucks or something?'

'Maybe he did.'

'But he didn't tell you?'

I didn't know what to say. Max had a way of knocking you off your feet, watching you fall. This is why I was learning to like him less every day, although, in a way, more. He was born likeable, I reckon, with his perpetual grin and his refusal to take anything too seriously. 'I bet he did a bit of fighting,' I said, perhaps to spite him. 'Put on the bayonet, and gave it to them. He was a fighter, our Ern.'

Max just listened, watched, as the sound of knitting needles filled the giant vacuum of the rooftop, sky, universe.

'As kids,' I said. 'You know, pretending to be pirates and . . .' Descending. 'The Jesus house, I told you about that? They'd decorated one wall with swords, and a musket, and some African masks. We'd get them down, dress up, go out into the backyard (always kept so nice) and have our little war.'

Ern as Sir Wolseley, me as a Zulu.

'He'd point the musket and say, Ethel, when I say, you gotta fall down dead. Charging across the lawn with his sword, cutting down the aggies (it was as sharp as anything – what they reckoned Jesus'd need a sword for I don't know).'

Max was still searching the city. 'Perhaps he *is* coming?'

'Jesus?' I asked, and Merl said, 'When?'

'It makes as much sense as anything. I could put the light on him: his face, from hills to sea, gazing down and saying, Oi, you, Harris, you're not on the list.'

'Surely you are,' Merl said, smiling.

'Ern always had a go,' I said. 'He learnt from Dad. *He* was a trier. Always something new … despite his business going belly up.'

They waited. Then Merl said, 'A lot of that going on.'

'This fuel pump,' I said to Max. 'It sent him broke … but when he read about this reliability trial …' I filled them in: the Indian, the test drives around Eastern Creek, then, day one. 'All of them lined up. Dad in his goggles and overalls, determined to win. Thirty, forty bikes revving.'

I remembered the morning. The sign above the road: *Esso Reliability Trial: Australia's First Desert Bash*. Dad saying to me and Ern (something like), Don't worry, I've got it in the bag. 'Then the pistol fired and they were off! Dad was right at the front … but then they disappeared from view.'

'He'd win this money and you'd all be rich?' Max asked.

'That was the plan.'

'And what happened?'

I wondered whether I should tell him. I wasn't sure if he'd believe me, anyway. 'It's a long story.'

'A long night.'

'What I tell you – you gotta *believe*.'

'I do, don't I?'

Mostly, I thought. 'Yesterday you had me in prison.'

He sat back and took in the sky, full of marked-down stars, shades of yellow, white and blue. 'I can't be responsible for what Mary says.'

'You didn't argue much.'

'What's the use? What would you be doing in prison?'

At that point Merl told us about her youngest son, who had been in Yatala, but only for a few weeks, because his boss had bought and sold shares illegally, and they'd thought he was involved, but he wasn't (just the office boy), so they arrested him, and oh, it was a terrible time, the shame, seeing your son's name in the newspaper, after having brought him up to do the right thing. Shame. That's the worst thing of all.

'I don't know, Ethel. Maybe you murdered someone?' Max said.

'Who?' I looked at him.

'Ern. Maybe you killed him for his poems?' He was grinning, but I just laughed. 'Maybe I killed the neighbours and buried them behind the shed?'

Then things settled, and eventually Max said, 'I told Mary to check her facts before accusing people, so she made a few phone calls, and it was some Malley woman from Bundaberg. You've never lived in Bundaberg, have you, Ethel?'

'No.'

'So I told her she'd need to apologise.'

'D'yer reckon she will?'

'Not a hope. Either way, that story, about the trial . . .?'

I didn't feel like telling him. Dad and Ern seemed so far away. So long ago. Me and my brother, up and down the driveway of the Jesus house, taking turns in Ern's go-kart, until one of the neighbours said, 'Are you kids meant to be in there?'

Ern: 'We got permission.'

'From whom?'

'Mr Alexander.'

Looking at us suspiciously. 'He doesn't let anyone in here.'

'He let us.'

He'd heard the pipe organ, I guessed. I'd told Ern not to play it, but he never listened. Switched it on, set out some music, played some scales and a Czerny exercise he'd learnt.

'Better ways to spend your life,' Max said, standing, removing his helmet and coat.

Merl sat up. 'Where you going?'

'Get a drink. Come on, Merl, you're just wasting your time.'

'But we're *meant* to be here.'

'Suit yourself.'

We made for the fire escape, but Merl wasn't far behind. 'We can tell them we stayed all night.'

'What about a coffee?' Max asked me, almost apologetically.

'It's late,' I said.

'Big city, bright lights.'

We helped Merl down the stairs, and she set off for home, still concerned Göring might arrive, and we'd be in bed. And *then* what would the papers say?

We walked back along North Terrace. Deserted, mostly, apart from a few drunks coming out of the Adelaide Club. The Establishment watering hole, Chesterfield couches and gin, what shares to buy and sell from and to whom, both boys at Saints, doing nicely, and a third pre-selected for Frome (by the way, we were in London, met Shaw, but the bombs!). Around the corner into King William Street, a few late trams sparking, arms hanging out of windows, the promise of Keen's Curry on the number 34 to Prospect. Hardly any cars. A few trucks, delivering papers and milk. Stopping, backing up to loading docks, more men in overalls throwing boxes to each other, a Capstan puff, a sit-down for five minutes, because what was the rush? The city, the world at war, was going nowhere.

Right into Hindley Street. Past the Theatre Royal, and a variety show to raise money for the boys. Past the bookshop,

and there, in the window (Max pointed out): *the gift of blood.*
'Juvenilia,' he explained.

An early verse poem, although rubbish. He wanted to buy the old copies, burn them, but didn't have the money. Still, he seemed proud to see it in the window. Max Harris. Local boy made good, or as good as you could make with poetry.

'The Jindyworobaks,' he said. 'With a little help from Mum.' Still forking out for his literary ambitions. '*The thunder broke and it was not as other thunder, the invitation to the hilltop, the vein slightly throbbing.*'

Perhaps Max was really a pornographer. And perhaps poetry was the closest he could get to being filthy. 'What's it mean?' I asked.

'What's marina mean, boult upright?'

'But Ern's not here, you are.'

'The poet shouldn't give it away. *It's no matter, here I am, You are he, my love is not shame, but its course, is a force, temporarily disabling all the limping stars.*'

It sounded like a love poem. Max? Love? And then, for a moment, I thought, What if it's for me? A whole book, but he tells me about his throbbing vein. Love, not shame, a force strong enough to disable the stars, hanging above the Miller Anderson & Co. rooftop.

'Not bad,' I said.

'Not good.'

The way he stared at me. No? He had a thousand women to choose from. And anyway, there was Von.

'*Into thy hands I commend the spirit, hormone to hormone, ovum to sperm, blood to blood to where you're going, Amen.*'

What was he saying? Hormone? Sperm? Blood? 'That's quite racy,' I said.

'You reckon?'

'Sperm to ovum.' I hadn't meant to say it, but it slipped out. The message seemed obvious, didn't it? I searched his face, his eyes, for clues. Hardly in the poems, but that was the point. 'You've memorised the whole thing?'

'Bits.'

'I'd like to get a copy.'

'I reckon that's the last one left. I got rid of mine.'

'Pity.'

'Not really. I'm just doing the world a favour. That's why I look for proper poets now.'

I wasn't entirely convinced. Had he given me the gift of blood? He moved his hand, touched my nose, and I knew. *'Your sister, her blood and mine will make us all truly one. Ours is a common sun.'* I felt weak. The breeze, the shadows, and the sound of the muffled orchestra from the Royal. Was this what it had come to?

But then he moved further along. Pointed and said, 'Look!'

*Angry Penguins*, Autumn 1944. Ern's name plastered across Hindley Street. Well, a poster someone had made up, with Sid's picture, as well as five copies of the journal. 'How do you feel about that?' Max asked.

'He'd be so proud,' I said, and this time I was gushing. 'I never guessed, my brother. I wish he were here, Max.'

Because I could see him, in front of the bookcase, saying, Eth, what's an ecliptic?

Dunno.

Is it like an eclipse?

Look it up.

Which he did. And said, It's the path the sun follows. See – and showed me a picture of the sun moving through the sky. I said, That's a bit like you, Ern.

How?

Brightening everything up, I said. Pinching his cheeks.

He seemed taken by this idea and said, I'm gonna build a solar system.

He searched the house for materials. Found some cardboard, scissors, strings, and every time we returned to the Jesus house, he worked on it. A few weeks later, a scaled-down solar system hung from the ceiling. Different colours for different planets. A big yellow blob in the middle. He was so proud; showed me how it revolved, each planet in order, taking as long as it ought, no more, no less. The whole world, and us, in it, summarised in a model.

Except, a week later, when we returned, it had gone. I guessed the cleaner had removed it. I said to him, Next time we'll make it in our shed. But he said there wouldn't be a next time. And found the ripped-up pieces in the bin.

'Wonder how many they've sold?' I said to Max.

'Plenty, I bet. Now we just have to wait, see what people say about Ern.'

This, I thought, might be the most frightening thing of all. What if they didn't understand? What if they hated him? Poor Ern. Perhaps, then, it'd be best he was dead. Perhaps that was why he hadn't published his poems.

Max produced his hip flask, unscrewed it, raised it and said, 'To Ern!' Drank, and offered it to me, and I did the same (after cleaning the lip). 'To Ern!'

141

# 17

I could see Dad, sand in his eyes, the Indian cutting across the desert. Stopping for water, checking his compass, wiping muck from his lips, before continuing. I could hear him saying, You're not gonna get me, you bastards. I could smell him, Old Spice giving way to the desert heat: four or five days' growth, tired eyes (from sleeping on his old swag), greasy hair and yellow teeth. But determined.

Page seventeen of Lodge's *Deserts of Australia*. As I stood, between rows in the Union bookshop, admiring the orange sand, desert pea and dead sheep. I turned the page and saw the telegraph line hobbling across the hummocks, civilisation surging in little amperes of First Eleven and Stalingrad. Dad, out there, somewhere, determined to win. Money that'd keep us in school shoes and holidays (nothing much, Newcastle, perhaps) for years to come. He always believed he'd win; that this was his birthright.

I gave up on the book, replaced it and returned to the launch. Mary, at a table of undergraduates, laughing along with some joke. Unusual. She was usually a misery, always caught up in other people's philosophies. Spilling her drink, sucking on a cigarette, saying things like (probably), She's obtuse, to say the least.

A dozen others stood around, not so much to honour Ern, I guessed, as their own contributions. This had come to worry me. That *Angry Penguins* wasn't much chop; a collection of intellectual driftwood that Max had thrown together. And perhaps Ern was just a novelty. I sat next to Von and said, 'This is it?'

'Long time coming,' she managed.

'Max said we've already sold seven hundred. All around Australia.'

'Encouraging, but ...' As she sat, thinking. 'Just because they've ordered doesn't mean they're going to sell them. If they don't, they'll return them for credit.'

I hadn't realised. Should've. The unopened boxes around Max's flat. 'But, chances are ...?'

'I'm sure Ern'll be a big hit.' Smiling her smile.

Max stood and said, 'Let's get going.' And again, introduced himself, the *Penguins*, the highlights of the issue.

Von said, 'How's the accommodation?'

'Fine.' Although I lied. The bathroom, with mould between the tiles. Drying off my feet and treating them with tinea powder, just in case. Towels that smelt like dog. I'd tried to wash them, but the machine was broken, and Max had said, 'It's not like it's gonna kill you.' He'd filled the curry-coloured bath, thrown the washing in, added some powder, taken off his shoes and socks and got in and trampled the whole lot (apparently an old Mount Gambier trick). Hung them out to dry (saying the sun'll clean anything). The kitchen that'd become a china Somme, piles of plates waiting for me, apparently. Perhaps that was how I was meant to pay my board?

'It'd take one hell of a woman to tame him,' I said to her.

'You're coping.'

'I'm trying, cos I'm a guest.'

As I thought of Ern, calling for water, and me, cursing him. Perhaps it was best people lived alone. The older you got, the less you tolerated. But to see Max's old socks, blooming, sweetening each of his four rooms. A person had to have *some* standards.

Max was on to 'Culture as Exhibit' – *Come, we will dance sedate quadrilles* – as the small crowd listened.

Von leaned forward and said, 'I still don't understand those poems.'

'Maybe they weren't meant to be understood.'

'Why else would you . . .?' As she lit another cigarette.

Minx. I'd told Max what she'd been saying. 'She reckons I should've gone home by now, that I'm sponging off you – but it's all for Ern.'

'You can stay as long as you like, Ethel.'

Von said, '*You* don't understand them, Ethel.'

'Mostly.'

'*Milord had his hands upon the snowy globe* . . . What globe?'

'We had one in our lounge room.'

I couldn't see what he saw in her. But they walked around the university, sometimes holding hands, and he kissed her when she left. 'Max needs someone stable,' I said. 'Someone to clean up, give him the environment to think, and write. Someone who won't challenge him.'

'What the hell are you talking about?'

'He needs someone who'll make a good wife.'

She shook her head. 'You're *still* giving advice?'

A few minutes later I had a turn. I realised this could be the beginning or the end of Ern Malley. I started with a story. Max's advice (only I knew Ern). I said how, when he was born in 1918, in a hospital close to the docks in Liverpool, he was a weedy-looking boy. How one doctor had said he wouldn't live more than a few days (his wheezing lungs, even then), 'But Mum wouldn't give up. She sat with him, day and night, for three weeks, until he decided to give life a go. That was our mum, bless her heart.'

I scanned the room. Max was right; they were all listening. Richard and Bertha and Brigid, the shop girl, a couple of kids, even. 'I remember very little about Liverpool, but Dad told us times were tough after the first war. He was out of work, spent his days roaming the streets . . . And that's when they decided to come to Australia.'

I hadn't told Max about Liverpool. How it was strange, wasn't it, growing up with Scouse parents, and their grating accents, as we kids became other (bronzed, happy) people, unknown to them. Like all kids perhaps; drifting away from the dock that had been the only dock. The only street, house, room that any of us ever knew.

'We moved into our place at Croydon, and Mum promptly died. No one really explained to us kids. One minute she was there, the next, gone. We were kept from the funeral.'

Intrigued, or were they bored? But to understand the *Ecliptic*, you had to understand Ern, and what had made him.

'There was a house across the road. Big place. Fancy. No one lived there because the owners, the Alexanders, reckoned Jesus would return and He'd need somewhere to stay.'

Some seemed confused. But they had to know.

'Me and Ern would play inside, cook food, sleep there. One day Ern was taking a bath and Mr Alexander arrived, up the stairs, saw him, dragged him out by the ear, across the road (with not so much as a stitch), stopped on the footpath and slapped him, hard, right across the face. Well, this is what I want to tell you: I was Ern's protector. So I got this Alexander squarely in the ribs, and down he goes, can you imagine?'

Blank faces. I wondered why. It was a good story, and I reckon the first time I'd told it.

'Dad comes out asking what's happening, sees Ern naked in the middle of Dalmar Street, and asks what's going on. I point at Alexander (groaning, on the ground) and say, He tried to kill Ern.'

I could still see the welt, and Dad shouting at Alexander, calling him a fruitcake, keeping a house meant for Jesus.

'Anyway, that was me and Ern, always watching out for each other. He was a sensitive child. He'd suffer in silence, but he was thinking things. If I hada known he was poetic . . .' I offered the book, as proof. 'But I should read, shouldn't I? After all, we've got to sell a few copies.'

Max was confused; Mary, Von, the Exiles. Maybe they didn't want the real Ern. Maybe they wanted the one they'd made in their own heads.

'*I have pursued rhyme, image and metre, Known all the clefts in which the foot may stick, Stumbled often, stammered, But in time the fading voice grows wise, And seizing the coordinates of all existence, Traces the inevitable graph.*' I looked up. '*The inevitable graph* . . . he knew, especially at the end, when he lay coughing, constant headaches, his heart racing, like any moment he might explode. And what did he do? Wrote. Put down his understanding of life, from the docks to Dalmar Street, the trams to a thousand broken watches (all of them, ticking away, reminding him of his limited time).'

A few people left. Maybe I'd said too much? But it was their duty to listen. They'd come, in search of Ern.

It was then I noticed him – this Elliott fellow. Coming in, surprised to see me, and Max, and the shop set up for the launch. What was he after? A book about Byron? Probably. He avoided eye contact and disappeared down an aisle.

I raised my voice. 'Ern was the real thing. An authentic Australian. Someone who'd help out, give his right leg. He was forged from misfortune. Lost his mum early, and then later, this business with Dad . . .'

A few more left, without buying a book.

'Our father entered a motorbike race, which ended badly. For a time he was winning but . . . he never came back. Ern and I were left alone, orphaned.'

Elliott emerged with a book, noticed me, and I said, 'There's a picture of him in here, Mr Elliott. Would you like to see?'

'I have. Ern, is it?' Turning to Max. 'Or someone else?'

'Ern was my brother,' I called.

He shook his head, put down the book and walked from the shop. I wasn't having any of that. I followed him, as Max followed me, warning me to let it go. But I walked in front of this man, handed him the book, and said, 'Perhaps you could try reading it.'

He took it. 'I could, and perhaps you could try telling the truth.'

As we both waited – a dozen or so faces watching from the window.

'You see, *Ethel*, I checked. There was no Ern Malley living in Dalmar Street . . . that's where it was, wasn't it?'

I was back beside the incinerator, ready.

'I have a friend who works for the council, he checked.'

Max, Mary, Von, with her arms crossed.

'I lived alone,' I said. 'Ern was in Melbourne. He got so sick he asked to finish work, and he got the train back to Sydney.'

Elliott was unfazed. 'How old did you say your brother was, Ethel?'

'Twenty-five.'

'And he was a motor mechanic?'

'Among other things.'

'And he wrote this?' And returned the book.

'I've tried to explain,' I said, but he just turned, walked off, and said, 'Nice work, Max.'

# 18

The first was a crocodile, with fat lips and bulging eyes. The label said it was three thousand years old. This poor man, sitting in the beast's mouth, gazing out, terrified. Maybe he'd just been bitten in two, swallowed, and wasn't yet dead? Pots and pans, and reliefs showing natives, all square-faced and angry. Maybe they'd just sacrificed someone? Not a good-looking people. With rings through their noses and lips and ears. But the exhibition (*Treasures of British Honduras*) had cost a quid, so I was determined to make the most of it. A small dog on wheels, and a hole where there'd once been a bit of string to pull it. The label explained it was a popular children's toy. Like something we'd had as kids. Ern's cart: a bunch of bits and pieces thrown together in the shed. There was a human skull, but it wasn't so shocking. A big hole where someone had knocked him or her on the head. Worse ways to go. Maybe they needed rain? And another skull, this time crystal. The label explained that it'd been found by a woman called Sarah Foster-Thomas. This seemed familiar. It said she'd found this skull (priceless, hand-ground from a piece of quartz crystal over three hundred years) buried under an altar inside a temple in Lubaantun. Foster-Thomas, apparently, was the daughter of Arthur Thomas, the British explorer who, in his twenties, had uncovered a dozen pharaohs.

*Thomas?* As I tried to remember. Ern sitting in the lounge room beside the wireless, reading. Saying, My arse she did.

What's that, Ern?

He showed me a picture of Sarah Foster-Thomas holding the crystal skull in the air. Some people have got a nerve, eh, Eth?

How's that?

She said she found it, but she didn't find it.

No?

Listen: *In a letter to his brother in 1913, Arthur Foster explained that he'd recently purchased a crystal skull at an auction in Glasgow.*

I waited. It was some sort of women's hour, advice on cooking hogget so it wasn't too tough. I turned it down and said, What d'you mean, Ern?

See, she's a fake. Says she *found* the skull, but at the time she was only eleven years old . . . and no one on her dad's expedition remembered *her* being there.

Standing, staring at a relief of a warrior with his tongue sticking out, I remembered. This Foster-Thomas had toured the world, charging people a quid a pop to see the skull *she'd* discovered.

People are stupid, if they believe that, Ern said.

They should arrest her. Although I wasn't sure she'd done anything wrong, apart from telling a story people had chosen to believe. But that wasn't her fault.

Nice-looking skull, Ern said, examining his magazine from different angles. Going on to explain that she'd made hundreds of thousands, and now, when people were asking questions, was refusing to give any of it back.

Good on her, I said.

It's not right.

Everyone tells lies, Ern, don't they?

No.

You do, I do. Or if not lies, half-truths.

I've only ever been honest, Ethel.

Rubbish.

All of the books he'd stolen from the Jesus house, kept under a rug in the shed so Dad wouldn't find them. But he did, of course, smacking him around the chops and demanding he return them. Along with a selection of His jumpers, shirts, underwear.

Now, here was the same skull, on display. Had this Foster-Thomas woman sold it to someone? Lent it, to gain credibility? Either way, if this was it, it should've been made clear to people. To just put it there, and pretend it was something it wasn't. Where was the *morality* in that?

It couldn't stand. So I approached an attendant, explained that I had some concerns about this skull, and asked him to fetch someone from the museum. He said everyone was probably busy, but I asked him to try anyway. Ten minutes later he returned with a small man with wire glasses and a bald patch. I told him about this Foster-Thomas and he said, 'It'd hardly be in the exhibition if it wasn't authentic.'

'I remember my brother telling me,' I said. 'This wasn't discovered at Lubaantun, as your label suggests.'

'Your brother?'

'Ern, Ern Malley.'

'Who was . . .?'

'A mechanic, but that doesn't matter. I remember him telling me that this woman couldn't have discovered this skull. She was only a child . . . and no one at the dig even remembered her being there.'

'I'm not an expert,' he said, 'but it seems unlikely—'

'Exactly, that an eleven-year-old ... meaning somehow, Mr ...?'

'Lyons.'

'You're not telling the truth.'

He seemed to pity me. Obviously I was some sort of mad woman, let out for the day. Making up some story about a brother who ... god, I have no idea what he thought, but he said, 'Well, Mrs ...?'

'Malley. Ethel Malley.'

'I'll pass on your concerns to the museum director.'

I knew he had no intention. He just wanted to get rid of me, but I could still see Ern, in his old chair, saying, The world's changing, Eth.

Me agreeing.

We're just lucky we were brought up to be honest, and decent.

Yes, *decent*. That, I thought (still do) is the most important thing. Then I might've said, It's important to be honest with people, Ern.

It is.

Tell them everything. Better out than in.

But he didn't take the hint. He was his own relief, baked by a thousand years of sun, hard, unchangeable, hiding secrets he was willing to take to the grave.

This little man, this Lyons, turned and walked off, but I followed him and said, 'You should put up a sign, or remove the skull until you've checked.'

He moved faster; as I did. He motioned to a guard, who started walking beside me. But I said, 'It was bought at auction, Mr Lyons.'

He nodded and the guard took my arm, and pulled me away, but I pushed him, and he fell back, and I said, 'I can do a lot worse.'

Had. Beside the incinerator. It just came over me, like a sunburst. This sudden gulp of anger, like someone drowning, gasping for air, unwilling to take their last breath.

But people were watching, so I decided to let it go.

Walking back across the museum lawns, I wondered if there was any point. The big dinosaur bones they'd laid out for the kids to play on. Dead. A fossil, a footprint, a million years old. Who cared, really? Gone, all of it. Life was about the living. Ern, although he was dead. Max, with his army greatcoat; Mary, with some sort of knitting needle through her hair.

Terry (we never called him Dad), and Mrs Royal (she insisted). Arriving a few days after Dad's memorial (they never found his body, but after three weeks, assumed he'd died). Both of them walking up the drive of number forty, as me and Ern (our Aunt Carol had got us cleaned up, best clothes, knees washed) stood on the porch waiting. Mrs Royal was first (always). She offered her hand and we dutifully shook and she said, This is a nice place you've got here, Ethel . . . and, how are you, dear? She looked at Ern.

Not that she cared. Terry was always four steps behind. Always smiling, winking, raising an eyebrow. At first, me and Ern thought he was simple, but soon found out he was her fifth limb. Obverse. Opposite. A foil. If she growled, he grimaced in mock horror; if she gave us the silent treatment (maybe once a week) he'd come out of his shell, compensating for her mood; if she obsessed about a broken glass, he'd break another, just to show how little glasses mattered.

Mrs Royal said, You've had a rough trot, I know, but my husband and I aim to bring a bit of stability back. You'd like that, wouldn't you, Ethel?

I had no idea what was standing on our porch, so I just said, Yes.

We went in, and she sat on her arse as me and Ern made tea. It didn't feel like number forty anymore. Dad, singing his way from the bathroom to bedroom, nothing but old potato sacks, his guts hanging halfway down to his knees; Ern tuning into some jazz, an old driftwood sculpture the boys had made and placed in the middle of the table. As we came in, Mrs Royal said, This is pretty, what is it?

Dad made it.

She touched it, and it almost fell over, but Ern saved it. I said, It's not meant to be played with.

Her eyes, steaming, already. But she calmed. Early days. It'd take some time to get things as she wanted, but she would, I knew, even on that first afternoon.

Me and Ern in the kitchen, waiting for the tea to draw, Ern whispering, We don't have to have her if we don't like her, eh?

I reckon we do.

We should have some say.

Pouring the tea, taking it in, Terry studying a picture of Dad and saying, He liked fixing things up, did he?

She shooshed him, but he didn't care.

And Ern?

They had a few projects, in the shed. I spoke for him.

What sort? Looking at Ern.

He didn't reply.

They made stuff outa driftwood, I said.

I'd like to have a look at that. Really enthusiastic, sitting forward, his hands on his knees. So I told Ern to take him out to have a look, and I was left sitting with Mrs Royal, who said, There's no use pretending, is there, Ethel? You've had a bad time of it. With your mother, and now your father ... who meant well, I'm sure. But ...

He was trying to get money for us, I said. He said, if he won, I could go to a nice school, like St Margaret's in Burswood.

*If*, she said.

He woulda won.

Really?

But something bad must've happened. Maybe with his Indian?

She decided to let it rest. She was, I guess, working me out, how I might be a problem, and what it'd take to fix me.

I made my way towards the university, but stopped in the middle of a courtyard. An old stone building on four sides, and what looked like a stable, although there were cars in it now. A dead lawn, and me, like a thousand-year-old Honduran, descending into the mouth of a crocodile. Calling for Ern, back on the bank, reaching for me. Carn, Eth, get out, swim! I thought, I could stay here, like this. I could just walk, sleep under a tree, eat from a bin, become my own Jesus, head home to the house across the road. Or just stand here, waiting for Ern. Who'd appear from around the corner, and ask about the poetry, and I'd say, I got it published for you, Ern.

But something made me continue. It always does, doesn't it? You place one foot in front of the other and keep moving. Why? There's no reason, really. But every reason. You can write, or not write, but not writing is dying (if you're that way inclined). Believe, or not believe. And which is better? Even if everything you believe in is a fake? Proddy hymns and crystal skulls. Max. Von.

I walked back to the Hughes Building, and Max's little office. A broom closet, almost, that he'd arranged for editorial meetings, somewhere to work. He often slept on the floor, but even then he couldn't stretch out. A table and three chairs, more piles of papers, blocking the sun. A dead aspidistra from the twenties (I'd offered to get rid of it, but apparently it was symbolic of something). I heard Max say, 'Bullshit.'

'That's what they reckon.' An unknown voice. Young, well-clipped but working-class. 'They're from Sydney.'

'So what?'

'One's called James McAuley, the other, where is it ... Harold Stewart.'

Max said, 'Now everyone's getting on the bandwagon.'

'They reckon they sat down one Saturday afternoon and made the whole lot up. Dictionaries, encyclopaedias, bus timetables.'

I barely breathed. I wondered what Max was thinking. He said, 'Why?'

'Why do you reckon? They're taking the piss, Max.'

'But I haven't even heard of these fellas.'

'Well, they've heard of you. It's just what's going around. Believe what you want, Max.'

I heard a chair move and turned, scampered down the hallway. Hid in a stairwell, walked back, went in to face a despondent Max. 'You look like Death,' I said.

And he barely smiled.

# 19

The man in the shop examined the book and said, 'You a fan?'

'I know him.'

'Fair enough.'

*Fair enough?* What did that mean? That there had to be some reason for buying it? 'Popular, is it?' I asked, as he placed *the gift of blood* in a brown bag, like some sort of pornography, or hard liquor.

'Appeals to a certain type, but not the average man or … anyway, you ask Maxie.' And he turned and served another woman.

I walked along Hindley Street, sat at a bus stop, took the book out and flicked through. *This age had brought me twenty years till the heart must say 'regret'.* Maybe by saying one thing you said many; by writing for one, all. I'd spent a lot of time thinking about this, reading poets from Dante to Eliot, as I sat alone, lost in a world of words, like Mr McDonald.

*… be young no more, forget the gentle thrilling and the unknown fears …*

To be honest, Max wasn't so good. Maybe this is why he didn't like anyone seeing his work. No Ern Malley, describing the world in a fantastic way. But, a noble attempt. So I took out my pen and wrote inside the cover: *Dear Max, Thanks for Ern, and the Penguin. My brother would be shaking your hand, if he could, Love from your close friend, Ethel.*

Ern, I think, was born to it. Always a reader. Once, Mrs Royal took us to town and we walked down Pitt Street and Ern saw the Angus and Robertson store. Come on, Mrs Royal, just for a minute.

We haven't got time, Ern.

Five minutes, as he grabbed her hand and dragged her towards the door.

A few steps behind, Terry said, They used to make us recite Henry Lawson. Mrs Royal ignored him, as usual, like he was some retarded child she'd inherited, or made, and had to tolerate. Although he didn't seem to care. Just smiled, walked along slowly with his hands behind his back, whistling.

The minute Ern was in the door he ran, and she called, Five minutes!

Can I buy one?

I haven't got money for books.

For other things: a permanent wave, Swiss chocolates, but not books. So Ern was off, and Terry (who I found in Popular Mechanics), and even Mrs Royal, examining the Classics, because, as she said, They're good for you. I found Ern in Poetry. Ern and his dirty little secret. I said, What you reading?

Shakespeare. And he showed me. Henry V trying to convince his troops to attack the French. He read me a few lines, from the bit about the breach to holding our manhood dear, and said, That's the best, isn't it, Ethel?

I had to agree. Shakespeare had earned his reputation. Poetry, but nothing too nancy. Gore, blood, action, but also beautiful words to describe it. Compared with Max's 'Progress of Defeat' *(death is bourgeois)*. What did that mean?

Not bad, I said to Ern.

Do you think she'll let me buy it?

No.

I could offer to work it off.

I saw the poet in his eyes. A kid that hadn't been led to any water, but was thirsty anyway. Who'd discovered words, like a half-eaten pastry thrown in a bin, and picked them out and tasted them and *wanted* them, like a baby wants milk, like Max craved admiration (in the end, anyone's). I wanted my brother to have the collected works of Shakespeare, but it was a big book, three quid, and there was no way she was going to buy it. I said, Haven't they got it in the Jesus house?

I want my own.

Now that Mrs Royal had taken over from (what she called) my hopeless father, we weren't poor. Hopeless, not in a personal way (she explained, I'm sure he was a very nice man), but hopeless with money, and anything practical. She'd fixed that. Sold off half the shed, invested the money in clothes, planted vegetables in the yard, taken us to the Legacy shop for new (old) clothes, paid all of Dad's debts, bought us new shoes to replace the ones with holes, even started a bank account for me and Ern.

Then she was standing behind us, saying, We gotta get on.

So we got on. My brother, with his poetry denied. Like everything, denied. Then there was a Depression, and war, and he was always doing what was expected. He might've been a great academic, or poet, but that wasn't to be. Just watches and carburettors, more's the pity.

Walking along Martin Place, I noticed something down Ern's

pants. At the back, held in by his belt, big and uncomfortable. I knew what it was, and said, How are you going to get that home?

No reply. He'd find a way. Keep his back to Mrs Royal and Terry. Until we lined up for the bus and she said, You first, and Ern said, I get in last.

Why?

I'm scared of buses.

Nonsense, go on. Manhandling him on to the bus, seeing the box-shaped extension to his lower spine and saying, What's this? Producing the collected plays and looking at him with horror. You little thief!

I'm sure Ern didn't see it that way. If you wanted something, and were denied it, it was okay to find another way to have it. If the world stood in your way, you went around. Why was it okay that some rich cow from Potts Point could enjoy Shakespeare, but not a kid from Croydon? When did theft become wrong?

I didn't steal it, he said, after she'd removed us from the line.

You didn't pay for it.

I need it.

Why?

Because I like it. I might be a poet.

Mrs Royal was having none of it. She dragged him back the shop, placed the book on the counter and said, My child (because she'd started thinking of us as her children) thought I'd paid for this, but I hadn't.

The shop girl didn't seem to care, placing the book on a shelving trolley, but Mrs Royal said, You need to apologise to the lady.

No need, she said. It happens all the time.

You need to *apologise*.

She said –

There was a hand across the back of Ern's legs, and he smarted, and I saw the tears coming. Felt them. The girl seemed shocked, and said, It's no problem, I can put it back.

What do you say?

Sorry.

Full sentence.

Sorry for taking the book.

She seemed happy enough. Wrong had been made right. She would've liked to continue the punishment, but that would have to wait. To mould his character more, but that might take years. So she led us out, along the road. Ern, with his head down, sobbing, like he always did when he pissed his pants, before I gave him a hug and told him it happens to everyone.

Of course, that night it was on. She said, If I let you get away with that, there'll soon be worse. You'll be stealing cars, and I'll have to visit you in Long Bay.

Wrong. All he'd wanted was the words. To see how they'd been chosen, welded or nailed together, given a bit of paint and presented to the world. Instead, he was sent to bed without food. Terry brought him some anyway, and I did, and he ate more that night than usual. And that was the template for our adolescence – the art of compromise, of living without the sort of love Dad had dished out.

Love. All poets needed it. Even Max, who was so embarrassed by it he had to talk around it. *The strain is that of death betrayed; for we cannot be afraid who may not love nor die again.*

As I sat at the bus stop, I searched the volume for clues: *We were dead, you and I, and close, as never before, we walked hand in hand . . .*

I returned to Max, hands behind his back, staring out of his office window, surveying the lawns. Like Hitler, I thought, about to make a speech. Same height, even the same haircut, seen from the back. I heard him before he heard me. Mumbling. '*Swamps, marches, borrow-pits and other areas of stagnant water serve ...*' He turned, noticed me, and tried to smile. 'What you been up to, Ethel?'

I had the feeling he was tiring of me. The book had been written, published, launched and sent out to the world. Why, then, was I still in Adelaide? I'd explained, how I'd grown to like the place, and how there's more – isn't there, Max? – we can do to promote Ern's work. A signing with the poet's sister? I'd suggested this at a few bookshops around town, left Max's number with them, but hadn't heard. I'd rung 5CL, said, '*Angry Penguins*, the Max Harris journal, you've read it?' And someone had replied, 'I don't think it would interest our listeners.'

'I got a present for you,' I said, holding the book behind my back.

He was only half-interested. Sat, crossed his legs, waited, and I gave him the inscribed book. He tried to smile, read my scribbles, flicked through a few of the poems and said, 'You saved it from the trash.'

'No,' I said, sitting beside him, both of us hemmed in by his cave of books. 'There's some nice writing in there, Max.'

'You reckon?'

'Good as anything Ern wrote.' Although I wasn't sure I believed this. Ern's voice was unmistakeable. Max's, easily confused with a dozen other poets.

He put the book down and said, 'Some of Ern's stuff stays with you, but this bit, about swamps, marshes, borrow pits ...'

I'd never liked 'Culture as Exhibit'. Not one of his better poems. But he hadn't had the luxury of being able to select the best; just what he'd managed to write. So it was unfair to judge.

'I had Ray Leaney in here,' he said. 'The editor of *On Dit*.'

I always knew when he was curious about something. He'd pinch his septum, sometimes play with the little hairs up his nose. Look down, think a thought through, and then share it. 'Ern must have copied some,' he said.

I was surprised. 'From whom?'

'Ray reckons it's from a book about tropical hygiene ... word for word.'

Could've been. Poets stole, poets borrowed. 'He's seen this book?'

'Not him, but these other fellas.'

I knew who he meant. The poets, from Sydney.

'They reckon ... Na, it's not worth it.' As he tried to decide. Looked at me, looked at the ground.

'Go on.' Because I knew it would have to come out.

'Ray reckons these fellas, Stewart and McAuley, wrote *The Darkening Ecliptic*.'

I couldn't believe it. Knew it, already, but still, to hear it from Max.

'They *wrote* it?'

'That's what they're claiming.'

'The nerve!'

'They reckon they wrote it as a joke, to get to me, to bring me down a notch.'

'Why?'

He explained how the traditionalists hated the modernists, how they were determined that all this symbolist rot meant nothing, except the poets were idiots. How they sat, one Saturday afternoon in Victoria Barracks in Sydney, and concocted the whole lot. From other poets, timetables, military manuals, newspapers, but mostly from their own sense of the ridiculous. Then he said, 'Those lines about swamps and marshes, they're from the *Manual of Tropical Field Hygiene*' – and he checked a note he'd written – 'by CS Tanner, Government Publishing, Canberra, 1938.'

'Well, might've been,' I said. 'Maybe it had something to do with Ern's work.'

'The work he wouldn't tell you about?'

'*He* wrote those poems.'

'You saw him?'

'No, but he must've. Why else would they have been hidden? And who are these fellas to say? They didn't find the poems – they only said all this *after* I'd sent them to you, Max. And you'd published them.'

He thought it through. 'They must've seen copies . . .'

'I reckon.'

'Then thought, hi-ho, off we go, let's have a bit of fun with Maxie.'

'Rotters.'

'How many months since you found them, Ethel?'

'Last September, I reckon.'

'And these fellas said, apparently, last week . . .' He seemed glad. Maybe he'd doubted Ern, for a minute, but returned. These bastards had taken my brother's work and were trying to destroy it.

'If there was no Ern, there was no Ethel,' I said.

'That's right.'

'No Ethel, no Dalmar Street, Sydney, Australia . . . we might as well say the whole lot's made up!'

He returned to his book and re-examined his poems in the light of a renewed faith in the power of words, and truth.

'I reckon that's what he might've done,' I said. 'He was an invalid. Couldn't do much physical. So it begins, Max. The answers to the mystery of Ern Malley, poet-soldier, reaching up (I can see him now) to the bookshelf above his desk and finding (by chance) a manual on tropical health.'

Max reached over to his desk, took the latest copy of *On Dit* and threw it in the bin. 'I must tell Ray, and we must write to these fellas, Ethel.'

'I'd like a word with them.'

'Set the record straight, before people start believing them.'

And his look, that said, there can only be one Ern, eh, Eth?

# 20

That night, Max was moody, grazing the *Ecliptic*, his own poems, as if trying to work something out. I attempted to make conversation, but he said he was tired, and fell asleep on the lounge. Like some sort of doubt had persisted. Maybe he was confused about McAuley and Stewart. Why would they want to cause harm? Why not write a letter saying they disagreed with the way poetry was going? Why pretend they'd written Ern's poems?

The next morning he seemed better. I was waiting out front, and he came out and said, 'You coming to uni?'

'Why not?' Smiling.

'You wouldn't prefer to stay home? I could give you a few bob, and you could buy some steak, for tea?'

No, I said, I'd like to come.

Which was fortunate, because it was his easy day, and in the few hours he had off in the afternoon we headed down to the Barr Smith lawns, much changed in the few weeks since my arrival. Now there was a network of trenches snaking around the trees, and people digging. A collection of spades and shovels and barrows, and it seemed like it was expected. In the same way they'd sandbagged the Mawson Laboratories, taped all the windows on Union House.

So we worked, and as we did, someone (a big, rugged engineering type) said, 'If I could see any sense in it.'

I said (as people noticed me, and wondered) that the point was to show some patriotism. And the engineer said, 'Why?'

'There's a war on.'

'Why dig *trenches*?'

Someone else said, 'Because the vice-chancellor said so.'

'Well, he's an idiot, too.'

I thought this seemed wrong. If we'd been caught saying the same thing in Germany we'd be shot. 'There are men in uniform doing their bit,' I said, 'so it's not too much to expect us to do ours. Considering *we're* not fighting.'

'I can't,' another woman said. 'My neck.'

*My neck*, my arse, I thought.

And someone else: 'I'd happily go, but they'll need doctors, and I graduate next April.'

This seemed fair, but it didn't explain the majority: in the bar, coffee shops, joining the fencing club, ra-ra rugby, let's beat Melbourne. 'My brother was in the army,' I said, as I dug, but only managed to scrape a bit of dirt.

Max worked too, but stopped, lit up, smoked for a few minutes, tried again. 'What do you reckon he did, Ethel?'

'It's hard to say.'

And his look – *it is, isn't it?*

'I think something to do with engineering.'

'Something very *secret*?'

'Possibly.'

'Something you or I, no one could know? Like . . .?'

'Well, some secret weapon.'

'Of course. This bomb they reckon they're building. Blow up a city with a handful of uranium.'

I tried to work out his face. He might've meant it. Might've though Ern was that smart. But then again. 'I would've known.'

'But that's the whole point . . . you wouldn't have.'

This was going nowhere, so I said, 'Unless he helped drive the trucks.'

'Maybe.'

'Even they'd be sworn to secrecy, eh?'

'They would, Ethel.'

'But probably something less exotic. Dams.'

Max sat against the side of the trench, only a foot deep. 'Cos he wouldn't be able to tell you about that.'

'He would but . . .'

His face – I could tell. What had happened to my Max? The one I'd met at the train station all those weeks ago? The excited Max, the bohemian, the rebel, the never-follow-a-rule Max? He'd come to this. Cynical Max. Doubter Max. Someone whose face I couldn't recognise or understand.

'Either way,' I said, scraping, 'I reckon he woulda been doing something with his hands.'

'What's the fucking point of this?' someone said, throwing down their shovel, climbing out of the trench and walking away.

'Not bombs or dams,' I said, 'but perhaps the wireless or . . .' As I descended, saw Ern and Dad at the dining table, newspaper spread, bits of balsa cut ready for joining. Dad taking two bits, spreading glue, handing them to Ern, who carefully pressed them together, as Dad said, Perfect . . . now hold them tight for a few minutes. As he studied the instructions, found the next parts, fiddled, working out how they connected. Ern saying, We should paint it red.

And Dad, No, only the Baron was red, everyone else was grey.

But no one'll know.

*We'll* know. We should aim for historical accuracy.

They worked for hours, over several weekends (and a few school nights, if Dad wasn't too tired). Until it was finished, painted red (Ern always got his way), taken into the backyard, where Ern climbed a tree and launched it, and it flew, a few little loops, before coming to rest on the roof. And Dad: Look at that Ern! It flies too damn well. Me, up a different tree, watching, because these times were all about Dad and Ern. Not that I cared. I liked the way they had planes and driftwood and someone's old motor mower to fix, and me and Dad had ... well, I'll tell you about that later.

So there was Dad, up his ladder, onto the roof, crawling across to the biplane (although everyone knew von Richthofen had three wings). Reaching, grabbing it, but losing his footing and falling into a camellia bush. Me and Ern straight over, checking for broken limbs, although the only thing broken was the plane, in little balsa shards, the wires hanging loose. Ern saying, That's okay, Dad, we can fix it up, better.

'Or chemicals,' I said to Max. 'Maybe that's what he was doing? Mixing DDT, spraying it in swamps and bother-holes ... he was good with chemistry, as I remember.'

'Didn't you say he left school early?'

I had to think. Perhaps. Perhaps just the little experiments he made in the shed, the vinegar and bicarb. The magnesium that could burn, if you heated it enough. Maybe that's what I meant. 'They coulda taught him,' I said.

'They coulda, but they didn't,' Max said, throwing away a cigarette, picking up his shovel and digging. 'Tojo could be here any minute.'

'They coulda,' I said.

'DDT's top secret?' As he dug, thrusting the shovel into the earth.

'Of course not.'

'So he woulda told you?'

'He was sick . . . perhaps a bit in the head, Max.'

'Is there much of that in your family?'

'*What do you mean by that?*'

He stopped, waited, surveyed me. 'Nothing.' And continued.

'Go on, Max, say it . . . say what you mean.'

Stopping again. 'It's all a bit confusing, isn't it, Ethel? In the army, but no one seems to know anything.'

'He joined. He knew he was sick, but he did his best. What about you, Max Harris? What have you done?'

He threatened me with his eyes. 'What have I done? For you?'

'No, for the war. Where's *your* uniform? Nothing wrong with you.'

'I'm exempt . . . everyone here's exempt.'

'That doesn't make it right. You could *choose* to fight, all of you. You could put your studies on hold. But you like it here.'

Now, there were even more listening, and someone said, 'The world doesn't stop for a war.'

'Yes, it does. Everything stops. Except you lot, and you, Max, with your poems and journal. How does the world need any of that right now?'

I had no obligation to these people, their university, their trenches. So I climbed out, cleaned myself off and headed up the hill to town. Max didn't say a word. Didn't come after me. Didn't care. And I thought, so be it.

I made it as far as the art gallery. Wandered, admiring the colonial works, all sheep and wheat, grapes and dead pheasants on tables. Then, to the early eighteenth century, a succession of small people in big landscapes (life, I guess), wandering Roman ruins, seeking paths through dark forests. Late nineteenth century: Renoir, Matisse. Although were they the real thing? What someone says, and others believe; what can be proved, or not. I studied one – the brush strokes, which might've been unsure. Was the faker showing his lack of technique? Good enough, still, that no one would notice.

A desert. Not a bad one, I thought, sitting, with the day going through my head. A bird in the foreground, and a mirage in the distance. And Dad, deserting his Indian, wandering, calling for us. Ern? Ethel? Because, in the end, they decided, the course hadn't been set out clearly enough. He'd misread a direction, driven a hundred miles south-east, instead of whatever it was. Ran out of petrol when he couldn't find the refuelling stop. Wandered, dehydrated, confused, until . . . *Ethel? Ern?* Slowly realising he might never see us again; the bills, unpaid; the house gone.

Then Max said, 'Which one do you fancy?'

I pointed.

'The desert, eh?'

'Yes. Just thinking about Dad.'

He sat beside me. '*Nature has her own green centuries which move through our thin convex time.*'

'You've remembered all of it?'

'Lots. There's a poem for every occasion, Eth.'

'Yes, there is.'

He cleared his throat, as a prelude to apologising, perhaps? 'I was thinking . . . so far, these poems have been written by Ern, Elliott, McAuley, Stewart. Everyone's had a shot.'

'But only one did.'

'Agreed. But my problem . . . not yours, or Ern's, is why people would say . . .' He noticed a modern piece, and pointed it out, but couldn't be bothered getting up. 'It's a strange situation, Ethel.'

'It is.'

'But I want you to know, I believe in Ern. *That taunts the living life, O those dawn-waders . . .*'

'*In?*' I said.

'Yes.'

'But he was a man.'

'I know. In a uniform, unlike me.' He smiled.

I looked ahead. 'I'm the one should be saying sorry.'

'Doesn't matter, Eth.'

We barely noticed the art. Maybe it didn't matter. The artists were dead; that was the only reason they displayed them. Culture didn't care for the living. Not this sort, anyway. It had become so much wallpaper.

'They have their reasons,' I said, 'but I don't care. We've done our part, haven't we?'

'Yes.'

'And it's there, the *Ecliptic*, if someone wants to check, in a hundred years. No one has to read it, but they can. We've made a record, Max.'

'Exactly. If nothing else, a record.'

'That this man lived and thought and died . . .'

Max said, 'We might have to watch these fellas in Sydney.'

'How's that?'

He handed me *The News*, open to page three, an article circled in red. 'Mary just gave it to me.'

*Harold Stewart and James McAuley have perpetrated Australia's greatest literary hoax. Tired of the modern jabberfest that poetry has become, they set about teaching the movement's leading exponent in Australia, Max Harris, a lesson he wouldn't forget . . .*

The article explained how these men had concocted the absurd, shoddy, rough-sawn poems and glued them together in their spare time, sent them to Max and sat back and waited for the response. *They*, McAuley and Stewart, were Ern Malley. No explanation, of course, why Max had never heard of them. That was easily explained.

*. . . both men also created the fictional Ethel Malley, sister of Ern. Having discovered a bundle of poems after her brother's death, she sent them to Mr Harris in Adelaide, who declared them masterpieces and set about publishing them in the autumn number of his modernist journal,* Angry Penguins . . .

I couldn't believe what I was reading. Now *I* wasn't real. I, Ethel Malley, was a fictional character, invented by these two turds. The nerve! *They* had made me, and Ern, and his poems. *They* had orchestrated the events of the last few months. All to make Max look stupid.

'How could they say this?' I said.

'They've seen the poems, and my introduction explaining the events, so they've had to improvise, work you into the story.'

'But they'd know *you'd* make it clear?'

'Perhaps, but their aim is to discredit me. So I say, I know Ethel, she's staying with me, and they think the nation will laugh even louder.'

*'The nerve.'*

'I gotta give it to them … it's clever, ambitious, creative. I don't think anything like this has been done before. I mean, trying to convince people that what's real, isn't, and what isn't, is.'

It seemed confusing. You couldn't deny the existence of real people, could you? 'Didn't they think I'd say something?'

'Probably hoping you do. Then they claim I'm the hoaxer. I dreamt you up.'

'But that doesn't make sense.'

'It makes perfect sense. By the time the whole thing's revealed, they're famous, I'm a fool, you're a fool, Ern's a fool, they've made their point. *That's* what they're on about, Ethel.'

I thought about it. About the pictures. Real, but not. 'It's a game then?'

'Yes, they're improvising. Every time we put out a fact, it becomes part of their story.'

'We could take legal action?'

'We could, but they're probably betting on it all being over in a week. If we get a lawyer, they admit everything, apologise, but win.'

'Bastards.'

'I guess, Ethel, the only thing to do is play *their* game.'

'How?'

He smiled. 'Turn Ern into the mythical poet.'

# 21

What he meant was, instead of fighting these fellas with facts (easily enough done), why wouldn't we play them at their own game? Take advantage of the publicity, of the myth that was stirring, because, at the end of the day, mystery novels always outsold biographies. We wouldn't be manufacturing Ern, as such – more, exaggerating. This wouldn't have to be any sort of hoaxer's hoax, just a gentle gilding of the lily. Ern wouldn't mind. I didn't (I told Max). *He* certainly didn't.

So the following morning, Max and I walked down North Terrace towards the offices of *The News*. 'It seems it could all be cleared up with a note from you,' I said.

'It could,' he agreed. 'I say I've never heard of them, never received so much as a submission. They're not poets (and that'd hurt them, because they claim they are).'

Then, a loud thump. We turned and, at the intersection of King William Street and North Terrace, saw a boy lying on the road, squirming, as the driver of the car that had just hit him came over, knelt, shook him, talked to him.

'He's okay,' Max said.

'Should we help?'

Soon there were six or seven people, and someone, a doctor

or nurse perhaps, was taking charge, ordering another man to stop traffic, another to call for help. He talked to the boy, who was stretching, lifting his body, trying to stand up. The driver, meanwhile, had turned away, started crying, as someone consoled her.

'What should we do?' Max said.

'We'd just be in the way.'

I'd been here before. Remembered how a person could go from discussing the weather to lying, minus their words and movements and smiles, and breath, even, on the road. I must have gasped, because Max put his arm around me; must've cried, because he squeezed me. The boy had stopped moving. I watched, desperate for anything. A leg shifted, a hand raised, but there was nothing. Come on, I thought, move. A small roll of the head on the road, the rising and falling of his chest. Nothing. As the man in charge turned the boy, moved closer to his mouth and listened.

'He's okay,' Max said, still holding me.

No, he wasn't. I remembered from the last time. People could be talking, then still, then dead. That quick. Before you could reach out, say anything, prevent it happening. It could be something simple, like not looking right before you stepped on the road, or thinking you weren't that high up a ladder.

I just watched, but he wouldn't move. As the man blew into his mouth, pumped his chest, as cars slowed, stopped, watched, the whole intersection became some scene from a film.

'No point watching,' Max said.

But there was, because we owed him that much. To care, to be concerned, in these moments. To put off living our own lives for a few minutes, delaying the purchase of bread and paying of bills.

As the doctor worked. But the boy refused to move. Come on, I thought. Get up! 'Get up!'

Max looked at me; and another woman, and she said, 'Doesn't look like he will.'

'He will,' I said.

Then the man stopped, and there were so many people we couldn't see the boy anymore. I knew he was dead. Death just decides to happen; it doesn't wait for anyone's opinion. Like a branch falling from a ghost gum during a drought. And me, crying, avoiding the hysterics I could feel percolating. Rumbling, like a Hawaiian volcano. Ready to erupt. Like when you read the end of a novel, and the person you most like dies of tuberculosis and you want to call the author and protest.

Max walked me around the chaos, and I caught a glimpse of the body, covered with someone's jacket, and heard the sirens, too late. Saw the feet and ankles and a bit of muscle. Socks, low, like he might've been just about to pull them up. All of this, perfectly workable, ready to stand, get back on the crumpled bike, tell the driver (who was sitting on the gutter, screaming) it didn't matter, cycle home to his mother, who was probably still making jam, no idea that her life was over, just as surely as her son's. All of this, because of a bad left turn; all of this, on a sunny Adelaide morning; all of this, as the birds continued squawking, and the 34 to Rostrevor drove around the mess to try and get back on time.

Max said, 'That's just shitty.'

I agreed. Shitty.

A few minutes later we arrived at the newspaper, asked for Sid Carpenter, and were shown up. He was standing at his window, staring along North Terrace at the drama. 'Doesn't look like it ended well.'

'Only a kid,' Max said, shaking Sid's hand, because he knew him from his copyboy days.

We sat on a couch and Sid wagged his finger at Max and said, 'He would've made an excellent journalist.'

Max shook his head. 'Maybe at a proper newspaper.'

'We do some solid stuff.'

'Lost bunnies?'

'Graft – Playford and his mob, they'll keep us busy for years.' He sat, leaned back and said, 'So here's our fictional woman.'

'I'm quite real,' I said.

'I can see. Let's get it straight. Stewart and McAuley wrote these poems—'

'Ern,' I said.

'They sent them to you, Max, you reckon they're shit hot – excuse me, Ethel – and you publish them as the next big thing?'

Max agreed. That's what they were claiming.

'That's how I came to write the article,' Sid explained. 'I got this phone call from Sydney, and this fella says, Are you Carpenter, the arts editor, and I say, Yes, how can I help you? And he (it was almost like he was giggling) says, This Max Harris you got in Adelaide, we played a trick on him.'

'Bloody nerve,' I said, but Carpenter barely flinched.

'And he says, Me and my mate dreamt up these poems and called them *The Darkening Ecliptic*, and filled them with a load of bullshit from textbooks.'

Max was happy to wait.

'Then I got a copy of *Angry Penguins*, read the poems and wrote that article. I did like the poems, though, Ethel, if your brother wrote them.'

'Of course he wrote them. You don't believe . . .?'

'My job's *not* believing, Ethel. I'm the unpriest of Adelaide. Where there is faith, I sow doubt.'

I really didn't know where to start. The argument was so ridiculous, so easily disproved, but here we were, talking about it like these men might have written the poems, like Ern might've been invented. 'He was my brother,' I said.

'You'd know. Anyway, then they reckon this letter, from Ethel, they dreamt her up too.'

'*Am I real?*' I asked.

'You are.' He took a moment. 'And you've never met this Stewart and McAuley?'

'Of course not.'

'Both being in Sydney, you might've crossed paths?'

'Are you saying . . .?'

'I'm not saying anything.'

'I'm in it *with them*?'

Max sat forward. 'No one's saying anything, Ethel. Are they, *Sid*?'

But he just sat, arms crossed.

Max explained the timing. How many weeks since he'd received the letter, and the poems, and the next letter, and how our correspondence had developed. 'At no point during this time did I, you, anyone, hear from Stewart and McAuley. Only *after* the poems were published . . . *several* weeks after. Enough time for them to dream up Ethel, write the letters, call you. Problem being, Sid, if journalists are gullible, and willing to print unchecked information, these sorta hoaxes will happen.'

'Wasn't unchecked, Max. These men *claimed* to have written the poems and invented Ern Malley, and you, apologies to you, Mrs Malley.'

179

We were getting nowhere. This man, this Carpenter, was a fence sitter. I said, 'Surely your next step, Mr Carpenter, is to ask these gentlemen for proof of authorship.'

'Should I ask Ern, or you?'

'I have the original manuscripts.' I produced them from my handbag. The ones I'd sent to Max. I laid them, one by one, on the desk. 'There you go: "Egyptian Register", "Young Prince of Tyre". See, in his hand.'

He examined them, but didn't seem convinced. 'Very neat.'

'He was.'

And stared at me. 'So, tell me about this brother of yours.'

I remembered what Max had said. In this, the battle of the Erns, we had the upper hand. All we had to do was gild, but as he'd also said, you couldn't gild that which could be checked. All Ern needed was a gentle push. 'He was a very nervous child but Mum, who died when he was only young, kept him under her wing.'

Carpenter started taking notes, and asked, 'Do you mind?'

'Of course not. I suppose, in the life of most creative people, there's some sort of *problem*.'

'How's that?'

'Something unresolved, that they spend years mulling over.'

'And with Ern?'

'He was always secretive, right up to the end, which is why I only discovered his poems by chance, and spent time deciding whether he'd want the world seeing them.'

'Like Brod and Kafka,' Max said.

'When I found out about Max, and forwarded the poems, I knew I'd found someone who understood my brother. And, if he published his work, would do it with sensitivity.'

Carpenter seemed more convinced. After all, if Stewart and McAuley had gone to some trouble, I'd gone to a shitload. Inventing lives. I would've had to be insane, surely, and I clearly wasn't, and Max clearly wasn't stupid. '*Unresolved*,' I said.

He stopped his Pitman, stared at me.

'Mum had died, Dad needed money, so he entered the Esso Reliability Trial.' I explained, from the shed assembly, the starting line, the days without hearing. 'It didn't end well, Mr Carpenter.'

'What happened?'

'No one's sure but . . . there he is, driving into the desert . . .' And with a certain wistfulness. 'Realising there was no one in front of him, behind him, stopping, getting off, checking his fuel . . . but less than a gallon.'

He seemed intrigued. Took notes, to check, but it was all there in the archives, poor Bob Malley, dead at thirty-three, no body recovered. 'Some said there were Aborigines involved.'

'How's that?'

'Dad crossing sacred songlines.'

'Right.' Scribbling.

I stood, walked to the window, noticed the ambulance driving away, the last of the crowd dispersing, cars and trucks and trams continuing like nothing had happened. 'Ern had an interest in long jump. Schoolboy champion, state finals, invited to nationals, six years straight. But . . . he had a fall.'

'Bad?' Sid asked.

'From a ladder. He was fetching a toy plane off the shed roof . . . three operations and spinal fusion, so no more long jump. But he took up chess (learnt, from a doctor, during his six months in hospital) and could defeat all comers. See, he had this competitive streak.'

'And what about school?'

I returned, sat and said, 'He would've liked to go to university, but that wasn't an option. Study arts perhaps, become involved with theatre, write for the student paper, all that, but it wasn't to be. He had to put his mechanical gifts to good use.'

Sid seemed happy. He had an angle. Life stands in the way of poetry, and it's only years later, on his deathbed, that the world learns about Ern Malley.

'He was happiest as a child. Never really progressed, I think. Just accepted the changes that life brought. Various jobs, until he signed up.'

'He fought?'

'I believe. But he was very secretive.'

'On active service?'

'Possibly. But I suspect, something covert. Intelligence. Or the development of certain ... technologies. See, he always tinkered.'

'Weapons?'

'It's funny, Mr Carpenter, but after he died, I found papers in the shed.'

Now, he seemed intrigued.

'Some documents, in Cyrillic.'

'Russian?'

'Yes. A whole box full. I thought of contacting the army, but then wondered, what if he wasn't meant to have had them?'

Max was grinning, I was sure, but I didn't check.

'So I burned the whole lot.'

'But you don't want me printing that?'

'I suppose not. The army might come knocking, eh?' I smiled.

'So, he might've been translating them? Did he ever—'

'No, Ern didn't get his Leaving. He wasn't a *smart* man. In the sense that you or Max are smart. But as a child he loved reading, not that we could afford books. That was our Sunday afternoon, down the library, Ern on the ground with . . . military history. He was always interested in that.'

More notes.

'I don't know what else I can tell you, Mr Carpenter. Ern was complicated. He'd always lock the toilet door, put a towel between the gap, so no one could hear.'

'What?'

'I think Ern is there, in every poem,' Max said. '*I am still the black swan of trespass on alien waters*. I think that's how he saw himself. That the world was apart from him – that he was disembodied.'

Rising, from the asphalt, years too early.

'*I have shrunk to an interloper, robber of dead men's dreams.*'

Silence, as Sid scribbled.

'It'd be interesting to know what our friends, Stewart and McAuley, know about the real Ern Malley,' Max said.

And Sid agreed, it would.

'Or whether they've come up with a new story yet.'

We left, down in the lift, back to North Terrace. There was no sign of the boy, his messy socks, a cowlick his mother tried to wet down every morning. By now, I guessed, his parents would know. His body would be on a gurney, in a fridge, cooling. He'd still be in his shorts and shirt, with jam around his mouth.

'How did that go?' I asked.

'Fair. But it's the small things, isn't it, that make a person real?'

I agreed. Kneecaps green with grass. The flapping sole of old shoes.

Max touched my hand and squeezed it. Nice. But what did it mean? The warmth, the fat fingers. Max, the lover, denied his passion, because of *her*. And now, the gift of blood coursing through my veins as much as his.

'What's next?' he asked, but right then, I didn't care. 'This can't end without an apology.'

'I agree. It's our turn now, isn't it, Max?'

# 22

This Carpenter was an idiot. Hardly a journalist, hardly factual, hardly funny, although he'd tried. A page three article titled 'The Importance of Being Ern'. A picture of Oscar Wilde imagining both versions: my brother, a soldier with a question mark where his face should be; Stewart and McAuley, larrikins, grinning with their thumbs up, holding a copy of *Angry Penguins*. And dumb, mindless explanations like, 'Ern in the country, Ern in the city. But who is Ern? And does the average Australian even care?'

Was it too much to expect a journalist to do his job properly? Investigate? Instead of, 'These knockabout soldier-poets from Sydney reckon our Max is a bit of a twat. Ridiculous poems that make no sense; literary "soirees" where university types sit around all night drinking wine, listening to jazz, as the war buzzes around their ears.' Too much to expect that the public might want to know *why* there was a hoax? My comments had been through the wringer and emerged as, 'Ern's "sister", Ethel Malley, told this reporter her brother was a sensitive soul, always busy with a volume of poetry, full of boyhood visions of Elysium Fields. But I checked again, and there was no one on the couch! Maybe she was a ghost?'

Still, what could you expect? Adelaide! Nasty little place, with its few ex-pastoralists, living in the leafy east, running everything, while the boilermakers were fed a diet of football and cricket, cheap carpet at Solomon's and green, turgid slop at the pie cart – pea soup for the masses, enough to soak up a lifetime of grog (they'd need it). But what annoyed me most was how these men were ridiculing Ern. They had no interest in the real man, what he'd struggled to achieve. Ern was like a balloon, deflating, as the newspapers and wireless rustled up a sort of anti-culture lynching, with Ern the strange fruit.

I wasn't going to take it. That morning, on the way into town, I said to Max, pull over here. I went into a post office and filled in a telegram. *From Ethel Malley. To Harold Stewart and James McAuley, Victoria Barracks, Sydney. Dear Sirs, my name is Ethel Malley, the sister of poet Ern Malley. The real one. I'm awaiting explanation, and apology, and seeking legal redress. 24 hours. Yours, EM.*

Max stood behind me, reading. 'I think it'd be far more effective to wait and—'

'*Wait?* While they continue this nonsense. While the world laughs at us?' Showing him the newspaper. 'The longer we leave it, the sillier we look. People believe this rubbish, Max.'

'I doubt it. Look—' showing me the picture ' – a couple of fools, no one's going to take them seriously.'

'They have! They shouldn't be allowed to get away with it. They're breaking the law.'

'Which one?'

'You can't say something that isn't true.'

'They want you to get your hackles up. Then they try again, and Carpenter has another go, and on and on.'

'It can't stand.' Paying for the telegram.

He didn't stop me. Knew, perhaps, there were limits and risks to our strategy.

We arrived at the Hut. I sat and studied the actors: Max, script in hand, and a young boy called Ronald, playing eight-year-old Archie. Max was blocking him, but he was clumsy, and forgot the moves almost as soon as he was told. His mother, Rhonda, sat a few seats down from me in the auditorium, watching. She said, 'He seems to be getting it.'

'The boy can act.'

'He's had lessons. His teacher reckons we'll see him in the West End one day.'

I didn't think so. He was a stolid sort of boy, a foot-dragger, a mumbler. He opened his arms to Max and said, '*I say, Pappie!*'

Absently, Max replied, '*What is it?*'

'*I want to ask you a thing.*'

'*What is it?*'

Max showed him where to sit, and he did, awkwardly; how to hold his hands, and he tried, but looked like a nun. I could see Max becoming frustrated. But not angry. I could imagine him as a father, a good one, breathing life into a cardboard son. Ours, perhaps. Yes . . . *ours*. Little Wilfred Harris. Part poet's son, part Malley-struggler. I wondered what he'd look like. This one? No, leaner, smarter, quicker, more attractive. Little Wilfred, with his blonde, wavy locks and red cheeks. Top of the class, crack mathematician, piano prodigy.

Ronald/Archie said, '*Will you ask mamma to let me go out in the morning with the milkman?*'

'Yes,' I whispered. 'Yes, *son*, you can go out with the milkman.'

Max said, '*With the milkman?*'

'*Yes, in the milkcar. He says he will let me drive when we get onto the roads where there are no people. The horse is a very good beast. Can I go?'*

'He's got it down pat,' the mother said.

I just smiled. She didn't need encouraging.

Max: '*Yes.*'

'*Ask mamma* . . . ah, I forget what's after that?'

'*Ask mamma now can I go. Will you?*'

And the boy tried the line, but murdered it.

But mine wouldn't. *My boy.* Trying it on my lips. Handsome but cheeky, although not rude; just enough to prove he was a free spirit.

'*He said he will help me—*'

'No,' Max said, '*He said he will show me the cows he has in the fields.*'

'*He says . . .*'

Stupid boy. Too fat for his frame. And dull; you could tell, from the eyes, although Wilfred . . . Was that the best name? I'd always wanted something Irish? Seamus? But Wilfred would do, for now.

'*Eleven. Nine red and—*'

'No! *Eleven. Eight red and three white.*'

I thought Max was going to lose control. The boy only had a few lines, and he'd forgotten most of them. Like his blocking, stage manner, everything. He was an idiot, too, spoiling the play Max had put so much work into. The Adelaide premiere of *Exiles*. Not that the creaking bitch deserved it. *Showboat*, or *No, No Nanette*. The intellectual equivalent of its fascination with kicking balls and growing monster pumpkins.

'Ronald,' the mother called out, 'you must try harder.'

'I am.'

'Mr Harris is waiting.' And to Max. 'He had bad news today, his brother in France—'

'Very good,' Max said. *'Do you understand what it is to give a thing?'*

The boy stood, motionless, thinking.

The mother said, 'He's like a lot of good actors.'

'How's that?' I asked.

'Don't learn their lines till the end. There are more important things – the emotion, the motivation.' And she called, 'He needs motivation, Mr Harris.'

I wasn't sure that's what he needed. Talent, probably. Max mustn't have either, because he said, 'We can't really progress until he knows the lines.'

'He's been busy with football.'

Max was building a head of steam. I could tell by the way he made a fist, lifted it, then opened his fingers and massaged his neck.

Poor Max. First, his Richard had dropped out and he'd had to step in and take his place, learn his lines (up all hours). Then he'd discovered *this* was his Archie.

'Alright, let's try again, Ronald. You here, me here, I move towards you and say, *It is yours then forever when you have given it. It will be yours always. That to give.'*

Archie said, *'How could a robber rob a cow?'*

'No, not yet. *But, pappie?'*

'That's right. *But, pappie?'*

*'Yes?'*

*'How could . . .'*

*'. . . a robber rob a cow? Everyone would see him. In the night, perhaps.* Go on, then.'

'*How could a robber rob a cow?* Ah . . . sorry, Mr Harris.'

Max threw back his head, walked around the stage, mumbled something to himself, and the mother stood and called, 'He's doing his best, Mr Harris. At very short notice.'

'*His best?*'

'You could always find someone else?'

Max knew, perhaps, there was no one else. 'Right, continue, Ronald.'

As they fumbled along, like this, the mother turning to me and saying, 'He should really be a bit grateful. It's not like Ronald is getting paid.'

'No one's getting paid,' I said.

'Still . . .' She brushed imaginary crumbs from her dress.

Wilfred would've had the lines down, the blocking, the intonation. He'd be standing backstage, and there'd be a dozen girls gathered around him. I tried to imagine him as Ronald, but couldn't. But could imagine Max as a father. Devoted. Setting to rights the many wrongs of his own ballet-purged childhood. Because Seamus, or Padric, would be a ballet dancer too. Long, slender limbs, his flat belly and angel arms. Lifting some frumpy-looking girl.

But this boy said, '*Are there robbers in Rome?*'

'No! *Are there robbers here like in Rome?*'

'Same thing.'

'It's not.'

'It's close,' the mother said.

'Close isn't good enough. This is James Joyce. *Joyce.* You've heard of him?'

'Of course.'

Bullshit, I thought. Even I'd heard of Joyce, read a few pages

190

of Max's *Ulysses*. Rubbish, really, but apparently the best Ireland had to offer. Apart from Colm. Sweet boy, his high cheeks all aglow under the Sadler's Wells spotlights.

But first, first I'd have to make him. *We* would. Late night in the Austin, a back street, or in Max's bed, half-asleep, the feel of his legs against mine, his breath, his unshaved face . . . By which time I'd be awake, stretch out, allow full access.

'*You wait and ask here when she comes back. I won't be here. I'll be in the garden.*'

Max was shocked. 'Jesus, you got it right.'

The mother stood. 'There's no need to be rude, Mr Harris.'

'T's just . . . shocked.'

Max. If I haven't told you, a very attractive man. With his godlike curls, brown eyes, wide, unforgiving shoulders, leading down to an ironing-board chest. Residual nipples, as he had described. And legs, girder-like, but tapering at the ankles. There's nothing worse than unrefined ankles. So Mediterranean. Filthy.

'He's got a long way to go,' Max called to the mother.

'He's worked all weekend on the lines.'

'Really?'

She stood again, walked forward, and approached Max. 'A bit of gratitude wouldn't go astray.'

'Well, that's not going to help us on opening night.'

'Fine.' She grabbed Ronald by the arm, dragged him down the steps, the aisle, and out the theatre. Max said, 'We're not finished yet,' but she said, 'Oh, yes we are.'

Max turned to me. 'That's it.' Threw the script to the ground and took his jacket from the back of a chair. I shot up, tackled the steps, and was next to him. I gave him the script, took the boy's, and said, 'Let's just get this right. *I say, pappie.*'

'Ethel.'

'What?'

'No lead, no Archie, Bertha and Beatrice hate each other.'

'So?'

'No one gives a shit, why should I?' He walked towards the wings, I grabbed his arm. '*I say, pappie.*'

Maybe it was just to humour me. '*What is it?*'

'*I want to ask you a thing.*'

For ten minutes, he, me; Wilfred, the boy we'd share. As I became Padric. As we all became, by practising. Dropping our own persona, slipping on a mask, saying the lines over and over, until they were convincing. Then the performance which, of course, you had to sustain, for weeks, years, a whole life, perhaps. We got to the end and I, now Bertha, said, '*Tell me, Dick, does all this disturb you?*' I led my Richard to the lounge, and we sat. '*Because I told you I don't want that. I think you are only pretending you don't mind. I don't mind.*'

His hand in mine. '*I know, dear . . .*'

'*Remember, you allowed me to go on, I told you the whole thing from the beginning.*'

I held his hand tightly, felt each of the fingers, the meaty bit, up along his arm. Then I lifted my hand and stroked his face. '*He asked for a kiss. I said: take it.*' I took his neck with my fingers, pulled him closer, and kissed him.

He pulled away. '*And then?*'

'*He kissed me.*'

And again, this time hard, long, as the lines tumbled to the ground.

We could do it, I thought. Here. On the stage of the Hut. I felt like it. Hot, below, ready. Looked him in the eyes, dropped my hand, on his pants, but he didn't move. Rubbed it a bit, feeling it harden. He stood (and I could see the bulge, going to waste) and said, 'I didn't think you . . .'

I waited.

'It was just the poems.' He turned, and ran from the stage. A completely unconvincing exit.

# 23

I still remember that night. Yes, I do. I remember it. *I remember it!* Me and Ern (him, having crawled into my bed), lying, whispering to each other. I switched on my torch, opened my *New Testament* and read: '*In the beginning was the Word, and the Word was with God, and the Word was God.*' And Ern said, What does that mean? And I said, The *Word*.

Which Word?

Whatever God says is the word. So if he says, Let there be light, there is, because he's the boss.

He thought about this. The power of the Word. And if one was powerful, many were more powerful, surely? And if a bus timetable had power, then surely a poem? I can't be sure he thought any of this, but it seems logical, in retrospect.

Someone can't just say, Let there be light . . .

He did.

But you need a globe, or a candle, or the sun.

*He* doesn't.

All this, in the days when I still thought I could introduce my brother to religion. Another failed experiment. He just lay there, staring out of the window at the billions of stars, and said, If he can do all that, why can't he find Dad?

I had to agree. It seemed reasonable. Making a whole planet, universe, working out the best way to propel fish through water, eagles through the sky. Couldn't he just keep an eye out for a stray motorcyclist?

He didn't cheat, Ern said.

No.

We gotta tell them.

We had. Written to the papers, politicians, police, saying it wasn't true. Received responses saying there was evidence. But what evidence? We hadn't seen any. And now he was dead, and we didn't have a mum or dad, and we'd be stuck with Mrs Royal and her puppy dog for the rest of our lives.

Why would he have wanted to cheat? Ern asked.

He wouldn't, and he didn't, I said. Don't believe that, Ern. Don't believe the lies people are telling.

I won't, Ethel.

He got lost, that's all. It's a big desert.

I know . . . I seen the pictures. Maybe even God couldn't find someone out there.

That's it. Even him. Dad just went the wrong way.

He hadn't (as people were saying) died cheating. Driving out into the desert, two days, then stopping at a waterhole, pitching a camp (apparently they'd found the canvas and food), and waiting. Until the other riders headed a thousand miles north, turned around, and came back. By which time he'd have set off, and would be a day ahead of them, and miraculously, would cross the finish line in superhuman time. That's what they reckoned. That's how he planned on winning the trial, before everything went wrong, and he went mad, wandering the desert, never to return.

How can they know that? Ern asked.

They can't. Although, I'd often thought of how much Dad really wanted that money. Could the thought have crossed his mind?

Even if he hada done it, Ern said, he wouldn't have made a mess of it. He would've won, and told us later, with a big grin – remember how he used to grin?

I remember.

Then Ern was crying, because he just wanted Dad back, and couldn't have him, and was stuck with the old bitch we both hated. And people would tell lies about our dad forever.

When we get older, we can go look, I said.

As he lit up. Can we?

And find proof he lost his way. We can tell everyone they're wrong. How will that be?

But then Mrs Royal was in the doorway, light on, What on earth are you doing? Confiscating my Bible, making a big drama over nothing, as Terry stood smiling.

Then I heard them. From the lounge room. Max and Von, still drinking wine, still listening to Toscanini, still talking, laughing, hushing their voices. She'd come over just as I was going to bed. She'd said to me, Go on then, *Ethel*. We'd hate to keep you up.

*We'd.* Her and him. One minute leading me along, another, pretending I didn't exist. Like some sort of Mormonised sex maniac. I pulled my bedsheets up, placed my ear against the wall and listened.

'When do you think she'll finally leave?'

Bitch. She was trying to get rid of me. Had been for weeks, saying, 'Surely, if the thing's finished, what's the point?' I explained it wasn't finished, and people were just getting interested, and that more appearances were likely. So I whispered into the wall, 'When I'm good and bloody ready.'

The rustling of newspaper, then Von said, 'It's obvious *she* couldn't have written them.'

'You reckon?'

'Max . . . she couldn't write a recipe.'

'Well, it wasn't McAuley and Stewart.'

'But didn't Ern work at Victoria Barracks?'

'She reckons.'

'Couldn't they have been in it together, and Ern's died, and she's found the poems and sent them to you, and now *they're* claiming . . .?'

Silence. As Max thought it through. A trio of hoaxers, divided by death, and ego?

'But then they'd have to explain Ethel.'

Max wasn't really thinking this, surely? It didn't make sense. I'd told him, Ern had never mentioned McAuley and Stewart. Anyway, the poems *sounded* like Ern, they were full of our childhood, his worries and fears, his loves and hates. They were dripping Ern. Unless, of course, she was right. Was Ern's *Ecliptic* only one of two copies?

No, I thought, put it from your head, Eth! It couldn't have been. Ern Malley was Ern Malley. I was his sister. I had my young ear to the wall, listening to Terry (in our living room), defending us. Don't be ridiculous, Julie. Of course he got lost. What proof is there he . . .? And *her*: There's plenty of proof . . . the police have said they're sure.

Ssh! Rot and nonsense. You're always so quick to think the worst of people.

And you, so naïve. Stop and think . . .

The Word. As it was, and is, now, Von saying, 'Either way, something doesn't add up.'

'You overthink things.'

'You underthink. You're too nice.'

'At some point . . . if someone tells you something, you believe.'

'Rubbish. Think about it, Max. Ethel Malley. Ern, dying in the sunroom . . . like some sort of bad movie.'

She'd wait. Max believed in Ern, and me, and wouldn't be convinced by this sluttery.

'Well, you explain it,' she continued.

'Like Ethel said. Her brother wrote some poems, she found them.'

'Max!'

And Mrs Royal: *Terry!*

What?

He'd been camped there for six days.

So what?

Waiting. He knew how long it'd be until they were heading back.

No one can know that.

I'd had enough. Got out of bed, upending Ern, stormed down the hallway and said to this Royal woman, Lies! All of it! Our dad wouldn't do something like that.

And Terry, to her. See, I told you, keep your trap shut!

You keep yours.

It had descended into (another) argument between them. Shouting, throwing things. So that, after a while, I led Ern back to bed, and we snuggled together, listening to the chaos.

'There's one other option,' Max said. 'Perhaps *Ern* was the hoaxer.'

'Go on.'

'He hated *Angry Penguins*. He wrote the poems and meant to send them to me, but then got too sick, and maybe he thought, I've got a better idea. I'll pack them in my case, and Ethel will find them and send them to me (ours is the only journal of modern poetry) and off it'll go.'

Enough! I stormed out and found them, semi-entwined, her leg between his, and his pants unpopped, like they could come off any moment. But right now, that wasn't my concern. I picked up the phone, dialled the operator and said, 'Victoria Barracks, Sydney, please.'

Max stood. 'Ethel, what are you doing?'

'I thought you *believed* me.' I waited, glaring at her, the meaty bits of her legs revealed. She was grinning. 'Do you mind?' I said.

'What's your problem?'

'You!'

'I know what your *real* problem is.'

Max turned to her and said, 'Leave it.'

'No,' and she sat up, 'I think it needs saying. You, staying, because you think Max will come into your room one night and—'

'Von!' he said.

'You told me . . . she's sex mad.'

I turned to him, and said, 'You told her?'

'I just . . . well, it seemed sort of strange.'

'*You told her?*'

I just grasped the phone. 'Hello, I'm looking for Harold Stewart? This is Ethel Malley calling.'

A long pause, then, 'Are you having a joke?'

'Sister of Ern Malley ... I assume you know who I am, and Ern.'

'Ted, that you? You're entitled to a laugh, but it's late ... you woke me, you arsehole.'

'I said my name's Ethel Malley. I'm ringing to ask for an apology from you and your friend.'

He waited.

'Well?' I asked.

'Listen, whoever you are, we wrote the poems as a joke, and quite frankly, it's all got a bit out of control.'

'My brother wrote those poems. I'm seeking legal advice about your—'

'Seek all you want, it's over.'

'It's not. I'd like you to explain why you thought you could say my brother—'

But he hung up in my ear. I wondered if I should try again, but there seemed little point. Max was staring at the ground. She was still grinning. I said, 'If that's what it's come to.'

I went to my room, fetched my case from under the bed, and began packing. Max watched, saying, 'Carn, Eth, it's all got a bit messy.'

'*You*, you're the one I trusted.' Glaring at him.

'You still can.'

Packing, Max pleading, but I was having none of it. I latched my case and pulled on my dress, my shoes, and searched the room for anything I'd forgotten.

The Word. You had to have faith, or the whole thing would break down. No Jesus, no God, no Bob; no Ern, no Ethel, no Max. 'My brother was a genius,' I said. 'He wrote those poems,

Max. Whatever you choose to believe, whatever anyone says, including you!'

I took my case and left the house. Max came after me, and her, a few steps behind. He said, 'Where are you going?' But I wasn't about to tell him, and at that point, didn't know. She stood behind him, arms crossed, grinning, and I said, 'He's all yours.' I walked across Hackney Road, Botanic Park, the back of the zoo. After half an hour I made it to King William Street, stood looking up at the roof of Miller Anderson's. No spotlight, still. There never would be, I guessed. Adelaide wasn't worth invading, or bombing, even. It'd crumble, but not via Jap bombs. All it needed was a mirror.

I found a taxi, and said to the driver, 'Somewhere cheap, but clean,' and he said, 'Somewhere that charges by the hour?'

# 24

The driver pulled up in front of Wilson's Motel, North Adelaide. Someone had planted a palm tree, but its fronds had burnt and dropped. A high fence, a crow and the remains of barbed wire. I got out, helped myself with my bag and said, 'Stay there . . . no need.' As four lanes of traffic roared past I thought I heard him say, 'If you want a taxi, get them to call Charlie.'

I registered and stumbled to my room. Let myself in (musty, like some sort of crime scene no one had got around to cleaning) and opened a window. The No Vacancy sign blinked, so I pulled the curtain, but that did no good, and I wondered if I should ask for another room. There was a pool six feet from my front door. Half-full, more fronds floating beside deflated toys, rubbish, a sort of oil slick. Loud, too, with the highway a few feet beyond this, protected (but not really) by the wall that leaned towards an infinity of Astroturf and Capstan butts.

I locked my door, pulled back the bedsheets and collapsed onto the mattress. I felt defiant, proud. Max had threatened me, I'd responded. I didn't need him anymore. It was obvious where his bread was buttered. He was a man about town. Of *this* town, with its phoney piper promising a lowland of utter disappointment. Yes, the bedside lamp didn't work. The wireless had a signal, but just trots, and church. As I rested, listening: *'Onward, Christian Soldiers . . .'* Singing along, white noise lost in the traffic. *'At the sign of triumph Satan's host doth flee . . .'* Little Eth, making the words, raising her voice to Jesus. Me and Ern, in fact, on any one of a hundred Sunday mornings Mrs Royal sent us to Sunday School. Old bitch. Sent *us*. She never worried about God. Would just send Terry to deliver us into the arms of Jesus. Walking along Lang Street, our new dad saying, Maybe it'd do me some good?

And Ern: Dad reckoned it was a load of turd.

Terry smiling, like he'd just passed a kidney stone. Me too.

For the feeble-minded.

Amen!

So, why do we gotta go? I asked.

Because *she* says so.

But you're her boss, aren't you?

What do you reckon?

A man should be; a man is the boss. Doesn't God say so? Aren't women just ribs?

But Terry just pulled a twig from a branch. Well, it can't hurt.

*'Onward then, ye people . . .'*

Then someone thumping on the wall.

'Mind yer business.'

'I'm tryin' to sleep.'

I didn't think anyone'd be able to sleep here. Air brakes, an amplified phone ringing from a car yard, music from the PA around the pool.

But, I thought, at such moments you still have memories. They're always with you, running around your head, like Ern, making circles in the church hall, and the poor teacher (she was a Scot, incidentally) calling, Ernest, sit down!

Eventually he did as he was told, and she described Paul roaming Asia Minor, what happened on the way to Damascus, then Rome, arrest, and his head hacked off by a guard. Ern saying, That'd be a mess.

Her replying, He didn't feel a thing.

No?

Because he loved Jesus.

So it didn't hurt?

No. Jesus washed away the pain, the fear.

Although Jesus hadn't stayed in Wilson's Motel. I turned down the music, but still sang, '*Like a mighty army . . .*'

We were in the Jesus house. It was late at night, and so we didn't get caught, Ern had lit a candle. He was sitting studying *On the Origin of Species*, examining finches' beaks, saying, Dad reckons that God wouldn'ta bothered with all this.

He was smart, my Ern, and nothing was wasted. I'm sure Darwin ended up in the *Ecliptic*, somewhere.

And if he didn't make finches, he didn't make nothin'.

Ern! If you reckon there's no God, there's no point living.

Why?

Because when you die, what'll happen?

And then, from the hallway, a voice. *You want to know?*

Christ, we shit ourselves. Jumped up, saw the tall figure standing in the doorway, searched for an exit but realised there was none. *Your body is offered up*, the voice said.

I don't mind saying now, we were petrified. The long arms, and big hands, the low drawl, the yellow glint from a single eye. We just waited. If he stepped forward, we could try running. He might get one of us . . . Who was he? Jesus? Had it happened? Had He returned, wiped away Croydon, Sydney, Australia, the world, come home for forty winks before He started on Japan?

I think Ern might've pissed himself (but, later, he said he hadn't). I could see his hand shaking, and he said, We know we're not meant to be here.

I've told you once, the voice said.

We haven't touched anything, I said. If you let us go, you'll never see us again.

He stepped forward and said, You're interested in Darwin, Ern?

Christ, he knew his name. Did he know mine? Had he been watching us? Then he said, You're probably wondering what Darwin's doing in this library.

Of course. Mr Alexander. The holder of ears, the God-bodily of our nightmares. But at least he wouldn't kill us, would he?

He was a clever man, Darwin, he said, coming in, sitting in the big fella's armchair, lighting his pipe.

I know you said we should stay away, I said.

How was he clever? asked Ern (who probably hadn't pissed himself, because you couldn't discuss evolution with wet pants).

He had a daughter called Annie, Mr Alexander said, inhaling, sitting back, studying the ceiling. She got sick, and he prayed for her. Very sick, Ethel. Looking at me.

Shit, he knew me too. How? Had he been listening at our window, watching us with binoculars, following us home from school? He said, Did you pray, Ethel, when your mum got sick?

I sat on the rug. It was comfortable enough. Yes, sir.

And what about you, Ern?

Who'd sat on the couch, and gathered his knees under his

bum, and said, Every night. Me and Ethel used to pray together, but it didn't do no good.

*Any good*, Ern. Jesus forgives a lot of things, but not poor grammar. Anyway, Darwin did the same. Prayed and prayed, but Annie just got sicker. He had the best doctors, but they couldn't do anything. He asked God to help, and do you know what God said?

No, I said.

Nothing. He was silent.

Shit, I thought. He was, wasn't He? No matter how many times we worked our way through the *Old Testament*, prayed, sang, even. God was silent, and Mum died.

So, she fell asleep in the arms of God, he said.

Like Ern, *all one body we*, me singing, the thump on the wall. No reply. From the universe. No God. Just silence, except for the PA and the tinny music and the clunk of the neon's solenoids.

Mr Alexander might've known about our mum. Maybe that's why he was telling us the story. He said, And then, after poor Annie was buried, and life moved on, Darwin had to decide if he still believed in God.

What happened? Ern asked, because I suppose he was thinking of Mum too, and how, after, he stopped believing in God, and I believed even more.

Well, it's obvious, isn't it? he said. He ends up writing *that* book. It says people were made a different way, and if that's the case, there was no God.

He changed his mind? Ern asked.

We can't know. Maybe he didn't want to publish it. Imagine this (and he sat forward). Imagine he still *believed* in God, but *knew* this is how animals evolved, and he thought, What if I publish it, and God gets really annoyed, and he says to Annie, Well, your Dad's a right one, isn't he? And he throws her into hell? *Imagine that?*

But he still published the book? Ern asked.

He did.

The church hour ended and they started playing country music, so I turned it off. My thoughts turned to Darwin's book. How many people had hated it? Had written letters to the editor saying this Darwin fellow must be mad. Drawn cartoons, laughed, found reasons to doubt him, hate him. Not that I'm saying Ern was any Charles Darwin. But it made sense. Anything worth saying, thinking, writing, publishing, is going to cause trouble. That doesn't mean it shouldn't be done, but it does mean you'll need internal fortitude. And you will doubt. And show weakness. But that's when you should stay the course.

Mr Alexander said, Funny thing is, it still sells as many copies as the Bible.

But is it right? I asked.

He indicated, and said, I built this for the day He returns. I hardly reckon.

So why have you got his book? Ern asked.

He lit up. Ah! He'll want to know what people have been saying. And just because you don't get an answer, doesn't mean no one's listening.

Sitting there, on that bed, I felt someone was listening. The motel was its own desolate universe, but one that included Croydon, Ern (waiting until I went out, taking his pen and paper from under his bed, scribbling). And what were the chances anyone would care? But this didn't stop him. The best writers scribble in a void, unconcerned about a phantom readership.

Like wireless church. Although there were probably plenty listening. Country hour. No one. Still, they twanged away, because that's what humans do. Make, breed, multiply, fill the world with twelve-string trash.

So desolate. But beautiful. As I slid the window open, and smelt a salt and vinegar breeze, exhaust (plenty of it), beer, even, from some nearby pub. Yes, a little epiphany. That if you *believed* in Him enough, you could *become* God. Author of your own world, a cardboard solar system, all the planets caught in each other's orbits. *Onward, Ethel.* Golly, golly, golly. I was alive, and on this planet, at this moment, and life was as good as it'd ever get. Even at its shittiest, it was perfect.

Mr Alexander kept talking. Relit his pipe, started again, explained how the Romans would skewer Christians (in the bum, out the mouth) but how they wouldn't feel it, because Jesus was beside them, saying, Ten minutes, I'll have a room ready in my father's mansion. Would you prefer east or west facing?

Ern asked why he'd built a house for Jesus, and he said he'd made millions from importing tobacco, and didn't have a family, so thought he might as well. And Ern said, What if He never comes? And Mr Alexander said, That'd be okay too.

# 25

The next morning, I was more determined. This could all be fixed, the critics silenced, Ern put back on his pedestal, beside the little urns on the mantelpiece: Mrs Royal, in a fine china vase she'd chosen especially, and Terry, in a bakelite box she'd bought for him. I'd often wondered if I should take them out to the backyard, sprinkle them, be done with it. But no, I suppose I had to show some sort of gratitude. After all, if not for them . . .

So I had a shower, dried off and put on a wrinkled dress, laddered stockings, powder, lippy. Checked in the mirror, smiled, said, 'Come on, Eth, it could always be worse.' Although, things were no better in the light: the pool-hall windows, the rising damp, and worrying stains on the bedhead. Still, it was only for a night or two, until I decided, while I waited for Max's apology.

Out into the morning. Across the car park and down Main North Road toward the bus stop. The whole stretch was covered with car yards, little flags blowing in the breeze, bumper-to-bumper bargains, for two, three miles along what must have been the ugliest road in Australia. Cyril Rhodes ('A Name You Can Trust') had plenty of Austins (Sevens, mainly) honey-combed in a paddock of polished panels, a Vauxhall and beat-up Fords and Asters. You're probably wondering how I know so much about cars. Well, Dad, again, sitting at night studying the brochures he collected. All of the latest, and he'd say, How about this one, Eth? Showing me a picture of a Morris Oxford, and I'd say, That's a nice-looking car, Dad, but then he'd say, What's the point, with what I earn? All this time, the wheels turning, until he saw the ad for the Esso Reliability Trial.

He'd say, Four cylinder, 933 cubic centimetres (that's the engine capacity), top speed sixty miles an hour. Imagine that Ethel, Ern? We could go driving. Goulburn, perhaps, or Canberra – they reckon that's worth a look-see. Just staring at the glowing monster. The chrome, the gravestone-shaped radiator grille. Well, not to be – putting the brochure with the others, hiding them in the buffet, because it's best not to see what you can't have.

I noticed something strange, walked into another yard, down the back, towards a special ('Must Be Sold Today'). A man came over and waited with his hands behind his back. 'I reckon I know you.'

'Unlikely.'

'No, let me think . . . you're from Strath?'

'Sydney.'

'Ah . . . well, you got one of those faces.'

'So they tell me.'

'You're after a car?'

Dad had eventually saved enough and bought one. By then, it had a hundred thousand miles, torn upholstery, and over-heated every time you went up a hill.

The salesman said, 'If you wanna make an offer?'

But I was too busy, on the back seat, wrestling with Ern. Dad drove, oblivious, arm out the window, head in the clouds. Past the Northern Beaches, stopping for ice cream, a quick dip (he never came in, couldn't stand the salt water).

'I wanna get rid of it,' the salesman said. 'I need the room.'

'Beautiful.' As I walked around the old Riley Nine, ran my hand across the paint work and said, 'She's seen better days.'

'Agreed, but that's a good price. And a good car for getting around town – a single woman, like you?'

But I was back in Croydon. 'Dad'd put it in the shed of a night, just tinker,' I said. 'Polish it up. It meant a lot to him. We'd never been able to afford a car.'

'Give me a price then.'

'Me and Ern, I remember it like it was yesterday – gazing at the world going by. Because when you're a kid, Mister . . .?'

'Bernie, Bernie Jackson.' Extending a hand, although I didn't bother.

'When you're a kid your whole world's your street and neighbourhood, and suddenly . . .'

'My thoughts exactly. You know, Missus . . .?'

'Ethel.'

'Ethel, we are the very first generation to know freedom.'

He probably wasn't sure about me. I didn't care. It was 1922 again, we were heading up to Katoomba in a neighbour's Austin Twelve, and the radiator was hissing, but Dad just said, Smell that eucalyptus, kids. Both of us breathing in big lungfuls. That's the *real* bush, the real Australia.

'So, you're not buying?' the man said.

'Oh, no.' I looked at him, for the first time, perhaps. 'I can't drive, Mister . . .?'

To the bus stop. No point dawdling. The old rattler arrived, I got on, searched my purse and realised I didn't have any change.

211

Only twenty quid, and I knew how stroppy drivers got. But he just said, 'Na, it's a nice day, lady. It's a free ride.'

A free ride. A good omen. All the way into town, this little pub-struck city with its whitegoods shops and motor mechanics on every corner. An overgrown village, the promise of endless perms receding into evenings of low-setting sun and whitebait, a new Australian singing, somewhere, thinking we'd like to hear a bit of a wog, although we didn't.

I got off on King William Street and wondered who I should tackle first. Of course. I extracted the newspaper, and read the bile by this Carpenter fellow. *Battle of the Erns* and *Ern for Each Season*, *The Importance of Ern*. Piffle. But what could you expect? I returned to the *News* building, approached the desk and said, 'Mrs Ethel Malley for Mr Carpenter.'

'Is he expecting you?'

'Yes.'

She rang, and then said, 'He's busy, Mrs Malley. Reckons you should make an appointment.'

'That's not possible. I'm returning to Sydney this afternoon.'

'Reckons he's got meetings all day.'

My arse. But I'd learnt – there were ways. So I turned on a coughing fit, sat on a sofa, and searched my bag for a lozenge. Pretended to suck it, pretended to recover, and this little missy said to me, 'Are you okay?'

'Thank you . . . just getting my breath.'

And waited, and waited. She whispered something to her offsider, then went out a back door. Easy. I took the stairs, up eight flights, out into a familiar hallway, then into Carpenter's office. He was on the phone, looked surprised (as he might) and said, 'Mrs Malley. I'm busy.'

I flattened the paper on his desk, pointed to the headline and said, 'In what way does this resemble journalism?'

He told his friend he'd call back, examined his handiwork and said, 'It was just a *light* take on the matter.'

'Light? You think this matter's light? My brother's dead and these two clowns . . .' I opened to the picture, tapped my finger on their faces. 'It's libel, Mr Carpenter.'

'It is not.'

'I, and Mr Harris, have contacted a lawyer.'

'You have not.'

I just glared at him. 'I would've at least expected the benefit of the doubt. The editor of a major—'

'Sue?' he called over the top of me. 'Can you get someone in here to show Mrs Malley out?'

'That's your reply?'

He sat forward, fixed me with his beady little eyes and said, 'Someone's having a joke here, Mrs Malley. I don't know who . . . and I can't tell, can I?'

'I'm telling you!'

'Sue?'

And there she was, in the doorway – Sue, I guessed – with another man.

Carpenter said, 'When you've got something sensible to say, Ethel, come see me again.'

I could've jumped over the table, strangled him. I would've happily done time for it. But this man and woman had me under the armpits, directing me towards the door, as I called, '*He* was a soldier. Fought to keep the likes of you safe.'

Waiting at the lift. 'I'm perfectly able.'

But they escorted me down, out the front door, and watched

me walk away. Like I was some sort of lunatic, unbalanced.

There was no point dwelling on it. I thought of going to see Max. Could I? Would he have me removed from his office, building, life? I sat, defeated, watching the mid-morning crowd, all so busy. I felt a little tear, wiped it, realised I was descending, and stopped myself. Ern, I thought. I tried my best.

He said, Would he have felt much pain, Ethel?

As we cuddled, again, in the cold. Knew we were safe, because we could hear the old girl snoring.

Na, just like falling asleep, I said. Probably wandered, felt confused. Lay down to sleep.

As I thought of the *other* version. The one going around school, and in the newspapers, apparently, although Mrs Royal never got them. How, apparently, he'd waited several days, planning it. Plotting it in his head. How far each rider had gone, when they'd turned, how far back they'd come. All this time, less and less water, the footsteps that suggested he'd walked a mile east, two west, round the tree he'd camped under. Tristan saying in the lunch shed, They reckon your dad went mad, Malley.

Bullshit.

They reckon he was gonna cheat, but lost his nerve.

I'd fought him, to shut him up, but mostly to avoid hearing his version of events. I got in trouble, of course. Had to explain to Mrs Royal why I'd punched him. I'd said to her, He reckoned Dad was cheating.

The Bavarian Café on Grenfell Street. Maybe the Germans had been here, because there was a cuckoo clock and plenty of pictures of the Alps and the mad king's castle. But it seemed more Adelaide than Munich; dead flies on the windowsill, a warmer full of pies and pasties (although there was a slab of bienenstich). Tea. Presented in a mug, with a chip where your mouth went. But there was no point complaining. And anyway, it must've been rough running a Bavarian café with the war on. Forests, little *fachwerk* houses in their valleys, but nothing that would actually suggest, you know, *him, them*. The girl (in an un-German frock) brought a doughnut on a plate. It was stale, of course, so the act of eating it made me feel more, not less, depressed. Chalky dough, watery tea; could it get any worse? Then the thought of another night at Wilson's, and I knew it could.

A girl turned up the radio and a voice explained road closures, broken mains, a cow loose on Marion Road. I thought of Ern. So far away. No perspective in his 'Perspective Lovesong': *a night when the planets were wreathed in dying garlands*. Instead, a study of Munich Station, its iron-framed roof heavy with snow. *Princess, you lived in Princess Street, Where the urchins pick their nose in the sun* ... Where was Lois, in the middle of all this? Hadn't she heard? Didn't she feel the need to defend Ern? As I imagined some boarding house, the both of them sunning on a balcony, Ern scribbling, reciting: *I have remembered the chiaroscuro of your naked breasts and loins* ... Her laughing, pouring him more wine, as oak leaves settled in their laps.

I overheard some old bloke with a double-cut roll say to his friend, '... which says everything that needs saying about this so-called *modern poetry*.'

My ears pricked up. I'd become accustomed to ignoring the jibes. Leaving delis and seeing the puns on posters; a few overheard words in the gallery. Thought, given time, and a lack of oxygen, it'd go away. But someone was keeping it alive. Carpenter, of course, but others.

The friend replied: 'These fellas in Sydney invented Malley to make a point . . . and good on them. Who's actually read any of this stuff? Years ago, you read a poem, you got a story. It was entertaining, bit of a laugh. But now it's just someone growing a lobster claw for a hand, or eating nails. They're having a lend of us, this mob. University types, sitting about all day.'

The old bloke said, 'I reckon there's something wrong with them.'

And on, predictably. Ern, Max, the lot of them, lazy trouble-makers with enormous chips on their shoulders and 'if you ask me, they should all be locked away. Put them in the army and send them to France. That'd soon sort them out.'

Enough! I stormed out, along a few grimy streets, saying to myself, Deep breaths, Ethel, deep breaths. Down to Botanic Park, behind the zoo, stopping and thinking of kicking a pine tree standing in my way. On, finding a crowd gathered at Speakers' Corner. And standing on a couple of boxes, daggy old pants held up by suspenders, some man said, 'These young sons of the Eastern suburbs (certainly not Clovis!) prancing about in leotards, writing poems, pretending none of it's happening. Nothing. But we're fighting for our lives up North, aren't we, ladies and gents?'

There was agreement, and a polite round of applause.

'And as for Ern bloody Malley . . .'

My blood boiling in my veins, and I called out, 'My name is Ethel Malley, sister of the late Ern, author of *The Darkening Ecliptic*. Given time . . . you, what's your name?' I glared at the man on the boxes.

'Nielsen. Rus Nielsen.'

'Given time, Mr Nielsen, Ern's poems will outlive you, all

of us! They will leave a sort of greatness that you and your type will never understand.' I explained Graves', Max, the journal, the fallout. Rus Nielsen listened intently, but then said, 'Why would these fellas in Sydney be playing a joke on you, Ethel?'

'Not me. Max Harris. They're trying to bring him down a peg.' I explained this – the poetry-haters, the critics, the failed authors, all determined to destroy Max.

A younger man in the crowd said, 'I've read some of your brother's stuff, Ethel (if it *was* him, you're not having a joke, are you, love?), and I reckon it's rot.'

'It's rather impenetrable. Wouldn't you agree, Ethel?' Nielsen said.

'No.'

'I mean, some of it doesn't really make sense.'

'It's not meant to. It's poetry.'

'What I mean is, if people pay for a paper or magazine, they at least want to understand—'

'Poetry is different. Sometimes, one has to read a poem three or four times, *then* it becomes clear.'

One man said Ern sounded a bit of good, and he'd like to meet him, share a beer, have a laugh. Then, out of the crowd, the familiar locks, the piercing eyes and unpressed suit. Max took a few steps forward, stopped short of Nielsen and said, 'You reckon you're an expert on poetry, do you, Rus?'

'Let me guess?'

'Hardly a son of the East, but I'll have to do, won't I?'

'Come on, Max. You can fool some of the people . . .'

'I do my best.'

'See, ladies and gents!'

'Shall we talk facts, Mr Nielsen?'

'Righto.' The murmurs, the occasional clap, the blokes and sheilas on his side. 'So Ern's sister, Ethel, reckons we're barking up the wrong tree?'

Max just looked at me – no smile, nothing. I said, 'I was defending Ern, you, and *Penguins*.'

Max said, 'Thanks, Ethel.' He returned to Nielsen and said, 'Rus, it seems you've already made your mind up. You hate people who love culture because you don't understand it yourself. And instead of trying to (these things, like anything worthwhile, take some effort) you find it easier to destroy the people involved, to laugh at them, to call into question their motivations. And like Hitler, you agitate people into a frenzy, telling them it's okay to hate what they've always hated, because it's somehow *different*, and we can't tolerate difference, can we, Rus?'

Max, my hero, again. 'Ethel, there's no use buying into it, this idiot knows what he's doing. If you people choose to go along with it, so be it. You'll get the society you want, but in the end, might not like it.'

'So that's my fault?' Rus said. 'A little bit arrogant, wouldn't you say?'

'See, tactic number one. Identify the enemy and characterise as a moral danger.'

'Now you sound ridiculous.'

'Use of emotive language. Short, simple words.'

'What, you writing an essay about me, Max?'

'Reduce everything to imperatives. Black and white. Are you with us or against us? No complexity in any argument. That's another thing Hitler does.'

'So, I'm Hitler now?'

'Sometimes it sounds like it. When you pick on people that

can't stand up to you, feel intimidated. After all, Rus, you're still here. What's Ern got? Nothing. He's dead. Shame on you, *mate*. Shame on you.'

And for a moment, Rus was silent. Then, 'Max, I think you've made your feelings clear. You claim this McAuley, this Stewart, are the real hoaxers?'

'Yes, if you'd bothered doing some checking. Although that might've taken a bit of effort.'

'Bad as that Carpenter,' I said.

'How's that, Ethel?' Rus asked.

'Making a joke out of it, instead of printing one of Ern's poems, explaining it, perhaps, saying how it fits into the scheme of modern poetry. Something, instead of this comical piece he printed.'

Max said, 'How you keeping Ethel?'

'Fair,' I replied.

'Where'd you go?'

'Wilson's.'

'Jesus, that dump.' Then silence.

'I went to see Mr Carpenter, but he had me removed from his office. I guess he thinks I'm mad. But these poems meant everything to my brother (not that I know, for sure, but they must've). He was a quiet, pensive man. He would've liked to work on his writing more, but he decided *others* were more important. His fiancée, Lois, in Melbourne, me, Dad, in the days after Mum died and there wasn't much money around. But he never talked about his poetry much. He wouldn't big note himself. He always said, the ones with most to say are those . . . well, I wouldn't want to speak ill of arts editors, or academics. There was one (no word of a lie, Mr Nielsen) who was so egotistical he believed Max had written the poems to make fun of *him*. So you see we've had it from all sides, but the thing is, Ern was my little brother, and it was my job to look after him, protect him, and I did that, for years, until nature took its course. And that's the worst thing of all, isn't it, Mr Nielsen? When you love someone, and want the best for them, and hear other people saying . . .'

'Well,' Nielsen said, 'seems like there might be more to this than meets the eye. Max, what's next?'

'The best thing a person can do is get out and buy these poems, support Ethel.'

The crowd wasn't happy – no blood, no winner, no loser, everything muddled and made complex. So they drifted off, mumbling among themselves, dragging their tails towards someone who'd started up about Marx. Then piss, from a possum in a pine tree, and everyone scattered. A distant elephant blared, and it was all over.

After, Max came up to me and said, 'Well?'

I took a moment, smiled at him and replied, 'I've got some unfinished business, Max.'

I stormed down King William Street. Didn't wait for the lights, nearly got collected, but didn't care. All you had to do was stand up to a bully, and they backed off. It's all Terry had to do, but he hadn't. Content to languish in his own impotence, daily receiving critical appraisals of his life, body, prospects, ideas. He could've said, Those kids can do what they want. No, love, I'm going down the pub, and won't be back till late . . . The idea that we could waste a life, because we couldn't imagine offending someone. Even people we didn't particularly like.

Into the university, through the throng. 'Outta the way!' Into the Draper Building, upstairs, and into Elliott's office. No one, of course. But his secretary, completely unaware, said he was in the Staff Club.

Down in the lift, directions, into a bar with leather couches and no races. Ten, twelve people, perhaps, but I didn't care. There, in the corner, beside some woman. His wife, perhaps? Or was he having an affair?

'I've been down at Botanic Park telling people about you,' I said to him.

'Do tell, Ethel.'

'About what you've been saying.'

He put his drink down and said, 'This club is for university staff only.'

'Stiff shit. I said that people who aren't creative shouldn't criticise those who are.'

I think he'd had enough. He motioned for help.

'And shouldn't make statements unless they have facts. Saying my Ern didn't write the *Ecliptic*. How dare you!'

It seemed it might happen for the second time in a day. Elliott said, 'Are you going to continue following me?'

'Perhaps.'

'In which case I should report this to the police?'

'If you like – or, alternatively, write an apology to me and Mr Harris explaining how you didn't have the facts, misjudged. And have it published. Maybe Mr Carpenter, at *The News*?'

'I'll do no such thing.'

'Why?'

'Your *brother*, you say?'

I felt the urge to jump on him.

'Your brother's not Max Harris, is he?' And he smiled at this woman.

That's it. I moved, but a hand took my arm, pulled me back, walked me from the room. As I went, Elliott said, 'I can tell a Harris from a mile. How much did he pay you for the story . . . or is it a favour . . . how are you repaying it, Ethel?'

Nasty little man. I stood out front, watching him through glass panels, receiving a meal and tucking in, laughing with his *friend*. He didn't look up, but I knew he knew I was watching. Then, when they'd finished, they exited through a back door. I thought, I haven't finished with you either, Elliott. Not by a long shot.

Deep breath. I walked up the hill, in the back door of the art gallery, past the Impressionists, Conder, Streeton, and all the others who were happy painting Australia as it looked. Anyone could do that. But how it *didn't* look? I shouldn't have ever doubted Mr Nolan. Now, I knew, we needed him and his Malley-like landscapes. I wondered if he'd suffered the same outrages. I'd heard from Max that he'd gone AWOL from the army, hid, lived at Heide as a wanted man. Yes, Sid was some sort of Ern. Someone you could admire.

People are liars, I kept repeating, trying to think of where to go next. Max? No, not yet. He needed longer to stew in his own self-doubt. He'd come around, eventually. Maybe, now he knew, he was already waiting under the great man's kilt? A Rodin. Although, who could tell? It looked Rodin. But maybe it was his brother, or admirer. I'd read (a magazine at the dentist) that there were more fake Rodins in the world than real ones. And who was checking?

*Of course.* I almost ran to the front door, down North Terrace, into the museum, the crystal skull. Read the label again. It couldn't have been. Couldn't have. Liars!

I heard Max's growling voice. Action-reaction. Ern, pleading for the truth. Peggy, commiserating her son. Mr McDonald, lost in the novel that he'd lost in the refusal to say, No more school! I am a writer! I will write! I noticed the case wasn't stuck down. Looked around. It was time to make a point. I lifted the lid, placed it on the ground and slipped the skull into my purse. *Nothing. So. Easy*. Replaced the case, turned and made for the door.

Walked out.

As easy as that. Along North Terrace, feeling better than I'd ever felt in my life.

# 26

Back to Wilson's, the bed made (although the sheets smelt no better). Same mould, same dead flies, same traffic, louder, it seemed, in the late afternoon. I took out the skull and examined it, ran a finger around the eye sockets, jaws, teeth. A beautiful piece of work. One crystal, formed over millions of years, ground to perfection. Whether using a machine, or hands. Maybe it didn't matter. But it did. Fifty years old, or ten thousand. A glint, when it caught the sun through the yellow windows; red, orange, blue; maybe a touch of neon, as the sign clunked to life, again, and the shadows lengthened, the room cooled.

What would be happening now? The director calling the police, contacting his agent in London, explaining 'it's just been misplaced . . . we're having a look-see now.' Until the press got a sniff. Carpenter and a few of his mates asking if what they'd heard was true. The Mitchell-Hedges skull, gone, in the middle of the day, and where were the guards, the alarms?

Still, that was *their* problem. I sat on the bed, placed it on the table and gave it a little clean. This'll teach them, I thought. Trying to pass off fakes. I switched on the wireless and there was more church. '*Who, when they were come down, prayed for them . . .?*'

I didn't care. There was no one to pray for me, or Ern, just these little devil people, chasing us down North Terrace. The God fella finished and the news came on: 'A major theft at the South Australian Museum this afternoon.'

Put that way, it sounded bad. A *major* theft. It wasn't so major; there were plenty of other things worth more. Not so much a theft as a protest (it wasn't like I wasn't about to give it back).

'Police say the thief snuck into the museum between one and one fifteen, lifted the case and walked off with the skull.'

Again, not so much *snuck*, and it wasn't like there was anyone to stop me.

'There are concerns the skull was stolen to order. That it will be taken out of the country, sold to an investor. Police are contacting forces in the United Kingdom.'

Jesus. It was just a fake, like something you'd keep in your buffet: claret glasses, a decanter. The United Kingdom? No, typical journalists, making a mountain out of a molehill. Stuff must've gone missing every day. I cradled the skull and rubbed it for good luck. It *could* get me into a bit of trouble, but like Max said, If people won't listen . . .

'Two men saw a woman in her late twenties walking out of the museum at approximately one twenty, although neither got a clear view of her face.'

Good. Good. That was that. No harm done.

'*I am verily a man which am born a Jew.*' Yes, a Jew. That's all. *You'd* forgive me, wouldn't you? I know not what I did, done. Just a second, and I had it. Hadn't planned to. Didn't mean to. You understand, don't you? People make rash decisions.

'*And I persecuted this way unto the death* . . . Listeners, I ask you again, are you free of sin?'

'Well . . .'

'Are you ready to meet your maker with a clear conscience?'

I found another station. Took a deep breath, placed the skull under the bed, but thought better of it, in the bathroom, changed my mind: the drawer, back under the bed, under the sheets, the pillow, studied it again and thought, You rotter! And put it back in my purse. Then the announcer said, '. . . and finally, tonight, the premiere of the Theatre Guild's *Exiles*, by James Joyce.'

Perfect. I had to get out. Rushed to the bathroom, foundation, rouge, lippy, brush through the hair, and I was ready. A nice night out (all the time, wondering what else the news report was saying). I took my purse and tried to decide what to do with it. Hide it? Where? Wasn't much of a room. What if the girl came in to change the towels, or someone broke in?

No, only one thing to do. I had a shawl, so I arranged it over my shoulders, and the purse. Stepped out and caught a bus back to town.

The Hut was nearly full. The stage was set with a table and couch, smokers' stand and jug of water. Low, muted light and piano music (nothing too heavy, a bit of tinkering). I settled in towards the back. Placed my purse in my lap and covered it with my shawl. It seemed I'd made a mistake. This, not uncommon when Eth got angry. I could be like this, as a child, mostly. Remembered raging arguments with Mrs Royal when she wouldn't let me stay out past eight with a few of the girls. Said things I regretted, and later, had to apologise.

An oldish woman sat beside me. 'You like Joyce?'

'Well, to be honest, I haven't read a lot of him, but Max, the director (I think he's playing Richard) lent me his *Ulysses*.'

She settled, read the program, and another woman sat beside me and said, 'Hello, Ethel. I wasn't expecting to see you.'

'Von.'

'After our little . . .' She smiled. 'Max'll be glad. He was upset about all that.'

'Well, maybe . . .' Although I didn't want to concede anything, not yet, anyway. 'The play's all ready to go?'

'I think. Max has been working on his lines. Couldn't find another Richard. And this kid, he's no better.'

What could you say? The place was nearly full – four hundred, maybe more. A few army uniforms, wives in long frocks, and I said, 'I wouldn'ta thought that sort'd be here.'

'The Guild's got a good reputation. And Max, of course. Last year they did *Enfants Terrible*. It was a big hit. Full houses every night. People came from Sydney and Melbourne.'

The woman on the other side agreed: outstanding. If it wasn't for Max, where would Adelaide be? Shaw, perhaps? But probably Rattigan, and lashings of Shakespeare, because that way you knew what you were getting.

Von said, 'That's what you've gotta understand about Max.'

'What's that?'

'He doesn't do things by half.'

And the woman agreed.

'Straight in – everything he does. Like with Ern.'

'I think he's finished with Ern.'

'No, hardly started. That's what I'm saying. Nothing by halves. He seems to have attached to Ern, found a purpose. And you, too.'

'I don't know about that.'

'I do.' She stopped to offer me and the other woman a butterscotch. 'I can see it.'

'What?'

'The way he looks at you.'

'Nonsense . . . how?'

'When he talks about you (which he does all the time – Ethel this, Ethel that).'

'What do you mean?'

'I can't say, Ethel . . . but you know, don't you?'

'What?'

'You *know*. You must.'

The stagehands were adjusting chairs, tables, props. The woman was reading, but I reckoned she was listening.

'You mean he's . . . attracted to me?'

'*Is he?*' Her eyes glowed. 'You know how you feel, Ethel. How *do* you feel?'

I wasn't sure what to say. The truth? Then she'd start laughing. A denial? How could I deny it? 'We're good friends, I hope.'

'You are.'

'We have a common interest in poetry. Ern.'

'And?'

'That's all.'

She crossed her arms, smiled. And then, quietly, 'Max is not a person you can half-like, Ethel. He has a magnetism, a sexual attraction.'

I paused, watched the preparations, clutched my crystal skull. And with a sort of whispered indignation: 'There's been nothing . . . absolutely nothing.'

'But that's not true, is it?'

'Nothing!'

She almost laughed. 'I know how you like your bun buttered, Ethel.'

The woman stood. 'The toilet, I think, before it starts.' Wriggling past.

'I think you've got it wrong,' I said. 'My only concern is—'

'*For my brother, Ern,* I know what you're gonna say. But I don't believe you, Ethel. And maybe it's not all your fault. Maybe it's him.'

I wondered if it'd be best to leave it there. Maybe Max had feelings for me I hadn't fully appreciated. Maybe they'd fallen out of love. 'None of us can see the future.'

'Oh, *Ethel.*'

Was I that deserving of her spite? Ethel, the imaginary woman, fed a story about how the poet loved her, although it hadn't really crossed the poet's mind. I felt a tear, opened my purse and searched for my handkerchief, and she said, 'Jesus, Ethel!'

I realised: the skull.

'*You* took it?'

I closed the nib, refused to answer.

'They're looking all over the city. Why'd you do that?'

Again, I refused, panicking, thinking what to say. Should I get up, run? But where? Wilson's? Explain? How could you explain?

'Ethel?'

Would she run off, call the police? That was one way to get rid of me. But I didn't think she would. 'It's not what you think it is.'

'It is. I saw.'

'It's . . .' I turned to her, moved closer and explained. The anger, the fraud, the opportunity. 'Next thing I was walking down North Terrace, not even sure what I'd done.'

'Nice work, Ethel.'

'Ssh!'

'I think we've underestimated you. I've never met a crook.'

'*Ssh!*'

Over the next few minutes, the woman returned, the lights dimmed, the actors began. Max, in a tweedy suit, trying his best Richard Rowan. '*But do you feel that happiness is the best, the highest that we can know?*'

And a stale Beatrice: '*I wish I could feel it.*'

I wished too. Something. Love. Lust. Jealousy. But all I felt was fear. This woman, beside me, the keeper of my secret. She leaned over and whispered, 'What are you going to do with it?'

'I don't know.'

And a few minutes later, 'It's all over the news.'

I didn't answer. But felt this *thing*, hot and heavy in my lap. Saw the cell door closing, felt the heat from the camera flashes, the looks of the prison hags as they sized me up.

'It might be worth millions.'

'No, it's a fake.'

'Is it really?'

*Really?* Of course. Although, I could be wrong. But no, I remembered what Ern had said about this hyphenated woman, and her games. Her skulduggery, her greed, her friskiness with the truth.

'Is this the first thing you've stolen?'

But someone shooshed her, so she just sat there, smiling, occasionally elbowing me and giving me the thumbs up.

Then Max saw me. Stepped forward, said a few lines. His eyes stopped, moved between me and Von, and he seemed confused, but said, '*The asthmatic voice of Protestantism.*'

Von sat up. 'That's not right.'

Beatrice waited for her line, but it didn't come. Max just stood, wondering, perhaps, why we two were sitting together. She wandered over to him, whispered something, but he didn't respond. Then the prompt, and he managed, '*For some help, within me or without, I must find. And find it I will.*'

The play limped on like this, all the way to the end. Still, there was a standing ovation, because, I guess, that's what this sort of audience did. Max was watching me. I felt uncomfortable. Stepped past Von, walked down the aisle (faster and faster) and out the front doors. Towards the Barr Smith lawns, and somewhere, behind me, Max: 'Ethel, come back, I've got to talk to you.'

But I didn't have to talk to him. So I ran, and heard him running after me, Richard Rowan, in a pinstripe suit and leather shoes, knocking across the cobblestones. 'Carn, Ethel, this is silly.'

But I didn't stop. Just clutched my purse, gathered my shawl, and headed up the hill, sure that every copper in Adelaide was after me.

# 27

And there he was, in costume, standing beside his car. Smoking, as he always did when he was anxious. Pacing, looking up, half-smiling. I walked across the car park and said, 'Was it a good night?'

'Shithouse.'

'Why?'

'I was so busy trying to pull it together, I didn't have time for my own lines.'

The traffic had eased; there wasn't so much noise. Only a few cars in the park, a woman coming out of a room, and Max said, 'How did you end up here?'

'The taxi driver thought I was a prostitute.'

A few minutes later we were in a sort of visitors' lounge. Wood-panelled walls, candelabras with most of the globes blown; a library with books about stagey romances, Ecuador, how to fix a tractor. Max opened his flask, took a swig and offered it. Although I didn't. He said, 'The other night . . .?'

'You've been very helpful. Things have changed. I wouldn't expect *anyone* to keep believing.'

'How do you mean?'

'All the evidence to the contrary. Although I've said, again and again, that Ern's the real thing.' I tinkled the keys of an old Bösendorfer, similar to the one we'd had in our lounge room. I remembered Dad and Ern pulling up in the drive, tooting the horn, and me going out to see the car, the trailer, an old piano. And Dad, What d'you reckon, Eth?

Does it work?

It will.

Dad getting up, opening the lid, playing a few notes, although they twanged, clunked, or did nothing. A bit of work she'll be playing. We can have singalongs, eh?

As Ern got up, tried to play, but only made more of a racket.

I tried this one. Opened some music and played a chord. Not bad, although flat. I kept at it, sung a few lines, and Max said, 'I didn't know you could.'

'Self-taught.'

After Dad had rebuilt the case, got a tuner in to fix it. Then, of an evening, me and Ern'd bang away, then I'd tell him to piss off while I did some scales – for an hour, longer, a song or two – before Dad came in and started singing along, Ern croaking. All of us, for another hour, perhaps; the window open, neighbours walking past and sharing a few bars.

'They were good times,' I said to Max.

'What?'

I told him, kept playing the old beast in the Wilson's drawing room. I sat, and he came up behind me, put his hand on my shoulder, but I couldn't let that stop me. Playing, singing, '*And tho' 'is education had been free* . . .' For a few minutes, the chorus together, and when we returned to it, joyful, as it had been back then, Dad with his hand on my shoulder, Ern in the gap between us, reaching for notes that were far too high.

I stopped and said, 'Just about the best piano ever made, the Bösendorfer. They had one on the *Titanic*, and I bet it's still sitting at the bottom of the sea, waiting for a singalong.'

Now the music had stopped, Max removed his hand from my shoulder.

'Dad and Ern were walking down the beach' – and I turned to him – 'and lo and behold, Ern says, Look, Dad, it's a piano! They run over, there it is . . . straight off a shipwreck, or maybe someone'd dumped it. Either way, what were the chances?'

And what could I do, but start again, this time from memory. '*After the ball is over* . . .' For a few rounds, until Max returned, started behind me – Ern, who took a solo, '*After the break of day.*' I could still hear his alto, before he became a tenor, a baritone, and eventually, told us that singing was for *ho-mo-sexuals*.

When we finished, I said to Max, 'Ern had a fine voice. Me and Dad told him he should take lessons, but he wouldn't have a bar of it.'

Max sat again, returned to the nipple, wiped his mouth and said, 'Hundred memories, eh?'

'I guess.'

'So it must be strange, to hear people say things?'

I sat beside him. 'What Von said – I heard. That Ern wrote the poems as a joke, and knew, when he was dead, I'd find them.'

'She was trying to work out why these fellas in Sydney . . . see, Von's scientific. She proposes theories, then looks for evidence. Theory number one: Ern Malley and his poems. Two: Stewart and McAuley. Three . . .'

'What?'

'You coulda done them, Ethel.' He smiled.

I laughed. 'Me? I can't write a shopping list.'

234

'Hypothesis number three. You *can*, and you *did*.'

'Max, that's funny. If only I *could*. Imagine. I'd be scribbling all day, sending it off to the papers.'

'That's how Von works. You shouldn't make too much of it. What she lacks (that we don't, Ethel) is a bita faith.'

'Exactly.'

'An understanding of poetry, and how it comes out of a hole in the ground. Not to the university professors, but to the common man. Like Ern. She doesn't get it. Most people don't. So they want explanations that aren't there. They invent hoaxes: Elliott, McAuley – see, they're jealous, Ethel. *They* wanna be Ern, but they can't be, so they explain him away.'

I sat back. This seemed more satisfactory. Ern as the arbiter of good taste and common sense. 'I could tell you a hundred stories about Ern.'

'Go on.'

'He felt things deeply, Max. The smallest things. A sensitive soul, which is never good for anyone, I guess. You were a sensitive soul, Max?'

'For a time, but the dorms at Saints took care of that.'

'How do you mean?'

He thought. 'The first day I arrived in the boarding house, Ethel . . .'

'Go on.' I held his hand.

'I unpack, we go and eat, and then they say it's time for a shower. So off we go, and Jesus, when I arrived . . .'

'What?'

'It was all one big shower . . . no curtains, dozens of boys with their kit off.'

'What did you do?'

'Took off my shirt, walked in, still wearing my potato sacks. Thought I'd got away with it, then one of them looks at me and says, Hey boys, this one's still got his dacks on. Then they were all laughing, dozens of them. I just wanted to melt, wash away, down the plug hole.'

'So?'

'It was out of my hands. Three or four of the biggest apes held me, and one whipped off me dacks, and there I was, naked, dying of embarrassment.'

Poor Max. He was still there, holding his cake of soap, wondering what to do with it. I was glad he'd opened up, at last. I wondered if he'd told Von all of this. Would she care? Or just form some hypothesis about his behaviour?

'It went on like that,' Max said. 'If you weren't tough, you didn't survive.'

'You should've asked your parents to move you.'

'I did. Dad wouldn't have a bar of it. Said boarding would do me good. I never worked out what that meant. *Do me good*. I think he meant, stop me ending up a poofter. Ballet, poetry – that all had to be gotten rid of. And was, mostly. Although we had a poet's club, and all of the little Oscars came along, and they gave us a room and a little press to print our stuff . . . so they weren't all apes.' He smiled. 'Although it's scarred in my brain, Ethel.'

'What?'

'You know. I had no idea people kept that sort of thing in their pants. I'd seen Dad a few times, but that seemed harmless, a few nuts and bolts you kept handy in case you needed them.'

'You should have to carry these puddings around.' I checked they were still there. 'I remember, too, from school . . . and I'd wonder how they didn't put their back out.'

Both of us, giggling, like a couple of kids.

'Luckily mine never ... well, like a pair of camellias, kept clipped. But others, Jesus, Max, you could suckle a whole village of Africans.'

I know, the wrong thing to say, but it was just me and him, and four walls, and we kept laughing because, at the end of the day, your bits are about the most ridiculous thing of all.

'Not like you can leave them home,' Max said.

'No.'

'Although they do come in useful.'

'Max!' I pushed him away, he swigged, and it ran down his chin, like a thirsty baby. He smiled, laughed. He seemed happy; happier than I'd ever seen him.

But then it settled, because you can only talk about that sort of thing for so long before theory becomes practice, and we weren't ready, yet. 'Ern was no different,' I said. 'He was scarred by the smallest things, Max. This one time, Mrs Royal came home with a dog ...' I noticed the clock. One-fifteen. Should I start the story? Did he want to get home? 'Unlike her, because she was an old battle-axe, but for some reason ... maybe Terry had convinced her, though God knows how. Either way, she comes home with a dog and it jumps all over us kids and we fall in love with it ... you know the way? Next morning there's a big shit at the front door and Mrs Royal curses it, cleans it up. Next morning, next day, two, three times a day. Ones and twos, Max. Ones and twos. Meanwhile, Ern's fallen in love with this dog. It sits with him, sleeps with him (until *she* comes in and moves it), follows him around the house. It only wants him, because he only wants her. But the shit continues. Mrs Royal locks her outside, Ern lets her in. Finally, the old cow says, Enough! Takes the dog by the collar and leads her out, down the drive, and puts her in the car. *Terry! We're taking it to the RSPCA.* Well, you could imagine Ern, shouting and crying, pleading with her, but God, she was a heartless woman. I can still see them, backing down the drive, Terry apologising to Ern out the window, Ern trying to open the door, get his dog back.'

Max sat back. 'I bet you two were glad when she died?'

'Well, that's another story.'

He paused, cocked his head, then said, 'I got it.'

'What?'

'You. Only you knew Ern. So you gotta write something about him. Him, the boy, the man, so people will know him. Then there'll be no doubts.'

'D'you reckon?'

'Sitting here, listening, it all makes sense. Where the poetry came from.' He looked at me, but no longer me – Ern, again. It always worked this way. Me. Ern. Ern. Me. Who was he most in love with? Or were we indivisible?

'This'll shut them up, and draw some attention to your brother.'

'Do you think?'

'Tomorrow. A thousand words, tops. A few memories: the man, the mystery. We'll make Carpenter publish it. Elliott can shove that up his arse – we'll demand an apology from him too, eh, Ethel?'

I was overcome. All of this faith, again. God bless Max, again.

'Come on,' he said, 'let's get you out of this shithole.'

He almost dragged me, almost took my arm off.

'And then, I was thinking, Ethel, you and me, on a train to Sydney. We'll go see these fakers, have it out, once and for all. What do you reckon?'

'I reckon.'

'I'll write it for *Penguins*. Bit of a shitstorm, what d'you reckon? But that's okay, they started it, we'll finish it. Two tickets, I checked. Coupla quid. No bastard's gonna say we don't matter – we don't exist! We do, eh, Eth?'

# 28

The next morning Max drove us to the university, parked in the vice-chancellor's spot, and we walked to his office. Nook. Whatever it was. The dead aspidistra was growing, I swore, but Max didn't agree. How could something grow with no water, cigarette butts and cold coffee? But it even had a small bud. All of which I took as a good sign.

Max had it planned. I'd hand-write the Testament of Ern, give it to him, and he'd type it onto two-ply. Then, when we were done, he'd take the duplicate and run off a few hundred on the spirit machine. All done in a morning. So I started page one, and he went off to the bar while I worked. Returned half an hour later, and put the carbon in the machine. 'Bet you didn't know I could touch type?'

'Where'd you learn that?'

'Don't ask.' But then explained. 'After I met Von she told me they were running a secretarial course at Saints Girls' and it might come in handy if I wanted to be a journalist. So every Monday afternoon I sat with a dozen girls and practised my drills.' And then, he explained, the reaction when he got back to school, the dorm, as he lay in bed and the other boys said, How'd yer typing go, Maxie?

Men learn it too.

No, they don't.

If you wanna work for a newspaper.

They got cooking classes next week. We all pitched in and bought you an apron.

This, he explained, was probably not the best way forward for a delicate child. In the end they responded by holding him down and stripping him, powdering his face, applying lippy (stolen from the History tutor), and throwing him into the quadrangle. Again, little Maxie, stranded by life, branded an out-sider. Regardless, he explained, typing came in handy. 'I've never been easily put off.'

'I can tell.'

'I've always assumed, if *that* sort say something, the opposite must be true.'

Although, he said, he was the best footballer at Saints. 'I played every position, captained the team for three years straight, then went back to the dorm and read Rimbaud. Eventually the boys got used to it.' He sniffed the spirit in the machine, smiled and said, 'God's little consolation.'

He got started. A cigarette hanging from the corner of his mouth, eyes darting between my words and the keyboard. I just wrote, remembering – gilding perhaps, but I was the only one who'd ever know. Anyway, there were always two versions of a life: the one we'd had, the one we'd wished for.

*At age nine, Ern took a liking to the piano. He'd run his fingers across the keys, then start playing, note perfect. Something he'd heard: a song, or advertising jingle from the wireless. I said to Mrs Royal (who, by this time, was looking after us on behalf of the government), He's got a real talent, hasn't he, and she agreed, but said, There's no*

*money for lessons. So Ern taught himself, and was always quick with a*
*song or a Beethoven sonata (he could do them too), but he never became*
*the musician he might've been – because of her Royal Highness.*

Max stopped typing, turned to me and said, 'You sure you
want to put that in, about Mrs Royal, the piano?'

'She's dead.'

'She was your mother, of sorts.'

'She was never our mother. Just someone the government
paid to look after us. If we're gonna have the truth, let's have it
*all* out.'

So he kept typing, and I kept writing.

*Ern, me, both of us, would lay awake in bed, and Ern would say,*
*I wish she (Mrs Royal) would die, and I'd hush him, because imagine*
*if she overheard. But I did become worried what would happen if Terry*
*(who was a half-decent person) died before her. He held her in check*
*(for instance, with the belt, when she was incensed). And then, of course,*
*this came to pass. Terry had a stroke while we were at school, and there*
*she was, waiting at the gate to tell us, like it hardly mattered. Oh,*
*yes, he's popped off. Like that. Popped off. Won't be with us any more.*
*Heartless woman. And home we go, and she says, After we bury him,*
*I think we'll be making some changes.*

Max stopped and said, 'I reckon a thousand words might
do, Ethel.'

'How many so far?'

'Nearly that, and Ern's only ten years old.'

'Right.' He had a good point. If it was too long no one would
bother, then we would've wasted our time. 'Just finish this story?'

'Righto.' Typing on new ply.

*I, apparently, was a bad influence. If I could be gotten away from*
*Ern his attitude might improve. What she meant by attitude, I don't*

*know. He was a bit angry, but she denied him everything, from the piano (locked, only opened on the weekend for an hour or two) to new clothes. Always from the poor box. Repaired, but you could tell. Faded, too tight, too long, with that smell. Anyway, we were separated. I had to start sleeping beside her in the double bed. And she stank. Like she'd never got herself entirely clean in the shower. Every night, for several years, lying there, as she snored, rolled across the bed like a beached whale. Sometimes I'd get out of bed, go into Ern, and we'd talk. About her, the world, and how unfair it was. Mum, Dad and Terry all cold in their graves, as this old cow snored between warm sheets. Was that what we should expect from life?*

I couldn't stop myself writing. It was all gushing out, like it had been bottled up for years, and now . . . But Max lit a new cigarette and said, 'How's it travelling, Ethel?'

'Just this bit . . . it's important.'

'Then, maybe, skip to the poetry. That's what we want to say – Ern, the poet?'

*My and Ern's life changed one night in 1933. I was lying awake, as usual, and Mrs Royal (in a deep sleep) gasped, grabbed her chest, her mouth open, her tongue half out. I knew what was happening. I thought, should I call an ambulance? Should I? As she wriggled, kicked her feet a bit, then settled. Breathed, deeply, gasping. Then, eventually, stopped. Then I called Ern, and we looked at her, and I felt for a pulse, but there was none, and Ern said, Maybe we oughta called an ambulance? I said, Nothing they coulda done – she woulda been dead by the time they were here. The whole thing over in no more than an hour.*

When he got to this bit, Max turned to me and said, 'You sure you want to put that in, about Mrs Royal's heart attack?'

'Why not?'

'It's not really relevant to Ern.'

243

'Of course it's relevant. After she died, everything changed. He got his job repairing watches, started to live. To *live*, Max.'

But he didn't seem so sure.

'It's almost like . . . you let her die.'

'*No.* What could I do?'

'Call for help?'

'I did, eventually.'

'*After* she was dead?'

'As soon as practicable.'

'It doesn't sound like that. I was just thinking, if the police saw it.'

'You think? It could be taken the wrong way?'

'Well, it could be taken . . . *a* way.'

'Alright, if you think.'

Continuing. Writing. Typing. Max said, 'This'll do the job, Ethel. Everyone'll know about Ern. And perhaps, if the poems take off, we could expand it into a biography?'

'You reckon?'

'Yeah. People like biographies of writers . . . especially ones that died early, tragically. Big market for that.'

*Ern was greatly affected by the loss of our father. I believe it was this event that made him the poet he was. In a way, his writing was an attempt to reclaim him. But the more he wrote, the more he realised it didn't work this way. But this never stopped him.*

I had a sore hand, but I refused to stop. Max needed the toilet, fetched a coffee, sat down and kept typing. By now, the sun was coming in the big windows. Hot on our faces and hands. Max was sweating, but I'd found a nook, a shadow, entombed by the smell of a hundred volumes sent in for review.

*The manner of our father's death was traumatic. Ern never*

*recovered, although I believe many of the facts were kept from us. Yes, he did become disorientated during the final leg of the Esso trial; he did get lost, run out of petrol, wander the desert for days. He did, eventually, lie down beneath a bloodwood tree, and die. These are the facts, although for years, others have told a different story. That he was preparing to cheat, waiting till the others returned on their final leg, at which time he'd go ahead of them, win, take the money. But, in the meantime, these so-called journalists say he wandered, half-mad, into a pub, told the drinkers he was a local stockman (they knew better), drank himself blind, all the time learning the other contestants had dropped out of the race, and everyone was waiting for him.*

When he got to this, Max said, 'That's an awful story, Ethel. That's what they were saying?'

'Yes, Carpenter and his mob . . . dogs. All the rumours, but as you know, Max, he, they, don't let that stand in the way of a good story.'

'But there was no proof?'

'Just a broken compass, a few bits and pieces. These people in the pub, they didn't see my dad. They made up this drinking story, and it stuck, and me and Ern were saddled with the shame. Even now, when someone mentions the Esso Reliability Trial, it's, Oh, that fella that thought he could trick them.'

When the biography was done, Max pulled the last sheet from his typewriter and said, 'Elliott can shove this firmly up his arse.' He opened a drawer, produced a bottle of brandy and two filthy glasses, and poured two very stiff drinks. 'To Ern!'

'To Ern! I said I would, brother, and I have.'

Then, to work. Max turned on the duplicator (he'd explained, the first two issues of *Penguins* had been all purple). Lined up the first page and started. As we sat, the smell of spirit in our nostrils, down our throats, becoming giddier, and happier; the little motor whirring, sucking in paper and spitting it out.

'Did you mean what you said about the biography?' I asked.

'Of course.'

Then I thought about it. Would Ern bear that much scrutiny? The little boy, sitting on the back steps, in his own (always in his own) world? He hadn't asked for any of this. So I said, 'Maybe it's not such a good idea?'

And he agreed, it wouldn't be right (although he said he'd gone along because he only wanted the best for the Malleys).

Page after page. The finished testament was closer to two thousand words. So then we set to binding them, and by half past we had a pile – fifty or sixty, perhaps, but enough. Max slipped a copy into an envelope and addressed it: *Sid Carpenter, The News, North Terrace*. And then, with his little Maxie grin, took the rest under his arm and said, 'Come on.'

Firstly, every pinup board around the university. Under every lecturer's door – although Elliott wasn't answering. A pile for the refectory, the Union bar. Then up to the city, and all of the major bookshops: Preece's, Angus and Robertson. A pile beside the few remaining copies of the autumn number. Back to the university, and we stood, for an hour, handing out copies to anyone who'd take them.

By four, we were down to ten copies. We went to the Union building, climbed to the roof and threw the rest out across the university. Stood, watching, this little Sophie Scholl and her brother, as each copy fluttered, pirouetted its way to the ground.

Until, finally, we were finished. 'That's the best we can do,' Max said.

I agreed. The best. But not all. I wouldn't rest, I said, until

Ern was acknowledged as the great poet he was; Dad, the great tinkerer.

As we walked back past the museum, Max said, 'We got a lot of work ahead of us, Ethel.'

'I reckon.'

'And we can't do it with you in prison.' Indicating my purse.

'How did you know?'

He didn't reply. Maybe it was Von; but maybe, just maybe, he'd guessed, when he'd heard it on the wireless. Maybe I'd become *that* predictable?

'Is it wrapped?'

'Yes.'

'Come on.'

We went in, past the spot where the skull should have been, a note from the police asking for anyone who had any information. We stood reading it, and he smiled, and said out loud, 'What sorta person would do something like that?'

'Criminal,' I said. 'People like that should be shot.'

'Hanged.'

Down the stairs, along a hallway, and he asked for it. I handed it over, explaining how it wasn't right, displaying fakes, but he just shooshed me and said, 'So what? If people are stupid enough to believe.'

He cleaned off the fingerprints with the rag it was wrapped in, went into the Men's and returned a few moments later. 'Come on.'

Out of the museum, back across the parklands, to his house, where we spent the afternoon packing.

# 29

The taxi dropped us, and we stood in front of number forty. 'Well, here she is.'

I don't know what he was thinking. Plain, ordinary, not a place you'd associate with one of – no, with Australia's greatest poet. But that was the point: greatness came from shoe boxes, laddered stockings, coal mines, a little fruit shop on Parramatta Road. 'This is where we grew up.'

Max lit a cigarette, stopped to take it in and said, 'Not what I expected.'

Through our little picket gate ('Dad put that in when we were about four or five'), past an orange tree ('Ern'd climb it, but he'd always rip his clothes on the thorns and then Mrs Royal'd be on at him – make him sit there, half the night, with a needle and thread, fixing it') and onto the porch. 'I'm so glad we came, Max.'

'It's very middle-class.'

'Nothing posh about us, Max. No St Peter's College.'

'We weren't posh. That was a scholarship. If we hada had this . . .' As he studied the neighbours' yards.

'Now, if you wouldn't mind, Max, I try to avoid smoking in the house. Ern did, of course, but he wouldn't be told.'

My brother, sitting a few yards away in a canvas chair, looking at us. Who the hell's this, Eth?

I could've told him. The man who's published your poems, Ern. But even then he mightn'ta been impressed, mighta said something like, Bit full of himself, isn't he?

No, Ern, he's the nicest man.

What, you fancy him, Eth? Grinning.

But the chair was empty, and had been for some time. Since he'd got so bad he couldn't come out of his room. 'He enjoyed sitting there,' I said to Max. 'Said he liked to listen to the birds. But I'd often look out and see him talking to someone going past. I think that's what he was after . . . company. There's only so much you can say to one person, isn't there, Max?'

He just flicked his cigarette into the garden.

Entering, bags left in the hall, and I said, 'And here, to your left, the sunroom, where he'd go of a morning, and here, the lounge . . . come on, then.'

We went in, and he stood, astonished. 'Like it's set for a play.'

'Which one?'

But he wouldn't say. Just turned circles, taking it all in. He sat on the lounge, and sunk into it. I must admit, it was just as bad as the one at Wilson's. But he didn't say anything. I approached the Bösendorfer, opened the lid and said, 'This is it, Max. Hours and hours.' I sat, played a few bars, sang a few lines. 'They were good times, at the beginning . . . *Somebody's pinch'd his wings and toes, I had a bit of parson's nose* . . . Any requests?'

'Nothing comes to mind.'

'*It's a long way to Tipperary* . . .' Pounding the notes, although now I was Ern, hands criss-crossing, turning to Dad and taking the octave: '. . . *it's a long way to go* . . .' Ern, in his old recliner, lit a fag and looked at Max like, he fancies himself a bit, doesn't he, Eth?

You be quiet. Always thinking the worst of people.

Max said, 'Considering she washed up on a beach, she's in good nick.'

'Dad put a lot of work into her.'

And Ern, protesting, because he had to help sand the wood, help with the varnishing.

'It paints a picture,' Max said, examining the old candelabra (not a fancy one), the mantle clock that hadn't worked for years, the hole in the rug near the front window where the dog had tried to dig a hole. I wanted to tell him about that, too, but supposed there was a limit to his interest. Wanted to say how Ern had told *her*, You can't take her, Mrs Royal, she's a good guard dog. Wouldn't let no one get in.

She's also a good shitter. Give her here.

I'm not givin' her up.

You'll do as you're told.

Out the door, the car, the RSPCA. Me and Ern sitting, watching, studying the hole in the carpet. As she sat in the front with our dog in her arms (so happy to be going on an outing). Terry driving, as always, as commanded. Ern saying, I hate her! I hope she dies soon, today. I won't help her, Eth. Before running out to try and reclaim his dog.

No, don't think what you're thinking. There was no way I could've helped Mrs Royal. It was quick and clean. God took her, in the same way *she* took the dog. See, it makes sense. God is dog backwards. What you do to one gets done to you. Amen.

'He could play all of these,' I said to Max, showing him

the pile of manuscripts. 'Self-taught. Like I said, no money for lessons. He was possibly a genius.'

'That's crossed my mind.'

'If they hadn'ta called him up ... *Goodbye Piccadilly, Farewell Leicester Square ...*'

He still didn't join in. Just like on the train from Adelaide. A group of six or seven soldiers singing, and me, '*It's a long, long way to Tipperary but my heart's ...*'

This was – is – the funny thing about Max Harris. Dispassionate, you might say. Just at those moments when you might expect a person to open up, let his or her defences down, become the inner Ern – just at those moments, he'll back off, close up, give little or nothing away. Not sure why. Like if he was happy, for a moment, something terrible might happen.

The soldiers sang it over and over, me joining in, one of them saying, 'You got a good voice on you, missus.'

'It was my brother's favourite. He always sang it. Played on the goanna.' Another round, and then: 'He was in the AIF as well.'

'Yeah? What battalion?'

'Second Third.'

'Don't say. We were fighting with them. What was his name?'

'Well ...' I wasn't sure I wanted to discuss it; not here, not now. I didn't want to ruin a nice evening. Or afternoon. But Max said, 'Ern Malley.'

The first soldier turned to the others and said, 'Malley ... doesn't ring a bell.'

Things settled, and as we tackled the Blue Mountains, Max said to me, 'You'd think someone mighta remembered him?'

'Lotta people in a battalion, Max.'

'But someone like Ern?'

'What?'

'Just sayin'. You woulda thought *someone* . . .'

Back at number forty, in the lounge, I said, 'How about a cuppa?'

After I put on the kettle I showed him Ern's sleep-out, and he said he'd prefer the lounge, and this suited me, as it's hard, isn't it, sleeping in a dead man's bed? He stood staring at the stretcher, the imprint of a body, the old army sheets and rug (Mrs Royal, Legacy), the few knick-knacks I'd left, in memoriam.

'This is where it all happened?' Max said.

'I guess so, although like I said, I never had any idea.'

'He must have hid it well.' Sitting on the stretcher, searching every corner of the room with his little brown eyes. 'It's hard to imagine how he could write all those poems and you didn't . . . I mean, you'd think you mighta walked in on him once? Maybe he only worked at night – after you were asleep?'

'Maybe.' I crossed my arms. 'Maybe I saw, but didn't notice.'

'How?'

'Assumed he was writing a letter, although he wasn't.'

He just stared at me. 'Still, it's good to see where he wrote. Although, it's not that inspirational.'

'No.'

'He must've travelled, Ethel.'

'How do you mean?'

'Astrally. He must have risen from his bed, floated to Melbourne, Innsbruck, all over the place. He must have had a good imagination.'

'I guess that's how all writers work.'

'I reckon you're right.' Still looking around, trying to work out Ern Malley. Ern on his bed, saying, Piss him off, Ethel. Man's room's a private place.

He's just interested, Ern.

Piss him off!

Max checked under the bed, but there was nothing; on the shelves, nothing, except the old soccer ball. And he said, '*Farsa?* What's that mean, Ethel?'

'Couldn't tell you.'

So he took out his notebook (as he always did at such moments) and wrote it down. I said, 'Ern found it on the beach when him and Dad were collecting. He reckoned it'd come all the way from Chile.'

'Don't say?'

'And one day, he reckoned, he was going to find the owner, return it.'

'But he never did?'

'No.'

'That's how it works, eh, Ethel? Mean to do something, but time gets away from you?'

'That's the kettle boiling,' I said, and went out and switched it off, realised he hadn't joined me, returned and found him searching the bottom of the wardrobe.

Shit. The envelope! He'd removed the rubber band, and the photos, and sat studying them. I took a few steps closer and saw the various shots: the boy, only a toddler, playing on his front lawn; five or six, on a jungle gym; in a park (the photo had been taken from a distance, and it was blurred, but you could tell it was the same boy); as a nine-year-old, leaving his school, turning to look at me, as if, somehow, he knew who I was; a year or so older, playing in the ruck (another bad photo, the shot obscured from where I was hiding the camera); and several of the same boy mowing the lawn for his dad, pruning, for his mum. Max said, 'Who's this?'

I reclaimed each of the photos I'd hidden (I wasn't expecting company). 'A friend's son.'

'Right.' But, of course, his suspicions right.

'You ready for a cuppa?'

'Coming.'

A few minutes later we were sitting around the dining table, if you could call it that. You could squeeze six people around it, arm to arm. Old, wobbly, scratched from a thousand plates, burnt by hot mugs, plates of suet. 'This place is full of memories,' I said. 'I've been wondering if I should sell it. Find something smaller, with less garden.'

'You can't,' Max said. 'Your whole life's here.'

'That's the problem. Every day you've got to look at it.'

He waited; wanted the details, I guess, although I wasn't sure he deserved them.

'It's upsetting, Max.' I felt like crying. 'Like he might walk through that door at any moment. Say hello, ask what's for dinner. If I had one of those new places, with the double-brick, I could get on with ... but you're right ...' Sighed. Because that'd be like burying what was left of Ern. Some family moving in with their kids writing all over the walls; some wogs, cooking tomatoes all day, the place smelling of garlic. No, I couldn't do it.

'It's early days,' Max said. 'Course the place is full of memories, but they'll fade.'

'Not sure I want them to, Max.'

'Well, you choose how you remember. Could become a

shrine to Ern – if the journal sells, if people take to him. A line out the door. The Ern Malley Memorial House, seven and six a ticket. Yes, folks, this is where the great man slept . . . stand back there, son, don't touch his bed.'

Max could always get around you. I smiled, reached across, touched his hand. 'D'you reckon?'

'Of course. Like Lawson's house. People visit that.'

I squeezed it. 'You know how to cheer a person up.'

'No point getting gloomy, Ethel. I can feel Ern here, beside me, talking to me. How are you, Ern? Good thanks, Max. Nice job you did on me poems. No worries, Ern, any time. People seem to like them. Some, that is. Well, Mr Harris, you tell them others to take a long walk off a short jetty.' He smiled, sipped, squeezed, but then reclaimed his hand. Pity.

'Memories, everywhere,' I said. 'Dad, standing on this very table with a bottle of beer in one hand and a pile of bills in the other, saying, No way out, Ethel. Stumbling, then he was on the ground. Just about broke a bone.' As I noticed where he'd fallen. 'But he got himself up. Cut lip, black eye. Cleaned himself off (me and Ern, shoving him in the shower). Then we made him a coffee and he sat here drinking it, reading the paper, and he said, Christ, listen to this: the Esso Reliability Trial . . . See, that's how it works, Max. When God closes one door . . .'

He didn't seem convinced.

'Then he was off, fixing up his Indian.'

Max drained his tea, said to me, 'What about your grandparents?'

'Both sets in Liverpool. We never saw them. They never came to visit. Which seems strange, doesn't it, Max?'

'Why?'

'Knowing they had grandkids in Australia.'

'Maybe there was no money?'

'Maybe.'

'In which case, they'd write, or phone, wouldn't they?'

Enough of the past. 'You'd like a shower, wouldn't you, Max?'

'Wouldn't say no.'

So I set him up in the lounge room beside the Bösendorfer, made up his bed while he was in the shower. Returned to Ern's room, stripped the sheets and rug, because they'd do, and sat on the stretcher and said, 'You're gonna have to make more of an effort, Ern.'

# 30

Later, Max told me he couldn't even remember that day at Victoria Barracks. That's how much it must have affected him. To have to come face to face with a set of lies (and liars) that took Ern, his poems, our efforts at publishing them, that took clear, demonstrable facts and twisted them in the most malicious (and deranged) way. No wonder he blocked it all out.

It all started across the road from the entrance to the barracks. The high walls and unwelcoming gates, the several guards, up and down, rifles across shoulders. Men coming and going on foot and in cars, trucks, artillery. Max: 'Not that I would've minded.'

I didn't enter into it. We'd had the discussion the previous night, sitting on the porch, drinking our sweet tea. I'd said, 'It's funny how the army rejected you.' He'd said, 'What do you mean by that?'

'Your age. You seem fit.'

'I was offered up to the gods of war, but they didn't want me.'

I was going to leave it at that but thought, No, why not? 'I could understand if you were studying Medicine but … *Commerce?*'

'I had a condition.'

'Oh?'

'I don't want to talk about it.'

Mrs Kynoch had walked past, and waved. I'd said to Max, 'Although I respect your privacy—'

'Christ, Ethel, you keep on at a man. I'm telling you, it's a chronic condition.'

'But you tell me everything.'

'No, I don't. Do you tell me?'

'Yes.'

'You do not.'

'Most things.'

'Well, there you are.'

We'd left it there. His choice, of course. If he wanted to keep some distance. But I felt like telling him, there's nothing I'd keep from you, Max Harris.

Some sort of siren went off inside the barracks. To Hell and back, the sound of men running, more marching, although it was hard to tell from where we were sitting. Under a giant Moreton Bay fig, a hundred yards from a playground, full of soldiers and their wives and kids, a few spread out, picnicking. Boys climbing trees, pretending to shoot each other (as their dads had described, I guessed). The girls sitting in groups talking. That's what I've always liked about girls: careful, calm, considered. Always in tune with other people's emotions. Whereas boys . . . horrible creatures (as I imagined Ern, halfway up a tree, throwing sticks at me).

Max checked his watch. 'They're late.'

'They'll be here.'

'Half an hour.'

'Stewart sounded half-decent, although . . .'

When I'd rung, the previous afternoon, and he'd come on, saying, 'Ethel, I'm not willing to have it out.'

'Mr Stewart, I'm back in Sydney.'

A long pause.

'With Max Harris.'

'You don't say? *The* Max Harris?'

'We were wondering if you and Mr McAuley had a few minutes tomorrow?'

Then he'd gone away, and I'd waited for three or four minutes, and he'd come back and said, 'I suppose that'd be alright. There's a park across the road from the barracks.'

Further away, other men had set up for a barbecue, and the smell had made it over to us. Max said, 'I'd kill for a snag.'

'Just tell me, Max, if I get irrational.' I clutched the handle of my bag, ground my feet into the grass, searched the gates for the so-called poets. 'Although I don't reckon we should go easy on them.'

'No.' Smoking, calmly, watching the kids play.

'After all, they're liars, and they've caused us a lot of trouble. I think we should demand a printed apology . . . Max?'

'Eh?'

'A printed apology?'

'Yes, I guess, although I think you'd be lucky.'

'The least we could expect.'

Then he sat up, leaned forward on his knees and said, 'If it gets legal, it could be messy.'

'So?'

'Look at what happened to Dobell last year.'

'That was different.'

'It ruined him, they reckon. Someone said he said he'd never paint again. Does a picture, ends up in court, because other idiots don't understand what he's trying to do.'

'Disgraceful.'

'But it happened, and Dobell was a serious soul, quiet, shy.'

'This is different.'

'I guess.' Gazing out across the acres of park. 'As much as I believe in Ern, I don't believe . . .'

And with that, they appeared, one (Stewart) looking like Joshua Smith himself; McAuley taller, lankier, with blonde hair and a fat face, teeth all crooked and yellow. I thought, How could it be? How could *this* be Ern Malley?

But I stayed civil. Mainly because I'd promised Max. But I felt like grabbing them by their collars, shaking them, demanding an apology. They got closer, and I saw their features, and grins, like this was the tail-end of some joke they'd enjoyed.

Stewart sat, but McAuley lit a smoke and stood, some distance away, surveying the scene. 'This is like a spy novel.'

Max didn't take long. 'That's what you work in, is it?'

'Can't say, Max.' As he sized him up. 'It's good to meet you at last.'

Max couldn't agree. 'We thought it was time to get to the bottom of this.'

'Of what?'

'It's all got a bit confused,' Stewart said, turning to me. 'You're Ern's sister?'

'Yes.'

'*Ern Malley* . . . you're his sister?'

'I am.'

He stretched back, lit his own cigarette and said, 'Fair enough.'

'What's *that* mean?' I remembered my promise. Civil. We hadn't got far, so I decided to back off.

'His *sister*,' Stewart said. 'I never really thought about Ern's family . . . just that bita background we made up.'

'Made up?'

'Yeah, made up.'

'Alright,' Max said. 'We've come all this way, I guess we should hear what you've got to say.'

Then Stewart said, 'We were avid readers of *Angry Penguins*.'

I wasn't sure if Max was flattered; but he just waited.

'And poets, too, aren't we, Jim?'

'Absolutely.'

'We sent you samples of our work, Max, but never heard back.'

'No? I'm sorry, sometimes I get so many submissions.'

'Anyway, Max, over the past few years we've noticed that poetry has changed.'

'How's that?'

'From something accessible to something . . . silly, we believe, don't we, Jim?'

'We do.'

It was almost staged; like they'd written a script, learnt the lines. Like they were pretending to be another Stewart and McAuley.

'So,' McAuley continued, 'a lot of poets we've spoken to find this modern movement is taking over the pages of . . . well, for better or worse, it's very much in favour. The trend. In Europe. But, to us (and we've always shared our work, discussed it, offered criticism) this type of poetry (no offence intended to *Ern*, Ethel) lacked any real connection with the average man or woman.'

261

Max said, 'The average man or woman?'

'Someone you'd meet buying your groceries.'

'You'd meet me, Ethel, Ern . . . Eliot.'

'No, Max. Now we're just tossing words around. Years ago, kids would be reciting Lawson in class.'

'Times move on.'

'Can't recite "Perspective Lovesong".'

'That's ridiculous. So Picasso should still be painting Spanish landscapes?'

'That's not the point.'

'It is, exactly.'

'It's not. Painting changes, but words, people *rely* on words.'

'What the hell does that mean?'

I looked at Max. Civil, I said, with my eyes. But there was a fury, little cyclones, little tornadoes in his head, stirring him up (he tried a deep breath, but it didn't work). I wasn't sure that Max Harris was up to this. And as it turned out . . .

'Anyway,' Stewart continued, 'we thought, we're entitled to our say. And if we just say it, who'll listen? No one. But if we do it *creatively*.'

I'd already had enough. What were these two: mates, soldiers, spies, lovers? Why were they writing poems when they should be fighting a war?

And McAuley. 'So we sat down one Saturday afternoon and made up Ern, and his poems.'

'You did not,' I said.

'*Ethel*,' Max warned.

'How can you say that, Mr McAuley? He was my brother, a soldier, like you, and he was very sick with Graves'. Now he's dead, and you're saying these terrible things—'

262

'Ethel!'

I stopped, but glared at them both.

McAuley wasn't easily put off. 'I'm not sure why you're doing this – Ethel, Max – but it's a strange sort of joke.'

'Joke?' I said.

'The poems were made from bits and pieces, as you've discovered. Training manuals, encyclopaedias, things we remembered. Cobbled together, although I think we did a decent job.'

At least I could agree with this. Despite everything, the poems would last. But not because these liars had claimed authorship.

'To cut a long story,' McAuley said, 'we sat down with a typewriter (and I'll admit, we'd had a few drinks, and were feeling mischievous) and invented this story – Ern, the dying poet.'

I waited for Max. Could, should, we let this continue? He said, 'You invented Ethel, here, so your joke would seem believable?'

'Exactly.'

'She finds her brother's poems in a case (as you did, didn't you, Ethel?) . . .'

'Yes.'

'And sends them to me? *She* sends them to me? *You* send them to me?'

'Yes,' he replied. '*We* did. Because we wrote them'

'And here I am, sitting in a park, with at least one person lying to me?'

'Believe what you will, Max.'

'Max,' I said, 'I think we've heard enough. The *nerve* of these fellas.'

We were getting nowhere. Max seemed agitated. Like *I* was the liar. But I'd only ever told the truth about Ern, and his poems.

So, time for facts. 'The bit you fail to explain – Mr McAuley, Mr Stewart – is how Ern's poems arrived on Mr Harris's desk several months before you claimed to have authored them.'

Stewart thought about this. 'We were in no rush.'

McAuley was gazing across the park.

'And when we heard that *Ethel* ... well, let's just say, our poems had been sitting around our office for months. It's not inconceivable that someone, Ern, perhaps, took a copy a long time before we'd completed them.'

'Now, come on,' I said.

'If you want to look for holes in our story, Ethel, but we're just saying what happened. The poems had laid around. Someone could've seen we were using them as a joke on Ern, and decided to get back at *us*.'

I turned to Max again. 'Do we really have to take this?'

But he'd become vivisector. 'So, Ern came into your office, found the poems, saw you were playing a trick on him, copied them, passed them off (in an elaborate story involving, in the end, his own death) as his, I published them, Ethel herself was convinced?'

'No, simpler than that,' Stewart said. '*We* wrote the poems, to make a point about your little magazine, Max. And now it's all come back to bite you.'

'What the hell does that mean?'

'Now you look silly. Now you've been hoaxed.'

'Hoaxed!' I said. 'How dare you, you nasty little man, wearing that uniform – you're a disgrace to your country. Why aren't you out fighting?'

He pointed to Max. 'Why isn't he?'

'He has a faulty heart, a murmur. But you, and you:

pretending to be soldiers, sitting out the war in your office, bored, so that you feel the need to torment others in the most personal, humiliating way. That, even now, you have the nerve to sit there and claim *you* wrote the poems my brother . . . I can *prove* they were his. The references to our childhood, his trip to Innsbruck (he went there four times!), his relationships – with Lois, did you know about Lois, in Melbourne? He loved her deeply and planned on marrying her, before you *shat* upon his life, his memory.'

McAuley said, 'We're due back, Harry.'

They offered to shake hands, but we refused. Max looked like the Hindenburg, after the crash – the smoking remains of something perfect, and beautiful. Like all of the helium, the life, the love had been sucked out of him. The apparent poets walked back towards the gate, and I followed, and Max followed me at a distance. 'You've given your side, and here's mine. Ern always wanted to write, but couldn't, because he had to go out and earn money. But at the end he managed to get down what he'd always wanted. His *Ecliptic* was his legacy, although if it wasn't for people like you there would've been more.'

'How's that our fault?' Stewart said, crossing the road.

'There's only one thing can make this good,' I said. 'An apology, in every paper in the country. Saying it wasn't you who wrote those poems. The truth.'

They passed through the gates, and I stood, shouting at them. 'You killed him, you two! He died of the shame. You raped his wasting body, you bastards!'

Two soldiers approached me and I braced, ready for them. I turned to Max, standing on the other side of the road, arms crossed, waiting for me. 'Come on, Ethel, this is getting us nowhere.'

As we walked back towards the bus, he said, 'See, this is what finished Dobell.'

'What can we do, Max?'

'I don't know. But I wouldn't hold my breath waiting for an apology, Eth.'

Arrogant. That was the word. Even on the phone the previous night, when Stewart had started laughing and said, 'You reckon you're Ethel?'

'I am Ethel.'

'But we got your name out of the *Women's Weekly*. Ethel Polkinghorne, the columnist.'

I was ready to jump down the phone. Then he'd said, 'I can't believe that Max actually thought they were proper poems.'

'And them claiming,' I said to Max, 'that those poems were made up from books, and had no real value, whereas anyone can see they're beautiful pieces of writing, aren't they, Max?'

'Yes.' He crossed his arms again. 'Although it's hard to imagine anyone hating me enough to . . .'

So, you can see how he might have forgotten it, I suppose. Blanked it out. Some things are safer to forget, to write over in your memory of how things happened.

My little Dobell, struggling up the hill. 'In the end, you'll be the hero, and they'll be the fools. Time has a way of settling these issues, even if we can't . . . get a resolution.'

# 31

First, down Byron Street. I wondered if he'd had the same problems as Ern. Things had seemed so much simpler a few months ago – the virgin poems emerging fully formed, singing their song across the Santa Ana, the sound of summer hoses, someone's incinerator smoking out the yard. But now, with grey-blue skies, the words scattered far and wide, all the hope had gone out of the thing. *I have been bitter with you, my brother*, although it might've been something from the paper now, a gas bill, a timetable.

Max and I walked to the Legacy shop and found Peggy busy behind the counter. She hugged me, asked how I'd been going, and who was this dark, handsome man? I said an old friend from Adelaide, and she (surprisingly) didn't say any more. But she did say: 'You just disappeared.'

'It's been hectic, hasn't it, Max?'

'It certainly has.' As he examined the jackets, hoping for something wearable, uncovering David, who looked up at him and said, 'This is my cave.'

Max knelt down. 'What's in there?'

David thought about it. 'Want a look?'

'I reckon.'

So Max crawled in, and the jackets fell across the entrance, and we heard whispers, and Peggy said, 'Wanna cuppa?'

We went out back, Peggy put on the kettle, and I said to her, 'What have you been up to?'

'Same old routine,' she said, unpacking a box of belts. 'Don't know why I bother. You never get any thanks.'

'No, like everything these days. People are so preoccupied.'

'I know there's a war on but ...' She used week-old tea leaves, said Legacy didn't supply coupons and she wasn't using her own. We returned to the shop and she asked David if he was behaving.

Max said, 'We're looking for the Holy Grail.'

'Not again.'

As I suspected: Max, the man-child, refusing to engage with the real world. Six years old still, as most men were – remained.

'Jesus had it at the Last Supper,' David said.

'He's gone a bit religious,' Peggy said. 'I think it's *her*.'

'Shelley?'

Then she leaned forward and whispered, 'Things have got worse.'

'What has?' David called, from his cave.

'Mind your own business.' And quieter. 'Michael tried to ... you know ...'

'*No?*'

And quieter still, holding her cup to warm her hands. 'Shelley found him *hanging*.'

'Jesus, Peg.'

'Cut him down, called an ambulance, and they managed to save him.'

'What, he hadn't be there long?'

Some old girl entered, skimmed the books and asked if we had any detective novels. Peg checked, then said, 'No, but if any come in we'll put them aside.'

She said thanks, looked at some ties, then left.

'What you doing down there?' Peggy said to David.

'A pit of snakes,' Max said. 'But we got over them, didn't we, David?'

'Vipers.'

'And now we're after the Grail. Who wants it, David?'

'The Knights Templar.'

Then Peg quietened again. 'They had him on a machine for three days, and they were gonna turn it off, but he rallied.'

'Good.' I squeezed her hand.

'And now he's back home, and Shelley's looking after him, which makes it difficult, with no money coming in.'

David appeared from the jackets and said, 'Lions!' He ran once around the shop, and Max emerged, following him. Then they disappeared behind the women's frocks.

'Anyway, it's all very gloomy,' Peggy said.

(And more whispers, from the frocks, as African drums – a sort of bongo David had found in the toys – started pulsing).

Peggy said, 'That's for sale, Davy.'

No response. Maybe she didn't care. 'I was thinking of getting a job, Ethel.'

'Doing what?'

'Those factories out west – they're making shells, artillery, they need people. Either that or . . .' She stopped, because there was silence from the savannah, and she was sure David was listening. 'You two okay?'

'*Oga boga, oga boga*,' David sang.

'Well, to be honest,' I said to her, 'if you're not getting paid for this . . .'

'Exactly, although who would look after Davy all day?'

'Well, I suppose I could.'

'No, it's not your job. I could look after Michael, and Shelley could . . . I dunno, it's all such a mess, Ethel. If he'd just get up and . . . how do you make someone, Ethel? I mean, how's life so bad?'

'It's not, Peg.'

'He didn't get it from me, I'm chirpy enough. Although his father . . . he was adopted, so you don't know what's in *that* closet, do you, Eth?'

'No.'

'Maybe . . . *David*?'

'Yes?'

'How about you let Mr Harris come out and have a cup of tea with the adults?'

'He doesn't want to, do you, Max?'

'Of course not. Cup of tea, my arse. Those darts are tipped with poison, David. If they so much as graze your arm.'

I was tiring of Michael and Shelley and their problems. Always Michael. If he chose to be that way what could you do? You couldn't feel sorry. So many people in situations they *couldn't* control. Maybe, I wondered, if Peggy and Shelley didn't pander to him so much he *might* get up, make something of himself. And as for this *suicide*. Staged, no doubt. 'Do you think it was . . . you know, a call for help?'

'How do you mean?'

'Like, he didn't really *mean* to.'

'We've given him all the help we can.' She sat back, thinking. 'Luckily, *we're* the strong ones, eh, Ethel?'

Max emerged from his cave and said, 'He's busy writing.'

'He always scribbles,' Peggy said. 'End up like his father.' And she was off again, telling us about Michael's childhood and how, perhaps, something had happened that she never knew about. And I thought, time to go. But Max was sitting beside the books, and he noticed one, took it off the shelf, found his notebook in his pocket and checked something. 'That's strange. *Farsa.*' Consulting the Spanish dictionary. 'It means fake,' he said to me.

'Fake?'

He seemed intrigued, checked again. 'Fake.'

'What's fake? The soccer ball?'

'And at the time this word was written on it?'

'Yes. Why do you ask?'

'Floated across the Pacific . . . *Farsa* . . . in permanent marker?'

'What do you reckon?' Peggy asked me.

'How would I know?' As I glared at Max.

Peggy made Max a cup of weak tea, and David called, 'How do you spell exhausted?' Max said, 'E-g-g-s-o-r-s-t-e-d,' and I growled at him, but he just said, 'As good as any.'

Half an hour later, I said, 'I guess this steak needs a refrigerator, doesn't it, Max?'

'I reckon, Ethel.'

'Anything I can do, Peggy, let me know. Davy, if your gran needs a break . . .'

He glanced up from an old *Gulliver's Travels*. 'I'm okay here. I can hide.' And lighting up, saying to Max, 'Can you come back, mister?'

To the land of Lilliput, in the Legacy shop. 'I'll try . . . soon.'

But I think David knew what that meant. No, I won't return. I'll get on with my life, and I'll leave you here, in your little cave, to work things out for yourself.

'Mr Harris will be returning to Adelaide soon, won't you, Max?' I said.

So David returned to his book.

Peggy said, 'Oh, before you go . . . that box.' She went into the back room, found the half-unpacked box of Ern's things and handed it to me. 'Someone's written . . . ERN.'

As I remembered. 'Right ... Ern?'

'You may as well take the rest . . . doesn't look particularly saleable.'

We headed home, but the word kept going through my head. *Saleable*. So we rested at a bus stop, opened the box and had a look. Firstly, a shirt. Ern's. Collected a few days after he'd died. I sized it up on Max and said, 'That'd do you, Max.'

'Not my style.'

'There's a war on, we can't afford style,' I told him.

He didn't seem convinced. But just because someone had died, you couldn't afford to throw away all their stuff. 'I bought him that to cheer him up. He was just lying around, and one day I said, Come on, let's get the ferry to Manly.'

I'm not feeling up to it, Ethel.

Get up! (And I pulled him up). Pop this on.

I found pants, braces, a tie, an army belt, and again, I offered it to Max, who just said, 'What would I want that for?'

And then, a manila folder. I couldn't remember it. Maybe it had already been in the box, or maybe I'd just scooped it up? I opened it, examined the first page: a curry-coloured newspaper clipping from 1942. Our troops were making headway in New Guinea, and the Japs were fighting back. Two hundred and ten casualties in a single day, and twice as many wounded. There was a picture of a soldier on a stretcher. I couldn't make out the face. Perhaps it was Ern. 'Perhaps,' I said, 'he was there?'

'D'you reckon?' Max asked.

'Why else would he ...?' I examined the clipping, the picture, and wondered if these were Ern's legs, arms, the side of his face. 'The timing's about right,' I said. 'That's when ... well, 1942, I didn't hear from him until six months later.'

'Could be,' Max said.

A few more clippings, like this – battles from around the same time, and place. And on one, an underlining: *The whole troop, who'd recently been returned to the front, were attacked, with one casualty.*

The significance, I thought. And Max, 'Why would he underline it, Eth?'

I studied the article, but there was nothing specific, not even a battalion number, no names, all anonymous. And this time, no picture to suggest Ern, or anyone.

Then, a pile of recipes. I said, 'Why would he want these?'

'He didn't cook?' Max asked.

'No ... although, come to think of it, towards the end, he did cook a couple of cakes, and biscuits. I just assumed he'd got bored.'

Recipes for Afghans, Anzacs, Cornish fairings and digestives; yellow cake and pineapple upside-down.

'Funny,' I said, 'I can't remember him using a recipe.' I saw him, with the mixing bowl, remembered asking, What you up to?

Save some money doing it this way.

You should be in bed.

The way he took his time, mixing, adding chocolate chips, talking to himself, If only we had a bit longer … Me saying, We've got all day, Ern, but him just looking at me like I was stupid.

Next, a carbon copy of form 123A-7B MEDICAL DISCHARGE. *Name: Ernest Lalor Malley; Address: c/o Victoria Barracks, Sydney.* Rank, serial number, eye colour, and the rest. And then, *Reason for Discharge: Medically Unfit for Service.* Although no mention of Graves' Disease. Any disease or illness. There was a spot ('Diagnosis or Condition'), but no one had filled it in. Maybe they'd been in a rush, or forgotten? 'Never seen that before,' I said, reading it aloud.

'You'd think they'd say,' Max said. He tried to look at the form, but I folded it.

I kept searching. I wondered what I'd find next. Then, a photo of an unknown soldier. Medium height, brown hair, good teeth. No name, just a small 'L' written on the bottom.

'Do you recognise him?' Max asked.

'No.' I stared at it. Thinking, *Lois.* Max, too, who saw it from a different angle. Thinking. Looking up at me. Down at the photo, the folded discharge, the recipes for butter cookies.

'Like you said,' Max said, 'that brother of yours, he was a man of mystery, Ethel.'

'I wouldn't say that. Just liked keeping things to himself … but don't we all?'

'Sometimes.' Lifting his head a little, a little cocky.

'Well, enough of that,' I said, closing the folder, reclaiming it. 'I don't want to get sick on rancid steak.'

# 32

The next morning we were up early. Dressed and out the door by eight. Along Dalmar Street, up Croydon Road, back down Queen Street, past Karl McDonald, who called, 'Ethel, you see the paper?' Up to his porch, where I introduced Max. Karl smiled strangely, then read: '*To the Editor, sir . . .*'

He had some sort of bird, and although it was a hundred yards from my house, you could hear it of a morning, when the sun came up, squawking (the bird, not Karl). It, he, she, whatever it was, woke me. I'd often thought of saying something, but you don't, do you, if it's a good neighbour? Still, I couldn't understand how he could live with it.

'*. . . in respect to what has become known as the Ern Malley affair, my colleague, Mr McAuley, and I, were recently honoured with a visit from Mrs Ethel Malley of Croydon.*'

Karl said, 'You're famous, Ethel.'

'Those bastards . . . in the *Herald*?'

'Yep. *Mrs Malley was somewhat enraged that we, the perpetrators of this so called 'hoax', had the nerve to doubt her existence. She seemed real enough. We explained the genesis of the poems we'd sent to Mr Max Harris of Adelaide.*' Karl said to Max, 'You must be pretty pissed off?'

But he didn't seem to be. Just sat, feeding cuttlefish to the bird, smiling. 'I'm getting used to it – Karl was it?'

But he just kept reading. '*In an effort to counter our invention, Mr Harris has been doing some inventing of his own. Ethel, of Croydon, as we described her, has come to life, a sort of not-so-modern Prometheus made from the nuts and bolts and gathered limbs of executed criminals.*'

'The bloody nerve,' I said.

'*She has had life breathed into her, given clothes, taught how to walk, what to say, by her own Victor Frankenstein, Mr Harris.*'

Max laughed. 'Beautiful! I couldn't have done it better.'

'*We write today, sir, to thank them for their visit. For travelling to Sydney, taking the time to see us, before returning to their own sea of ice. We wish them well in their continued dramatic ventures. Particularly Mr Harris, whose recent South Australian production of Joyce's* Exiles *failed to excite the local critics.*'

Karl stopped. I waited for Max's reaction, but he just said, 'I think it's nearly run its course.'

'Aren't you angry?'

'What's that going to achieve? The more we give them the more they'll use. The more they'll invent.'

'We can't let them get away with this.'

He seemed surprised. 'What should we do then?'

'Get a lawyer.'

'To prove what?'

I thought about it. To prove ... Ern existed, although I wasn't sure anyone was saying he hadn't. 'We should start by replying to this garbage,' I said, taking the paper from Karl's hands, cursing the morning and the bird and all of Croydon with its slumberous, heavy air.

'The modern Prometheus? How do you feel about that, Ethel?' Max said.

'What's that?'

'My monster. They're saying you're my monster.'

'Bastards. You can write something, Max? Something clever. You're smarter than them.'

'Apparently not.' He continued playing with the bird.

Karl said, 'They published one of Ern's poems the other day.'

'I bet they did.'

'Something about a vegetable universe. I didn't get it myself, but I showed it to Roy and he said you'd showed it to him, and it was a nice bit of writing.'

I lit up. 'Yes, I showed him, after I found them, before I sent them to you, Max. He can vouch for them.'

But Max still wasn't convinced. 'What would that prove?'

'That *I* had them first. That Ern must've written them.'

'But what's it matter? You know who wrote them, I know. In twenty years' time the only thing that'll matter is the poems.'

'He's right,' Mr McDonald said. 'Roy reckons they're a bit a good. Said he wished he could write something like Ern Malley.'

'He said that, did he?' I asked.

'Yes.'

'Well, you tell him, Karl, that means a lot to me, and it would to Ern, I reckon.'


We continued into the morning. I pointed out the many features of Croydon, Burwood, all the way down Lang Street, towards Parramatta Road, again. Thinking about the manila file. Arriving home the previous evening, telling Max I needed a lie-down and locking myself in my room. Examining each of the recipes, the discharge notice, the details of the battles I guessed he'd remembered. Unless these too were fake?

Although there was more. Another photo, of Ern and another soldier, arms around each other (in a sort of blokey way, I think?), full uniform and kit, with the jungle in the background. But this other soldier's face had been cut out – a neat little, anonymous circle. And on the back: 'Me and . . .' Although the name had been scribbled out so violently it had made a hole in the photo paper.

'Nice spot,' Max said.

'It is. I've never gone far . . . beyond Adelaide, that is. You probably think that's pathetic?'

'No. Travel doesn't make you happy, necessarily. Broadens your view, but a person can decide to be happy wherever they are.'

'Too true.' I touched his arm again.

'I guess I should be heading home,' he said.

I didn't reply. Didn't want him to go, but realised there was no reason for him to stay. The hoax would soon be forgotten. I could get on with stewing peaches, and him, getting his next *Penguins* ready.

'Be funny,' he said.

'What's that?'

'We've been together for so long. And through a bit, with all this Ern Malley stuff. Your bloody brother, eh?'

I smiled. *My bloody brother*. Although I felt there were three of us now.

'Be quiet without you,' I said.

'You can come visit. Maybe we'll organise another event in Adelaide.'

'That'd be good.'

'You could read . . . you read your brother so well.'

'I knew him so well . . . like myself. Two peas in a pod.'

Perhaps. Although I'd found more in the folder. Another poem. His – every word, every forensic trace of grammar and spelling. Slightly shocking, perhaps, but definitely in the style of the *Ecliptic*. Set down here for truth's sake, so please, don't judge, dear reader.

*Take the day by the horns of Artaxerxes, and hold them tightly, lest they get away, Wrestling the beast to the ground, there, to penetrate the mysteries of its mythology, psychology, physiology, Especially this, when the dusk, in the jungle, is still warm, and thoughts turn to buggery, The stars all aglow with engorged lips, filling a screen we seldom see, but long for, every night of our astral dreaming (and others!) . . .*

No, you didn't need a lot of imagination.

*And then, when we run out of script, we'll improvise the night away, planting unproductive seeds that might substitute for sunnier, salad days . . .*

I couldn't really tell. Smut, perhaps? Either way, another side of Ern. Not that I *hadn't* thought he was human, a man of the flesh (like I've said, there was plenty of evidence).

Just then Max said, 'What did you make of those clippings?'

'Well . . . I was thinking of checking with the army.'

'Probably a good idea. That was some heavy fighting.'

'Yes. A lot of action. Although he hid it well, didn't he?'

'Wonder why?'

'Maybe there was some . . . shame involved?'

'How do you mean?'

'Maybe he killed some people, and didn't want to remember?'

'Quite possibly. Although one thing still intrigues me.'

'What's that?'

'This incident. What d'you reckon all that's about?'

'Might never know, Max.'

# 33

Twenty minutes' walk from Central, but it did me good, seeing the city come to life, buses so full they leaned towards the gutter, thousands of men in brown suits. What did they do all day? Write proposals or order shipments of steel or pepper, bits and pieces of the lives we clicked together, like Ern's Meccano? Were they happy going into their offices, setting out their lunch, a thermos of tea, sharpening a new pencil, because the old one had worn down too far? Happy? And did it matter? They had something to do. The most important thing of all. Because, left alone, a woman (or man) tends to dwell on life too much, find patterns that aren't there, think people are saying things they're not, worry about money, when there's more than enough. Like we were designed to fret – to see ghosts, risks (although risks were always overstated). Keep busy. That's what I needed to do, now that I was home, Max gone. More time at Legacy, perhaps? Or bowls? I'd tried that a few times, but wasn't much chop. War work? The Cheer-Up Hut needed ladies to make tea and biscuits, and now I had the recipes.

Either way, I had my old life back. It felt good, okay, reasonable, as I walked along Pitt Street, seeing what was in the windows. Petticoats, shoes (all leather), handbags. Just me, for the first time in a long time. Since Ern had appeared at the door and said, Still got me room, Eth?

Ern?

I've had enough of Melbourne.

I didn't know . . . what, you had problems?

No problems, Eth, just thought it was time to come home. Coughing. Again, a minute later, and that night, Well, there is something, Eth.

What, Ern?

This Graves' business, it's progressed. I saw a doctor and he reckons I should . . . what I mean is, he doesn't reckon I'm gonna make a hundred, Eth.

That's how it had happened. But now, he was gone, Max was gone, the poems, everything. Maybe I could write a book about the Ern Malley affair? Set the record straight, once and for all. Provide the necessary background in the form of a biography? Yes, that was an idea. Max could help me, and edit it, publish it. What would those two so-called poets do then? Who'd look a fool in fifty years? Not me, or Max. Yes, that's what I could do – as I looked in a newsagent's window, priced foolscap, went in and bought three hundred pages.

Good-o! Decided. Legacy, and the Cheer-Up Hut, could wait. Maybe someone could pop around to Dalmar Street and cheer *me* up?

Without Max. This would be strange. I'd got so used to him. His face, when I went out of a morning; his rancid flat; his life, full of random, strange moments, all dedicated to the god of words; the way he got up at three every morning to piss (although he was a young man, he had an unreliable prostate); how he interacted with people (everyone he met liked him); how he was so aware of his history, and how it informed his views about the world. Max was, and is, so damn smart!

But gone. I'll always remember him, standing on Platform 17, the smell of noodles and acetone from the Chinese laundry, a million men (I exaggerate) leaving their trains and heading for work, reading papers as they walked, because a lot had happened in the world since last night. He'd said, 'You gonna be okay, Ethel?'

'Of course. There was life before *Angry Penguins*, there'll be life after.'

'I'll let you know about McAuley, and his mate.'

'Gone, forgotten,' I'd said. 'Like they never existed. We did right by Ern – published the poems, gave the world something to remember him by.'

'That's the main thing, you reckon?'

'Of course. He didn't live for nothing, Max. He was a man, and he breathed and shat and worried, and pissed his pants, too.'

Max had just taken my arm, kissed my cheek and said, 'The old place is gonna seem empty. You're welcome any time.'

'Soon, when I get bored of things here. Too many memories.' I felt all teary, but he squeezed my arm. I said, 'I lost my mum too early, my dad, my brother. They all left me, Max. But you don't have any say over that, do you?'

Then the train was waiting, and Max had to get on, and I didn't have time to tell him what I wanted to.

All the way to the Mitchell Library. Up the sandstone steps, along a few passageways, overcome by the scale of the place. Silence, everywhere, the world explained in Garamond. I asked where I'd find the newspapers and a man pointed, and almost smiled, although I couldn't be sure. Into another room, with racks (like some giant tannery of facts) spreading from wall to wall. The smell of acid-eaten paper, and ink, and someone's powder and cologne (a little too heavy). I asked at another desk. 'The *Herald*?' And another finger, indicating the history that had died, and was forgotten, except for when someone like me came along. A billion Erns and Ethels who'd lived and died and populated the earth with more people who had in turn reproduced, grown, made candlesticks and served coffee, before expiring. So what made me, or Ern, special? Nothing. Standing, smelling the highlights of these lives, I guessed we were all destined to be forgotten, and writing poems (generally) didn't help. Publishing journals. Getting killed in wars. Curing rare diseases. Nothing much helped.

Was it? Yes, it was. Roy McDonald, sitting at a desk against the wall, surrounded by a little ocean of papers; drowning in them, moving them around, but going under. I walked over and whispered, 'Roy?'

He smiled when he saw me. 'Ethel!' Took my hand, squeezed it and offered me a seat. 'What are you doing here?'

'I'm after some information.'

As was he, explaining how he'd given up on the novel as a form (despite never having finished one) and turned to non-fiction. A biography of William Bligh. 'When I first went to London,' he said, 'I walked past his house. Little place with a few flowers out the front. I wondered how he'd gone from that to the *Bounty*, and the Rum Rebellion.'

I told him how interesting that sounded and how I, too, was thinking of writing a biography.

'Yeah? Who?'

'Ern.'

'Ah . . . you reckon there'd be a market?'

'If his poems last.'

'Right. A biography?' Although he didn't sound sure. 'Problem is, persuading a publisher.'

I told him all about Max, and his journal, and how I could get it edited and printed, but he just said, 'What's the good if people won't buy it?'

'But they would. Everyone's heard about Ern now. Haven't you?'

'Yes . . . plenty in the papers about him.'

'Well, you're the learned one, Roy. Maybe *you* could write it?'

'Dunno, Ethel. Up to me arms in Bligh.' He showed me his research notes. Hundreds of handwritten pages, scrawl, and I thought, this seems familiar. 'But I must say, Eth, I enjoyed reading his poems.'

'You bought a copy?'

'Yes. I was very proud. I mean, I was part of the discovery, wasn't I?'

'I should've given you some credit.'

'Don't worry about that – I didn't do anything. But they looked handsome, set in New Roman, on crisp paper. *I* felt proud, so I bet you did?'

'Very much so, Roy. It took a lot of work, and of course, there's been this controversy, but I suppose you can't have anything worthwhile in the arts without a bit of controversy?'

I didn't mean anything. Like, maybe a lack of controversy led to an eternity of unfinished books, and ideas. Or that he'd never know that thrill, the look of type on paper, the binding, the cover (and I explained, how exciting, Mr Nolan!), the launch, the customers, all of it – I didn't mean to say that he was, well, second-rate. Although he was.

'What was your favourite?' I asked.

'Let me think, that last one, the little testament. Because I thought it was Ern's testament.'

'It was.'

'And said more about him than the others.'

'It did.'

'I read it over and over, and each time, found something new. Those lines, what were they?' He gazed up into the sky-lights. '*I have pursued rhyme, image, and metre, Known all the clefts in which the foot may stick* . . . See, only a writer could know that.'

'Exactly. And those horrible men saying they'd made the whole lot up.'

'Always people like that, Ethel. But I saw those poems at the start, and knew, they were Ern.'

I thought about it. 'And you'd write something to that effect, would you, Roy?'

'Of course.'

'Something brief, saying how you've been an English teacher, and could recognise Ern's words?'

'Of course I would, Ethel.'

My mind ticked over. Those two bastards, brought down to earth. 'Could you write it now?'

'I guess.'

One thing Roy was, was accommodating. So we discussed the letter in some depth, and as I went looking for my news-paper, he got started.

All of the dying newsprint made me think of Carpenter, and his horrible paper, and where it all ended up. Time, I thought, would be on my (and Ern's) side. I searched for the *Herald*, July 23, found a table, spread it out and started reading. Avoiding the gossip, Pea-No-Lia, even *Ginger Meggs*, it wasn't long before I found it: *The Army has released few details about the incident reported on Thursday last. The soldiers, from the same battalion, were withdrawn from Active Service and returned to Australia. An Army spokesman would only say that incidents of this type occurred from time to time and had to be regretted. Men at the front were under great pressure and often responded in inappropriate ways. In this case, both Ernest Malley and Louis Fauske have been counselled.*

Then, I felt sick. I had a bad feeling. '*Ern.*'

And it got worse: *The Crown Solicitor is deciding whether to proceed to trial. The men's actions contravened several regulations, and according to Major Daniel Hardy, "It's not so much the act, as the neglect of duty".*

*The act?* I thought. Ern? No, he'd never shown any signs. Although he'd never liked sport, and read a lot, and maybe that led to . . . God, I couldn't think about it. Or maybe they'd stolen something, or went too far in the line of duty? Killed someone they shouldn't have? Or disobeyed some order? Maybe they thought it was unreasonable? Then I remembered the poem, and felt even worse, if that was possible. The horns and the . . . no, Ern!

I tore the article from the paper, folded it and put it in my pocket. In with the discharge, the photos, the poem which, for now, I didn't fancy re-reading. Then I returned to Roy, thanked him for the letter, left the library and headed for the GPO. I bought a stamp, and envelope, and addressed the letter to the editor of the *Sydney Morning Herald*. Posted it and wondered why. Wasn't the fight over?

Then I noticed a table covered with dozens of phone books. I thought about it. Even if I did contact him, would he talk? Or would I like what I heard? Wasn't it better *not* knowing? You needn't, Eth. You shouldn't. You really shouldn't. But if I didn't, I'd never know. I'd be sitting in the lounge, lying in bed, for the next twenty years, wondering.

I searched the phone books, found Melbourne. Faske, Fauske ... B, C, D, E, F, G, G, H, I, J, J, K, L ... Wrote the number on the back of a receipt, turned to the phones and thought, No, not knowing's good too, then, there's always the chance. No! Walk, Eth! So I did, into the box, sat down, fished some change from the bottom of my purse and slipped a few pennies in the slot. Dialled. Rang. Rehearsed what I'd say. Hello, is it Louis, or Lewie?

'Hello? This is Ethel Malley, calling from Sydney.'

'Ethel?'

'*Malley.*'

There was a pause. 'Ethel Malley?'

'Yes. Ern Malley's sister.'

'Oh. Ethel.'

'Yes. I just rang to ... the thing is, I found Ern's ... *medical* records. Are you there?'

'Yes.'

'And I noticed, among some of his possessions – he died, you know?'

'I know.'

'I found a few newspaper articles, one of which—'

'I'd appreciate it if you didn't call again, Ethel.'

'Sorry?'

'I'm sorry about Ern. And everything. But it's all over, and I don't want to discuss it. I think I'm owed that. So, I'd appreciate it, okay?'

'I was just interested . . .'

Rude! He'd hung up. I sat, phone in hand, angry. Should I? Yes. I wasn't going to be treated like that. So I tried again, and he picked up the phone, replaced it, and I was left sitting, again. 'Bloody nerve.'

What to make of that? Didn't want to discuss what? Why? And what, exactly, did Mr Fauske think Ern owed him?

# 34

I know I shouldn't have, but there I was, the next day, back in
the shop. Me and a cup of tea, and my pile of foolscap. I wrote:
*Biography of my Brother: Ern Malley.* Underlined it a few times,
drew a box around it, little stars in the corner. Then, thought
about how it might begin. *The late Ern Malley is best known today as
the central figure in a literary scandal that overtook the country* . . . No.
Lead into it. *Ernest Lalor Malley was born in St Margaret's Hospital
on the banks of the cold, windy Mersey River on 14 March 1918. As the
war still raged* . . . No, too clinical, nothing to get the reader, no
connection (Max had taught me all of this). What about, *This is
the story of my brother. To look at, not a remarkable man, but as these
pages will show* (okay, a touch of the Copperfield) *he was a generous,
creative and, as it turns out, much misunderstood person.* Perfect. So,
I wrote it down, then sat admiring the hundred or so words.

'David, don't do that, love.'

He stopped removing the wheels from a truck and said,
'When's she coming back?'

'Soon.' I continued. *Ernest Lalor Malley was a war child, taking
his first breath (of Mersey air) as the Germans retreated across the
Rhine* . . . I'd have to check that, but it sounded right. A world in
chaos, and Ern clearing his lungs of Malley mucus.

'I'm bored,' David said.

'Only boring people get bored.'

He glared at me.

'I can't control what your grandmother does. It was an emergency.'

'What emergency?'

'Your father's sick.'

'What happened?'

'I don't know. Why don't you read a book?'

Emergency, perhaps? She'd got a phone call, an hour before, saying Michael had been taken to hospital again. She'd turned white, fought for breath and said, 'What's he done?'

I thought I heard, 'He's tried again.'

She'd gathered her things, asked if I'd watch David, and ran from the shop.

The boy said, 'He's probably hung himself again.'

'Nonsense! Where did you get that from?'

But he just looked at me like, You're a bit simple, aren't you?

I had enough problems of my own without buying into this. 'No one's done nothing,' I said. 'Probably an accident, but he's okay . . . I suppose.'

*Ern was always a secretive man. Never loud, or angry. As I plan to show, he was a delicate child, and felt things acutely.*

'I'm goin' down the shop,' David said.

'You are not.'

'I got money.' He showed me.

The till, I thought. Slippery little eel. Waiting until I was out back. 'Where did you get that?'

'It's mine.'

'Tell me the truth.'

'*It's mine*. I brought it from home.'

'Your dad's ill in hospital and all you can think about . . . No! Your gran wants me to watch you, and I will.'

He just sat, shitty, but I didn't care. Someone had to show some discipline, hanging or not.

*I'd like to show the darkness and light. The generosity, but difficulties. This will be a truthful book. It will challenge the commonly accepted view of Ern Malley . . .* I thought, Should I? I took the poem out of my purse, to check. Laid it flat and read: *Take the day by the horns of Artaxerxes, and hold them tightly, lest they get away, Wrestling the beast to the ground, there, to penetrate the mysteries of its mythology, psychology, physiology . . .* I could only recognise one word. Penetrate. So, how honest was I willing to be? Like Max had said, the truth is painful, but necessary. *Especially this, when the dusk, in the jungle, is still warm, and thoughts turn to buggery, The stars all aglow with engorged lips . . .* It seemed certain. There wasn't much else the words could mean. And 'L'? Who else? I checked the photo again. Thought, No. Tore the sheet from the pad and went to screw it up, but stopped. *And then, when we run out of script . . .*

Then David was gone. Out the door, down the street. I sprung up, ran after him, caught him outside the newsagent and squeezed his earlobe. 'What's the game, boyo?'

'There's the deli. They got Jaffas.'

I led him by the ear back to the shop and deposited him in the storeroom. Sat him down, placed a book in his hand and said, 'Try something like that again and I'll smack you so hard you won't sit down for a year.'

He pulled a face, but I didn't care. 'Got it?'

'My dad's sick, and you're beating up on me.'

'You want me to?'

That did it. I returned to my spot. Sat, picked up my pen and continued. *The story really begins with my parents' decision to move to Australia. I, of course, have little memory of this, except a dim recollection of Liverpool's grey skies, the sound of gulls, everywhere, fish and chips by the river. Perhaps that's why Ern always liked the sea, beachcombing with my father, Robert Malley, along the Northern Beaches . . .*

I checked on the boy. Turning pages, but not reading. Just looking back at me. 'You're mean.'

'You're a terror.'

'What if he's dead?'

'Then *I'll* take you home.'

This shut him up. 'I had foster parents,' I said, 'and they beat me and my brother every night.'

'If you touch me I'll go to the police.'

'Not if you're locked in the cellar. We were fed scraps of meat – only let out to go to the toilet.'

'You don't scare me.' Sneering.

'I don't mean to. I'm just saying it as it is. So, if he's dead, watch out.'

The bell rang and Mr Dalrymple came in. He placed a box on the counter and said, 'More for the shop, Ethel. Where's Peggy?'

'Had to leave, an emergency . . . *Michael.*'

'Oh.' He knew. He saw David and said, 'How you keeping, young fella?'

'*She* won't let me do nothing.'

'Don't say?'

'Dad's probably dead, but she doesn't care.'

'Little David here,' I said, 'tried to run away, and wouldn't come back when I called him.'

'That won't do,' Ron said. 'If an adult tells you something . . .'

But he just scowled and returned to pretending to read the book.

'Dad's not dead,' Ron said. 'Probably fell off a ladder or something.'

But David's eyes said, Unlikely.

Ron sat beside me, read the title and asked, *'Biography of my Brother?'*

'I thought, to set the record straight. You know, with all this controversy.'

'Yes.' He was clueless, but always encouraging. 'I'd buy a copy.'

'Would you?'

'For you, Ethel. A woman, by herself. In need of some financial support, I'd guess?'

God, not now, Ron. 'Not really.'

'Right . . . still, I'd buy a copy, if you finished it. Considering Ern was a Returned Man. We – you, me, all of us – have to stick together, don't we, Ethel?'

'Yes. He was proud of the uniform.'

'Listen, if you need help, I know a fella . . .'

'How's that?'

'Works for liaison. He'd be able to help with any details.'

I thought about it. 'About . . .?'

'You wanna make yer book factual, Ethel. Ern mighta left a few bits blank.'

'He did.'

'Well, he's just down the road ... coupla blocks, if you're interested?'

I studied the poem, saw the clippings in my purse, and decided. 'I suppose we could go ... now?'

'If you like.'

I gathered the boy, the keys, wrote a note (*back in an hour or so*) and we set off. Down Parramatta Road, a short-cut, a park I'd never seen, and Ron pointed to a four-storey building and said, 'That's it.'

Faceless, grey, covered with little windows that didn't open. David slowed and I said, 'Come on.'

'I wanna know what's happening with my dad.'

'You'll have to wait.'

'Where we going?'

'Stop sooking,' Ron said. 'Your gran wanted you watched, so we're watching you. Now, hurry up.'

'Make me.' He stopped. Ron returned to him, threw him across his shoulder and kept walking. The boy complained, but Ron didn't care. Just walked. The boy started kicking, but he kept going. Into the foyer, and said to the man at the desk, 'We're here to see Captain French.'

We were admitted, climbed three flights of stairs and arrived in an office – rows of civilians and soldiers behind typewriters, the sound of rollers and bells and chatter. Ron led; I followed. He stopped, placed David on the ground and said, 'Had enough?'

'*Yes.*'

'Another word, I promise ...'

Into a side office, and this man, Simon French, in a pressed uniform. Ron greeted him and asked after his father. The captain said, 'Ron saved my old man's life,' and Ron said, 'I didn't do anything of the sort. Just killed a coupla Huns who were in the way.'

'A couple?' French said, turning to David. 'Did you know your grandfather's a hero?'

'He's not my grandfather.'

'Seven of them, in a trench – shot three, bayoneted four, wasn't it?'

'Shot four,' Ron said, looking at David, who, at last, fell silent. 'Come on, young fella. Let's leave Ethel to find out about her brother.' And he took David, and went and sat outside the office (telling me, as he went, that anything I said to the captain would be hush-hush, private, you know ... *confidential*).

People have selective memories, don't they? Or little memory. Or none. Some, poor dears, lose it. Like Ron, who, when I asked him once, said he had no memory of that day. (Old-timers', I think they call it. Cruel. That was one of the first signs.) But I can recall well enough. I sat, spread the documents on the table and said, 'This is rather *delicate*, Captain.'

He just waited, arms crossed.

'My brother, Ern Malley, was a private ... Mr Dalrymple said you might be able to help me?' I noticed the door, half-open, and saw Ron sitting talking to the boy. Who was listening. Intently.

'Ern Malley?' the captain asked.

'Yes.'

'I know about Ern. Question is, Ethel, do you want to know?'

'Well, that's why I'm here.' I showed him the medical discharge, the clippings, the poem even. 'My brother was a poet. Quite a clever one, as it turns out. He recently died of Graves'

Disease.' I didn't feel I could go on, but made myself. 'I was thinking of writing his biography and thought, if I were to be truthful . . .?'

'Even if . . . I mean, you've probably worked out, there was a bit of drama. We tried to keep it from the press.'

'I'd like to know.' Moving the documents around the desk.

'Got it all here somewhere,' the captain said, standing, searching a filing cabinet, producing a folder. He sat, spread a few sheets of paper on the desk and said, 'Only because you're his sister.'

'I appreciate it.'

I saw David sitting, laughing, as Ron told him a story. He said, 'What happened then?' And Ron sat back and said, 'You seen how long them bayonets are?'

I waited, and French said, 'According to this, it started in early 1942.'

'What did?'

'Ern and . . .' – he leaned forward to read – 'Louis Fauske were on guard duty.' He stared at me, daring me to stop him. 'About two-fifteen, it says, their sergeant went to check on them and found them . . .'

'Oh.' I didn't know if it was too late to turn back. I heard more laughing from outside, and now David was sitting at Ron's feet, waiting for more of his story.

'Anyway, in the interests of decorum, the sergeant warned them off, said it should never happen again . . . sometimes, that's how these things are dealt with. Then time passes. But a week later . . .'

'Again?'

'This time it got reported. It couldn't be ignored. There

was a hearing, and they were told they'd be discharged and sent home.'

'*Medically* discharged?' I asked.

'Yes. Coulda been dishonourable, but how would these men continue living? They were given a form, like this one' – examining it – 'and told to go away.'

'Go away?'

'Lips sealed, Mrs Malley. But I thought I could trust you. And as Ron said, this is all between us.'

'Yes, you can.' As I descended, unable to get the thought from my mind – the palm leaves, the vines. 'Will anyone ever find out?'

'Couldn't say. As long as everyone stays mum. I guess, some-day, someone will say something. Or, this stuff, it's only sealed for fifty years. I assume you *won't* put it in Ern's biography?'

'No, Captain, I won't.'

'Because, you know, it was a favour to Ron. If it ever comes out, I didn't show you.'

'Of course. Fifty years, you reckon?'

'Well, forty-eight now, and counting.'

I thanked Captain French. He asked if I was okay, and I said better out than in, and he grinned again and said, 'That seems to be the consensus.'

We walked back to the shop, David hanging off Ron's every word. Luckily, as I didn't feel much like talking. Ern, crumbling, like one of his plaster statues left out in the rain. But, did they really do anything so wrong? God put the damn thing there, and didn't provide an on-off switch.

Ron took David into the deli and bought him a pack of Jaffas, and when we returned to the shop Peggy was inside, sorting Ron's latest donation.

'All good?' I asked.

She just said, 'He's getting better each time, Eth.'

# 35

*Dear Editor*

*In 1921 a 'new' Renoir was discovered in a French attic. Apparently painted in 1893, stored, and forgotten, 'Sunset over the Loire' was, according to the artist's wife, one of Renoir's lost masterpieces. Problem being, it was painted by Eduard Belmiro, an Italian faker with a taste for Impressionism. The work fetched £72,000 at auction in London before an astute dealer questioned its provenance. There followed a prolonged court case in which the faker, now under arrest for a series of questionable works, admitted (with a certain amount of pride) his handiwork, although refusing to return any of the money which, he claimed, he'd already spent. He was sentenced to seven years' gaol.*

*Why, sir, do I mention this? Lately, it seems, fakery has been back in fashion. The soldier-poets McAuley and Stewart claim to have 'created' Ern Malley (in the very best Belmiro tradition). Malley was, they have claimed, their attempt to comment on the state of modern poetry by 'throwing together' a yarn about an unfortunate poet who scribbled these poems in his final days. But Ern was no Prometheus. He was a poet, and a very good one, as seen from my point-of-view. Thirty-seven years as a teacher of English literature and poetry has given me some insight into authenticity and, I would like your readers to know, Ern was the 'real thing'.*

*So now I believe it is time for McAuley and Stewart to do what Belmiro did – lay down their weapons, write their mea culpa and set history straight. Every word of the* Ecliptic *is Malley. I can hear Ern's voice, recognise the references to his childhood with Ethel, see the streets of Croydon in his versifying. It's all well and good to have a bit of fun, but in the end, history demands truth. And, I'm sure you'll agree, the law does too.*

*Yours,*
*Roy McDonald*
*Burwood*

I was pleasantly surprised, as I'd forgotten Roy's letter. I tore it from the paper and placed it on the table. Re-read it, among the crumbs and dried gravy, and thought, There you go, McAuley, your turn. Although, what if they had something better? What if they ... *knew?* Still, someone needed the last word. I had Ern, they had a typewriter; I had the poems, the pictures and documents, the memories, they had a book about DDT. Maybe it'd take years, but I had time. Grit – plenty of that. I knew I'd get them. I'd wait by the school gate, confront them, drag them into the mud and make them say sorry. Just as I'd done for my brother a dozen – no, a hundred – times.

*Chapter 1 (continued): After the death of our mother, our father kept struggling. These were some tough years. We became used to men knocking on the front door, asking if we had some work. Sometimes, Dad would let them mow the lawn, or fix some furniture he could fix himself. Then, he'd allow them to sleep on our back lawn. Me and Ern would look after them, taking them tea, rugs. Sometimes Dad would let them make a fire, and we'd all sit around, with Mr Smyth (over the back) complaining the smoke was getting on his laundry. Ern would yarn for hours, me, listening.*

Ern, leave them alone, they don't wanna talk to you.

Where do you go the toilet?

More laughter. Wherever we can.

Where's your wife and kids?

They'd fall silent, and eventually, one of them: My missus is staying with her mum, in Ballarat. Explaining how, since there was no work, they'd lost their house, car, the lot.

And Ern, That must stink.

Yeah, it does, Ern. Stinks. But we're gonna paint your gutters tomorrow, so that'll keep us busy.

I can't remember them needing doing, or Dad having the money to pay them. We had old bread, and jam and dripping, but as Dad explained, we had a roof over our head, which was more than they did. Anyway, how could you turn people away? What would that make you? You'd still have to wake up in the morning and look in the mirror, and like what you see.

All the next day, these men up a ladder, Ern taking them barley water (it was hot, and the roof was tin). Dad wants to know if you want a beer.

Later, son. Tell him there's a few spots yet.

Sometimes we had other people at the door. Mormons. There was a house full of them nearby. Dad said we should call the pest exterminator. Ern would say, What's a Mormon? I'd say, No moron, like you.

Two of them at the door. We come on behalf of the Prophet. Who?

Listen: 'Awake, my sons; put on the armour of righteousness.'

And Dad: You lot are allowed to have a coupla wives?

As Ern snuck from the room, out the back door, around the side, grabbed one of their bikes and rode off.

Says Mormon: No, sir, that's a myth. Most people, like my father, have one wife.

Most?

Ern, riding up and down the street, ringing his bell. Dad: Ern, get back here now!

Mormon One running after his bike, Ern heading up Dalmar Street: Awake, my sons!

A knock. 'Hold on!' I covered my writing. 'Coming!'

I opened the door to see Peg: standing, waiting. Surprising, really, because she never came to see me. I let her in, put on the kettle and said, 'How you keepin'?'

'Not me that's the problem.'

'Go on.'

And she began. The previous night he'd sealed off a room with wet towels, turned on the gas, put his head in the oven. Then, fallen asleep. But a neighbour, walking past, had smelt it and gone in.

'I don't understand, Eth. We brought him up good.'

'That's all you can do,' I said, holding her hand, stroking it.

A cup of tea, some long, awkward pauses, then I said, 'David was well-behaved.'

'Really? He can be a terror.'

I didn't feel I was in the room. I could smell smoke, and hear the men on the back lawn, and Ern, laughing. I could smell bacon, because Dad had given them some, and I could see the first light of day. I could hear birds; I could sense the whole world beginning, and me, a part of it (whereas now, I just observed it, wrote about it, had an opinion on it). I felt that life was unsatisfactory, but could be satisfactory, if pursued differently. Enough light, as I lay in bed, to see the back of my hands. The books on the shelf (though not light enough to read the titles).

Then, Peggy was crying. I covered both her hands, but that didn't work, so I went around to her, rubbed her shoulders and said, 'Come on now, it'll all work it out.'

'It's cosa me, Eth.'

'No, it's not.'

I heard a sprinkler. No. Some sort of bird, and the men were laughing, and Ern was saying, You could make a bedroom in our shed, I reckon, but Dad was saying, No, Ern, they gotta get on. The first car of the day on Dalmar Street, and smoke, still, although it might've been a burn-off in the mountains. The first day of the world. Like something the Mormons had explained, when their God-of-many-wives made us. And crickets, I could still hear them.

'I wish he'd just get it over with,' Peg said. 'I want him to be happy, but he won't be. He won't change.'

'People don't.'

'Shelley's tried everything. Now they reckon they wanna zap him.'

'That sounds nasty.'

'Apparently it works.'

Ern, telling the swaggies they were welcome to stay as long as they wanted. And what did they do? Tie you down, use leather straps? How many volts? Was a thousand enough? Would that stop you wanting to kill yourself?

Peggy noticed my scribbles. She moved the paper, read them. 'This about Ern?'

'I'm writing about him.'

'Right.' Wondering why, probably.

'A biography. Cos it's hard to get your head around people, isn't it, Peg?'

'How's that?'

I wondered whether I should tell her. At that moment, that morning, lying in bed, life seemed so simple. People were all wired into each other; they understood and loved each other (even if they didn't really know each other); they were like the hundred moving parts of an Indian (and I can still see Dad, showing his bike to these men); they were like a driftwood sculpture, made from the leftover bits of other lives. I thought about telling Peg everything: about Louis, and Ern, and their *inclinations*. Imagined how good it would feel. The relief of sharing.

'I made a discovery, Peg.'

'Oh?'

'Ern was involved in . . . he was discharged from the army.'

'So you said.'

'Medically.'

'His condition?'

'As it turns out, *another* condition.'

'Right.'

'He met a fella, Peg.'

It seemed strange that her son was on the verge of extinction, but this (growing) realisation was such a shock. I could see it in her eyes, glowing; her mouth gaping like the little clown mouths in the booths at the Royal Show.

'A fella?'

'I think his name was Louis.'

'Ern was a poof?'

'I guess so.'

'Right.' Taking it in. 'Wouldn'ta thought, eh?'

'No.'

'Seemed such a, you know . . .?' She flexed a bit of muscle.

'Ern was many things,' I said. 'You think you know a person, Peg.'

She finished her tea, then said, 'Do you know what happened?'

I provided an abridged version. 'They were unclear with the details, but maybe that's for the best.'

'Well, Nan, what was her name, Alcott? Her husband, what I mean is, one day he was there, with her and the kids. The next he's off living with some fella half his age.'

Here was the problem. That the sun came up, and the day became clear, easily understood, cut into pieces and examined, weighed, described in memos. Nothing was left of the night, and the swaggies had packed up and gone, leaving the lawn like no one had ever camped there (apart from the smoking fire). And Ern was in bed asleep and probably wouldn't remember a thing of what happened.

'I wasn't gonna say anything,' Peg said, 'but David told me he heard . . .'

'. . . what?'

'He says to me, Eh, Nan, did you know Mrs Malley's brother was a poofter?'

She smiled, and I laughed, so she guessed it was okay, and joined in.

'Eh, Nan, she said he was in trouble because he'd gone into the jungle to . . . what d'you reckon, Nan?'

'What did you tell him?' Laughing so much I had to put down my tea.

'I said they were probably washing the dishes.'

'Washing the dishes! Ern never washed the dishes.'

'I wouldn't be so sure!'

As we cackled, and Ern, sitting listening, said to me, What, you're gonna tell the whole neighbourhood?

Peg's okay.

'So, he was sent home?' Peg asked.

'Yes.'

She seemed consoled by this fact. That men were unpredictable, unstable. 'I never understood all that. I mean if you think about it, people are designed to . . .' She lifted a single eyebrow.

'God, Peg, don't talk about it.'

'I guess it was the jungle. And the stress . . . Japs taking pot shots at you all day.'

'Don't talk about pot shots.' And we started again, unsettling the table and the tea dregs, until she spilled hers and it wet my writing, but I didn't care.

The phone rang. Unusual, this time of day. Any time, really. I often wondered why I bothered with it. It only brought bad news. But I answered it, and heard Max: 'That you, Eth?'

'Max?'

'How are you?'

'I'm good.'

There was a rustle of papers, a clunk of the phone, and Mary's voice, perhaps, then he said, 'I just thought I'd tell you, I'm in a bit of trouble.'

'How's that?'

'Just had a copper at the door, with a summons.'

'No?'

'You'll never believe it ... I didn't know whether to laugh or cry.'

'What, Max?'

'Ern's poems – some fella reckons they're obscene.'

'Obscene?' My heart dropped, the sun rose, it got warmer all of a sudden. I thought of Ern, the sounds that had given him away. *Obscene?*

'This detective, he reckons I had no place publishing them. Called them smut.'

'Smut? Ern?'

'I'm gonna fight it, of course, but I thought I'd let you know.'

'How are they, I mean, what bits ... are they *that* bad? A summons?'

'Well, it is Adelaide, Eth. I warned you.'

'Obscene? I wouldn'ta thought.' I tried to think of what bits might've been obscene. 'You can tell me, when I arrive,' I said.

I arranged for him to pick me up in two days, then returned to Peggy, sitting, reading about Ern. 'You'll never believe it.'

'What?'

'They're gonna take Max to court.'

'What?'

'They reckon the poems are filthy.'

This time, nothing so amusing. She said, 'You got a copy I can borrow?'

# 36

Adelaide had become my second (maybe first) home. The old girls at the train station, waiting, sipping tea, the man in blue, giving directions; the porters, standing in small groups, smoking – so hard to see how anything got done. But it did, somehow. That was Adelaide, everyone's son or cousin given a job because they were someone's son or cousin. Very cosy. Nothing too challenging; no need for progress (including culture, and that was the problem). Déjà vu. Max waiting out front of the station in his Austin. Same vest, same shirt, same cheap cologne. Same cigarette held the same way, same expression, same peck on the cheek, as he put my case in the boot, got in beside me and exited the No Parking spot.

'How you been, Eth?' As the lights turned from orange to red, but he went through anyway.

'Well. What about you?'

'Fit as a fiddle.' Speeding up along North Terrace.

The days, weeks, months, since I'd first arrived had changed nothing. Winter had come and gone, the plane trees had lost their leaves, stood naked in the little bit of rain the place could muster. Like the mad aunts, the three or four prostitutes (I guessed, they were everywhere, weren't they?), kids playing in the sprinklers.

'Papers still going on about Ern,' he said.

'Still?'

'Elliott's had a few letters to the editor. I've replied, but they haven't printed them.'

'Carpenter?'

'No doubt.' Cutting in front of someone who wouldn't hurry up, the inevitable toot, but he just gave the finger and called out the window, 'If you'd get out of my blind-spot!'

It was good to be back with Max. In Sydney, I'd felt alone. With people I'd known for decades, but *alone*. But Max. Max had saved me from myself. He was good-looking, and hardly anything annoyed him. Impervious to the summer rain. His attitude that he was right, the world was wrong, and the sooner others came around to *his* way of seeing things ... He shot in front of a bus, slowed, turned without indicating and said, 'Dramas all around.'

'Tell me.'

We waited at the lights. 'I was getting the next edition ready, and cramming for my final exams ... you always know it's time.'

'Why's that?'

'The jacarandas bloom, the hayfever returns.' He set off. 'Anyway, in come these fellas ...' He reached in his pocket, found a clipping and presented it to me.

*The News, Tuesday 5 September 1944. Indecent Writings Alleged in 'Angry Penguins'.* 'Indecent? What's so indecent?'

'Ask Ern.'

'The nerve ... *Maxwell Henley Harris, 23, university undergraduate, was charged in the Adelaide Police Court today with having published indecent advertisements in the publication* Angry Penguins.' I looked at him, and him at me, avoiding the road, as usual. I guess he knew the tight corners and short turns well enough. 'You mean they actually charged you?'

'Yep. I'm sitting there declining verbs when one of them, tall bastard, walks in, sniffs the air (I guess he thought I was smoking something), looks out the window and says to me, You Harris?'

'*Rude.*'

'Yes, I reply. Can I help you?'

'We'd like to have a talk with you. And there's me thinking, shit, what have I done? Didn't occur to me it was something I'd published. I mean, it's not the *Herald*, is it, Eth? Anyway, he says, Are you the editor of a magazine called *Angry Penguins*? I'm thinking, Okay, it's not a girl but . . .' He slowed, waited for roadworks, became impatient and punched the steering wheel a few times.

'What did you say?'

'I said, Not exactly, and I explained how there was a committee – me, John, Sunday and Sid. I told him how they were in Melbourne, and I just did the editing, and he said (all pompous, like he owned the place, silly little man – his name was Detective Apeldoorn), Are you responsible for the publication of the magazine?'

We moved a few inches. Max called to a group of workers standing about: 'What's the point of all this?'

No one replied. He said, 'Take it easy fellas,' and one of them gave him the finger.

'Dickhead!'

'Max!'

'So I told him: people send in their work, we decide, I edit it, set it in type, we publish it – see, that's the bit he was interested in – who published it.'

I could tell Max was worried. The lines on his face, the perspiration, the way he clenched his jaw – all new to me. Some old Max I'd never seen. Parading, showering, trying on his tights as his Dad stormed in, and he stood, ashamed.

'Then he says, In the Autumn number of *Angry Penguins* there was a section *you* were responsible for publishing. Work by one (and he checked) *Ern Malley*?'

'*Ern*?'

'I told him, *we*, the committee, had agreed on a special issue in honour of the late Ern Malley, and I told him about you, the submission, but he didn't seem interested. He just said, So *you're* responsible for the production and distribution of this magazine? I said, *We* are, the committee, but he didn't listen.'

We moved off. Along Hackney Road, but the car spluttered, and he pulled over. Then it stopped, and he tried to restart it, but it wouldn't obey. He kicked the floor, punched the dashboard and said, 'If one more thing happens today, Eth, I swear, I'm going to kill someone.'

Yes, a very different Max – red in the face, blood pumping through the little veins on his forehead, spit flying from his mouth – like a cornered snake, ready to strike.

He tried to start it again. Nothing. 'It had to happen eventually.'

'What?'

'The old girl's let me down. Everyone's let me down.'

'I haven't.'

'No.' He managed a smile, and I felt good.

'Come on then.' We got out, he took my case from the boot, closed it, and started walking along Hackney Road. 'You coming?'

312

'We just gonna leave it?'

'It's not registered. Someone can have it.'

'You're gonna . . .?' I caught up with him, tried to take my case, but he wouldn't let me. He just said, 'About then I told him I didn't think I should be talking to him without a lawyer.' He struggled. I said, 'Should we try and restart it?' and he said, 'Not worth the effort, Eth.' Continuing, tripping on branches, walking past a tree with a limb that looked indecent. 'He said, You can please yourself about that, Mr Harris. All officious, like I'd murdered someone. But I didn't even know why I was in trouble. I mean, Ern? He just wrote a few poems. Mostly harmless. Not . . . indecent (I'm thinking).'

He was struggling. I couldn't bear it. I took the case from him, and he didn't argue.

'I asked him, Is this on or off the record? Then he got all serious and said, We've been instructed to make inquiries in connection with provisions of the Police Act with respect to (*with respect*, what an idiot) an immoral or indecent publication.'

I couldn't keep going. Sat, under a pine tree, and wiped the sweat from my face. Max sat beside me, looked back at his car and said, 'I suppose I oughtna leave it there?'

'It might be something minor.'

'Yes.' Although he was caught up in other thoughts. 'I don't mind telling you, Eth, I was pissing my pants. I couldn't work it out. I thought Elliott might've said something. Wouldn't put it past him, although I'm the one should've gone to the police.'

'Exactly! So, they took you . . .?'

'In a police car, like a common criminal.'

'*Max*. I feel like it's *my* fault.'

'Rubbish. By this point I was angry. Very angry, Eth. Ready

to fight back. So they took me in, and there was this room, and out comes a magistrate and looks at me like I'd just raped someone, and says, Harris, is it?'

'Rotten bastard.'

'I say, Yes, Max Harris (wasn't about to call him Your Honour). Then he says, You've violated Section 108 of the Police Act. I say, What is this, Russia? *Silence!* And I reply, I refuse to say anything till I've seen a lawyer, and what's more, until I know what I'm meant to have done wrong. Anyway, that shut him up.'

The traffic went past, slowly. I could smell the oil from the pines.

'Anyway,' Max said, 'he told me there'd been complaints from different people and the Crown Solicitor had decided the poems weren't decent. I said that's absurd and he said, You're quite disrespectful, aren't you, and I said, Only when it's warranted, *sir*.'

I didn't get it, any of it. I was no artistic expert, but I could tell: people were entitled to write what they want, and read it, and if you couldn't, well, then it'd be like Hitler making everyone read *his* book. It wasn't like there was anything shameful. Ern didn't have it in him. I'd read those poems a hundred times, and hadn't noticed anything indecent.

'So, nothing else from our poets?' Max asked, calming.

'No, although Mr McDonald wrote a nice piece in Ern's defence.'

'I don't think that's the end of it.'

'I hope not. Ern wouldn't want us to give up, Max, would he?'

'No.'

'After what he went through with the army.' I realised. Stopped.

'What's that?'

'Nothing.'

'Did you find something out?'

'I just meant, those two using his name for that . . . joke.'

Max reclaimed his article and kept reading. '*Detective Apeldoorn said he interviewed Harris on August 1 this year in company with plainclothes constable Cameron Smith. Harris said he did not know what the author of the poem "Sweet William" intended to mean.*' He looked up. 'Can you help me, Eth?'

I thought about it. Knew it – knew them all. '*Down the staircase of flesh, To where in a shuddering embrace . . .*' I said. 'But that's not obscene.'

He continued. '*One moment of daylight let me have, Like a white arm thrust out of the dark . . .*'

'And the arm is . . .?'

'A dick.'

'Surely not?'

'If you want to see it that way. I said to Apeldoorn, what bits exactly do you object to, but he didn't know. He just seemed glad he was able to stop all this *poetry*. God damn it, those young people with their penises and abortions.'

'And breasts and clitorises!'

'And fucking, Eth, fucking. People putting their arms where they're not welcome. Their Sweet Williams, if you know what I mean?'

'I know exactly, Max. Everyone does. These so-called *creative* types, homosexuals, lesbians, child molesters.' I leaned towards him, smiling, laughing, taking his hand. I said, 'Maybe Ern *did* mean it that way?'

'We can only hope.'

315

We walked back to the car, determined to start again.

'But worse,' Max said.

'Surely not?'

'*Though I have your silken eyes to kiss, And maiden knees, Part of me remains, wench, Boult-upright, The rest of me drops off into the night.*'

'Pity,' I said.

'Listen, none of this dirty talk, or Apeldoorn will be after you too.'

As we went, Max said, 'There was a time when the coppers came to our house, in the Mount.'

'Really?'

'I was terrified.'

'What did you do?'

'I'll tell you, one day.'

We got in, and of course it started first go, and I said, 'Just cos she's running rough, Max, doesn't mean you should give up on her.'

# 37

It wasn't a shower you'd trust, but I guessed you'd emerge cleaner than when you went in. Possibly. The mould between the tiles, setting seed heads, the spores coalescing around my feet; a sliver of soap, but I'd learnt from last time, and brought my own. Standing, washing away the night, the Max-smelling sheets (he didn't bother changing them any more), the catty rugs and lounge suite, although there was no cat – perhaps humans smelt this way, given long enough.

I cleaned the Ethel bits. My bosoms, like a dromedary in my twenty-ninth year. My belly, bulging with tea and cake, the recipes I was still to decipher. And lower, down, into what might've belonged to an old woman, although I wasn't. Secret, from all except Ern, who'd come into to the bathroom when I was twelve, and say, Where'd you put my sherbet?

Get out! Covering myself, although I guess he didn't see me as a girl – just his sister, Eth, with new bits growing here and there. Piss off!

Dad, she won't tell me.

He arrived, but stood outside the door (luckily), as Ern continued. I gave it to you.

Covering my bits. Get the hell out! I wouldn't come in on you.

Then Max came in. *Jesus*. It was steamy, but it was meant to be private. Difficult to see much, but enough. He said, 'You don't mind, do you?'

'No.' Turning away.

'Quick shave . . . promise I won't look.'

I didn't reply. What could you say? I trust you. You can look if you want (because, I thought, wouldn't it be funny, if he slid back the door?).

He lathered up and started working on his whiskers. 'This Apeldoorn character . . .'

'Yes?' Trying to sound nonchalant, like it happened every day.

'After I came out of court, he says, You, Harris, follow me.'

'You didn't go with him?'

'Shouldn't have, but you know how it is with authority, you feel intimidated.'

'Wouldn't have thought *you'd* be intimidated?'

'Well, anyway, I follow him down these stairs . . .'

At some point I'd have to turn around. Risk it, turn off the water, step out, towel myself. I imagined this happening. Him dropping his pants, boult-upright, me saying, It's all very free and easy these days, isn't it, Max? In fact, as this thought overtook me, I could feel changes in my body. The nether regions. Like someone had started a lawnmower, and was about to tackle a quarter acre of Santa Ana. That's how I felt. Ready to be mowed.

'Anyway,' he said, 'he leads me to the cells and opens one and says, Step in, and I joke, You're not gonna lock the door, are you, Detective? He says, Oh, no, Mr Harris, just a quiet spot, so you and me can have a few words.'

I could see he'd finished one side. And if I could see that, what could he see? Turning away, still, gathering courage. Before moving, inch by inch, into his line of sight.

'Then he says, Just a quick word to the wise, Maxie ... you know, *Maxie* ... he was tall, seven foot, standing over me, real close, and he says, In this town, fella, we have certain standards. And I say, What are they? And he looks at me like, Wanna be a smart-arse, eh? And he says, We believe in decency. I say, So do I. We don't like smut ... like you think yer better than us. I've never said that. You don't need to say it. It's all in your little *penguin* business – abortions, erections – think that's funny, do you? I didn't write it. But you published it, which is worse. This Malley, he's dead, but you, you take his stuff and next thing it's in libraries and bookshops and people, *decent* people are in there with their kids, and they pick this stuff up ... I said, This *stuff*? He says, Yeah, stuff. I wouldn't call it real poetry. I've read the *Rime of the Ancient Mariner*, that's a good one. But all this ... I tell you, Eth, he was an inch from my face, like he just wanted to clobber me.'

'You should've walked out.'

'No, I was enjoying it too much. I said, All of this so-called filth, it's what you've seen in the work, Detective? And you're able to recognise it? He was about to explode. I mean, Detective, abortions, perverts, I guess you've seen plenty of those? And then, Ethel, he says, I'm looking at one now.'

Max howled with laughter. He only had his mo to go, and brandished his shaver like a sword. 'You reckon I'm a pervert, Detective? Why else would you have published this rot? Because it's modern poetry – people are reading it all over the world. It's the latest thing. Not here it's not.'

He kept shaving and I realised he wasn't interested in what I was showing him.

'So I said, It looks like we get to meet in court, Detective, and I'm looking forward to it. So am I. And that was that, Eth.'

He finished, wiped his face, turned to me and saw everything. Didn't seem so surprised. 'You got it all on show there, Eth.'

I thought, if it's going to happen, now's the time. The door, the embrace, the stiffening (I'm wondering, will this ever be published, and will there be another Apeldoorn coming after me?). But no, he just said, 'Funny, eh? Few months ago we barely knew each other, now we share a shower, sort of, eh?'

Was he about to do it? I felt like saying, Come on, Max, let's have a crack, but realised that might make me a tramp. He just dried his face and said, 'I had him worried, Eth. You could tell I was getting under his skin. He didn't like smart-arses and, I must admit, I can be one, can't I?'

'In a nice way.'

'I left him before he had a stroke, but like I said, I'm looking forward to the next chapter.'

And with this, he walked out.

I dried off and sat on my bed. Maybe he didn't feel the same way. Despite having made things clear to him, there wasn't even a small sign, a stray glance, a kind word, a rough hint at other things. Nothing. I went out and he was sitting at the table, reading my notes. 'You don't mind, do you?'

I'd told him about the biography, and how it was going to be comprehensive, warts and all, the real Ern. He read a small section and said, 'This is intriguing.'

'What's that?'

'This Esso Reliability Trial. Your dad was really gypped?'

'He was.'

'*After having changed the signs* . . . they found that out?'

'They did.'

'Cruel.'

I sat, and started on the remains of my orange juice. 'There was a group of them, and they'd decided to split the earnings. So they got ahead of him, moved the signs, told him the wrong directions. He got lost, and died. It was manslaughter, but that never came out.'

'Why?'

'No proof. My word against theirs. This other fella, I think I put it in there' – and I checked the scribble – 'his name was Moore, and he saw all this, and wrote me a letter, explaining, but he refused to testify.'

Max seemed confused. '*Moore*? Like the butcher?'

'Yes . . . no, not him.'

'Right . . . maybe you should've gone to the police?'

'We've seen how much good that does, haven't we, Max? Anyway, they let him go, they knew he was lost, but they just kept going, and when he disappeared' – and I read – '*the rest of the men said they didn't feel up to joining the search and returned to the hotel where they ate a meal, drank, into the night, and then went to bed, to sleep off their adventures and count their winnings.*'

'We couldn't publish that.'

'Why not? It's true.'

'They'd sue us, Eth.'

'How? *They* know it's true, *I* do, *we* do. What's the problem with that?'

He still wasn't sure about something. 'In the meantime, we, I mean me, *I* have to deal with Apeldoorn.'

'I wouldn't worry, Max. I'm here to support you. We'll be vindicated, demand an apology, maybe even seek compensation.'

He didn't seem convinced.

'People can't be allowed to tell lies. These so-called poets, we've got them on the run, but I'm not finished with them. By the time I'm through they'll regret their little joke.'

He read some more, said, 'So this biography, it's *all* like this?'

'Is that a problem?'

'Just, if we can't prove these fellas – I mean, that's a big claim, Eth. That they killed him?'

'I don't care. I've spent enough of my life keeping quiet. It's time things were out in the open.'

I was wearing a nightie, and realised it was open at the top, revealing everything. Max noticed, and maybe, this time, it crossed his mind. I waited, but he didn't act. Maybe we were at cross purposes? I didn't attempt to fix the buttons. Just sat, all out. What'll be will be, I thought. But instead of standing, kissing me, sliding his hand down my nightie, he said, 'We can't fix the whole world.'

'Enough of it.'

'I mean, in a way, I'm getting a bit tired of . . . you know.'

'You mustn't.' I patted his hand, squeezed it, but it didn't do any good. 'We've still got a long way to go.'

'The letters to the papers, it's still on the wireless, and I get calls from overseas, people wanting to write articles about it, and I say, No, that's all done and dusted, but they say, What about this trial, and I say, I don't want to talk about it.'

'I didn't know you felt this way, Max.'

'It just goes on and on, and nothing changes.'

We just sat. Him reading, me waiting. I did up my nightie –

there was no point. Anyway, did I really want this man? 'So what are you saying?'

'I'm not saying anything. I want to keep going, sort out all this *indecency* business. There's only one thing indecent about this place, Eth.'

'What's that?'

'The people running it . . . and living in it.'

'All of them?'

'Most of them. They wouldn't have started this action unless they thought they'd win. Unless they *really* wanted to. But you gotta have faith, don't you, Eth?'

'Exactly.'

'In the cause?'

'Too true.' Although I wondered what the cause was.

Then he stopped, taken by a thought. 'Guess what I did?'

'What?'

'Got engaged.'

'Engaged to . . .?'

'Who do you reckon? Me and Von. We're gonna tie the knot.'

'Oh.' Equal parts shocked and disappointed. Von? Really? 'That's marvellous, Max. Congratulations!'

'Thanks, Eth.'

I stood, went over to him, hugged him, felt the old chaff bags rubbing on his shoulder, returned to my seat. 'You and Von are a perfect pair. Wonderful. How . . . I mean, when did this happen?'

He explained: a drive the previous week, a stop in Strathalbyn, a coffee outside the pub, the birds, the smell of freshly harvested oats, all so perfect. And it had just popped out. 'I said it before

I knew what I was saying. And she's accepted . . . I mean, it was all so quick.'

He was expecting joy, I guess, but I didn't feel it. Still, I was good at pretending. Her, and him. Him, and her. Together. Forever. And didn't I feel stupid? Me, with my fantasies? 'I've often thought, Max and Von, they'd be happy together. But one thing . . .'

'What's that, Eth?'

'I always thought, you, Max, were more independent.'

'I am.'

'I mean, someone who wouldn't go in for all that *traditional* stuff.'

'Well, just goes to show, Eth. Anyway, traditional? I'm getting married, not joining the priesthood. Lots of people get married. It's not that unusual.'

'No. Only . . . it's a bit old-fashioned.'

'Like me?'

'Yes. And me.'

'You? You're not old-fashioned. You're a fury, Eth. You're a tornado, a whirlwind. No one could pin you down.'

'No, I guess not.'

# 38

That afternoon, the Botanic Gardens, a slightly prissy café with ducks, and rats on the tables. Big bastards with muscly legs and yellow teeth, nibbling the remains of a rock bun. I shooshed the ducks, took in the view, and tried to focus on the positives. No Elliott, no Carpenter, no Stewart or McAuley, and no Mary Martin, with all her talk about bookshops. Just a row of bamboo, their leaves making music. Big oaks and elms, new buds and baby leaves straining the spring sun. This almost-perfect world, if it weren't for Von, holding Max by the arm, walking him across the grass into some sort of domestic nightmare I knew he'd come to regret.

Still, what could you do? They whispered, laughed, she kissed him on the cheek. Come on, Max, walk away ... *walk away*. Yes, he was a Renaissance man, with his fingers in a dozen tasty pies, but love, and love-making, and regretting, was the end of independence. He didn't get it. I'd told him, but he didn't get it.

Come on, Eth, positives! Pigeons parading the concourse in front of the pond, their little heads bobbing (like hers), beaks pecking (like hers), squabbling for food (like her). Deep breath. But nothing helped. She said something to him, and he seemed to be telling her off. She did it again, laughed, but this time he laughed.

I opened the paper, avoided the articles about footballers, and how Cawley had injured his hamstring, and something else about the perfect meringue. Oh, and the war did get a mention – Russian troops ploughing across Poland, bleary eyes and knives clutched, ready. As was mine. But I put it down, as she looked again.

And then, Letters to the Editor, and a name caught my eye: *Dear Editor, I, and my friend McAuley, have sent a copy of this letter to every newspaper in Australia. It is a response to a letter to us, the 'Ern Malley' poets, from Mr Roy McDonald, an English teacher, of Sydney. In which he claims we were not the authors of the poems titled* The Darkening Ecliptic . . .

I felt my hand shaking. Fury. Every paper in the country? But especially *The News*, no doubt. Especially for me and Max and the ghost of Ern Malley.

*How Mr McDonald claims to know Ern in any detail confuses us. Yes, he was real, but imagined. We made him. So how could Mr McDonald know him? Why, then, the claim in his letter that certain words, phrases, and events from the poet's life rung true?*

I put down the knife. Even here, these bastards had found me.

*Mr McAuley and I consider this matter closed. We wrote the poems in jest, but this affair has taken on a life of its own, and in a sense, consumed ours. The public ridicule, the idea that we are no more than the 'Ern Malley' poets, when we both have our own 'careers' as poets (but who knows our work?). No more correspondence, Mrs Malley, Mr Harris, or any of your supporters. No more imagined 'Ernites', rallied for the cause. We hope you continue believing in your delusion, and quite frankly, are satisfied that you have the last word.*

'Max, you gotta read this!'

Then, in a half-trot, he and Von joined me. They sat, and Max read. 'See, we win!'

'I wouldn't say that.'

'. . . *are satisfied that you have the last word.*'

'You don't think they will be?'

'That's what they say.' Reading, re-reading, with apparent satisfaction. 'Anyway, it all helps sales.' Which, he'd told me, had gone from strength to strength. A third reprinting, orders still coming in.

Von extended her hand across the table, showed me her ring and said, 'Do you like it?'

'Well ... I'm not sure. I think all that sort of thing is ... gaudy.'

'You do?'

'I mean, there are better things to spend your money on (no offence, Max). With a war on.'

'Doesn't mean people are going to stop getting married.'

'No ... and I've meant to say congratulations. Have I said that yet?'

'No, you haven't.'

'Well, congratulations. I hope it all works out.'

Her head tilted. 'You hope?'

'Yes. Kiddies, all that.'

Max almost laughed. 'Kids?' His surprise, his indignation moving between me and Von. She said, 'Three, I reckon.' He said, 'None.'

'Three.'

'One, eventually.'

'Two – the first within eighteen months of—'

'It's funny,' Max said, 'they reckon they've had enough, but why do they keep replying?'

'They want the last word.'

Von kept admiring the ring. I studied her face, then said, 'Children are a lot of bother.'

'You've had one?'

I thought about it. Decided. 'No.'

'Well.'

'Max will want time for his work, won't you, Max?'

'Yes.'

'And if there's one contraceptive to imagination, it's changing nappies.'

'He'll get by, won't you, Max?'

'Did you see the rest?' Max asked, showing me the paper. 'Up the top, the next column?' And he read. '*Only time will tell whether Ern Malley is real. Whether we or Mrs Malley have the correct version. While we have heard certain rumours, we never bought into them* . . . What on earth does that mean, Eth?'

Fury. I clutched my knife, ready to throw it at a pigeon. 'I have no idea what it means.'

'Was there something going around the barracks?'

'What do you mean?'

'. . . *certain rumours* . . . you must have some idea?'

'No.'

'It seems strange they'd say it. I mean, you could question it.'

I scanned the sky. Blue, damn it! The pond, full of scum, dissolved piss and shit and rotten vegetation. How could those dirty animals swim (or sleep) in it? 'Maybe he was gay?' I said.

Max sat back. 'You think?'

'No, I don't, Max! I'm saying, they're getting dirty.' I threw the paper away, ducks scattering, the pages blowing across the asphalt. 'If you choose to believe their filth?'

'I didn't say that, Eth.'

Don't call me, Eth, I wanted to say. Only my brother got to do that. Someone who'd stuck by me, as I, by him. Through thick and thin. Never doubting each other, whatever was said or done. Trust. Unlike whatever that rotten ring signified.

'Believe what filth, Eth?'

'Ethel, thank you.' My heart was racing. I had to let it settle. Remember where I was, who I was sharing coffee with. Max. Maxie. My friend. My best friend. My saviour. God bless Max, God bless Max. I took a deep breath. 'How dare they?'

'I was just asking, Ethel, what they coulda meant.'

'I'll tell you – they're planting little seeds, little, little seeds that might grow, set roots, everyone saying, Oh, Malley, he was a bit *pink*. Wasn't there that incident, where he and another soldier got caught in the jungle?'

Max was shocked. 'In the jungle?'

'We should get a lawyer, and challenge this.'

'We could . . . but we've already got a court case.'

'True.'

'Old Ern's keeping us busy, isn't he, Ethel?'

'Eth.'

So that was that. All of the paper had blown away, and Max said, 'Let it go. The more we feed it, the fatter it gets. We need to strangle them, Eth.'

'How?'

'Deny oxygen. Keep our mouths shut.'

I excused myself and headed up Frome Road into the city. The ancient oaks, the Humbers and Austins, like it had always been this way, and would be. A bench, a man in a suit, reading, and I checked if it was the *Ecliptic* – but no, just Hemingway going on about bulls, again. Along Rundle Street, and I didn't know where I was walking, or why. Among thousands of people going in and out of shops, reduced shoes and shawls and electric toasters. The words in my ears . . . *certain rumours* . . . You'd think they'd just say it: him and some fella called Louis, nudge-nudge. Cowards.

Before long I was in the cemetery. Headstones to the horizon, or at least as far as the train line. At the front, big, marble memorials, and people with hyphenated names because, I guessed, if you could, it was good to show your provenance. No fakery here. Not that it was doing them any good. Further back, smaller headstones, thousands asleep in God's arms. See, I could say to Max, this is what you're getting into. Making people, sustaining them. Tiring. Stick to the penguin, old boy. But it was no good. She had him by the balls. It was over. It always ended that way. Some of the headstones had faded – just bits of names and dates: *Hu . . . 182 . . .* Life's final indignity, or consolation. After all, no one remembered past their grandparents. And for me and Ern, not even that. These strangers, living and dying in Liverpool, too poor to afford the fare. But that was life. Make do.

Someone had tied a rope to a tree, but not (as you're imagining) to end life, but to swing. You could tell – two bits, and a stick for a seat. For the living. Visitors, their kids bored, or maybe locals from the West End? Either way, *the living*. Up and down, until the rope snapped. So you never could tell, even in a graveyard (although the smell from the crematorium gave it away).

Enough! I walked all the way home. It gave me time to think about how you never really bury people. Because they stay with you, all day, every day (if you've loved them). So that, in a way, you never lose possession. And everything you do and say and fight for is a memorial. You stand up for them (who was teasing you this time, Ern?) because they can't stand up for themselves. See, nothing changes. Ern. Sitting up in bed, the words coming, rearranged, shaped, calling for me to bring him his slippers (lazy bastard).

I returned to Max's. Let myself in (the key under the mat, although I'd told him it was the dumbest place to put it), made a cup of tea and went to lay down in his room. I must've fallen asleep, because when I woke (the room darker, and colder, the tea sitting untouched) I heard voices.

'Loada rubbish . . .'

'You don't *want* to believe, Max?'

Mary, of course. You couldn't mistake the growl she had when she'd found a bone, and started chewing it.

'Harry was sure, he checked the local *and* state records.'

'So?'

'The husband was Evan, Evan Miller.'

I sat up, but quietly. Minx! Why would she? On with McAuley and Stewart, no doubt. Determined to destroy me, make Max hate me, take him away from me.

'Here, plain as day – she married him in 1932.'

'At seventeen?'

'According to this, and she was probably pregnant at the time.'

'How could that be? She's never mentioned a kid. I mean, how could she have kept that . . .?' A pause, like he was thinking. About these lies, and why Mary was making it all up. 'A birth record, for a child?'

I couldn't let this stand. I stormed out and said, 'What's this?'

Max was horrified. 'How are you, Eth?'

'*Ethel*.' I grabbed the sheet of paper this *woman* was holding, tore it to pieces and threw it away. 'What child?'

Mary didn't seem to care. She lit a cigarette. 'You forgot to tell us, Ethel.'

'There was no child. You, too, are against me, Martin.'

'I was curious. I checked. Forty Dalmar Street, wasn't it?'

I could've hit her, with her arrogance, and grin, or was it sneer? 'You're working with them, aren't you?'

'Who?'

'McAuley and Stewart.'

'Don't be ridiculous.'

'Tell me! And Max. Go on, tell him, how you hate me, always have, and what you'll do to get rid of me. What did you do? Go see them? How did you arrange all of this?'

Mary started gathering the pieces, but I stopped her, pushed her, and she fell across the floor.

'What are you doing?' Max asked.

'Can't you see? She's one of them.'

'Who?'

'Our enemies, Max. She's with them!'

Me, raging, fists clenched, ready to destroy her. Max, between us. Mary, still on the ground, still smoking, like none of this mattered.

# 39

I knew he wouldn't come home after his exam, so I waited in the Barr Smith Library. The previous night he'd gone to his room, locked himself in, and I'd knocked and said, 'Could I get my nightie?' The door had opened, half an inch, and he'd slipped it out. Closed it again. I'd said, 'What's all this about?'

'I'm tired, I've got an exam in the morning.'

'Not talking?'

'Tomorrow ... perhaps.' Then mumbled, 'Never, hopefully.'

I'd returned to the lounge room and thought about this. We'd had arguments before. He'd come around, he always did. Unless, of course, he was changing his mind?

In the morning, he'd already gone. Written a note and left it on a pile of books: *aust. lit. exam 9–12.30. could you get milk?*

At least he was talking, or writing. But the old Max, he would've woken me, had a chat. He was losing his nerve. Back on his front lawn, in his tutu. Poor old Max. Though, he just needed cheering up. So I got dressed, walked to the library, found a copy of *The News* and sat near the door, waiting. Betting he'd arrive, any time. As I studied my watch: 12.30, 1.00, 1.30 ...

There was no excusing it. Checking on people behind their backs, manufacturing lies, throwing them around so they stuck, no matter what the truth. What sort of person was this Mary Martin? Not someone I would've thought Max would mix with. No boyfriend or husband, of course. Maybe she was a feminist, feeding off all those angry women in France and Britain. Determined to reduce me to my essence; facts. But there was more to Ern and Ethel than facts. We were myth. Every word of the poems, true. Not just a collection of dates, achievements, births, deaths, marriages. We had risen above the mundane. *She* was mundane, always sifting through her chemistry notes, her Trollope, her endoplasmic reticulum and Virginia Woolf.

Then he came in. 'Max!' He saw me, turned the other way and descended the stairs to the lower levels.

Bloody nerve! I followed him. 'Max?' Down to B1, books as far as I could see, but no Max. Not to be put off, I searched. Up and down histology and Imperial Rome, Seneca and the hydrology of the Thames. For ten minutes, until I found him in a corner, reading. 'Max?'

He barely lifted his head. No expression.

'We were going to have a chat.'

'I'm busy. I've gotta finish this paper.'

'Ten minutes?'

And another little voice: 'Ssh!'

'I don't like leaving things unresolved, Max.'

'It's due tomorrow.'

'Come on, you've never been that busy before.'

'Ssh!'

'Get stuffed.' That did it.

Max stood, said, 'Come on then,' and led me up the stairs, from the library.

As we went, I said, 'You're angry with me?'

'I'm not.'

'I can tell.'

We passed through the refectory, bought drinks and proceeded out into the sun.

'If you're angry, you should say.'

'I'm under a lot of stress. I've got exams, papers, *Penguins*, this . . . court case.'

'I wouldn't worry about that.'

'I got a call from my mother.' He sat on the wall around the Barr Smith lawns. Our trenches had been filled in. Maybe the chancellor had given up on Tojo. 'She says, What's all this about a court case? I had to tell her. She just about had a coronary. I said not to worry, you know, it's minor . . . but my mum, Ethel!'

'Come on. Small beans. Say yer bit, the whole thing's dismissed. We didn't do anything wrong, did we?'

He took a moment, then said, 'No.'

'So, therefore . . . we continue.'

He blew his nose, examined the result and placed it in his pocket. 'I got a lawyer . . . Eric Millhouse.'

'I thought *you* were—'

'Mum insisted. She said I gotta go see him. Apparently he's good.'

'So?'

'A lawyer. It warrants a *lawyer*. Like murder, or rape.'

'It's nothing like murder or rape. But even if, not that it is, *you* believe in free speech, don't you?'

'Yes.' Begrudging. Like a kid admitting he broke a window.

'So what's all this about?'

'A *lawyer*.'

'And what's the worst. If you lose?'

'A fine.'

'There. I'll pay it for you.'

'But I'll have the conviction.'

'Don't worry, that won't happen. We explain those few lines, pretend we never knew what they meant, say, indeed, who knows, Your Honour? And if that's the case, why are we all standing here arguing about nothing when there's a war on?'

'Apparently this Millhouse has got a good record.'

'There you go. Thing is, if you *believe* in what you publish, Max. Do you?'

'Of course.'

'Well, then, it's all good. In fact, better. Because this will be a cause. People will report it, and the importance of free speech, and you, Max, will become Australia's defender of the word.'

'You reckon?'

'You, you will be the first person to stand up for an author, and what he's written, and his right to say it – in the face of all these small, pathetic debutantes and public servants, all being told what to think by their newspaper, and Carpenter and his mob, and the intellectual dwarfs that run the place. You, Max, will be the Montgomery of the Barr Smith lawns!'

This idea seemed to appeal to him. He gazed up at the first few clouds of a change that was meant to have arrived days ago. 'I guess,' he said. 'It needs doing.'

'It does.'

'Now, before I get too old.'

'How would you feel in twenty, fifty years' time, when you wake up at night and regret doing nothing?'

He decided. Shook his head a few times and said, 'Sid and John arrive tomorrow.'

'See? Between the three of you, you can hold off anyone. Turn this against them. How will that feel, when you win?'

That was enough, maybe. I was happy for him to return to his work, but he didn't seem to want to. 'It's all about trust,' I said. 'But that Mary woman, you can't trust her.'

'She does it to everyone.'

'Well, I won't have her investigating me.'

And then he said, 'She made a mistake.'

I thought and thought. What was the use? 'Well, if you must know . . . me and Evan were married for a few months. But after you marry someone, Max (and let this be a warning), you see a different person.'

'How's that?'

'I'm not sure I'd like to say, or that it's relevant. But the man I married was not the man I left.'

'*You* left *him*?'

'Some men are like you, Max. Gentle, thoughtful. That's why I've always admired you. But others are . . . I had to go, in order to protect myself and little . . . to preserve the little dignity I had left.'

He was confused again. It always went this way. My attempts at truth (admittedly limited, muddied, but never an outright lie); his growing reluctance to accept me at face value.

'Be careful, Max. Evan was a proper gentleman . . . then he moved into number forty.' I felt guilty, for having kept it from him, but good, for having come clean. 'And the rest, I promise, you know.'

'All of it?'

337

And without thinking, I told him. Ern and Louis in the jungle, the discharge, the disgrace. I described my interview, and how I was shocked. 'Not that it changes anything.'

'I had my suspicions.'

'How's that?'

'Clues, in the poems . . . *the sole clerk of my metamorphoses.* If you use a bit of Freud, and Jung.'

'Why didn't you say?'

'You don't, do you? *Hey, Eth, that brother of yours, bit of a poofter, was he?*'

I had to laugh. Max always made me laugh. He didn't seem to care; took it in his stride. 'Anyway,' he said, 'half of those poets in Europe, they're fighting on the other side.'

'Eh?'

'Auden, Spender – all in bed together.'

'Metaphorically?'

'Sometimes. But don't worry, Ern's secrets are safe with me, Eth. All of them.'

'And yours with me.'

'And yours with me.' Smiling, although I wasn't quite sure what he meant.

# 40

Max parked in Grote Street. We walked through Victoria Square to the police courts. Stopped, a hundred yards short, to see what we were in for. A small crowd, a few journalists, and Max said, 'It's all on.'

'Is there a back entrance?'

'Why?' Smiling. 'Carn, Eth, it's our big moment.'

We crossed the square, dodged a tram, a few taxis, walked towards the court, and I saw Sid Carpenter watching us, smiling. 'What do you expect to achieve today, Mrs Malley?'

'What do you want?'

'Do we finally get to find out who wrote the poems? Was it Mr McAuley, or Stewart, or did *you* have a crack, Ethel?'

Max took my arm and led me towards the steps. 'Don't say anything. He just wants a headline for this afternoon. Are you going to give it to him?'

But I couldn't help myself. 'We hope to defend my brother's work against the philistinism of Adelaide, and its so-called artistic set, and its so-called journalists.'

Max pulled my arm again. We had to squeeze past more journalists, calling more questions, a few passers-by, intrigued to see who this Malley woman was, and this Harris, the publisher of perversion and indecency. But I couldn't help it, raising my voice, 'All of these people making fun of Ern ... but he was a great poet.'

Inside, Max turned and said, 'You can't say anything, Eth. You still don't know how they work? They take what you say and print it, *differently*, to mean something else.'

'I know.'

'Well, ssh.'

'That Carpenter, I could murder him.' Before realising where we were, and how many policeman were standing about listening. 'Let's just get on with it.'

John Reed was there. A nice enough young man, with a broad, handsome face. The whole thing didn't seem to faze him. He just smoked (before someone told him to put it out) and said, 'This is gonna be the making of Ern.'

'How do you mean?' I asked.

'Ern. The poet. The Australian Whitman. We're gonna make him proud, Mrs Malley.'

'Ethel, please.'

And Sid Nolan. I thanked him for the cover, and said how much I liked his other paintings and how, in a way, he was to art what Ern was to words. Real, but not. The thing, boiled down, like suet. Not to everyone's taste, but do we, Sid (I felt I knew him well enough), go through life trying to please everyone? In which case you please no one. He explained how he was trying to keep a low profile. How the army wasn't quite through with him, for leaving his post, his barracks, his war, and spending his days lounging in the grass at Heide. I told him Ern'd had a similar problem. 'I guess,' I said, 'some concession should be made for creative people.'

340

'Exactly.'

'In a way (this is what I've learnt from the Ern Malley affair), Australians hate anyone who claims to be creative. Art, after all, is made elsewhere. Olivier acts, Eliot scribbles, Jimmy Stewart tells American stories, but what about us, Sid? What about our stories?'

'That's why we're here, Ethel.'

I liked him straight away. As I did any man willing to piss in the pool, and say he hadn't.

We were shown into the courtroom and led to the second row of about ten, and sat – me, Max, John, Sid – and further back, I noticed, as the court filled, Mary, beside Von (chattering like a pair of witches), Carpenter, even Elliott. All of them, their knives sharpened. God knows they wouldn't do anything to support Australian letters, but to bring it down, question it, shit on it?

In front of us, Eric Millhouse with his clerk, sifting through papers, smoking a cold pipe, turning and smiling and saying, 'Don't worry, Max, coupla hours ... day or two. How's Mum keeping?'

'Good, I reckon.'

'She coming?'

'Na, it'd kill her, seeing all this.'

And opposite, Ted Williams, from the Crown Law Department, sitting quietly, occasionally checking his nails, paring them back, wiping them on his striped pants. And beside him, Detective Apeldoorn. Max pointed him out and said, 'That's yer problem, Eth.'

'Nasty little man.'

Apeldoorn. The apple tree. He whispered to Williams (all the time, avoiding eye contact), as Eric Millhouse said to his clerk, 'Where were those lines?' and the clerk replied, 'They're somewhere.' They searched, like a couple of school kids who hadn't done their homework, or had, and had forgotten to bring it.

'I've never been in court,' I said to Max.

'Me neither. Although Mum took me to *Trial by Jury* once. It's remarkably similar.'

I guessed he was right. The elevated bench for the judge, the clerks and stenographers, a couple of policemen as window dressing. A high fan that clunked, a lion and unicorn and piping shrike, and a cross, minus its Christ. Like the lounge room of the Jesus house. Someone, I suppose Mr Alexander, had put one up. It seemed strange. Like, if Jesus did return, he wouldn't want to be reminded. Either way, Ern took it down and said, Good for a slingshot.

Put it back.

They won't notice.

But a while later, when we returned, Mr Alexander asked Ern if he'd seen what had happened to the cross, and Ern said, No idea, sir, and Mr Alexander said, You know, God sees everything.

Everything? Like, even when you're in the shower?

Even then.

Or on the dunny?

Everything.

Well, I don't know what happened to your cross, sir.

Alexander wasn't happy. He got one of the bibles down from the bookcase and read us a few parables or psalms or whatever they were, then said, Truth's more important than anything, Ern.

I guess so.

If someone trusts you, but you lie to them ... you wouldn't lie to Mrs Royal, or Terry, or your sister?

No.

If you tell me you didn't take it, I'll believe you.

I just stood, watching. Ern shaking, biting his lip (as he did at such moments), saying, No, sir, I definitely haven't seen your cross.

And that was that. Although, that night, in bed, I said, You better give it back.

Dad calling, Why aren't you two asleep yet?

I might've drifted off, but later, woke, as someone crawled in our window. Got into Ern's bed. I didn't say anything. No homilies were needed. A bit later Mr Alexander told us he'd found the cross, back on the wall, and it was funny, wasn't it, how some thieves broke in to put things back?

We were told to stand, and the judge came in. Sat, looked around the room and said, 'This is quite unusual.' And to me: 'You're his sister?'

'Yes ... Ern Malley's sister, Your Honour.'

'The mystery man, eh?'

'Well, not so mysterious. To me, anyway.'

'We'll see, won't we, Mr Williams?'

Who stood, seemed to agree, and sat.

'This case may turn out to be a waste of my time, so, Mr Williams, I hope you and the Crown Law Department have got very good reasons for wanting to censor these people?'

I took this as a good sign. Max leaned over and said, 'We could've done worse.' Sid winked at me, and John gave the thumbs up. Although it seemed a bit early yet.

'Well, let's get on with it,' the judge, whose name was

Andrews, said, gathering his own papers, scanning the room, saying, 'A few journalists . . . and you watch what you write. I've had enough tattle, sailing around the truth.' Then he said to Ted Williams, 'Get on with it then.'

Who explained the Crown was prosecuting charges of indecency against one 'Maxwell Henley Harris, twenty-three, a university undergraduate and co-editor, along with Mr Reed, and Mr Nolan – both gentlemen are here I believe?' Checking, and Sid and John raised a hand '. . . of the publication *Angry Penguins*, as well as indecent segments of various other publications, namely Mr Harris's earlier book of poems, *gift of blood*.' He produced a copy.

Max didn't seem worried. Sat, legs crossed, scraping a stain from his pants.

Andrews was already bored. 'Listen, Williams, make yourself clear. What do you mean by indecent?'

He had to think about it. 'I'll be offering a range of examples, Your Honour.'

'No, what do *you* mean? What exactly is your purpose? I mean, there have been a few authors, haven't there, overseas, who were put through all this, and in the end their right to write, if you like, was upheld. And the courts were seen as slightly pathetic. So before we progress, what is indecency?'

'Whatever might offend the majority.'

'So you claim the majority need to be protected?'

'No, yes, in a sense.'

'Even if that affects an individual's right to self-expression?'

Williams said, 'If I took my eight-year-old daughter into a bookshop and she picked up Mr Harris's publication, and read a few pages . . .'

'Yes?'

'We intend to show examples of how people . . .'

'Of how an eight-year-old might be affected?'

'Yes.'

'Good, well I look forward to hearing it, because I don't want my time or the taxpayers' money wasted.'

Max elbowed me, and I whispered, 'I know.'

Williams was allowed to say his bit. How the poems had been discovered, published, and how complaints had started coming in straight away. Andrews asked, 'How many?'

'To date, Your Honour . . . let me check . . . four.'

'Four?'

'Yes.'

'*Four?*'

'Four.'

'Righto, keep going.'

Williams claimed the poems were full of sex, but the judge said, 'My wife has a few novels in that vein, Mr Williams. I'm worried, now, that you might send Detective Apeldoorn around to my house.'

Laughter. Andrews didn't seem to mind. Max was loudest, almost slapping his knee, and Sid and John weren't far behind.

Williams said, 'But you didn't write the books, Your Honour, or seek to have them published.'

'But I've read a few purple passages, Mr Williams, and I'm still standing.'

'With due respect—'

'So, come on then, make it clear. What are we talking about?'

Williams was on firmer ground here. Evidence. He picked

up Max's book and read: '*The gift of blood, Scene one. The dream. The galvanised iron wall. The back of a barn. Very remote thunder.*'

Millhouse objected. Wasn't this about Ern Malley? Was everything Max had written or published to be examined? Hardly fair. 'If any of us, Your honour, had our every word questioned, we'd all look wanting.'

The judge overruled him. He seemed to be enjoying himself.

Williams continued. 'Two men, a German and a Jew, stand on a hill, and then . . . *the vein slightly throbbing. Here I am and here are you . . . I believe you shiver, why?*'

The judge said, 'What?'

And Williams: 'It seems rather obvious.'

'Not to me, unless you're suggesting I'm simple, Mr Williams?'

'No, of course not, but *the vein slightly throbbing*?'

'One of them had a headache?'

'I think not.'

'I think so. Of course, we could ask Mr Harris, but my understanding of poetry is that each person . . . *translates* it as he sees fit.'

'I'm not so sure—'

'Mr Williams, Mr Harris can't be responsible for the state of other people's minds.'

'I'm not suggesting that.'

'What are you suggesting?'

'That . . . I'd like to call my first witness.'

It seemed to be going nicely. Perhaps the Christ, absent from his cross, was watching over us. Mr Alexander. Mum. Dad. The Royals, even. And Ern, maybe he was beside me, holding my hand? Mary was smiling, and she waved to me. Von, too. The sun was coming in the stained-glass windows, warming us with all the morning had to offer.

Detective Apeldoorn stood towards the back of the dock, and the stenographer asked him to step forward. A clerk told him to place his hand on the Bible, and he swore to tell the truth (his truth). As Mr Alexander had made Ern do. Carn, Ern, if you're telling the truth.

Of course, I am. Don't you trust me?

Yes. So you've got nothing to fear.

The hand, shaking, on one of a thousand bibles, and Ern saying, Of course I didn't take yer cross.

Apeldoorn wasn't about to stray from the script. He opened his notebook, found the page and started reading: *'I interviewed Mr Harris on August first this year in the company of plainclothes constable Cameron Smith.'* He pointed him out. *'Asked whether he was editor of* Angry Penguins, *Harris said there was a committee of four – himself, Mr Sidney Nolan, artist, Mr John Reed, lawyer, Mrs Sunday Reed, homemaker.'*

Apeldoorn pointed out Sid and John and said, 'These gentlemen, from Victoria, although they weren't present at the time. Mr Nolan, I believe, is on a charge of being absent from—'

Millhouse objected. 'How can this be relevant to charges of indecency?'

Andrews said, 'Detective Apeldoorn, you have some experience in presenting evidence in court?'

'Yes, Your Honour.'

'So?'

'My apologies. If I may proceed? *Mr Harris wanted to know about the charges, and I explained. He seemed confused. I gave him the legal definition of indecency, but he wasn't sure, so I referred to this poem ... "Night Piece".'* He looked at the judge. 'Apparently someone is shining a torch in the dark, visiting through the park gates. To my mind they were going there for some disapproved motive.'

'Disapproved motive?' Andrews asked.

'Sexual congress, in a park.'

*'. . . to your mind?'*

'Yes. I've found that people who go into parks at night go there for immoral purposes.'

'You do? Unless they're walking, or attending a carols' night or . . .?'

'Those, I believe, are the exceptions.'

'What else have you got for us, Detective?'

Apeldoorn didn't seem happy. There were a few berets, and men who hadn't bothered wearing a tie to court. I guess he knew what that meant. 'I asked Mr Harris about several of these poems. "Sweet William". If I may, your Honour?' He waited, was given permission and read, *'And I must go with stone feet, Down the staircase of flesh, To where in a shuddering embrace, My toppling opposites commit, The obscene, the unforgivable rape.* He said he didn't know what all that meant and' – he read from his notes – *'You would have to ask the author. I would have to give it two or three hours thought to tell you what it means.* I suggested most people might think it is about rape, and he said, that's their choice and I said,' (reading again), *'Have you considered the effect the poetry might have on high school children? To which he replied, I could think of a good deal in the Bible that would have a worse effect.* I explained,' and Apeldoorn grinned, 'that the authors and publishers of the Bible weren't on trial, and he suggested they would be, if they were still alive and living in Adelaide.'

Laughter. I saw Andrews grin, but hide it. 'Stick to the evidence, Detective.'

'Anyway, after this discussion, Mr Harris was charged.'

Andrews seemed content. Maybe he was a lover of literature, maybe not. He said he'd like another read of the poems, and the court was adjourned.

We sat together in Victoria Square. Trams sparking, men on bikes, sleeves rolled up, although it'd turned cold. The grass was parched, thirsty for a drink, like us, after a morning of obscenity, muscular ideas versus starchy benevolence, the ceilings so high every idea had to rise, with warm breath, stirred by the fan, spread, fart-like, over the crowd, the town, the country, wanting a bit of scintillation. Ern's tits and erections, although, 'None of that was what he meant,' I said.

'How's that?' Max asked.

'None of those words meant none of those things. Ern wouldn't have it in him.'

But Mary Martin, busy with a sandwich, said, 'It seems hard to believe he didn't intend some of it that way.'

'You should sit with Apeldoorn,' Sid said, smiling, eating his own sandwich (I'd made a pile, mostly curried egg, because I wasn't sure if there'd be any refrigeration).

'Bullshit, but ... *boult-upright*. I'm not saying there's anything wrong with it ...'

'Not that you'd *know*,' John said.

If they were determined to crucify him, they would. That's how people worked. What had been said about Dad, in those days and weeks after the race. That he'd planned the whole thing, knew the day and hour the riders were due, and had no other motive but to cheat.

'Ern couldn't sleep,' I said.

'How's that?' Von asked.

'We'd just lie there at night, and I'd wake up, and he'd say, You awake, Eth? And I'd say, I am now, what about you? Just lying here.'

They all listened – gnawed on the bread (stale, but most things were in Max's kitchen) and wondered (I guess) what I was talking about.

'And I'd say, How long you been awake, and he'd say, All night. Can't work how to get to sleep. You just close your eyes. And he'd say, It isn't that easy. And I'd say, What, you worried about something?'

They were all listening. To me, Ern, in our room. Terry snoring, Mrs Royal tearing the sheet from him, cursing him.

'Bad like that, was he?' Max asked.

'Oh, yes, worried about everything. Which is why I'm glad he's dead. Not *glad* glad, but glad. All this would just about kill him.'

'Loada shit,' Sid said. 'Any other country he'd be on the wireless, in the papers.' He watched the schoolgirls walk across from St Aloysius.

'I'd say, Ern, there's no point worrying about anything, least of all whether you'll be able to get to sleep. Then he'd say something like, Eth, where d'you reckon all them homeless men sleep? See, that's what he was like, always thinking about others. If he was in there with Apple-Tree . . .'

'That's what I don't get,' John said. 'There's no case. A coupla old girls have read a few lines, had nothing better to do.'

'Exactly. Ern went for the pastoral, the stuff he read at Mr Alexander's place (he was the man with the house he'd built for

Jesus). Those poems were all about sheep and waterfalls and people going about their business. Where they get all this about *abortions*?'

'It could be read that way,' Mary said.

'And other ways,' I said, glaring at her, wondering why she was even sitting with us. 'So I'd say to Ern, Maybe they have shelters to sleep in? You know, like St Vincent de Paul, but he wasn't happy with that. He'd say, And if they haven't got money to send to their families, what do *they* eat?'

Ern knew the geography of insomnia better than anyone. If I woke, and said to him, How long? he'd say, Well, at one-thirty she got up for a pee, then the dog walked around a bit, sniffed in the kitchen, pulled those chops (I reckon) from the bin and had a go at them, then the wind picked up and it got cold, and I noticed you weren't covered, so I closed the window, and she heard and called – What are you doing up? On and on like this. Most nights, most of the night, I guess. I wasn't sure why. Maybe he was thinking about Mum and Dad. Maybe he talked to them, asked Dad how the Indian had performed, and what it was like in the desert at night, and if *he* slept.

Then Sid said he'd like to paint some pictures of Ern, and did I have any more photos, and I said, Perhaps, at home. I asked why he wanted to, and he said, 'They're the most interesting people, aren't they?'

'Who?'

'You know, the ones people don't get.'

'I get him.'

'But you were his sister. Most people ... they're more interested in Ern than the poems.'

'True,' Max said. 'Look at Lasseter. You should do him, Sid.'

'He was an idiot. What do you say, Ethel? Ern Malley, the paintings?'

'I think he burned all his photos,' I said.

And Mary's face, predictably, a grin no more than a tooth on a lip. 'Why would he do that?'

'You'd have to ask him.'

'He went out into the yard, piled them up, bita lighter fluid?'

'Yes . . . why, what are you suggesting?'

But Max was already onto it. 'Like Dickens. Took every letter he'd ever written, and burned them.'

'Well, I'll just have to imagine,' Sid said. 'Tall, was he?'

I told him. How my brother wasn't exactly an attractive man, with a too-square face (as an adult), too flat, his nose a volcanic eruption. Sid liked this, a volcanic eruption. 'He had thin lips,' I said. 'And he was always biting them, and they were always bleeding, and I was forever telling him to stop.'

As I spoke, Sid sketched. On the back of an envelope, with six squares for the six faces of Ern.

'He had almost no cheeks to speak of . . . like someone had sanded him down.'

But I could see him peering out of the window, the night that went on forever, the moon on his smooth face. Saying, I prayed to Jesus, Eth.

What?

That I could get to sleep. But I can't.

Maybe he doesn't help with that?

Doesn't help with much, I reckon. Like cancer, or getting lost, or anything. So what's the point of him?

None, really.

I better tell Mr Alexander.

Na, don't do that. It's all he's got.

'And all he had,' I said.

'What?' Max asked.

'Lasseter. His gold. Wouldn't have been any point arguing with him – if that's what he wanted. So what?'

Piddle. At my age, the worst thing. So I excused myself, crossed the square and headed into Moore's Department Store. Fancy, really, not that I ever went into such places. Stockings for twice the price you'd pay at Coles. Down to the basement, into a small, dark cubicle, and the bladder. Sighing, as I watched a fly trying to work its way free from a web. And then, someone came in, entered the adjacent cubicle and said, 'Got 'em on a string, Ethel.'

I knew who it was. 'Just came in for a bit of privacy.'

'The Esso Reliability Trial, wasn't it?'

I didn't reply.

'No one called Malley ever entered.'

She might've been more dangerous than I thought. A knife? Was this where they'd find me, Ern's sister, dead on the floor? 'You checked?' I said.

'I did. I rang them – couldn't remember anyone going missing.'

'It was a long time ago.'

'No Bob Malley on their records.'

'Mighta used a different name.'

'Why?'

Someone came in. We waited until they'd finished, washed their hands, left. Then Mary came out of her cubicle, knocked on my door, and I thought, If that's how you want it. Emerged, said to her, 'What have I ever done to you, Mary?'

'Just tell me, just say it: No, my dad was never in a bike race.'

'He was!'

'Tell me. If you do – I won't tell a soul. I haven't told Max.'

I didn't believe it. 'What do you want, money?'

'No. Just the truth.'

'I told you, he . . .'

'The *truth*, then I'll shut up. See, I *care* about Max.'

'My father entered that competition, got lost, died. Maybe they've lost the records, but why would I lie to you?'

'*Why?*' She smiled. She was enjoying it. 'That's what I was wondering. *Why?* So, I kept checking. Ethel Malley married Evan . . .'

'I told him about Evan, and why I hadn't mentioned him. People keep secrets.'

'They do, don't they? Ethel and Evan have a boy . . .'

I could've pushed her back into a cubicle.

'A small, Ern-like boy who, I believe, you've also forgotten to mention.'

'Keep yer mouth shut.'

'Now, as I understand it . . .'

'Quiet!'

I couldn't understand why she was doing this to me. Why she was making up more lies.

'I had the feeling, at the beginning, you were good at convincing people, Ethel. About Ern, and these poems he wrote . . . clever, wasn't he, *your brother?*'

'You leave him out of this.'

'Your brother? Ernest Lalor Malley. Should we talk about him?'

She was some sort of mad woman. I turned, walked from the

toilet, and climbed the stairs. She followed me, and said, 'You're entitled to your privacy, Ethel.'

I continued, past the underwear, petticoats, frocks. She followed, taunting me. 'If you tell Max, I won't. Better coming from you.'

I called at the top of my voice. 'Help!' Shouted, again and again. Mary just stood, refusing to move. Some sort of manager came over and I said, 'This woman,' pointing, 'has been following me.'

He didn't understand. 'You know each other?'

'No,' I said. 'I've never seen her before.'

'Maybe if we could just . . .?'

A few people had stopped to look, and I told them to mind their own business. Walked, at speed, from the store, and returned to Victoria Square.

'Did Mary find you?' Max asked.

I sat, and straightened my dress. 'Mary? No.'

John was lying on the grass, his hat across his face, and Von, too, her ring glinting on the Buffalo, but Sid kept sketching, and said, 'I'll draw you, Ethel, there must be a family similarity.'

'There's not!' I bit back. 'Not at all.'

But he just shrugged, and continued.


The Honourable David Andrews sat, coughed a few times and said, 'Righto, then, I had another go at these poems.' Showing a copy of the autumn issue. 'Mr Williams, I hope you're going to make a convincing case, very soon, because I've got murderers and rapists downstairs.'

'Yes, Your Honour.'

And turning to me. 'Mrs Malley, you coping?'

'Yes,' I replied.

'Looks like your brother's famous.'

'For all the wrong reasons.'

'I wouldn't be so sure. In that business, it's all good publicity, isn't it?'

'Yes, sir, Your Honour.'

It seemed like a good sign. Hopefully, it'd be over quickly, we could go home, all the crooks would crawl back into their holes. I could look after Davy, work on the garden, full of weeds where Dad used to tend it on a Sunday morning. Forking over the soil, pushing in the bulbs, and in spring there'd be a great display, everyone stopping to congratulate him, me and Ern sitting at the window, smelling the jonquils, listening. No, you've outdone yerself this year, Bob.

That's what it was like back then. Everyone for everyone. Decency everywhere. No talk or hint of *in*decency. Ern wouldn't have known what it was. Neighbours with buckets of peaches (you couldn't eat a whole tree full), talking about so and so's kid with polio, which was a shame, because he'd been a good runner. Me and Ern listening from the window, learning the way people spoke and cared about each other. Life was a little solar system, and we were all planets circling Croydon. Closer, further out; larger, smaller; but all with the same sense of thrall. Some red, some gassy (Mrs Kynoch, farting her way along Dalmar Street). This world was still hanging in Ern's room. His primary school solar system, held together by twine, his little paper planets with names, so you knew. Like Mr Moore, Peggy. Whenever there was a breeze they'd fly around the room, and make a scraping sound as they collided, and you knew there was a change coming.

Carpenter had gone. He was probably back in his office,

beating up a headline. But I didn't care. A few days, his words would be wrapping prawn shells, and Ern's would still be read. That's what Max had taught me: the long view.

'Detective Apeldoorn?' Andrews said.

He stood. 'Yes, Your Honour?'

'Ready?'

He nodded; then the judge invited Eric Millhouse to have a few words, and he said, 'Seriously, Detective, you must be wondering what you're doing here.'

'Pardon?'

'As a witness, to this case. You must be thinking, Why on earth am I wasting my time when there are criminals out there?'

'I'm assigned a job, I do it.'

'You can tell us. I bet you like getting a crim round the neck, twisting a few times?'

'Objection,' Williams said.

Andrews said, 'Mr Millhouse, we've met before?'

'Yes, Your Honour.'

'And I've had cause, haven't I, to remind you about relevance?'

'All I was saying, Your Honour, is that if Detective Apeldoorn agreed, and the prosecution agreed, we could forget these silly charges, head down the Cremorne for a quick pint, get on with our lives?'

'He's your witness, Mr Millhouse. If you don't want to ask relevant questions we'll move on.'

'I'm sorry, Your Honour. I have a few questions, few things I'm confused about.'

'Such as?'

'I was just wondering, Detective, if you made the nature of these charges clear to Mr Harris?'

Apeldoorn assumed his usual pose, feet spaced, so he wouldn't get blown over by the breeze from the fan. 'Mr Harris was confused, so I explained the charges. I pointed out the line, *Part of me remains, wench, boult-upright,* and asked him to explain, and he said' – reading – '*Do you know anything about the classical characters? When you know what they stand for you can understand the poem.*' Looking up. 'I said I didn't understand the reference, but wasn't sure that made it any less indecent, and he said, *The poem is no more indecent than Shakespeare or Chaucer.*'

'Have you read either, Detective?'

'No.'

'So this part of the conversation was lost on you?'

'I don't believe so, sir.'

'Shouldn't the Crown Law Department have sent someone with a broader knowledge of literature? No disrespect intended, Detective, but this is a specialised field.'

'I don't believe so. If something's crude, it's crude. I'll admit, I'm not the best read fella in the world, but I know vulgarity when I hear it.'

'For example?'

He smiled, waited, and said, 'No, I don't think that's going to work, Mr Millhouse. I'm aware of these words, but I'm not willing to use them in mixed company.'

'Only . . .?'

'I don't use them at all, thank you.' He glared at Millhouse, but he was unfazed. He was, I think, happy to destroy Apeldoorn. 'So, Detective, the final line of that poem, *You shall rest snug tonight and know what I mean* . . . could refer to?'

'I'd rather not say.'

'I'd rather you did,' Andrews said.

'Well, sexual congress. The author, I assume, is inserting his genitals into this lady's . . . vagina.'

A bit of giggling, but that had to be expected.

'But,' Millhouse said, 'it could just mean that she would sleep well. Maybe she's tired? A long day at work?'

'Perhaps, but I think not, when you consider the context.'

'Ah, *context*, Detective. But if that's the case, and this is a love poem, couldn't that line be excusable, indeed, necessary?'

'I don't believe so.'

'One thing leads to another, Detective, if you understand.'

'That doesn't mean it should be written about, in publications within the reach of small children in bookstores.'

'*Small children?* You honestly believe a small child, anywhere, would reach for this volume, study it in some detail, analyse the possible meaning of each line, become overcome with shock, grow up to become a deviant, a rapist? Is that what you're suggesting, Detective?'

'Perhaps.

'Mr Millhouse,' Andrews said. 'Stick to facts. The outcomes of reading this publication could only be guessed at. The point is, is it indecent?'

'Yes, Your Honour.'

'In reference to that line,' Apeldoorn said, 'Mr Harris replied, *If you're looking for that sort of thing I can refer you to plenty of books to fill your department with*. I explained that we were concerned with *his* book, and he said, *Our publication is intended for cultured minds which understand these things and place ordinary thoughts on a higher level*. He told me his firm only printed modern literature, of a type that would be *accepted these days*. I wasn't sure what that meant, but he said it would take three readings of half an hour each to understand the poems. I asked him why it would take so long and he didn't provide an answer. I then asked Mr Harris if he thought some people mightn't place an indecent inter-pretation on "Boult to Marina" and he said – *some people would find a bus timetable indecent.'*

Andrews seemed bored. He was gazing out the window, watching a few seagulls resting on a ledge. He managed to pull himself back into the room and say, 'It's all semantics.'

Apeldoorn seemed unsure. 'Excuse me?'

'Words, Detective. A couple of dogs running in circles, chasing each other's tail. I'm still no closer to knowing if there's anything *indecent* in those poems. Mr Millhouse, can you help me?'

'Certainly.' He popped a mint in his mouth and said, 'Detective, do you discuss sex with your colleagues?'

'Excuse me?'

'Sex? Do you?'

'Certainly not.'

'And don't believe it should be written about?'

'In certain contexts.'

'Such as?'

'Textbooks.'

Another fringe of laughter, and Andrews said there'd be no smut in his court room, and everyone fell quiet. Williams objected to the personal line of questioning, but Andrews allowed it, saying, 'Mr Millhouse, get where you're going, please. This is becoming tedious.'

'Yes, Your Honour.' And he read: *'Nay, but to live in the rank sweat of an enseamed bed, stewed in corruption, honeying and making love . . . or . . . my cherry lips have often kissed thy stones . . . or perhaps . . .'*

360

'Alright,' Andrews said. 'Enough, we get it.'

'Two of several dozen references to congress,' Millhouse said. 'And each with a certain Ern Malley quality. I've asked Mr Williams to summons this Shakespeare fella, and the sheriffs are out looking for him now.'

More laughter. But Andrews didn't stop it. Apeldoorn was about to explode. 'That's entirely different.'

'How?' Millhouse asked.

'It was tasteful. No mentions of penises and erections.' And he turned red. 'And tastefully done, not like this modern rubbish, this *Angry Penguins*.'

Now there was quiet. Millhouse said, 'As long as Ern Malley didn't write Shakespeare? Or Shakespeare, Ern Malley. That's it, is it? That we can't have any of that sort of thing here. In Adelaide. Today.'

'Nonsense.'

'Well?'

Apeldoorn seemed to have had enough. He sat, wiped his face with a handkerchief, and stared down at the ground. 'Am I the only one believes in decency?'

No one, not even the judge, answered. Even the stenographers, who sensed this needn't be recorded.

'Fifty years' time, what sort of world will we be living in?' he said, taking deep breaths.

Andrews asked if he was alright, and he said he was, and that he'd given all the evidence he could, and believed the poems were, indeed, indecent, but if we chose to see it otherwise – so be it.

Then he stood, shuffled from the room, and I felt sorry, and sort of proud, of Detective Apeldoorn.

# 41

We danced on the outer edges of this little galaxy. Me and John, as he told me about Heide, nestled in the bush on the outskirts of Melbourne. Two little meteorites we, trapped in the gravity of the hundred or so revellers at the Palais de Dance. Seriously, the Palace of Dance. Although it wasn't much of a palace – an old Nissen hut with skylights, floorboards that didn't sit flat (the odd occasional dancer tumbling). But it'd do, I guessed.

'Nothing that a bit of work wouldn't fix.' John Reed, co-editor of *Angry Penguins*, wife of Sunday (he'd shown me the pictures), tall, strong, confident, although no Max Harris. Max had the attitude *and* intelligence; John was more of an Austin, running on three of four cylinders.

'I should come visit,' I said.

'Love to have you, Ethel.'

I wasn't sure if he meant this. He'd described Heide as a cross between Dad and Dave and Montmartre; chooks in the early afternoon and Rimbaud. A place to cultivate life, and spirit, and avoid the deadening worst of Australia. Reached by train from Flinders Street, but a million miles from Melbourne; a love-nest and an office; a budget Shangrila, and home. That was most important, he said. Home. Somewhere that he and Sunday and Sid and Bill Dobell, and a hundred other drop-ins and drop-outs, could come and visit, stay, hide from the world (and in Sid's case, the army).

'Ern would've loved to meet you,' I said.

'He sounds like quite a character.'

'Yes . . . he would've fit right in at Heide.' I thought about this, my brother falling asleep under a plum tree in the overgrown garden. 'All he really wanted was a quiet place to work.' I was sure of it.

Unlike the Palais, the rings of Saturn going round and round, as me and John settled into an orbit of slow waltzing. 'It wasn't something you did,' I said, above the band, the five lost souls on their little stage, and a saxophone, wailing.

'Thing is,' John managed, as he tried to dance, 'you can't afford to care what people think.'

'How's that?'

'If you try to please people . . . if you want to be a poet you've gotta put your work first. Look at Sid. He's meant to be fighting the Japs, but he manages a canvas a week.'

I noticed Max and Sid sitting at a table in the corner, sipping some sort of green drink, involved in a conversation with an adjacent table – three women, strumpety, with big hats to hide the worst of their looks.

'Pity,' John said. 'If poor old Ern hada lived.'

Yes, I thought. *If.* But there was no point worrying. Life was for the living, and here I was, little old Eth from Croydon, in the arms of another woman's husband, sweat and grainy muscle, the ketones of his beery breath, the way, when you brushed up against him, you could feel what it might be like if . . . 'You liked his *Ecliptic*?' I said.

'Did I what, Ethel. When Max sent them over, and I first read them . . . although to be honest . . .'

'What?'

'I had my suspicions.'

As the number changed, but the dancers, us included, didn't miss a beat. Max and Sid, still sitting, although I'd asked them, a dozen times, to get up and dance.

'There was this fella in Melbourne,' he said. 'Like your mates in Sydney . . . thought we were full of it. I read the poems and said to Sunday, D'you reckon they're taking the piss? And she said, Could be. But then I re-read them and realised . . . they were too good to be a forgery.'

I didn't get it. Why did everyone think Ern was a joke? 'And you decided?'

'I wrote back the next day – and Ern was born.'

In a way, I had him to thank as much as Max. If he hadn't have liked the poems, it could've ended differently.

'No,' he said, 'Ern was an original, wasn't he, Ethel?'

'Too right.

'Probably the greatest discovery of my career. Years to come, they won't remember me or Max, they'll remember Ern.'

'No,' I said, 'you too' – although I guessed it unlikely. 'What's your favourite?'

He thought about it. '"Culture as Exhibit". That's a clever poem, Ethel. Hard to get yer head around. But if you give it a few readings . . . what was it, the floor of heaven, *inlaid with patines of etcetera*?'

'What do you think he meant by *patines*?'

'Who knows? Doesn't matter, really. It works, doesn't it?'

The music stopped. John excused himself, made for the

toilet, and instead of returning to our table, I stood by myself among the rubble of the heavens. Then, music. Me, the old lamp lighter, lost in the clang of the drums, the little pulse of bass, and the twinkle of ivories. Ern said to me, I remember.

I asked him what, and he said, when we were kids, and Mum and Dad (our real ones) took us to a dance like this. I tried to remember. Like this, still, among the movement; like David, lost in his corduroy jungle; people clanging into us, telling us (perhaps) to get off the dance floor. But me and Ern joining arms, pretending to waltz, like we'd seen in the magazines.

Now, me and Ern were watching me and Ern, all these years later. Ern was just staring, turning in his own orbit, mouth open, all aghast, like it was all coming back to him. What is it? I asked. No reply. Just round and round, as the earth and world tumbled. Ern?

I can see them.

Who?

Mum and Dad.

So can I.

I suppose we stood out, but I wasn't about to interrupt Ern in the act of remembering. He said, I wish Mum hadn'ta gone, and I said, That's right, it could've all been different, couldn't it, with a mum?

Now he was still.

They were good times, weren't they, Eth?

They were, Ern.

I never felt that way again ... never ... like I had that night. Seeing Mum and Dad so happy.

(I could see them now, dancing, so pleased to be in each other's arms).

I tried, Eth, but I never felt that way again. What about you?

Same, I said, cos it was true. You only felt *really* happy a few times in your life, and you spent the rest of the time trying to get it back, to remember.

The way she just went away, he said. Like it was . . . like she was going to the shops. And he started turning again, remembering. Like she thought it'd be best if there were no goodbyes.

This was right. It was all done quickly, and afterwards, you didn't talk about it much. Like it was best if we all moved on, found other interests, other mothers, perhaps. Perhaps Dad's biggest mistake – thinking we needed to forget. But you couldn't. No one can forget seeing their parents so happy, dancing, like we'd made them so, and it would last forever. D'you reckon we made them happy, Eth?

I reckon.

He smiled. That's good, eh?

It is, Ern. It is, I thought. Because no one could ever take that from us, until we finished, at which time, the circle was complete, and the planets could stop turning, the sun burning, us, working.

Me and Ern, and me and Ern, dancing together, in the thick of it. I noticed Max and John and Sid were standing, watching me, motioning for my return. Why would I? At such a moment? Dancing a little three-step they'd taught us at school.

Perhaps they thought it strange, this woman, with her arms around nothing, although it wasn't nothing, it was Ernest Lalor, my brother, my first, second and only true love. It might've looked strange, but it felt right. The way other people were watching me now, like I was mad. So be it! I closed my eyes – the breeze and me and rum and Coca-Cola – and said to Ern, I remember we got bored after a while.

We did, eh?

And found the kitchen, remember? Ate all those sausages, and the next day, remember, we were sick?

Yes, I remember.

We were terrors, Ern.

Too right, Eth.

You should write a poem about it.

I will, one day, Eth. One day, sting them, sting them, my Anopheles. Dancing, like the little mossie he was, over the swamps and marshes and borrow pits.

Then Max was beside me, with his hand on my arm, and he said, 'Carn, Eth, time to get yer breath.'

We sat down. The girls giggled and Sid said, 'Practising, Eth?'

'How's that?' I asked.

He showed me a picture he'd drawn on the back of a napkin. A woman dancing with her arms around a phantom partner. 'Don't mind if I use it?'

Max said, 'Who were you dancing with, Eth?'

'Ern.'

Although they said nothing, didn't even look at each other, but thought, I guessed, I was going silly. I said, 'You can't lose faith, Max. Mr Alexander did, and look what happened to him.'

Max knew all about the Jesus house. He'd read the chapter in my biography. How we'd played there, been caught, stole books, got to know this man, with his belief in a Croydon Jesus, due any day. He said, 'What do you mean, Eth?'

'One day me and Ern were playing in the front yard, and this moving truck pulls up outside the Jesus house. These men get out and open the truck and me and Ern run over and we say, What you doing? And one of the men says, Loading the furniture. So we watched, for an hour or so, as they brought out all the furniture, and pictures, and books, and packed them in cases and wrapped them in rugs and put them in the truck.'

John and Max listening, Sid sketching.

'Mr Alexander (who'd built the house, Sid, for when Jesus returned) arrived in his Mercedes and got out and we went up to him and said, What about Jesus? And do you know what he said – Sid, John?'

They shook their heads.

'He said, I can't wait any longer. So I said, What if he comes back tomorrow? And he said, I don't reckon. Could be a hundred years, a thousand, a million – and by then, the old place woulda fallen down anyway. Me and Ern (who, of course, had a vested interest) tried to talk him out of it. We said, Oh no, Mr Alexander, you can't give up on Jesus (although we had, years before). What if He returned tomorrow? How would you feel then?'

Max seemed interested, but to the others, it was just so much amateur band music, thumping away, slightly out of tune.

'I said to him, But if you *believe* in Jesus, Mr Alexander, why would you give up? He said, I haven't stopped believing, and I said, If you sell the place, you have, and he said, Well, I'll just have to take a chance on that. And that was it. He said he'd come and visit, but he never did. The place was sold to some New Australians. No kids. Just stuck to themselves. Which was sad. No more breaking in (although, in the end, he'd taken to leaving the door open for us).'

Max sat back with a drink and watched the dancers.

'Ern reckoned he must have been a bit simple, to build a house for Jesus . . . but we all do, don't we, Sid?'

'What's that?'

'Build a house for Jesus. Spend our lives doing it.'

Max must have felt sorry for me. He took my hand, led me up, and we danced. I'll be seeing you, Maxwell Henley Harris. He held me at a distance, as he always had. Hand in hand, but no arms touching, no body, no legs. I moved closer. 'This was a nice idea.'

Now, he didn't seem so sure. He had been, earlier in the evening, deciding we all needed a good shake-up. Clear out the grey cells, choo-choo on the A train, as we dreamed a little dream of Ern Victorious. Mary and Von had decided against it (thank god). Just me and the men, with their grim faces and red eyes from a day in court.

'Few more days,' I said, holding him closer still, 'and they'll have to eat our shit, Max.'

'If we win.'

'No, that's the beauty of it. Win or lose, we win. No more of this *censorship*.'

He waited, relaxed, said, 'What will you do, Eth?'

'Celebrate.'

'I mean, after?'

'Finish my biography. You still want to edit it?'

'Well, yes, but every day I get another dozen submissions.'

'Not as good as Ern?'

'Well, some are pretty decent.'

'But not as good as Ern?'

In his refusal to agree, I had my first vision of the future. Max as Mr Alexander, losing faith. I didn't like it one, little, bit. 'Max?'

'He's still the best, Eth.'

'Of course he is. There'll never be another Ern Malley.'

Closer. More than we'd ever been. Legs brushing, tummies together, my wheeze bags against his chest. Then (I couldn't help it, I swear!) I placed my head on his shoulder (although it wasn't even a slow song). He didn't resist (or encourage).

'Wouldn't it be nice if we could just stay like this?' I said. And then, without really knowing what I was doing, I lifted my head an inch, breathed on his neck, kissed it. And again, so that the flesh was between my lips – at last.

He pulled back. 'Ethel?'

I was in some sort of dream state. I took his head in the palm of my hand and said, 'It's alright, Max. We can agree to . . .' Wasn't sure about the word. *Make love* would do, but that was slutty. *Be close*, perhaps? But he stepped back and said, 'What's going on, Ethel?'

'Nothing.'

And turned, and returned to the table. I watched, as he sat, and tried to ignore me. Said something to the boys, then took his coat and left the hall.

# 42

It seemed nice, the way these Europeans did their coffee with milk, all frothy, lighter to drink. And sometimes, with some sort of bread or cake made from almonds. Nice. Although what wasn't so nice was Max, sitting across from me, stirring his espresso, studying the melamine tabletop, the stray crystals of sugar. 'It's just me,' I said. 'One drink's all it takes.'

He didn't smile, grin, seem angry. Nothing. 'What was it?'

'A Singapore sling.'

'Promise me, next time . . . never again?'

Contessa's, beside the police court. Lawyers and clerks and a few coppers with jackets over their uniforms. The owner, a Mediterranean, and his daughters or nieces, probably; his mother in the kitchen, his sons making coffee, the machine blowing steam every few minutes. Like I wished Max would. But he was holding it in. 'Not the first time,' I said.

'No?'

Good. Some reaction. It had been a long night, arriving home to find him already asleep in his room. So I slept in his spot on the lounge, but didn't sleep, really; just tossed and turned, wondering what he was thinking of me. And who could blame him, really? 'Ern must have been fifteen or sixteen,' I said.

'And one night he says, Come out to the shed, I got something to show you. So out we go, and he presents this bottle of whisky.'

Max was just listening. Thinking, perhaps, not another Ern story. But my whole life was Ern stories; him and me, together, forever, amen.

'He drinks a bit and offers me some and I try it and say, Not bad, eh? He says, Bloody oath, and we keep going and a few minutes later, literally a few minutes, Max, there's me on the floor, staring up at the light-globe, all the little sculptures dancing around singing.'

'And what about Ern?'

He was warming, venting, returning.

'Ern wasn't affected. He told me, later, he'd been stealing it for months, and trying it, a bit more every day.'

People coming and going, the till ringing, the little bells on the doors tingling with excitement, because Max was returning. Returning!

'Anyway, it didn't end well,' I said.

'Why?'

Was that a smile? I'd apologised for what I'd done, but he didn't seem to want to accept this. Thought, perhaps, this had been my idea all along. Get to know him, seduce him, get rid of Von, make him my lover. No. Nothing like it. It'd just been a weak moment, I'd explained.

'Well,' I began, gilding, or was I? I could never tell any more. Maybe it had happened this way, maybe not. But in the end, what did it matter? The story needed feeding. Naked virgins tossed into its caldera, the screams, and a hot, bubbling blow of steam as another coffee emerged. 'Ern tried to get me up, but it didn't work. Pulled and pulled, but I flopped and flopped, and then Mrs Royal was in the doorway. Shouting, storming off with the bottle, tipping it onto the lawn, calling for Terry to come out and deal with us.'

'Did he?'

'Just sauntered out, laughed, asked Ern where he'd got a full bottle, and Ern said he'd found it, and Terry believed us, because he always believed us, and she told him to stop being so soft and give us a good thrashing. Terry said, Kids experiment, but you know it's not right to drink at your age, don't you kids? And we said yes, and Mrs Royal stormed off calling him pathetic, and us, insufferable. Which we were, I guess. And when she'd gone in, Terry finished what was left in the bottle and said, She won't let me buy any grog. And we laughed, because we knew it was true. She never let him do anything.'

The table was cleared, new coffees offered, and refused, and Max said, 'You just gotta give me the full story, Eth.'

'I do.'

'Really? Ern, in the jungle?'

'I could've told you earlier, but I didn't want to . . . I mean, think about the *specifics*.'

He noticed the clock on the wall. 'Shit!' Dragged me – hand, arm, body and all – from the coffee shop, down Gouger Street, up the stairs of the police court, and in. The foyer, with the last few entering – John (asking where we'd been), Sid (still sketching, always sketching), Von, and Brian Elliott. Elliott?

It was my big day. Sworn in, offered a chair on a stand, and I sat, studying the court room from an entirely different perspective. The thirty or forty faces, mostly familiar, but as for the others, I thought, Who are you? What business do you have listening to me? Tweed jackets, a few coughs, snorts, someone laughing, although I wasn't sure why. We were big business. Articles in all the national papers: the professor (although he wasn't) in trouble for publishing pornography. John and Sid had gathered them, and we'd studied them, laughing until it became dangerous, at which time Max took them out to the incinerator and burned them.

Judge David Andrews appeared from a back door, and we all stood. He was a decent-looking fella, and it was almost like he was preparing for a day's fishing. 'Mrs Malley, how are you this morning?'

I told him I was fine, although I hadn't slept so well, worrying about what people were saying about my brother.

'Just their opinion,' he explained. 'I'm not on anyone's side . . . well, yours as much as theirs.' And he searched the room. 'Mr Williams, you ready to make sense?'

'Yes, Your Honour.'

'Mr Millhouse?'

'Likewise, Your Honour.'

'So, Mrs Malley, I'm going to throw you to the lions, as such, because I'm interested to learn about your brother. As I see it, people aren't *indecent*. And I'm sure he was a decent fella, having fought.'

'Yes, Your Honour. He was.'

'Mr Millhouse . . . thank you.'

Millhouse stood, blew his nose (he always did, for good effect) and said, 'Mrs Malley, do you consider your brother's poems indecent?'

'No.'

'Can you see why others might?'

'I can see, but I believe, Mr Millhouse, that poetry is open to interpretation. If a person chooses to see filth, well, that's their right, but to claim to know what an author means . . .'

'So, you think the poems have been taken the wrong way?'

'Yes.'

'And that they are harmless?'

'Yes.'

Millhouse seemed happy with this. And the judge, still watching birds at the window, tidying his desk, arranging papers, like he might be about to thread a few worms on the line.

'This seems to be the consensus,' Millhouse said. 'This article – ' and he held up a copy of *The News* ' – seems to suggest . . . well, maybe if I may read?' He adjusted his glasses. '*Dear Editor*, and on it goes, and here, *my name is Brian Elliott, and I am employed as a lecturer in Australian literature at the University of Adelaide.*'

Elliott sat, legs crossed, with his head raised, but slightly tilted, sort of superior. I remembered our first meeting, the claim of Max's authorship, his refusal to back down. Raised voices. Now he was wearing the same suit, same tie, I guessed. I thought, Australian literature? What do you really know, Mr Elliott? And now you've come, as some sort of hideous blowie, to hover over the corpse, lay a few maggots on what's left of Ern Malley.

'*I thought this an opportune time to share a few thoughts about the Australian poet, Ern Malley, and his publisher, Mr Max Harris.*'

This mightn't end well, I thought, but then remembered, Eric Millhouse for the defence. I looked at Elliott again. What's your game? And Max. What d'yer reckon, Max?

'*My first thoughts about these poems were that they were poorly written, pretentious, and on that fact, my opinion hasn't changed. But* regarding authorship, I've come to see that these were not the words of other people – whether Harris, McAuley or Stewart – but those of perhaps one of Australia's most original (now, already, lost) voices, Mr Ernest Malley.'

I saw Max sit back in his seat. And deflate, like a balloon that had been blown up for a thousand years, and suddenly pricked.

'Firstly, I've come to see that originality comes only in the most unexpected forms. And The Darkening Ecliptic, foremost among these. There was nothing that could be predicted about Mr Malley's ideas, words, phrases. Unexpected. I failed to see this. Now, of course, I offer Mr Harris, the poem's publisher (although not author), an apology. The idea that anyone could have faked such originality now seems absurd. Or would bother. Surely, any forger with this talent would have spent his efforts establishing his own credentials?'

I looked at Elliott again, smiled, but, of course, he didn't smile back.

'Secondly, what was to be gained by faking these poems? Was I, or others, meant to be made to look stupid? And was this, after all, the greatest conceit on my part? And what if there was no Ern Malley? Would the work be any less? Of course not. After the tenth, twelfth, twentieth reading, these poems become great.'

Now, a certain acknowledgement passed between Max and Elliott.

'Very interesting,' Andrews said, casting an eye at Williams and saying, 'You sure you want to proceed?'

'Yes, Your Honour.'

'You don't want to end up looking silly.'

'We'll risk that.'

Millhouse asked me more about Ern, and his methods of working, and I told him I was unsure, because my brother was such a secretive man. But I did say I'd found another poem, buried in a box in the shed, and he asked if I'd like to read it, and I said I would, and took it from my purse and began: '*And now that my soul might have joy in you, and that my heart might leave this world with gladness because of you, that I might not be brought down with grief and sorrow to the grave, be determined in one mind and one heart not to come into my captivity . . .*'

Everyone waited for more, but I said, 'Maybe Mr Harris might publish this, in his next edition?'

Max had his thinking look, his remembering look. I said, 'A very traditional poem, but maybe there are more in this vein – *later* poems?'

Then it was Williams' turn. He wasted no time. Straight for the jugular. 'It seems strange, Ethel, that half of Australia believes someone *else* wrote your brother's poems.'

Millhouse objected, and this was sustained, because half of Australia had no idea who Ern Malley was (although the other half had probably heard by now).

'Point being, Ern was, is, a magnet for controversy.'

'I wouldn't say so.'

'No? It seems strange that this is the first time a poet, a dead poet, has been taken to court for offensive material.'

I took a moment, straightened my dress and said, 'Well, in a way, Mr Williams, it seems unfair that Ern isn't here to speak for himself. Although he had a similar experience in school. Bigger boys would bully him, push him around – once, even, he got a black eye. So he was used to bullies.'

'Mrs Malley, I'm a Crown Solicitor.'

'Another way of saying it.'

Some laughter, and I felt proud, still sticking up for Ern, all these years later. He was on the front bench, short shorts, stick legs swinging, his big smile. God love you, brother!

'Mrs Malley,' Williams continued. 'Your brother isn't on trial. It's the nature of the words he's written.'

'Then he's on trial. Every word was Ern, and Ern was every word.'

Williams sighed. The judge asked him if he was *sure* he wanted to continue, and he insisted.

'Mrs Malley, the poems are vague?'

'Quite specific.'

'I would say vague, and for the purpose of disguising their meaning.'

'It's called poetry.'

More laughs.

'It seems to me, Mrs Malley, that Ern was having a few bob each way.'

'What does that mean?'

'He was saying without saying, making pornography without appearing to do so. Like a lifted eyebrow, or making suggestive noises.'

'I think you're confusing my brother with a horse.'

Then, the response was loud – like George Wallace at his best. So the judge quietened the room, and warned me, but I had no intention of listening. I hadn't asked for all this.

'Mrs Malley, sometimes when we're made accountable for our words . . .'

'What on earth does that mean?' Clutching my purse. 'Ern wasn't accountable to anyone, least of all you, Mr Williams. He was a creative artist. He owed that to himself, to me, perhaps, our parents, but not to you, or the Crown Law Department, whoever they are, and whatever role they serve in our society except to stifle the imagination of cleverer people – hear that, Mr Williams? Cleverer.'

'You seem defensive, Mrs Malley.'

'You seem ridiculous. Was your intention to bring me into the public spotlight, to show this *society* of ours that difference won't be tolerated? Is that it? That Ern was different? That he didn't like women, but men. That he didn't want to fight, but fix, soothe, help, love? Is that what you don't like, *sir*?'

The cat was out of the bag. I'd said it, and in the silence that followed, you could hear people gasping. So what? Stiff shit!

'What is your objection, Mr Williams? Here, let me do your job for you. You're about to say that the "Perspective Lovesong" is filthy. You're about to quote the line about naked breasts and loins. So what? Have you never seen one? Would you like to see mine, Mr Williams?'

And God help me, I didn't know what I was doing, but I was so damn angry I undid a few buttons, and the judge said, 'Mrs Malley!'

'He wants to see.'

'I'm sure he doesn't.'

'He does. This is what it's all about. Tits. Not saying the word, but the thought. Or a stiffy.'

'Mrs Malley!'

'It's not like men don't get erections. I've seen it, plenty of times. Ern had them in the bath all the time, and hid them with the flannel, but I know what he did. It's not the word, Your Honour, it's the object. We're scared of sex. Is that my fault? Ern's? The poem's?'

I heard myself and stopped. I felt my hands shaking, my

heart racing. 'Nothin' filthy about my brother,' I said. 'I won't hear it again. He was a decent man. How dare you call him otherwise, Williams, Crown Solicitor. You and your Goebbels and your propaganda and your belief you can tell people what to think, what to like, what's right and wrong. Yer just a miserable little cunt.'

This time I heard the gasps. Whose, I couldn't say, but I received a mouthful from the judge, and he said enough was enough, and I should take my seat. He said we should have a break and hear John and Sid after lunch. But I'd heard enough. Nothing good could come from this. Just people shitting on Ern's grave. And it had to stop.

We walked out, me and Max, and Von and Sid and John and Brian Elliott (Max actually holding his arm), into the midday sun above Victoria Square. A glorious day! Because what had needed to be said, for so long, had been. Poetry was one thing, but a technicolour spew was another. I felt happy. I'd stood up for Ern again. Beside the old incinerator, I'd taken some shitty little kid and thrown him against the fence. And he'd run off, whimpering.

Williams went past with his clerk. Head down, like every-thing that had just happened, hadn't. Like he hadn't meant anything by it, but had. So I said, 'I haven't finished with you, Williams.' And he turned and said, 'What was that?' And I said, 'I think you're hearing things.'

# 43

I wasn't going to let it stand. Why should I? Grimy little man. I should've fixed him when I had the chance. All this, I thought, as I stormed (again) towards North Terrace, *The News*, and Carpenter. That he could print anything, and it was up to me to find a lawyer, deal with him, disprove it. No. I crossed King William Street (a few horns, but what did it matter?) and heard a newsboy calling, 'All that's fit to print!' But what was news in this place? Europe in tatters, but whose kids were playing for the Burnside under-eights, who'd managed the biggest pumpkin, married the blondest girl (their names grotesquely hyphenated).

I slipped, almost twisted something, fixed my heel and continued past the graziers' bank, big steel doors showing the world where the money was, and who had it. I'd decided, enough of Adelaide! It was time to get back to Sydney. Although after the trial. I wouldn't let that rest, either. Carpenter. Comfortable in his little six-inch column. *The latest news from the Malley obscenity trial sees Detective Apeldoorn take the stand. A decent, well-meaning man reduced to tears by the poet's lawyers.* A picture of Detective Apple-Tree leaving court, the pain writ across his face, the caption: *Crucified for keeping the faith.* What faith? *Next was Ethel Malley, the 'poet's' sister. A few garbled words, an attempt to defend the*

*smut that, by now, most of us have sampled (unfortunately). The real
question being, who will wash these words from our footpaths?*

It wouldn't stand. No. This man would have to be told, made
to apologise. So I entered the foyer (again).

*The shock of the day was Mrs Malley's description of her brother's
'tendencies'. Many of us have thought the same about poets, affected,
languishing in the dock as their transgressions are numbered. Mr
Wilde himself, defending the indefensible. And now Ern. No more
secrets in the Malley family.*

He was willing to go as low as needed. Nothing about the
actual trial, the successes of the defence, the triumph of (what
I took to be) ideas above hysteria. This Carpenter man knew
what his editors, and boss, expected from him. It didn't matter
that Ern was winning – as long as they were selling papers. The
Allied Forces were finding killing camps all across Europe – but
no, none of this was worth mentioning, only Ern and 'his *friend*,
stranded in the jungle, making their own *amusements*'.

I said to the girl, 'I'm here to see Mr Carpenter.'

She glanced down at a photo of yours truly, and some sort of
written warning. 'I'm not going to let that stop me,' I said.

'We were told to say, Mrs Malley, that you weren't to be on
the property.'

'Told by whom?' I snatched the photo, tore it in half and
said, 'This man's written lies.'

A guard came up behind me. 'We can leave quietly, or I
can help.'

'This isn't Germany,' I said, waving my finger in his face.
'And where are your henchmen?'

He took my arm, but I shook free, and at that instant
Carpenter appeared from the lift, saw me, and hurried out

onto the street. I followed him, calling, 'I want to talk to you.'

He almost ran, but I kept up. 'What you wrote about my brother . . .'

'It's common knowledge.'

'You say his poems were filth, but this is the only dog shit on North Terrace,' I waved at the building '– and you, Carpenter.'

Then he went into some sort of coffee shop, locked the door behind him, waited for me and called through the glass, 'If you don't go away, I'll get the police.'

'Get them.'

He motioned for the shop girl to phone. The customers seemed shocked, and I wanted to explain: Do you know what sort of person this is? The proprietor, standing with a bottle of milk in his hand, his mouth open.

'Take responsibility for what you've written,' I said. 'If you step out now . . .'

'Go away.'

'Ern and I are entitled to some privacy, aren't we?'

He seemed to be explaining to his hostages. They gathered at the back of the shop, like I might break down the door, or smash a window.

'This pulp,' I said, producing the morning's paper, 'has nothing to do with the trial.'

By now there was a small crowd, and a photographer, taking pictures. I shooed him, but he wouldn't go away, so I returned to the shop. 'Carpenter?' I turned to the assembled and said, 'This man has been printing lies about me and my brother. Saying that me and Evan, my husband, had a child.'

*Mrs Malley is not all she seems. Some sort of fictional character, like her brother. The woman invented by McAuley and Stewart. She is a tintype, fleshed out enough to convince the unwary listener. She, the one who discovered Ern's poems in a suitcase, sent them south, to glory. A soldier poet? Who'd never put pen to paper? Producing masterpieces? Unlikely. About as likely as her story: the widow Ethel, dragging her chains around Petersham. With the boy she never told us about, and what happened to him, and the years behind bars . . .*

Couldn't stand. Wouldn't stand. No. No. No. 'How dare you?' I said.

He came up to the glass, and said, 'Every word of it, true.'

'You and that *Martin* woman?'

'No, Ethel. A few phone calls.'

I hammered on the door, and it wobbled. A few gasps from the much bigger crowd (the flashes), the diners retreating into a back room – like I was a common criminal, let loose on the streets of Adelaide. 'Lies!'

'Do you even *know* what's made up any more, Ethel?'

'Come out here.'

'And what's real? Your doctors, did you stop seeing them?'

Enough! I stood back, charged the door, but it didn't give. Fell to the footpath, conked the back of my head on the concrete and felt dizzy. Tried to sit up, but couldn't. Dizzy . . . lying down, closing my eyes, as people gathered around. Everything fading. Darkness. Then just voices. The door unlocking, someone telling people to get back, a siren, two . . .

I woke in a cell. Opened my eyes and saw bars on the window, blue sky, trees. Cracks in the walls, and a hand-basin with a dirty towel. I turned my head, and it hurt. A small lump at the back, radiating forward, around the sides, right through my skull. More bars, and beyond this, several figures seated around a table, smoking. One said, 'Don't worry, Bradman's got it all under control.'

'He's another crook.'

'A national hero.'

'My arse.'

Unmistakably, Max's voice. 'You think we should get the doctor back?'

'Na . . . she's alive.'

I could see them all watching. Max came over first, tried the bars and said, 'Can someone unlock it?'

More movement, then the cell opening, Max coming in and sitting beside me. And I said, 'Where are we?'

'The city watch-house.'

Then it all came back: North Terrace, the shop, the faces hovering above me. 'I got him good, Max.'

'Yeah, and you did a pretty good job on yourself.'

True. But it didn't matter. 'He was scared shitless.'

'He's going to press charges.'

'Rubbish . . . if he knows what's good for him.' I sat up, rubbed my head a few times and said, 'Did you read what he said about Ern?'

'What's it matter? The case is going well. A few more days – Andrews is on our side.'

One of the policemen came into the cell and said, 'A few forms to sign, then you're free to go, Ethel.' Smiling.

'That's it?'

'A court date, in three weeks.'

'But I was heading back to Sydney.'

'Not now.'

We crossed the road, and the parade ground, and sat on a

low wall watching fifty or so men marching. I said, 'Feels good when you get it off your chest.'

'What's that?'

'When Mum died we weren't allowed to say a word. Even the picture on the dresser disappeared. Me and Ern were only little tackers and thought Dad didn't want to remember her. But *we* did – we needed to. And every week, and month, and year, we forgot her a bit more. Do you know what that's like?'

Ern, looking in our parents' wardrobe, saying, Where'd all the dresses go, Dad? Because he liked to stand in the back, surrounded by the frocks and the smell of powder and sweat and bum, and Mum. He did this, all the time, until they were all removed. He'd even tried them on. Parading along the hallway in a dress, wearing fake breasts and lippy he'd found in a drawer. Till Dad came in, saw him, blew his top, dragged him to the bathroom and cleaned the lipstick from his face. Poor old Ern. And that night in bed, me saying to him, You can't get her back that way.

How, then?

I wasn't sure ... and still wasn't. Because he didn't tell us, allow us a proper remembering, dreaming, imagining (Mum watching me fumble my calisthenics). Nothing. Nothing was left to play with, in our minds. Even the last pair of shoes (although we realised, in time, found a pair, and hid them in the shed). Poor old Ern turning to poems, I guess. A neat way of remaking her (from the few faded photos Dad never found).

Max said, 'You're the one goes on about trust. Now you're telling me there are *more* poems?'

'I was keeping it for a surprise.'

'*Late* poems, you reckon?'

'I reckon. I mean, there were just some scraps, but they were quite different. Love poems, perhaps. I thought about this Louis character . . . maybe they were written for him?'

'The Princess of Princess Street?'

'We can always check. Anyway . . . *my heart might leave this world with gladness* . . . not a bit like the *Ecliptic*, eh?'

'No.' Looking at me doubtfully. 'I thought they sounded familiar.'

'What?'

'Those lines. So I checked.' He produced a small black book and showed me. *The Book of Mormon*. Leafed through to a marked page and read, '*And now that my soul might have joy in you, and that my heart might leave this world with gladness because of you.*' And looked at me.

'No?' I said.

'. . . *that I might not be brought down with grief and sorrow to the grave* . . .'

'That's just the same, Max.'

'It is. Comparative Religion IA. I chose to write about the *Book of Nephi*.'

I studied his face, trying to work out what he was saying. About Ern? Me? 'You don't reckon Ern . . .?'

'A late poem?'

'He stole it?'

'Well, he stole a lot of things, but mostly, he used bits and pieces, magpie fashion. But he never stole a whole poem, I reckon.'

I still wasn't sure what he meant.

'Thing being . . . if he's taken this?'

'What?'

387

'I'm confused, Ethel. I reckon you oughta tell me.'

'What?'

No reply. Ern, me. Me, Ern. 'Maybe he thought he'd get away with it? Max, I thought he was some sort of genius.'

'So did I.'

'But, you don't reckon ... the other ones?'

'It depends on who's written them, Ethel.'

'But the poems I found, you think they mighta been written by someone else?'

'I was reading your biography,' he said.

'Good.' That was better. One bad poem. I could throw it, tell them about the Mormon literature Ern had collected from the fellas that used to come to our door (a box full of it, under his bed, Dad always asking if he was about to turn religious).

'The bit about Ern starting school.'

'Nice.' I smiled. 'Did you think I did a good job of it?'

'At St David's, was it?'

'Yes.'

'Although, when we were walking past Croydon Public you told me ...'

'Ah, well, he started there, of course, but the bullies. All of those kids were horrors. Dad reckoned he'd get a better education with the Catholics, so he changed him over.'

'Right.'

I wasn't liking what I was hearing. He'd been checking, comparing facts. But wasn't it all about trust? 'What, Max?'

'If one's fake, what about the rest?'

The rest? All of it? Is that what he was saying? That Ern wasn't real, hadn't written the poems. 'If that's what you think, there's no point continuing the case.'

'But I didn't say anything, Eth.'

I wasn't going to take it. The ultimate betrayal. From Max. That'd be the end of everything. Was, it seemed. So I stood (but he didn't say anything), walked away (and he didn't stop me), turned and said, 'I'll see you back at the flat?'

'Right.'

# 44

We didn't eat, drink, nothing. Just returned home, retreated to our corners of the house, avoided each other. Max sat at the dining table and said, 'I've put these off too long.'

A pile of submissions that had been growing: a small mountain of poems, essays and book reviews for *Penguins*. John, he'd complained, did little of the reading. It was always up to him to plough through the sewerage in search of a wedding ring someone had dropped down the drain. As he sat, cursing each non-Ern, each pretentious take on Sartre, each book review by authors who couldn't get their own books read, mumbling, 'Why, I don't know.'

'Because you love it,' I said, from his room. 'That's how you found Ern.'

I thought the memory would get him going – opening the letter, reading, *Dear Sir, When I was going through my brother's things . . .* but he didn't say anything.

A cold night, with winds whipped up from the gulf. I sat at the window and wondered if I should stay. The police could come and get me – I didn't care anymore. All of this for a few poems, a few haters. But I owed it to Max, didn't I? To John, Sid, the many supporters. But why? Von? Mary? Carpenter? 'Wanna cuppa?'

'If you're making one.'

That was something. I emerged in my nightie and dressing gown, put on the kettle and sat opposite him. 'Anything any good?'

'*The poet's limbs, dangling in the multitude, the sure signs of Sirius as he skirts the Hebrides in search of electrical love . . .* Everyone sounds like Ern now.'

'Well, he might've written it.'

'Might've.' As he kept reading, and I made the tea, placed it in front of him, although he didn't seem interested. 'Maybe I should take a break from *Penguins*. I don't feel excited anymore.'

'Maybe it's time for you to write a novel? Autobiographical, perhaps, with you jumping in the Blue Lake?'

'No, this is what I do,' he said, sipping.

'Maybe the case has put you off?'

'Here, this one, from Mrs Ackland of Broome. *The heart beats with fibrillating love, for your fine limbs, and strong arms . . .* Jesus.'

'It might be a while before you find another Ern.'

This seemed to trouble him. 'I'm not gonna find him in here, am I?'

'If you look hard enough.'

'I'm sick of looking . . . you have a go.' He took three inches of submissions from the pile and threw them down in front of me.

'I wouldn't know . . .'

'Go on.'

I sat waiting, but he didn't apologise. So I had a go. More bad poems, a review of a Steinbeck novel. 'At one point Ern wanted to be a pilot. He wrote to the air force . . .'

'You never mentioned that, either.' He returned to a

submission, read a description of Mount Fuji from a butcher in Melbourne.

'He was never able. Dad told him—'

'Ethel!'

I waited. 'What?' And saw a man who was no longer able to do the thing he loved most. 'There's lots I haven't told you about Ern.'

'Really?'

'About how when Terry took us to—'

'Maybe, Ethel, I've heard enough.'

I just drank my cup of tea. 'Well, that's fair enough.'

'*As the beasts ate offal and wandered through the grey afternoon* . . . What sort of shit is this? Why would anyone bother? Beasts, and offal? Why? It's not like anyone's gonna read it, is it, Ethel?'

'Plenty of people will.'

'Really? You know what our readership is?'

'Lots, since Ern—'

'*Before* that, and after? Two thousand . . . and then a few hundred returns, maybe fifteen hundred. And as for the people who sit down and actually read this shit!'

'Max!'

'Next to no one. So why do I bother?' He upset his tea, and it spilled, soaking into the pile.

'Max?'

'The great poet, Ern Malley, the literary Jesus, resurrecting us all? Although he was just your little brother, little Ern, little pissy pants?'

He was scaring me.

'Eth, I pinned a lot on Ern. I thought he'd change things,

but it's just this shit – piles and piles of it – for the rest of my life.' He thought about this, bit his lip and said, 'Or is it?' He stood, gathered the manuscripts and ran outside. I followed, out into the cold night, the wind whipping up my dressing gown, a mist of rain on my face, in my eyes. 'Max?' He threw the lot in the incinerator, went inside, returned with matches, lit one and threw it in. The papers were already damp, but soon caught, and started burning. 'Now *that* feels good!'

'But how will you reply?'

'What do you think Ern would say?'

'I don't know.'

'I know. He wouldn't say a thing, and do you want to know why?'

'Max.'

'Because Ern Malley wouldn't know a poem from a peacock, would he, *Eth*? He might know how to put a watch back together, pull a *National Geographic* apart, but as for poetry. I used to *believe* in Ern, Ethel.'

'Max?' As I watched him crumbling, bit by bit, the rain soaking his black locks, his shirt wet, sticking to his chest, all little bosom, like Ern had, and pot belly.

'This man you keep describing . . . You and your little house in Croydon and Eth and Ern lying awake at night remembering Mum and Dad and the butcher and the races and the plums and all of it.'

'But it was *real*.'

'The front lawn you described' – as the rain got heavier, and made the papers smoke – 'the way this brother of yours rode down Dalmar Street with no hands and the way –'

'Max!'

He went in, returned with a box of *Penguins*, ripped them into pieces and fed them to the fire. One after another – and I made no attempt to stop him. If that's how he wanted it.

I didn't need it. I turned, ran through the house, out the front door, along the street, the sticks and stones cutting into my feet. But I didn't care. What was he saying? That he didn't believe – in the poems, that this man had existed? The world saying he was a fake – but he wasn't, wasn't, wasn't. Lying beside me at night, the moon on our faces, the smell of mock orange, Ern saying, You'll always look after me, won't you, Eth? Poor little thing. With his alabaster face. His eyes pleading, always pleading, this little boy of mine, taken away too soon. Not that it was my fault. I had to protect him, from Evan, from the blows, from the world, or he might've killed him. He might've. I couldn't allow it. As I crossed Hackney Road. Not a car to be seen. My nightdress sticking to my legs and tummy and womany bits (this, I couldn't stand, so I threw off my dressie, and ran into Botanic Park, its hundred acres of grass and pine trees and ponds). Looking back for him, because he'd probably be following (he always did, when we had our little tiffs). But I couldn't see him. Through the sheet rain, the limbs groaning and snapping, falling, thrown across the park. As I dropped to my knees, curled up into a ball, and rocked, moaning, Ern, Ern, Ern! Each of his words, each of the remaining autumn issues, gone, because in the end no one believed in Ern like I did.

I reached out to him. With my skin cold, pallid, pink and blue. 'Brother, where are you?'

Nothing. Just the roar of the wind.

'Get down from that tree, Ern. If you fall . . .'

Come and get me, Ethel.

'Get down!' One hand raised, imploring, the gusts blowing me back. 'Ern!'

Then the police were at the door of number forty, saying I had to go with them. But I was the one trying to protect him. Always, Little Ern. If not for me, then who? Everyone else, everyone had given up on him. No matter how much I tried to convince people, everyone gave up on Ern.

Maybe I should take a break, get my breath, before I tell you what happened next. I said, I think, at the beginning, that I would try and tell this story truthfully. Did I say that? Either way, I've tried. People have doubted me, invented sub-stories and alternative truths, claimed the sanctity of academia and records. But I'm the only one who's told the truth. And I'm glad you, dear reader, sitting in some distant future, have stuck by me (or are you reading the *Weekly* by now?). When the history of Australia is properly written, you will be remembered, like Ern, and his poems. Although one thing confuses me still. Why he left them in his case.

As the wind slowed, the rain eased, I walked home. Although what sort of home, I couldn't say. Perhaps I'd finish the last day of the trial, pack my things, return to Sydney, never to be heard of again. Then Max could get on with life, become an Adelaide academic, forget everything he'd ever believed in, settle into the Adelaide Club, marry Von, have babies and start the whole thing over again. Maybe that would be best. Maybe people shouldn't expect too much of themselves.

I walked in the front door and heard Mary. Just what I needed. Not much of a Mary, Magdalene or otherwise. Certainly no virgin, although you couldn't hold that against a person.

I stopped in the hallway and heard her say, 'You're lucky . . . when you think what she might have done.'

'She wouldn't have . . . I don't think.'

The wind was coming right through the house – from the back yard, with its smoking incinerator, out to the street. Through me, this grey ghost, standing in the hallway at two in the morning.

'They lived in Dalmar Street for three years before all of this happened.'

Max said, 'Bullshit.'

'Forget the poems. Who cares? And Ern. There was no Ern – you can see that now, can't you?'

'Of course there was. There's a birth certificate.'

I just listened. There was no point getting angry anymore. I'd lost Max. I'd lost my mother, my father, my brother. My brother. My brother. My brother. My brother. I can write it all I want, and people can choose to believe what they want, but he was my brother.

'And the boy.'

'No.'

'Look, Max, here . . .'

Silence. For a full minute, more, as the wind slowed, and the smell of smoke (Ern, finished at last) drifted down the hallway.

'I guess she was just trying to stop him, Max.'

I could see Max's face, but I couldn't see Max's face. Where had she got all this? The latest set of lies. But I was too cold, too tired to argue.

'Maybe it was an accident, Max?'

'Maybe.'

'Or he went too far, and she hit him, and killed him.'

And he said, 'You think that's what happened?'

'Yes.'

'She killed him, to protect the boy?'

'And that's her, in prison, see . . . nearly three years, while the kid's living out west.'

There was nothing left. Nothing. Now that Max had chosen her over me. And some ridiculous story that Evan (yes, I'd admitted) had . . . No point. He'd been sick. Little Ern. Graves' Disease. Pneumonia. Whatever you want to call it. Same effect, filling up his lungs so he couldn't breathe. And there's me, somehow, in prison.

So be it. The former things have passed away, Eth. Come on, old girl, time to go. It was good while it lasted. The letter I'd got from Max. The train trip, the arrival in Adelaide, and the way the city appeared as you came up the ramp. The smell of the place, the trams, and Max, standing with his smoke, waiting, grinning, always grinning. And what did he say the first time: Ethel Malley, is it? Or something like that. So glad to see me. The sister of the poet. So glad.

There was a baby in a pram. I noticed this. I always noticed babies. Because they were the whole package, begun again. Before anything had soured, any lies were told, before any disappointments (which is most of life), before screaming and arguing and people dying of diseases and the whole shitty lot that made you, finally, who you were. Thing being, no one asks for it to turn out a particular way. It just does. Yes, I noticed him or her in his or her pram, and thought, there you go, Ern, try again, have another crack, let's see if it's better this time round.

Funny thing was, the baby smiled at me. Now, how often does that happen? Never. Like it knew me, or remembered me, but it couldn't, because it was an Adelaide baby, and I was a Sydney Ethel. But it knew, sensed, somehow. Perhaps it was my boy, come back to try again, and he was saying, Hey, Mum, I think I got it this time.

I walked to my room, slipped off my wet nightie, and got dressed. Silently. Closed my case, returned to the hallway, and heard her say, 'I'm not saying it was her fault, Max. But she's lied to you.'

No, I thought, as I left the house. I haven't lied to anyone. The truth is so obvious. Me and my little boy. And people are taken away from you, aren't they, reader? No one asks – one day, gone. Some terrible accident, or Grandpa, in Liverpool, who leaned over to undo the gate, and had a stroke, dropped dead. What a release!

As I went I heard her say, 'If she's leaving, perhaps we shouldn't say anything?' And he agreed. Then she asked how I'd be in Sydney, on my own, and Max said, 'Nothing could ever stop Ethel. She's a marvel, Mary.'

I walked along the dark street, the sky clear, at last. The wind had dropped. It wasn't even that cold anymore. Now, I felt like I'd done what I'd come for: given the world the poems. Nothing could take that away. There'd always be a copy, in a library, and now, maybe, they'd be so rare they'd be valuable. And the myth of Ern would persist. And lesser writers would make stories from his.

# 45

There's only so much you can do to control a moment. The thought that kept occurring to me as I crossed Botanic Park, towards the whore of a city I'd come to know so well; carrying my case; my feet sinking into the muddy grass (no one had bothered with a path); in my best dress, my stockings wet to the ankles. Only so much. To make someone believe you, trust you, have faith in you. This, I thought, I've been doing my whole life. Offering. Followed by the doubts, and rejection. Not that I cared. I was me, in every atom and cell, every breath and word, as rough or embarrassing as it might be. Me, every time I passed wind, or offered an opinion that didn't make sense, rise to someone's standards. I was happy this way. So I could walk, admire the lopped branch that looked like a circumcised dick, listen to the crows arguing about a scrap of grey bread, smell the pine oil that still persisted on such a cold, wet morning.

I stopped and listened. Like a thousand people were gathering around, trying to say something to me. I wanted to hear them, but couldn't. Speak up! Ern, perhaps, a tribe of Aboriginal people, a family picnicking, Booth giving his inaugural Salvation Army oratory. 'What is it, Ern?' I said.

But he wouldn't answer. Terror of a man. Of a boy. I say all of this because I couldn't help that *he* was the one Dad loved. Fathers and sons, I guess, working in the shed, taking things apart, putting them together. And some of their sculptures were good. Two-storey people with wire heads and tyre bodies. Not that he didn't love me. We had our own special moments. He'd say to me, Righto, Eth, enough of this motorbike (or crystal set, or whatever it was). What d'you want to do on this beautiful Saturday afternoon?

How about the movies?

How about it? Let's go, my dear.

Then Ern would say, Can I come? And I'd say, No, it's just me and Dad, and he'd pull a sour face – but so be it. Me and Dad. Down to the Roxy. *Scaramouche* – and Dad snoring. But I didn't care, these were *our* moments. Every Saturday afternoon – well, every few weeks, months – maybe it had only happened a few times?

I continued across the gardens I'd see (I hoped) for the last time, past the zoo, with its groaning hippopotamuses, screeching monkeys, stench. But a nice stench. Honest. Like the smell of Dad's work clothes after a hot day (I, of course, got to wash them, while he and Ern, well, you know). Up Frome Road, past the hospital. There was a balcony, and all the injured soldiers would sit outside in the sun, smoking, watching people as they went past. I'd wave, and a few would wave back. Even from here I could smell the ti-tree and disinfectant, see the bandaged limbs, some with their eyes covered, which was the saddest thing of all.

I arrived on North Terrace and stopped at a café for tea and toast. There was a copy of *The News*, but I avoided it. Then I set off for the train station. A few more minutes, a ticket, I'd be gone. But then, I turned south, looked the length of King

William Street, wondering. Turned west. South. Something was making me, but I said no, crossed the road, then stopped again, and the voices were all around me, still, telling me, It isn't fair, Eth. He's doing it for you.

Go away!

Eth . . . he's first in the dock. After what he's done for you.

Quiet!

I thought and thought. There was a train after lunch, and what did it matter if I got home a few hours late? But why? After what he'd done, said, decided to think. Why?

Righto. Before I could think about it. South. Across Hindley Street, smelling of hops and horse shit, cheap perfume and semen, the bookshop, with its last copy of *the gift of blood*. One voice saying stop, turn around. Another, keep going. On and on, past Elder's, with its chaff and a little pyramid of kegs, across Waymouth Street, the still-singing newsboy, although I knew, now, there was no point worrying about public opinion. People would always believe what they wanted, what their meanest instincts told them. Across a trench-scarred Victoria Square and into the police courts, down the hall I'd already been down a dozen times. Stopping short of going in. Listening. Max, of course. 'I have no time for this, Your Honour. We've been over it again and again. In the end, the arguments Mr Williams has put are without merit. He has gathered the slurry of a thousand bar-room conversations, mothers standing outside schools gossiping, petrol station attendants – in short, people who never have or will read *Angry Penguins*. So if you're determined to find me guilty for publishing these poems, fine me, and let me get on with life. Frankly, I'm tired of it all.'

'As am I,' Andrews said. 'But I suppose we'll have to see this through . . . will we, Mr Williams?'

'I defer.'

'Do you? I thought this might take a few hours, but here we are, days later.'

A long pause. I wondered what was happening, but dared not go in. Why should I? I sat on a bench. Like one of those soldiers, with his eyes wrapped up, only able to listen, to try and make sense of the world from the words of the old girl who smelt like eucalyptus.

Andrews said, 'Come on then, Mr Williams. Maybe we can get out before lunch.'

A few chairs moving. I wanted to see Max's face, if Sid and John were still there, but dared not.

'Yes,' Williams said, 'there is a lot of sex going on, isn't there, Mr Harris?'

'It's going on everywhere,' he replied. 'As we speak. A thousand people, in this city alone.'

A bit of laughter, and again, Andrews did nothing.

'No, Max, if I can call you that – we've spent enough time together? I meant, in the poems?'

'If a poem's a reflection of life, then shouldn't it contain that too?'

'Perhaps. But the means, Max? These things can be suggested.'

'How?'

'I'm no poet, but one might say, *He kissed her with his eyes, and touched her face as if it was velvet.*'

'*Were* velvet.'

'Sorry. But my point is, there are ways.'

'In that instance, bad ways.'

'I never professed to be a poet.'

'Well, that's funny, isn't it, because you're professing to judge poetry.'

Good on yer, Max! Take him apart. Make him your Indian.

Williams took a moment then said, 'You're very good with semantics, Mr Harris.'

'As you should be – working as a lawyer.'

'But argue as you might, there's no denying some lines are not appropriate for general dissemination.'

'Pardon?'

'*Dissemination.*'

A few voices, and I could hear John's throaty laugh.

'Cos if you hada said that these officers would have to take you to the cells, in the basement, where Detective Apeldoorn took me, and they'd have to lock you up, and threaten you, as he did me. They'd have to say, Eh, you, Williams, wash your dirty mouth out or we'll do it for you.'

Silence. I wanted to go in.

'Which'd be a shame, cos you might feel very threatened, and like me, wonder whether you'd see daylight again, or like Ern Malley, who was also bullied as a child, you might actually piss yerself cos you're so scared.'

'Max—'

'Don't Max me. I've met you before, Williams. At school. Hanging around the showers.'

A few gasps, and Andrews settled the court and warned Max about what he was saying, and Max said, 'Quite frankly, Your Honour, I don't care. I'm a student, I'm young, I publish a magazine, I thought I was doing some good, it's led to this place, this dock, this ... it's led to me having a life I never wanted, all because I believed we were entitled to say what we want, as long as it doesn't harm anyone. And it hasn't, has it? Who's it harmed? No one. People choose to buy my magazine. No one's strapped in a chair and made to read it. And even if they were, what would they have seen? *The decimals of our deceiving age? A calm immortal frieze?* Beautiful lines. And so what if there is a dick? There's a million times worse being printed today.'

'Very impressive,' Williams said. 'You could publish that.'

'I will.'

'All of your university friends can read it, and be inspired with your lessons about free speech. Meanwhile, at Sigalis's milk bar, the ten-year-old boys can gather around a copy of *Angry Penguins* and read about—'

'No one believes you. No one's offended. The problem is, isn't it, people like *me*?'

'How, Mr Harris?'

'Unwilling to fight this ridiculous war. Because I and Mr Nolan and Reed and others refuse to get ourselves killed, you hate us? Because we busy ourselves with civilisation.'

Andrews said, 'I'm going to stop it there. I'm not learning anything new.'

'Ern Malley,' Williams said, 'was no poet. Ern Malley was a disguise for publishing pornography, and now you've been held to account, Mr Harris.'

'Ern Malley was a poet, an excellent poet, perhaps the best this country's ever seen. *That taunts, the living life* – listen to those lines, Mr Williams. Have you read them? I have, again and again, and every time they get better. That's how great poetry works. I knew, from the beginning, when these poems arrived on my desk, that I had to publish them, make this man known.'

'This man? Ern Malley? Who, I think you'll find, if you do some research, doesn't exist.'

'Nonsense.'

'Ern Malley, and his sister, Ethel?'

I stood, but stopped myself. Wanted to go in, but only took a few steps.

Williams said, 'Do you believe otherwise, Mr Harris?'

'I believe in Ern.'

'But do you believe he existed? Do you believe he wrote these poems? Because the rest of Australia seems to have decided otherwise.'

I waited. Silence. Come on, Max. Say it. I took another step. Max might've seen my feet, my legs.

Tell him. Tell him everything I've told you about Ern. Tell him about our dad, and mum, and what happened to us, and our dog, and Mrs Royal, and the men on the back lawn, and all of it. Max, please?

'No.'

As I heard this I took the final step, stood in the doorway, looking at him, and him at me. No words.

Williams said, 'So, if you don't believe Ern Malley existed, how can you stand there defending him?'

Max took a moment and said, 'Because that doesn't matter.'

'Surely it does.'

I knew I shouldn't have returned. I took my case, hurried down the hall, the steps, across Victoria Square. Max's voice in my ear: 'Ethel, come back!'

I turned, and saw him standing on the steps, beside John and Sid and Von. '*Ethel*.'

I heard a tremor in his voice (even above the trams, and

wind, and cars). Like Ern, calling to me, from the driveway, as Mrs Royal loaded the dog in the car. *Ethel!*

Me, running out, fighting with her and her pushing me away, onto the ground, as Terry tried to find a compromise, and Ern cried, and I held him – always Ern, always, always, till his, and my, last breath. I love you, brother. Love you.

The name in my head as I ran towards the station. Back down the ramp, to the concourse, the man in blue.

Ethel!

I was shaking. Terrified. I turned, and he was there. Max Harris, sitting on a bench. He said, 'I'll be in the shit . . . parked the Austin in the copper's spot.'

I noticed the times on the big board. Sydney. 12.52. My watch. 12.21.

'This is all very familiar,' he said.

'How did you get here so quick?'

He smiled. 'Eth, I told you, you never stop for lights in this town.'

I was having none of it. 'I have to buy my ticket.'

'Five minutes, to talk?'

I checked the board, my watch, Max Harris. Then sat and said, 'It'll be good to get home.'

'But it won't be much chop here without you.'

I took a moment. 'Not how it sounded last night.'

'All that . . . so much talk. But I would've thrown you out a long time ago, Mrs Malley, if I hadn't wanted you around.'

'Still . . .' Clutching my purse.

'I've often wondered, what you'd do, after Ern.'

I didn't see the point of answering.

'But now, I'm worried what *I'll* do.'

'You'll get by.' I had a tear, I know, and I couldn't avoid it, so I wiped it. 'We'll just have to get on with something constructive. I have plans for the shop.'

'Peg?'

'She's relying on me.'

'I know.'

'What with her son, and grandson, and life not turning out how they'd hoped. I'll go back, and do some good. I'll help the boy.'

We waited. Another tear, and I took care of that too. Glanced at my watch and said, 'I'll have to buy a ticket.'

'Can I come visit, soon?'

I turned to him, for the first time. 'Yes . . . I think I'd like that.'

'Maybe Chrissie. We can sit out on the grass and remember Ern.'

'But you said . . .'

I had to go. I couldn't stay. Not with Von, and Mary. But Max would always be my brother, my lover, my everything. What is it, when you put your faith in a person, and they don't end up being what you'd hoped for? What is it?

I stood and offered my hand, but now, believe it or not, after all this trying, he took me in his arms, hugged me, put his face on my neck (just like Ern!) and kissed me. Just like that. Like it wasn't such a bad ending after all.

As we parted he called, 'Dirty little bastard, that brother of yours.'

And I smiled. Cos he was right.

I approached the man in blue, stopped, thought about my destination, and bought a ticket for Melbourne. Looked back and waved at Max, who was lighting a cigarette.

I'd never see him again. Never.

# 46

It was a handmade, cobbled-together sort of city. Bluestone gutters full of horse shit and hay, rain, from the minute I stepped off the train in Spencer Street, the grey-blue sky I'd seen in the Innsbruck postcard. A European outpost, with a thousand bins full of fish heads and foetuses (I guess). But I liked the place. Could see why Ern might've. As I walked along Princess Street, singing to myself, '*When the unclean spirit is gone out of a man.*' I could see Max, waving to me, even blowing a kiss, although by then, I didn't read much into it. Never would again. The last of Adelaide disappearing under a railway bridge, the back of red-brick homes sprouting washing lines, cats perched on top of fences.

The tram, a short walk, then this neat street, with its angle-parked Austins, reminding me – always – of Max. A few double-fronted Federation numbers beside tin-sided cottages, and access lanes leading to yards full of bricks, tiles, timber and rubbish. Something more recent, with pink bricks and a picket fence. *Louis?* I wanted to call, but what were the chances? It was a dreamy place, really. Soaked with the smell of woodbines, and wisteria. A sort of bluestone Hampstead Heath, Keats and Fanny strolling in the sun (the Romantics all had a secret lover, all of them, all of us . . .).

I put down my case and waited at a bus stop, peered into someone's yard, and wondered. Would I see Louis and Ern walking down the street? Ern in his work-boots, ready for a morning of lifting wheat bags. Not holding hands, surely? No, they weren't that pink. Just like a couple of mates, or brothers. All along here – this path, this grass, this is where they'd come, where Ern would stroll, on a hot night, telling this man about his sister. Eth's as mad as a cut snake. She was married for a time, but it all went wrong. I didn't feel like moving from the shelter. Here, I was safe. My own little frock forest, the dozens of mothers he, we, had, have, at any given moment. Here, in a shelter, on Princess Street, no one knew about me, hated me, thought me a disgrace. Here I was a nobody. *A nobody*. Is that what it had come to?

I could overhear them – Ern and his friend. Ern saying, He was a violent man.

What was his name?

Evan. Poor old Eth, she put up with a lot, but in the end . . . it was too much for her, Louis.

Maybe they'd stopped, waited for a bus. Maybe Ern had looked in his eyes, and wanted to kiss him. Before saying, She might've put up with him, if not for Wayne.

Yes, it could've happened this way. Could've. Ern trying to make sense of me, as much as I tried to make sense of him, for these past months.

And then one day, Louis . . .

Go on.

This particular night, Evan had been drinking. He was letting the boy have it, and Eth had had enough.

The house was similar to number forty. Same frontage, and

hall. Same easterly sunroom, and westerly lounge. I remembered the night, and how it might've sounded. Slamming doors, pots and pans everywhere (cos it had started in the kitchen), poor old ... right, I guess I can say, can't I? Young Wayne, trying to get away from Evan, but this shit of a husband of mine catching him in the hallway, punching him, fair old punching him, and his jaw cracking, and him falling. Me calling for Evan to stop. But no. He kicked him. Fair old kicked, in the guts – and I knew, this time, he might kill him. So I went to the kitchen, got the bread knife, and returned. And by this time, Wayne, fearing for his life, had managed to stand, open the front door, and run away. But Evan had him again, and said (something like), You filthy little cunt (although he hadn't been doing a thing, not a thing!). He picked him up and threw him from the porch, and Wayne landed with a thump. Evan went after him, but I said, No, you don't. He turned and struck me across the face (God knows it was no shock, I'd had it a thousand times) and next thing I knew I was standing beside him, as he lay on the porch, moaning, the knife between his ribs, pleading with me like *I* was the problem. *Eth!* All breathy, as he started drowning in his own blood.

Now, if I stood, I could save Wayne. Leave this shelter, pick him out of the aggies, take him, protect him. But no, this other Ethel was already coming down the stairs, picking up her boy, carrying him in, covering his face so he might not see the gurgling man. But I could see. Her going in, closing the door, leaving Evan to die. Which took five or six minutes. None of which I saw – but did, now, sitting in my little cocoon. I saw him trying to call, but not having the breath, trying to stand, but falling, clawing at the wood with his too-long fingernails. I saw all this, for the first time. And the man becoming still.

Completely still. Lifeless, as the blood started draining from the wound, and his mouth, and his hand (reaching out, like he'd just found God) fell to the boards.

All of this, like I was sitting in a cinema watching a movie someone had made of my life. The real Ethel and the made-up, remembered, fake Ethel. But as for this small brown house – no one emerged. No one. It wasn't number forty, and there'd never be someone lying dead on the front porch (I guessed).

Anyway, no point staying. I picked up my case and continued. Down a slope, more of the same sort of houses, but no clues. I thought, perhaps, I'd smell biscuits and cakes baking, knock on a front door, introduce myself. But all I could smell was ground steel from a spring-makers, and cat-pissy rosemary, planted everywhere.

Soon the homes gave way to shops, and shops to State Street – a junction of several roads lined with coffee-smelling delicatessans and mattress shops and a single paper seller, asking me if I needed the news. 'I've had enough of that lately.' Along. A lino and carpet emporium, and an ice cart, the water pouring out, a man sitting with a cigarette, waiting. I stopped, put down my case and said, 'Ern, where are you?' And then I saw it. A big sign, in old-fashioned letters, hung high above the road: *Fauske's Bakery – Since 1897*.

I crossed the road and went into the shop. The sweet smell of bread and Lady Alice biscuits. There was a girl serving, and a man ordering. I studied a painting on the wall. Europe? Germany? It was Innsbruck – the same view, the same photo, but bigger. As I remembered Ern's words (or were they?). *Lois*. But why the lack of a 'u'? What did it matter now? I was here, committed. Bread in brown paper, presented as some sort of trophy, as the man left and the girl said, 'Can I help you?'

'I was wondering if Mr Fauske is here?'

'Hold on.' She went out back, called for him, and I thought, Shit, no . . . Although why else had I come? Why had I bought a ticket to Melbourne instead of Sydney? Why had I caught the tram, walked for hours? Why? But again, on the wall, an old photo of the Sphinx, and underneath in copperplate: *The hand burns resinous in the evening sky.*

'Can I help you?'

He was standing a few feet away. Shorter than I'd imagined, well-muscled, with brown eyes that seemed to retreat into the depths of his skull. Handsome, sort of, and my first thought was, I can see what you mean, Ern. I guess he thought I wanted to order a cake for a birthday, but I said, 'Louis?'

Then he tilted his head, much like Ern used to, and said, 'Ethel?'

I extended a hand, but he didn't shake it.

'Come on.'

He led me out back, up some stairs, along a carpeted hallway that fed into separate living areas. A kitchen, bedroom (was that the bed?), laundry, glassed-in reading room (was that them, sitting together, writing?) and finally, a sort of Edwardian drawing room with peeling wallpaper and what might have been gas lights, although when he flicked a switch, a single globe flooded the room. He showed me in, poured himself a scotch and offered me one. I guessed it might be best. A few moments later we were sitting, sizing each other up. I said, 'I know you didn't want to see me.'

'When something finishes, often it's best.'

Silence. Very uncomfortable. It was strange, because I

wouldn't have thought Ern would choose someone so aloof. Although maybe he was just shy? He said, 'Can I help you?' Like that. Like I was buying bread. Like he wanted me over and done with.

'I went to the army,' I said.

He dropped his head, maybe half an inch. 'And what did they tell you?'

The room was warm from the big windows at the front. There were a few pictures, and drawings – old, like they'd been torn from books and framed. One, some sort of poet. Keats, perhaps? I asked and he said it was, and I said, '*I have been bitter with you, my brother . . .*' And he smiled and said, 'Have you?'

This brother of mine. It was so hard to tell one thing from another. Maybe Max was right? Maybe he *was* me? 'At times . . . when I'd never hear from him. I guess, all that time, he was sick?'

'It came and went.'

'Because when he came back to Sydney he wasn't in good nick.'

He smiled. '*Good nick*?'

'His health.' Although his look indicated his own tendency for vivisection, like he found me funny, homely, perhaps. 'Was he?'

'What?'

'Ill?'

'Yes.'

Like that. Yes. Like, that's all I'm going to tell you. I didn't get this Fauske character. Why Ern was down here, living with him; why they'd been together for so long, in Kew, in the jungle.

'What do you want to know?' he asked.

'You lived here?' I noticed the heavy velvet curtains, like a set for a play; a candelabra with no candles; and a bookcase, full, haemorrhaging, like Mr Alexander or McDonald or all the other people I'd known who had let books rule their life.

'Not at first,' he said. 'After the war, and the discharge (I suppose you know about that?).'

'Yes.'

'After he moved to Melbourne. My mother was still alive, and she had no idea. She would've keeled over if she'd known. So I rented a place on Princess Street.'

I studied this princess. He didn't look queer, effeminate. Quite the opposite. Strong, bulky arms (God, as I imagined Ern in a rapture), perhaps from a life lifting wheat sacks. 'And you two?'

'Yes, we lived together.'

I didn't want to ask – the obvious. That is, you lived together because you loved each other? But it was the one thing I needed to know. 'You set up house?'

But he just said, 'It's funny, Ethel, how you're coming to life.'

'What do you mean?'

'From the hundreds of stories he told me.'

'He did?'

'Of course. He was always talking about you, and what you got up to. You two, and your dad, out in the shed with the Indian, and the race.'

He seemed to know it all, but was reluctant to give it up.

'Everything? Like the Jesus house?'

'Oh, yes, he was always talking about that. And the crazy man, thinking Christ would move in, and the library and books and conversations about . . . everything.'

Yes, he knew. Ern. Maybe, next to me, more than anyone.

I felt better. That this was someone I could trust. Forever, perhaps. Not some Max Harris, losing faith midway, but to the end – in the man, the spirit, the ghost, the body, the little pink legs, the willy, the dreams and nightmares, the pissy pants, everything. 'He told you about Mrs Royal and Terry?'

'He did. We'd sit at night on the back porch and he'd remember. He was happy when he did, Ethel.'

'Really?'

'Yes. And he was mischievous, wasn't he?'

'Oh, yes.'

'He always bragged about how good he was at shoplifting.'

'He didn't?'

'Reckoned he could get an Austin out of a showroom. Where do you reckon that came from, Eth?'

*Eth*. He knew me! Ern had told him!

'Well,' I said, 'we grew up poor, Louis. There was never money, so we had to make do. And Ern, believe me, he made do, not always legally. He got caught several times, but always seemed to keep it from the old bitch.'

'He told me about her – chasing him out the backyard with a rolling pin.'

He remembered who he was with, and waited. But he needn't.

'He'd tell me. Eth, he'd say, me and my sister, we'd just lie there of a night, and she'd tell me stories.'

'I did.'

'About these kids who'd lost their parents, and how it didn't matter because they'd become famous (him, a cricketer, her, a perfume maker).'

'Yes.' I returned. Always returning. That was my problem.

'I always tried to cheer him up. He could get gloomy, couldn't he?'

'At times.'

'I'd look after him. Any problems at school, I'd take care of them.'

He smiled again, but this time, differently. 'Let them have it, did you?'

'Did he tell you?'

'Bruises, a few black eyes, and didn't you break someone's arm?'

'Ssh!' I giggled. 'Nothing was ever said. The boy never told anyone. I got away with it, and he never bothered Ern again.'

'Eth, you're a marvel.'

'No.'

'Well, if you want to know, the way it happened . . .' He took a deep breath, thought about it. 'My mum died, and my sister, she hates me anyway, she said I could run the shop, she didn't want anything to do with a fag. That's what she said: a fag. So me and Ern moved in together . . . up here.'

Up here. The rugs all worn, covered in food and crumbs, plates left around the place, and a musty smell. These two boys, living some sort of attempted life.

'We'd sit in here of a night,' he said. 'Reading, listening to the radio. And one night we had an argument.' He was there, shouting, and I suppose Ern was shouting back, because he could give as good as he got.

'I couldn't even tell you what it was about, Eth, but next thing I'm throwing things . . . see' – as he pointed to a broken vase – 'that was one of them . . . my dad's. Next thing he storms out, and he's standing down there on the road, shouting up at me, and I went to our room, shoved a heap of his clothes in a case, and came out to that window and threw it down at him. It came open, and there were clothes everywhere. Blowing down the street, cars running over them, people laughing, and poor old Ern trying to pick them up, and me thinking, Good riddance to you, Malley.'

I could see this. My brother, a day or two before he arrived at number forty, refusing to talk about where he'd been and what had happened. 'He didn't say a thing about it.'

'No . . . although he was like that, wasn't he, Eth? A decent man, better than me, as it turns out. From the minute I threw that case, I regretted it. I knew I'd lost him, and I knew I wouldn't ever find anyone half as good.'

I felt this too. 'Louis, I miss him.'

He covered my hand. 'If I could do anything to fix it.'

This room still held the ghost of Ern. I could see him at the bookcase, reading each volume, asking Louis about it. 'You're a reader?'

'Not much. Most were my dad's . . . he loved poetry. All of the greats. He'd sit here of a night reading to me and my sister. That's how we got the love of it.'

My God. *The love of it.*

Louis poured us another scotch. We sat, for another hour, talking about my brother. We covered everything. The way he couldn't piss at a urinal, and always locked himself in a cubicle (and I explained, this is because of what had happened at school); the way his hands shook and he bit his lip whenever he got nervous; how his stick legs went all the way up to his tummy, and how they clattered when he was cold, and how he couldn't look strangers in the eye, and how he never said anything bad (really) about anyone, and how (I explained) Mr Alexander had given up on the Jesus house because this small, boy-like Christ had arrived, and taken root. At one point I said, 'What did you two do, sitting up here all night?' And Louis said, 'He was a nasty boy, when he wanted to be, Eth.'

'How?'

'The front window – he'd get eggs, throw them down at some old girl, then hide behind the curtains. I'd tell him to stop, but he'd go down to the bakery and get another dozen. One time someone called the cops, and they came and knocked on the door, and there's Ern, Oh, no, constable, we haven't seen a thing!'

'He was a rascal.'

'He never grew up, Eth.'

I waited; the window open, the curtain dancing, traffic. 'And when he died . . .?'

'It was weeks till I knew.'

'How?'

He took a letter from his pocket, unfolded it and handed it to me. As I drained my latest scotch, I read. *Dear Louis, My name is Karl McDonald. I live behind the Malleys in Croydon, Sydney. A few weeks ago Ern Malley came to see me. He told me how ill he was, and how he thought he might only have a short time. I'd known about his disease, but not much, as he, and his sister, kept pretty much to themselves. He told me that after he died, he wanted you to know. And he asked me if I'd write, once I knew. He gave me your address. He said I shouldn't tell a soul, because if Ethel knew it would kill her. He said he guessed I could keep a secret, and he could rely on me, as there wasn't anyone else. A bit sad, perhaps, but I made this promise to him. And one morning, last week, I was out in the back yard watering, and*

*I hear this scream from number forty, and I knew. Then Ethel came running out and said, He's gone, my brother's gone! I went around to her house and covered him and sat with her and made a cup of tea before the ambulance arrived. But he was gone. Peacefully, she said, although Ern reckoned it wouldn't end peacefully, and had accepted his lot, and in a way, just wanted it done. That was what he was like. He was a decent man, as you (he told me) probably know. He asked that I wait a few days before writing. He didn't want you coming up, or to the funeral (I went with Eth – it was simple, but nice). And he said for me to ask you to stay away from his sister. He didn't reckon she could take knowing, about how you two were involved. So, there it is, Mr Fauske. He had a smile on his face when I saw him. Maybe he was thinking of you – that's a nice thought to keep, I reckon. Yours sincerely, Karl McDonald.*

I returned it, and said, 'He should've told me.'

'He should've, Eth, but he was just thinking of you.'

I felt drowsy, slid from my seat to the floor and sat clutching my scotch. Louis stood, approached a drawer, took out a pile of papers then returned and sat beside me. The top sheet was covered in scribble: *Dürer: Innsbruck, 1495. I had often, cowled in the slumberous heavy air, Closed my inanimate lids to find it real . . .*

Then it dawned on me. 'You?' I asked, scanning the bookcase, the Eliot and Wordsworth, the Longfellow and Shakespeare.

'These are the first drafts,' he said. 'We worked on them, most nights.'

'We?'

'I'd sit over there with a pen and pencil, and I'd throw out a line, and he'd throw one back, and by the time we'd finished, with a gutful of scotch, we had a poem. *Now I find that once more*

*I have shrunk to an interloper* ... then Ern (giggling, generally, because he didn't have a poetic bone in his body, but enjoyed the game) – *robber of dead men's dream* ...'

Dear me. But not such a bad revelation. If Ern wasn't a poet (and so many now had decided he wasn't) then this was a suitable compromise.

'*You're* Ern Malley?' I said to him.

'No, Ern's Ern. He helped. God knows I didn't want anyone thinking I'd written them. And when I saw they'd been published under his name I thought, Good on you, Ern.'

'But he left your name off?'

'He knew. I didn't want the world banging my door down, writing me up, complaining about me, spreading rumours about *indecency* ... cos that's how it turned out, didn't it, Eth?'

'Yes.'

'In a way, it was lucky he died. He wouldn't have survived.' Smiling. Louis always smiled, it seemed. 'In years to come people will talk about him – isn't that funny, Eth? Ern. About *him*. This quiet little boy, hiding in the dresses (he told me all about it). They'll remember him as a genius. People all around the world – they'll write books about him. And we, Eth, we can sit back and have a laugh. Everyone can. Even McAuley and Stewart (bastards took them from Ern's locker). And the only idiots not laughing will be the ones who took it seriously. Imagine!'

# 1981

For some reason she stopped there. Her and Louis, sitting in Melbourne in 1944, less than a day after she'd said goodbye to me. That was all the story she'd wanted to tell, I guess. About her, Ern, Von, the trial. Louis, and whatever role he'd played. And after that . . . well, I'll come to that, but this is how I got the bad news.

I was sitting at home, writing my usual column. Strangely, I'd decided to write about the Malley affair (as it had become known): Ern and Eth, the court case, those last few days before Williams came in one morning, spoke to Andrews, and Andrews smiled and said, At last! The Crown has seen sense. All charges withdrawn! And me and Von dancing around – because John and Sid had already gone back to Melbourne. I'd decided to write about what made Australia unique – the latest De Niro film, or Michael Jackson song? The Eels, or Norwood winning a cup? Fraser, pretending to lead us into a post-Whitlam paradise of endless wealth and beach barbecues. My hypothesis being, we were a little bit less Australian every day. But in the days of Ern Malley (okay, perhaps I'm living in the past), people *were* Australian: the way they spoke, what they ate, how they cared for each other. I'd just started writing and Von came in and said, 'There's someone on the phone for you.'

'Tell them to ring back.'

'Said it's urgent – someone's died.'

Now you might say this is strange, but I knew straight away who it was. I knew, after all these years, I'd only hear at the end. In the same way Ethel had created, watered and pruned Ern, at the end. Like some Wagner opera where the inevitable death becomes the twilight of the story, the great affirmation. The discovery of sacred poems (because Eth was, if nothing else, a great dramatist). Anyway, then Samela, my daughter, came in and asked for help with a theatre review she was writing (another great irony, her taking Carpenter's job) and I said, 'I give up!' Stormed out, took the phone and said, 'Yes?'

That's how it happened. Although you're probably curious, aren't you, about the thirty-seven years in between. Because that's how stories work, don't they? We need a chronology, a thread, an understanding of what happens to people, and why. Well, I can't tell you why. In the end, I never really got my head around Ethel Malley. No one did. Never really understood why she threw so much into her own little crystal cult. Never got, all the following years, why she never replied to my letters. Not one. I guessed, perhaps, she'd moved on from those days in Adelaide during the war. Or become senile.

Then the voice said, 'You Max Harris?'

'Speaking.'

'And you knew a lady called Ethel Malley?'

Samela stood, hands on hips, whispering, 'Ten minutes?'

Covering the phone. 'Wait . . . it's about Ethel.'

'Who?'

'*Ethel* . . . Ethel Malley.'

But she'd forgotten, no doubt, gave a little huff, walked away, as Von appeared in the hallway and said, 'Ethel?'

'Ssh!' Returning to the phone. 'Yes, I knew Ethel, years ago.'

'Reason I ask is . . . well, I'm holding this book called *Angry Penguins*. Autumn 1944, it says. An old one. And it was in Ethel's handbag when I . . . when I found her, dead. In Centenary Park. Like she'd gone for walk and . . . dead as all hell she was . . . is.'

I could see the look on Von's face. Like she knew, too; like she was terrified. That Ethel was dead. And yes, considering what you've just read, you're probably surprised to hear that, but in the following years Von would often say to me, What do you reckon Ethel's up to these days? And I'd say, Maybe we could drive to Sydney to see her? And she'd say, You think? And I'd say, No, you're right . . . Point being, Von, who's the nicest person a man could meet, love, marry, cared about Ethel. Because, like me, she'd come to think of her as every bit as delicate and troubled as her brother. A little porcelain swan that might crack, just by touching it. During all those decades, we'd remembered her. As Elvis wiggled his hips, and JFK slumped forward; as Buzz and his mate walked on the moon – so long ago, most of a lifetime – we thought of Ethel. As we walked down the aisle (we sent her an invitation, but she didn't reply), as we brought Samela home from hospital, as I got dressed, every day, to go to work in my bookshop – she was always on my mind.

Then the voice said, 'I found your name inside the front cover, Mr Harris.'

'Really?'

'Underlined. And your address, and phone number in North Adelaide.'

Strange. As we hadn't moved to Stanley Street until 1969.

'It says: *This is the copy Max gave me the day after publication, in 1944.*'

Dear old Eth! All those years. Carrying me around in her bag. And did she stop and tell people about me, Ern, the poems, the trial? Did she say, You've heard of Ern Malley, no doubt? Well, he was my brother, and look here, see, this is a first edition of his work.

Von came closer. 'Is it her?'

And the voice, 'There were some clippings too, Mr Harris. Old ones. About you and her . . . we'll hold onto them if you like, send them to you.'

'*Send them to me?*'

Von was biting her lip. A habit (I always told her) she'd picked up from Ethel. She seemed ready to react, to cry, perhaps. Maybe it was because she'd beaten Eth to the prize (as it was). Because what love gives, it takes. Maybe she knew this, and had always felt guilty. I never asked. All those years ago when, after Eth left, and the trial was over, we'd had this raging argument, and I'd jumped in the car, driven to Melbourne, to Heide, and said to John and Sunday: Got a spare room? Stayed for six months. Drinking cheap wine till the sun came up, sleeping most of the day, composing odes under plum trees (just like Keats). And other things. Every day there'd be something different: Bill Dobell, Bracks, all of them. All of the people who made a culture (yes, that's what I'd say in my column – a day at Heide was worth a year at a state gallery, or a theatre, rehashing Shaw for the hundredth time).

But it didn't last. People got tired of each other, argued, bitched and back-stabbed, and I decided to leave. Thought, for a while, Von and I could go to Sydney and start again. But no, I went home, apologised, finished my studies, wrote more poetry, stocked Mary Martin's bookshop with the best literature from around the world (the latest *Angry Penguins* always at the front) and got on with the life everyone had expected me to live. As Dad died (although I wrote no poem for him); Mum (a ballad, still in my desk); as the Malley affair was forgotten, mostly. The odd, occasional interview in which I explained, and still do, how, given the same parcel of poems arriving on my desk, I'd do the same. If that included being made to look an idiot, so be it. Because (I'd tell anyone) the poems were good, and in the end that was all that mattered.

'When I found her I thought I should try heart massage, Mr Harris, but it was beyond that,' the voice on the other end of the phone said. 'She was cold. So I ran home, called an ambulance, and returned, and a few minutes later these fellas came and examined her and said, There wasn't nothing you coulda done.'

'Right.' I took it in. The old girl, dead. 'And she's . . .?'

'Gone to the mortuary, they reckon.'

'Thanks, Mr . . .?'

'McDonald.'

No. Couldn't have been. 'No relation to Karl?'

'My old man . . . you knew him?'

We spent a few minutes remembering. He told me he reckoned he'd seen a copy of this *Penguins* magazine in his house, and was headed home to look, and I told him his dad, and uncle, were players in the Malley affair, but he didn't seem to know what I was talking about, so I thanked him and said I'd stay in contact, got his phone number, and rang off.

I sat beside Von and said, 'They found her in the park.'

'What happened?'

'He didn't say. Heart, I guess. Or stroke. Either way.'

We sat, silently, as the crows started a shouting match, and someone kicked a mower to life, and the day seemed so ordinary, the same as a minute ago, a day ago, a lifetime ago – but it'd never be the same. Not without Eth.

Well, to keep it short, this is what happened. I caught a train to Sydney. Yes, agreed, something I should've done thirty years earlier, but it was too late now. It seemed Ethel had faced the final indignity: a death without love, friendship, someone to talk to, share her memories with. To say, Hey, Max, remember when we were on top of Miller Anderson's, and the spotlight, with no light?

How had it been at the end? Had she risen early, walked around Croydon, sat to get her breath? Had she looked along Queen Street, and remembered when she and Ern had gone cart racing, or Ern, reliving a detective novel, or Mrs Royal chasing them home or . . . one of a thousand things. Because so much of Eth's life had been remembering – trying to get something back.

Red-eyed, tired, but determined, I caught a taxi to Croydon. Got out at Ben McDonald's house, knocked on the door and greeted him. He walked down the road with me, into the park, and stopped at the spot. The same me and Eth had sat a dozen times. Talking about Ern. Like a whole lifetime wasn't enough to describe him. Ben said, 'Bit of a shock when I found her.'

'How was she?'

'Lying this way, with her legs out, like this, and a sort of peaceful look on her face.'

I sat and tried to guess what she might've been thinking. 'You didn't know about her?'

'Knew she'd been friends with Dad, but he avoided her – reckoned she'd gone mad. Lotta people did.'

'Mad?'

'Out in her backyard, singing at the top of her voice, calling for him.'

I explained the whole affair, as I sat watching the sun waning, the birds quietening, and guessed, perhaps, she was searching her bag, found the poems, read a few: a night with the planets wreathed in dying garlands. Yes, that's how it would have been, at the end. The Ethel moment of grace: released from, but reunited with, her brother.

'Anyway, I keep to myself,' he said.

'Yeah?' He must've thought I was as silly as Eth. Old man, in his tweed jacket, caught in a past of *Sullivans'* sentiments and dying roses on the hall stand. 'It's a pity, isn't it?'

'What?'

'People not looking out for each other anymore.'

Maybe he took this as a criticism, but I didn't care. 'I'm just as much to blame.'

'How's that?'

'I could've come back and checked on her, but I never did. I was always too busy, or thought . . .'

'What?'

'She wouldn't want to see me.'

'Well . . . people never hate you as much as you think they do.'

'Your dad and uncle, *they* kept an eye on her.'

'That was a long time ago.'

'Not so long. They knew the whole story, I guess.'

'What's that?'

But I didn't want to tell him. If he wasn't interested before, why now? I'd learnt that you couldn't convince people who didn't want to listen. That Elliott and Apeldoorn and Williams, and a hundred others since, were little hens, forever perched on an egg, regardless of its chances of hatching. And were there still. After Eth. After Ern.

At which point I walked around the corner. Croydon Road, Dalmar Street, Byron Street. Still waiting. Perhaps one day there'd been a Malley Street? Not likely. Now, a few days after Eth'd gone, the world had almost forgotten her. Like it had been in a rush to do so, and was relieved there was no reminder. Gone, all of it. Like the Jesus house. A pair of town-houses with garages built into the ground, big gates, a security system, fake turf and agaves, so no one would ever have to step outside. No more Jesus. And even this seemed sad. Like, if He returned, there'd be some cause for hope, that faith was real, and needed, and mattered. Faith. Or what was left after the wrecker's ball: homes with the impossibility of neighbours, and neighbour-hoods, and Jesus, and Ern Malley. I imagined him and Eth, walking across the road, breaking in, admiring all the crosses and books and pictures of Matthew, Mark and their mates, and the clean, unslept-on sheets and new pillows – all of it, because someone believed so much.

It was a nice afternoon, so I thought I'd retrace my steps, from that day in 1944. I went to Mr Moore's shop, but it had gone. More flats, more people locked away, dreaming of how much better life would be with Charles and Di married, or watching Tony Barber, and trying to solve the puzzle. On and on. Like Eth had, every day. The charity shop, a burger joint: visions of Marilyn Monroe and James Dean. But no Peggy, no frocks, no jumpers, no shoes, no books, no David, no Ethel, no nothing. All of these lives had become threadbare, and put in

430

the bin. Maybe that's how it is with people. We just live and die?

The sun was dropping. I wasn't sure where I'd stay the night, but I didn't care. I returned to Dalmar Street and looked around number forty, locked up, the curtains drawn, like Eth had known, somehow. And strangely, I checked the water, and she'd turned it off at the meter. She couldn't have known. Maybe someone had come and done it?

I checked the doors, but couldn't get in. There were gaps in the curtains, and I could see Ern's bed in the sunroom, still made up, the soccer ball. *Farsa*. Although what wasn't fake? All of us were.

So I went out to the shed. Went in, tried the lights, and they came on. Funny, but I couldn't remember it. Maybe it was because she'd had a clean-out. The old sculptures, the bits and pieces, the boxes – all gone. Except an old case, sitting in the corner (ELM on the front). I sat beside it and pulled out a pile of folders and clippings. Old, yellow, musty-smelling papers. Like they'd been left for a reason, so only they would be found.

Firstly, a four-hundred-page manuscript titled *Ethel and Max*. That's right, the book you just read. See, Eth *was* talented. She could write. Which means, perhaps, she could've written the poems, but we'll never know, will we, dear reader? The book started in Mr Moore's shop and finished in Melbourne, with her and Louis, sitting upstairs above his bakery. A simple, happy story I've spent the last two years editing. *In memoriam*. My way of saying thanks, and sorry, I guess. So, what I'd done for Ern, I did for Eth. Taken the dreams and made them real. Found a publisher, put them in your hands, so you'd know me and Eth and Ern. And do you? Do you know us all? Speaking to you through the ages? I've honoured Ethel's vision, her story, even when she strayed from the truth, added (her own touch) to history, placed someone somewhere they weren't, had them say something they didn't, made a suburban Prometheus out of thin air (but isn't that the whole point of storytelling?).

I decided then and there, in that mouse-pissy, sculpture-making, Indian-restoring shed, that I'd do this for Ethel. Although she'd never asked. Never sent it to me. Waited, so that I'd discover her masterwork in the same way she'd discovered Ern's. Chances were I'd never come, never find it. Maybe she knew I would. After all, all of life's great works are accidents. Nothing planned, or meant, can come to or from anything else. It's all a big accident.

There were plenty more surprises in the case. *A Biography of my Brother*. I remembered the first few pages. The same draft she'd begun in Adelaide. She'd got a few chapters in and stopped, mid-sentence: . . . *although as Ern grew he learnt to love the ladies.* Maybe she'd realised she couldn't lie. Except in a story, or poem. The biography put aside for the novel. Which was just as well, because even a cursory glance showed this document was flawed. That it somehow missed Ern, and what he was. Or, how she imagined him to be. Lines like: *Ever the brave soldier, my brother started out on the Kokoda Track in 1942, determined to kill a few Japs. With bayonet fixed and eyes aglow he fought, for six long months, for the freedom of Australia.*

Jesus, Eth!

The case was full. Even the lid, with an elastic strap to hold shirts and pants, and poems: *The Darkening Ecliptic*. But that was gone. Or was it? No. Of course. Handwritten drafts of each poem. The lovesong, the colloquy ('I have been bitter with you, my brother . . .'), all of them. The Testament. His and Eth's last words? *I have pursued rhyme, image and metre . . . stumbled often, stammered . . . But in time the fading voice grows wise, And seizing the coordinates of all existence, Traces the inevitable graph . . .*

Yes, the graph. And the initials at the bottom of each sheet: LF. Although I wouldn't know the truth about Ern and his poems until I'd read Eth's novel for the first time. And then I wondered. Had she really visited Louis? Did he even exist? None of it can be or should be known. A good story, admittedly, but only weakened by the truth. That they had sat of a night, co-authoring the cause of all this mess, laughing, giggling, coming together, making love. Well, reader of mine, I'll leave that to you.

The case was full, but I couldn't give up now. All of the answers, or lies, were in it. I needed to know. I'd waited thirty-seven years, come so far, worried so much, hated myself. Picked up the phone, dialled, put it down, picked it up again. For years. All to know what I knew, or didn't know, now. An art catalogue from 1974 with black-and-white photos of Sid Nolan's Ern Malley paintings. Maybe she'd gone to the exhibition? Followed Sid's career, as he became the greatest of us, loved the world over, rewarded with riches, while we sad few remained in our bookshops, and coffins.

Halfway down, copies of every *Angry Penguins* I'd ever published (before stopping in 1949). They were well-worn, well-read, and here and there she'd annotated them like I was still writing about her brother, leaving clues that she might pick up. Here, in Summer 1946, an article by Sid about Chinese watercolours. A box around the words *Chinese landscapes only ever suggest the real thing.* Of course, what Sid had meant literally, she'd taken poetically. From 'Palinode': *There are ribald interventions, Like spurious seals upon, A Chinese landscape roll . . .* Almost

433

as if she'd spent the intervening years seeing life as a version of a Malley poem. Was that it? Is that what Ben McDonald had heard, stepping out into his backyard? Ethel, lost in the ages, the ecliptic, floating around her head in the night, in their bed, these naughty Malley children.

A pair of shoes. I remembered these too. Or at least the story. Bob, determined to leave no trace of his dead wife, cleansing the house of every clue, every dress, every slip, every tube of lippy. But his kids stealing the shoes, hiding them in the shed, so there might be some reminder of who this woman had been. Kept hidden, for several lifetimes, because what was true for one was true for the other. A death certificate: *Robert Lalor Malley. Cause of death: Silicosis of the lungs. Silicosis.* As I imagined him, dying under a bloodwood tree, or ... sitting in bed, coughing up his lungs, calling for his son, or daughter. Like this, every day and night for weeks, and months, before the end.

Finally, the biggest pile. The *Collected Works of Chairman Max.* Everything I'd written up to December 1980. Articles, features, books, columns (separate, and collected in *The Angry Eye*). I had no idea where she'd got them all. From papers all over Australia. How could she have done that? My miracle worker?

A lawnmower. Who was mowing Ethel's lawn? Now I've got you thinking, haven't I, readers? Maybe this mystery will be Max Harris's masterwork? Maybe we'll all be remembered for the wrong thing? Maybe my life will be no more than Ern, the few scrappy poems I pulled from an envelope in 1943? But, I guess, that wouldn't be so bad. Better writers are forgotten ten minutes after they're dead. When it comes to posterity, I suppose you have to take what you can get.

I went down the drive, and saw this middle-aged man, half-stooped, prematurely grey, pushing his mower in long, neat lines. The same Santa Ana Ern had played on, pissed on, lost his dog on, jumped from the roof on. He turned and looked at me, like he wasn't quite sure. Then he switched off the mower, and the engine slowly died. Then near-silence, in the near-dark, in Dalmar Street.

'She died,' he said to me.

'I know,' I said.

He stared at me, and smiled. 'It's been a long time, Mr Harris.'

'It has, David.'

I felt good, that it wasn't *all* over, that there were signs of life, this late in the picture. David smiled and said, 'I thought you were gonna come back to the shop.'

'So did I.'

'I waited, Max.'

And then he came over, and we shook hands, and sat on the porch, as the sun set and the crickets almost drowned us out and the automatic sprinkler systems popped on and the street was empty, always empty now. David explained how he'd looked after Ethel, because she'd looked after Peggy, and his mum, and him, and the whole family, after his dad had finally done it. Found a rope, filled his pockets with nails. He explained that this was why she was so busy, becoming a second mother, or sister, as he grew up, finished school, met his own wife, had his own kids.

I said, 'You looked out for her?'

'Yeah. Took her shopping, did her garden, her bills. Kept her company. I'd promised Mum and Gran I'd do it, and I did.'

This made me feel bad. Because I could've done something, and I explained this and he said, 'Na, you were busy in Adelaide and she . . . although she never stopped talking about you, Max.'

'Really?'

'Never. Max this, Max that, he's just written a new book, he's about to reissue Ern's poems, with an introduction by TS Eliot.'

'She said that?'

'Didn't you?'

'Well, not Eliot.'

But it didn't matter. That was a far better story, and Ethel was the very best at telling them.

'It wasn't what you'd call a . . . complete life,' he said.

'How's that?'

'I mean, she was always dealing with what happened with Evan and the kid.'

I waited as he told me: Evan, and his daily grog, and fist, destroying the family. 'And Wayne,' he said.

The photos. I saw him, this boy, jumping from the roof, hiding behind the rosemary, marshalling an army of lead soldiers.

David said, 'You know what happened to him?'

'I think . . .'

'She was only in prison for three years. Mum'd go see her once a week, take her something . . . talk her through it. But it finished her, I reckon. Mum reckoned, we all did. Finished her.'

'What happened to Wayne?'

'Taken away . . . adopted out.'

Well, you think you know someone. You don't. You just get a better idea, but hardly understand. Eth was lead, made in a mould that restricted her possibilities. Not that she'd ever done anything wrong.

'This couple out at Emu Plains. The father was Returned, too. On crutches . . . shattered pelvis, in the trenches. So . . . she lost him, Max.'

But kept him, regardless.

'And when she got out of prison, she couldn't really accept it. She went strange, a bit mad, Mum reckoned. She'd get the train out there, watch him, you know, at school, playing in his yard.'

'Wayne?' I asked.

'How did you know?'

The photos, torn, yellowing, soft from so much handling.

'But Mum stuck by her, got her help . . . and later, she came good, although I don't know that she ever stopped following him.'

'Came good?' I asked.

'Better.'

'When?'

'Two, three years after she got out. Seemed to have a new purpose. Socialised with Mum, started at the shop. Like, somehow, she'd got him back.'

*Fuck.* Of course. She *had* got him back.

'Ern?' I said. 'What was he, twenty-five?'

'Ern? Her brother?'

'Twenty-six?'

'Na . . . Ern . . . mustn't have been more than six or seven.'

I didn't get this, but did, and didn't want to hear it. 'Six?'

'Didn't you know? He was only a little tacker, but apparently he'd pissed his pants at school, and he was so upset he ran home, and got knocked over by a car, on Queen Street.'

'Queen Street?'

'Yeah. Next to the park. She'd often go and sit there, and just watch that road, and remember him, I guess.'

'He was killed?'

'Yes. She never got over it. Little Ern.'

Eth! Why didn't you tell me? Why did you keep it to yourself? Why did you go there, and sit, and imagine it, a million times, and blame yourself for not being there: holding his hand, leading him home. It wasn't your fault, Eth (at which time, I think, I descended into tears, and little David gave my knee a squeeze).

'What did you think?' he asked.

'But, who was Ern?'

'Her brother.'

'No, *Ern*?'

He didn't seem to understand. Maybe I was the mad one? But all he said was, 'If you like, I got a room you can have tonight.'

# Acknowledgements

Joseph Campbell described myths as public dreams (and dreams as private myths). Even now, years after I discovered Ethel and Ern's story in a small shed behind 40 Dalmar Street, Croydon, I'm still not sure what to make of it. I can see Ethel, writing at her kitchen table in 1956, surrounded by memories of her brother; I can see her shedding a tear for her mum and dad, and many others you have (or shall soon) read about. I can hear her saying, 'Enough!' Standing, placing a lump of Mr Moore's brisket in a pan, and cooking herself a meal. Because despite anything any book has or ever will say, life just goes on.

The myth has a beginning, a middle, but no end. Originally, of course, there was me and Geoffrey Dutton, Sam Kerr and Paul Pfeiffer, not to mention James McAuley and Harold Stewart (poets who, for better or worse, wrote themselves into an Australian *Iliad*). In the wings, John, Sunday (and Sweeney) Reed, Albert Tucker and Joy Hester – people who thought Australia could, should be more than gristle pie and green lawn. Then there's Peter Goers (*Ethel and Max*'s first editor), Margot Lloyd (its second) and Jo Case (its third, its midwife, its champion). Chris Womersley, an early reader, and supporter. And my daughter, Samela, who's shown such generosity, such understanding, such good humour as the keeper of the myth. I'd like to thank the dozens, the hundreds who have written about Ern over the years – painted him (starting with Sid Nolan), set him to music, analysed him, tried to get to the essence (although you can't). I'd like to thank Liz Nicholson for the cover (Eth'd approve), Jesse Pollard for the riverless text. And Michael Bollen, of course, patching the boat in which we all sail.

Wakefield Press is an independent publishing and
distribution company based in Adelaide, South Australia.
We love good stories and publish beautiful books.
To see our full range of books, please visit our website at
www.wakefieldpress.com.au
where all titles are available for purchase.
To keep up with our latest releases, news and events,
subscribe to our monthly newsletter.


Find us!


Facebook: www.facebook.com/wakefield.press
Twitter: www.twitter.com/wakefieldpress
Instagram: www.instagram.com/wakefieldpress

www.ingramcontent.com/pod-product-compliance
Lightning Source LLC
Chambersburg PA
CBHW030928020726
47498CB00001B/157